Once in a Lifetime

Once in a Lifetime

GWYNNE
FORSTER

ARABESQUE®

Recycling programs
for this product may
not exist in your area.

ONCE IN A LIFETIME

First published by BET Publications, LLC in 2002

ISBN-13: 978-0-373-83194-4

Copyright © 2010 by Gwendolyn Johnson Acsadi

www.kimanipress.com

Printed in U.S.A.

Dear Reader,

This has been a very busy and rewarding year. In my travels to conferences and book signings, I met many of you for the first time and enjoyed the camaraderie. Beginning in June, Kimani Arabesque released my first collection of wedding novellas in an anthology entitled *Yes, I Do*. And there's especially good news for readers who are fans of the Harrington brothers and have asked me time and again to continue the series. In September, *Love Me Tonight* marked the first new book in the Harrington series in many years. Now, with the reissue of *Once in a Lifetime*, the very first novel in the Harrington brothers series, readers will discover how the eldest brother, Telford, found love and a ready-made family with Alexis Stevenson. Next year look for the second and third books in the Harrington series to be reissued—*After the Loving* and *Love Me or Leave Me*.

The really good news is that the Harrington series will continue with at least one novel a year. And be sure to look for Scott Galloway, whom you met in *Love Me Tonight*, to find love with Pamela Harrington's sister, in the fifth Harrington novel in September 2011.

I enjoy receiving mail, so please email me at GwynneF@aol.com. If you write by postal mail, reach me at P.O. Box 45, New York, NY 10044, and if you would like a reply, please enclose a self-addressed, stamped envelope. For more information, please contact my agent, Pattie Steel-Perkins, Steel-Perkins Literary Agency, email: MYAGENTSPLA@aol.com.

Warmest regards,

Gwynne Forster

Acknowledgments

To my agent, Pattie Steel-Perkins who, like an angel parting the Red Sea, eases my writer's path. I am fortunate to have an agent of such integrity and dedication to duty.

Chapter 1

Alexis Stevenson had spent most of her thirty years doing what was expected of her. She managed not to fall in love until she met a man of whom her family would approve. Her father expected his girls to lead the pack, and she graduated at the top of her high school and college classes. Indeed, as a model student, her grades were such that her college and graduate schooling didn't cost her wealthy parents a penny, although they provided her with a lifestyle that she neither needed nor wanted. But her academic successes came at the expense of a healthy social life. After she married Jack Stevenson, she exchanged her job as instructor in home economics at the State University for that of homemaker, spending most of her time either planning for or entertaining her husband's business associates, smoothing his rise to the top of the corporate ladder.

Her difficult pregnancy didn't lessen Jack's expectations of her as homemaker or as hostess to his never-ending parade of guests. Even when his boss's daughter announced that she was pregnant and that Jack was the father, she did the expected and gave him a friendly divorce. But when he sought and subsequently obtained a ruling that would allow him to stop supporting their daughter, Tara, when she reached eighteen, Alexis balked.

Now, two years after their divorce became final, two years of legal battling, she had what she wanted, custody of her child, though at an enormous cost—forfeiture of her entitlement to half of their joint property. But she would have given up everything she had for custody of Tara. However, she couldn't revel in victory over a father who cared so little for his child as to give up all rights to her in order to retain all of his wealth. She had been a fool to cater to him in his quest for status and power. But she'd learned a lesson, and in Jack Stevenson, she had a master teacher. What she learned, she learned thoroughly; it would never happen again.

No one, not her friends, her sister, her ex-husband or his relatives would believe her—daughter of a wealthy family and former instructor in home economics and health sciences at State University—capable of the decision she had just made. Too bad; from now on, she planned to live her own life, not anyone else's. She put the money Jack sent her for Tara into a fund for the little girl's education and prepared to support her child and herself.

Alexis looked around the house she'd lived in for the past two years, took Tara's hand and walked out, locking the door. All they would need she'd packed in her azure Oldsmobile Cutlass Supreme. She put her daughter in her special chair in the backseat, strapped her in, got in the car and drove off. *Today is the first day of the rest of my life,* she told herself, and put Sting's "Brand New Day" in the tape deck, pushed the button, said good-bye to Philadelphia and headed for Eagle Park, Maryland.

Four hours later, Alexis brought her Oldsmobile to a halt in front of number ten John Brown Drive, known for miles around as Harrington House. She put the car in Park, expelled a long, tired breath and stared at the sprawling white brick colonial house, its majestic setting proclaiming the status of its owners. An array of multihued pansies, irises, primroses, peonies and daisies along with well-spaced oak, birch and pine trees—green and fresh in the noonday April sun—gave the house a serenity and the appearance of a refuge. Well maintained, she thought, but not a human in sight.

"Are we gonna stay here, Mummy?"

Alexis glanced back at four-year-old Tara, the delight of her life. "I hope so, honey. I hope so."

Only the Lord knew what Telford Harrington's reaction would be when he saw her precious Tara. He hadn't asked, and she hadn't told, because she knew that would be the end of the best job offer she'd received in three months of frantic searching.

The picture before her beckoned, though she found the manifestation of wealth unsettling; she'd rather not return to the monied environment she escaped when she separated from Jack Stevenson almost three years earlier, but what choice did she have now?

"Let's get out. Can we, Mummy?"

"In a minute, love."

Staring at the unknown, she felt compelled to savor what might be her last minutes as a person free to do as she pleased whenever she liked. When she walked through that door, she would be a servant, a full-time housekeeper. She didn't mind it, nor did she resent it. She'd opened a new chapter in her life, and she looked on it as an opportunity, a lifesaver. A way to support herself and her child. State U now required all of its teachers to have a doctorate degree, which meant that, with only a master's, she had to find other work.

She got out of the car, took Tara's little hand and walked with her up the winding brick path to the door. It opened slowly. "You must be the housekeeper." The voice belonged to a dark-skinned graying man of indeterminate age who looked as if he might at one time have been a bantamweight prizefighter.

"Yes." She extended her hand. "I'm Alexis Stevenson, and this is my daughter, Tara." The man didn't fit the picture of

Telford Harrington that she'd formed in her mind's eye after her one brief conversation with him.

"M' name's Henry, and I'm the cook. Come on…" He noticed Tara. "She's yours?"

Shivers raced through her, but she steadied herself. After all, this was the cook, not Harrington. Still, he probably reflected his boss's attitude about things. Alexis nodded, as if having the child with her were of no consequence.

"Why, yes. She is."

Tara moved closer to Alexis. "My name's Tara. What's yours?"

Henry stared at the little girl and shook his head. "M' name's Henry, like I said. I don't know if this is gonna work, ma'am. Nobody told me nothing 'bout no little girls. Where's your stuff? Might as well get you settled in."

Nothing about his behavior eased her anxiety about Tara; indeed, he behaved as if she needn't hope for understanding. "How about giving me a tour of the house, Henry?" she called after him, hiding her concern.

"Soon as I put together something for you to eat. Course, if you don't like what I fix, feel free."

Henry gave them a lunch of hamburgers and French fries with ginger ale for Alexis and milk for Tara, enough to feed two more people and causing her to think the Harrington men were big meat eaters. Tara walked over to Henry, tapped him on the thigh and thanked him for her lunch. He looked down at her as though making up his mind whether he'd allow himself to be captivated, but Tara smiled and took the matter out of his hands.

Henry wiped his hands on his oversize, blue-denim apron and started out of the kitchen. "Come on," he threw over his shoulder. "This'll take a while. Ain't much changed here since the old man passed, and that was well-nigh twenty years ago."

Alexis glanced around the kitchen, enormous with Chinese-blue brick walls and kitchen cabinets, and a chrome sink, stove, dishwasher, grill and refrigerator. A round table with three curved-back Moroccan chairs rested in a white nook as if forgotten.

Hmmm. How odd, she thought as she walked with Henry through the dim living and dining rooms, rooms that obviously once boasted the elegance of their day. At the end of the hour-long tour, she'd decided that Telford Harrington lived much to himself. His bedroom contained a huge sleigh-style bed with a bedspread to match the tan-colored drapery, a beige-and-brown Tabriz carpet, mahogany desk, oversize brown leather chair and chest of drawers. What appeared to be a violin or a viola rested in a corner. A large black-and-white drawing hung over his bed. Nothing cheerful there. And nothing to calm her fears that he might send her packing, as would have been the case if his room were bright and cheerful.

Three other bedrooms, two of which belonged to Telford's brothers, met the criteria for a master bedroom with anterooms and private baths. Henry had placed her things in a different end of the second floor.

"You might want to ask Mr. Tel if you and your little girl can stay back on the other side in the room on the end by the garden. It's got an anteroom with a nice bay window, and your little girl could have that by herself. Course, I ain't saying he's gonna like none of this, but that's twix you and him."

She wished Henry would stop his frequent references to Telford Harrington's certain displeasure about her child. But she said nothing to that effect, only thanked him. She put Tara to bed for a nap, and walked around the gardens to get her bearings. She loved natural settings—gardens, forests, the ocean, places where a person could feel free. On an impulse, she cut a large bouquet of pink peonies and purple irises, put them in a water-filled vase and placed them on the marble-top walnut table in the foyer. Observing the elegance that the flowers added to the area, she moved the gilt-edged mirror from its dark corner in the hallway, found a hook and hung it above the flowers.

"Now that's *really* an improvement," she said to herself.

"The men won't like you making changes, ma'am," Henry

said, coming up behind her. "They like things the way they is."

"I can imagine. What are you planning for supper?" They wanted a homemaker, and she intended to turn that mausoleum into a home.

"Whatever I find in there." He pointed to the pantry. "Some chops, baked potatoes and beans, apple pie…something like that. They ain't hard to feed."

"I'll do the marketing from now on, Henry. We'll sit together, plan the menus and make out the grocery lists. Okay?"

"Don't matter none to me. Mr. Tel said I'd take care of the upstairs and the kitchen, and you see to the downstairs. Twice a week, Bennie comes in and does the heavy cleaning."

Just as he'd written into her contract. "Thanks, I'm sure we'll get on well."

She opened the windows downstairs, let the breeze flow through and immediately felt better about her new job. She found table linens, place settings and flatware and set the table in the breakfast room. Then she cut more flowers and put them on the table along with long tapered candles that she discovered in the linen closet.

Henry stood in the doorway scratching his head and shaking it. "Like I said, I don't know if this is gonna work. The men eat in the kitchen, and I ain't seen none of this—" he waved a hand around the breakfast room "—since Miss Etta passed. Course, like I said, that's twix you and Mr. Tel."

"How long have you worked here, Henry?"

"'Bout thirty years, since the boys were little. Why?"

She raised an eyebrow. "And you call Telford Harrington Mr. Tel?"

"Humph. I call him anything I want to. I figured that's what you'd call him."

She liked Henry, but she didn't think he'd appreciate her telling him that. "What time do we eat dinner?"

"You mean supper? Whenever they gets here…sometime 'round six or seven."

She'd have to work on that. Around five, she bathed Tara

and dressed her in a yellow pique dress, braided her hair and secured the ends with matching yellow bows. Then she showered, put on a floor-length yellow T-shirt that flattered her svelte and curvaceous five-foot-seven-inch frame, secured her permed hair in a French knot and waited for the verdict. Hers and his. Thinking of what she had to lose, tremors raced through her, and she groped her way to a chair. With three hundred and eighty dollars to her name, Telford Harrington would have to see reason or she'd have a problem.

She'd hung up most of their clothing when she heard the doorbell ring but, thinking that anyone who lived there would use a key, she didn't move from the closet. She couldn't. The colors of her clothing danced in a mirage before her eyes, and her feet would not budge.

Tara. She had to find Tara. If she'd gotten into something… She looked around for the child, didn't see her and walked quickly toward the stairs in time to hear a deep male voice— one she wouldn't likely forget—explain, "Well, hello to you, too, and who *are* you?"

"My name is Tara. What's yours? Do you live here?"

"I certainly do."

"What's your name?"

Alexis raced down the stairs and stopped, for he had looked up in her direction, and from that distance, his masculine persona, strong and heady, jumped out to her. Lassoed her and claimed her. She shook her body the way one rids clothes of wrinkles and got a grip on herself. "My name's Telford," she heard him say to Tara, though he'd locked his gaze on Alexis. "I'll be right back."

He stopped before reaching her and stared into her eyes. She tried to look away, but couldn't. He seemed to pull her to him the way a magnet captures steel, and she realized that she was closing the distance between them. Her whole body slammed on alert, tingling with a strange new vibrancy, with life, and a blaze leaped into his eyes. The expression burning in them nearly unglued her. She felt him then; oh, how she felt him! He rimmed his top lip with the tip of his tongue, bringing her back to herself and to a halt two steps above him. If she trusted her judgment right then, she'd swear that he shuddered as though tension seeped out of him.

"I'm Telford Harrington, and something tells me you're Alexis Stevenson." That didn't sound as if he was happy about it, either.

She took the hand he extended and shimmered with awareness from her scalp to the soles of her feet. He jerked his hand away from hers as if she'd scalded him. What a mess! Maybe she'd better leave right that minute and take her chances somewhere else.

"Yes," she said, as though leaving hadn't occurred to her. "I'm glad to meet you."

He remained there, a breath away, eye to eye with her though she stood two steps above him. "You didn't tell me you had a child. If you had, I'm not so sure I'd have hired you."

"You didn't ask me, nor did you mention it, so I figured you didn't think it relevant."

"If you had three kids, would you still think that?"

She shrugged. "I don't know what I'd think if I had three. I'm just thankful that I only have to support this one." She said that pointedly to ring his bell of compassion, if he had any.

He looked down suddenly, and she saw Tara pulling at his pants leg. "Mr. Telfry, Mr. Henry said supper is ready, and I'm hungry."

"Mr. Telford, honey," Alexis corrected.

She held her breath while she waited for his reaction. Tara reached up for his hand, anxious, as usual, to get her way. "Come on," she said, and he turned and let the child lead him down the stairs to the kitchen, where he stopped.

"Where's the food, Henry?"

"We're eating in the breakfast room tonight, Tel. New house rules."

He walked to the breakfast room, still holding Tara's hand, stared at the table and spun around. "What the… What's all this for? You're having a party? Before I get all the way in the house, I see the place looks and smells like a woman's boudoir. Now…"

She lifted her chin. "I'm sorry. Should I have set the table in the dining room? That seemed so formal."

"What's wrong with the kitchen?"

"It's the *kitchen*. Besides, that table has only three chairs. Why do you have dining and breakfast rooms, if you don't use them?"

Tara tugged at his hand. "Can we sit down?"

"Yeah."

"What about Henry?" Alexis asked him. "Doesn't he eat?"

"Ask him." He let his impatience show and picked up a slice of jalapeño corn bread.

"We have to say grace," Tara said and bowed her head.

To her amazement, Telford bowed his head and waited. Realizing that he wouldn't say it, she did, but she knew Tara would be disappointed.

"I don't like the pepper, Mummy."

"Then eat the potato and the pork chop, and remember, you do not complain at the table."

"Sorry, Mummy."

Telford looked at her, and she wasn't sure whether the fire in his eyes bespoke annoyance of or delight in her presence, though she suspected it was not the latter.

"You've been here, let's see, half a day, and in that short time, you've managed to get dust flying all through the house, change my furniture around as well as my eating habits, and you've got the foyer looking like a girl's dormitory. Ms. Stevenson, this is the home of three adult men and one grizzly cuss. We don't need this."

She leaned back, squared her shoulders and looked him in the eye. "'Wanted: a woman of taste, intelligence and refinement as homemaker for three brothers.' That's what your ad said, and I was expecting a man who could appreciate that in a woman."

"Yeah, but I didn't ask you to come here and change my life."

"Not to worry," she said in as casual a tone as she could manage, though she couldn't get her heart to settle down or her nerves to reassemble themselves. "You'll be pleased, and it's only for two years."

He looked toward the ceiling in an air of resignation. "Two years. We'll talk after we finish supper."

She'd thought they were talking about it right then. "Whatever you say, sir." She emphasized the "sir."

"Call me Telford, and no nicknames please. Henry calls me Tel, but that's because he can't remember that I'm no longer six years old. I don't accept that from anybody else. What do you want me to call you?"

"Alexis is fine."

"And you can call me Tara."

She watched Telford carefully to judge his reaction to her daughter. He smiled at the child—composed and at ease in her new environment with the strange man—and her heart raced a little faster. He may be annoyed, but he wouldn't take it out on her child.

"How old are you, Tara?"

"I'm four, but I'll be five this year. Mummy says I change ages every year, but only one time a year. Isn't that right, Mummy?"

She nodded. If Telford and his brothers accepted them, Tara would thrive in the environment. She reached for some lemonade, but Telford took the pitcher from her and refilled her glass.

"This is a lot more than I thought I was getting, Alexis. With a child this age among us, Drake, Russ and I...well, we'll have to learn a new way of living. Henry will, too."

"I...I'm sorry, but I've burned all my bridges."

He focused his gaze on her, and she could hardly withstand the intensity of it. There was no telling what those hazel-brown eyes were saying. "Then...all of us will have to give a little."

Five minutes later, Drake Harrington breezed into the room.

"Man, what the hell's going on here? Henry told me... Whoa!" He walked over to Alexis. "Things have definitely brightened up around here. First, I see flowers, and now I'm looking at a beauty who puts flowers to shame. I'm Drake, the handsome brother." He shook her hand.

A smile swept across her face. She liked his sense of humor and answered in kind. "So far, that would describe the two I've met. Does the other one live up to this standard?"

Drake's wide grin gave her a sense of well-being. "You mean old sourpuss? If Russ thought he was handsome, he'd do something to change that."

"Tut-tut," she said, barely able to contain a giggle. "You should show more respect for your older brother. Have you met my daughter?"

Drake's eyes widened. "Your... Well, who are you?" he asked Tara. He hadn't seen her, partly because he hadn't expected to find her sitting there and partly because he'd glued his gaze on Alexis.

"Mr. Telford already asked me that." She pushed her glass to Telford. "I drank my milk. Can I please have some lemonade?"

Telford looked at Alexis. "What do I do here? I don't know what's good for children."

Drake glanced at her and, when she nodded, walked around the table, took the glass and half filled it with lemonade. "Now who's your friend?"

With her face wreathed in smiles, she said, "Mr. Telford, 'cause I saw him first."

"Whew," Drake said, hunkered beside Tara's chair. "How do you like that?" He got up. "Looks like this one's yours, brother. I'd better eat before Henry gets antsy and doesn't leave anything for me."

Alexis noticed that Telford looked from her to Drake as if he expected something to happen. Then it dawned on her that he thought she'd fall for Drake, who obviously had a way with people and was probably famed as a ladies' man. She looked at Telford steadily and with as much dispassion as possible, hoping to convince him without speaking about it that, although she liked Drake at once, she was not and never would be attracted to him. By the time they finished the meal, Tara was leaning against Drake's thigh and talking to him nonstop.

If only Telford will accept us. I can't stay, contract or not, if he's not happy having Tara here.

"After you get Tara to bed, we'll talk," Telford told Alexis after sipping the last of his coffee.

Drake winked at her. "I'm going for a ride. See you later."

The two men stared as Tara ran to Henry. "Thank you for my supper, Mr. Henry," she said, smiling up at him. "Mummy said you're a nice cook."

The man had the grace to show embarrassment, and to Alexis's mind that was a good thing. He liked her daughter.

"You just tell old Henry what you like. I'll fix it."

"I like black-cherry ice cream," she told him, smiled and clasped her hands in front of her.

"First thing you know, I won't recognize the place," Telford said before heading upstairs.

For the nth time, she read *Puss 'n Boots,* and for as many times, Tara applauded constantly. When at last Tara was asleep, Alexis walked down the stairs and into the family room or den, where Telford waited for her.

Telford stood beside the gray-stone fireplace with a snifter of cognac in his right hand. How was he going to turn his life around to fit what he considered an appropriate environment for a little girl? No woman had lived among those four men since his mother died fifteen years earlier. Flowers, open windows in the spring and the breeze wafting through, a properly set dining table and a beautiful woman at its head. It reminded him of his mother, whom he had loved and, on many occasions, hadn't loved at all. He downed the Hennessy VSOP cognac and walked to the window that overlooked the garden, where he saw Drake dismount his horse and tether him.

"I wanted to be here when you started chewing out Alexis for bringing Tara," Drake said as he entered the den. "And don't say you hadn't planned to do it. I have a feeling she's just what we need."

"Who? Alexis or a four-year-old?"

Drake pulled off his riding boots, kicked them under a chair and poured himself a snifter of cognac. "Both of 'em."

"Sure. Alexis Stevenson and ten more would suit you perfectly, but don't make a move on her. She's the house-keeper."

Drake crossed his unshod right foot over his knee, and a grin burst out on his face. "Wake up, man, I saw what was going on."

Telford stuffed his hands into his trousers pockets and kicked at the brass andiron that graced the fireplace. "What do you mean by that?"

"Figure it out. Suffice it to say, she's not one bit interested in me, nor I in her."

"Glad to hear it. When you start after something you go like a bat out of hell."

Drake grinned. "By the time you know I'm going after it, I've done some thinking about it and made up my mind. Ready to move. And when I take off, I make time."

"Yeah, tell me about it. Say what you please, though, she can't stay."

His gaze caught Drake's foot swinging at a slow, even rhythm. "She stays, Telford, because you know you aren't going to ask her to leave. If you do, I'll oppose you."

Telford expelled a long breath. "Yeah, but she can't make the rules in this house."

"Let's wait and see. I wouldn't mind having a little order around here."

"I suppose you're planning to walk around fully clothed, remember to close the bathroom when you're taking a shower and watch your mouth when you talk. Et cetera, et cetera."

"Oh, hell. Yeah, I guess I'll have to."

"I was wondering where you were," Alexis sang as she glided into the room.

The simplest dress a woman could put on, and she looked like a goddess, soft, feminine and...and...for Pete's sake, what was he thinking? She refused the cognac he offered.

"Wine at dinner and a glass of champagne, occasionally, are my limit. You wanted to talk with me, Telford?"

Champagne, eh? "Yeah. Look," he began, rubbing the back of his neck, "have a seat. This is no place for a small child."

She sat forward, alert and anxious, and he had the feeling she'd spring out of the chair in a second. "Are you saying you want me to leave?"

Hearing her voice shake brought out his protective streak, and try as he would, he couldn't forget that by her own account, she was vulnerable. "Can you imagine what it's like for three men and a male cook living in a house this size together? On summer weekends, we hardly ever put on clothes, and I don't ever remember wearing bathing trunks in that pool out back."

Alexis stood. "Maybe you should have advertised for a homemaker with greatly impaired vision. You'll have to be just as circumspect around me as around Tara."

The howls of laughter from Drake accentuated Telford's embarrassment. He hadn't thought of that. He folded his arms against his chest, leaned against the wall and asked her, "Will I have to refrain from saying damn?"

"Yes, you will." He realized he'd raised her temperature level when she walked to within a foot of where he stood. "And there are a few other things we have to straighten out. My contract says two years, and I intend to stay for at least that long. If you're three blood brothers, you're a family. Families eat their meals together, so you shouldn't straggle in whenever it suits you. Say dinner's at seven, all of you sit down to the table at seven. Or six, or whatever time you decide."

"Anything else?" Telford asked her, and Drake eyed them the way a sleuth watches a suspected criminal.

"No hats on in the house or at the table, no boots beneath

chairs and no swearing. I don't want my daughter conditioned to accept such behavior from men."

She had hutzpah, all right, he had to hand it to her.

"Of course not," he said, sarcasm lacing his words. "She might one day go to college and live in a coed dormitory, and she'd be prepared for just what she found there—a bunch of naked men in the showers. Alexis, I would treat Tara with no less respect than I would my own daughter."

Drake got up, took off the Stetson he wore when riding, pulled his boots from beneath the chair and winked at Alexis. "You won't get any flack from me; unlike Robinson Crusoe over there, who enjoys his own company—" he pointed to Telford "—I love women. The more around me, the merrier. And Tara can stay here as long as she likes. She's just what this tomb needs." He left them and walked up the stairs, whistling "Knock About Sweetheart" as he went.

"Oh, yes," Alexis said. "I forgot to add that you shouldn't raise your voices in disagreement or anger."

His glare had to suffice, since he couldn't grab her and shake her till…till she was soft and…and warm and perfumed with the tantalizing odor of woman, till she… He brought himself up short and regrouped. "Alexis, don't push me too far. Don't ever do that. Never. You got that?"

She didn't give quarter, and in spite of his annoyance, he admired her. "I know this all sounds like a bad pill you have to swallow, and I'm sorry, but I figured you'd want us to settle everything now, and it's best to get these things straight in advance."

He'd had enough. "Do you think you've happened upon a houseful of barbaric, uncivilized men? If so, you'd better make a run for it."

She appeared thoughtful. "Barbaric? Uncivilized? Hmmm. I'm not sure I'd go quite that far. A little rough around the edges, maybe."

His glare broadened to a thunderous glower. "You trying to test my restraint?"

She lifted one shoulder in a careless shrug. "Wouldn't think of it. Anybody can see you're a paragon of willpower and self-control. Cool. Real laid-back."

"All right, all right. You and I both know what's going on here. If these verbal whacks are helping to relieve your frustration, by all means don't spare me."

Apparently less assured now, she avoided looking him in the eye for the first time. "You're assuming a lot, Mr. Harrington."

"Don't fool yourself." He poured half a glass of club soda, dropped two cubes of ice in it, offered the glass to her and, when she declined, sipped it slowly. "Let's get back to business. I was not expecting you to come with a child. You told me you were divorced, and I got the impression you were much older."

"If you'd asked my age, I would have told you. You didn't."

"I know, I know. But I always heard that women don't like to tell their age."

"Sorry, I can't help you there." Suddenly her demeanor seemed to change. Lord forbid she should try some feminine tactics on him. He wasn't holding still for that.

But she fooled him. "Telford, let's see this from my point of view. I sublet my house, packed some necessities, stored the remainder of my belongings, got in my car and changed my life by coming here. Where do I go if I leave here, and what will I do with Tara while I find another job and a place to stay? That's my dilemma, but if you don't want my child here, I don't want to stay, and I won't."

"I'm not asking you to leave. What do you think I am, an ogre of some kind?"

"She's obedient, and she's smart. You'll see."

And she was a beautiful, loving child who would soon have him and every other man around rolling over whenever she snapped her fingers. He looked at the hopeful expression in Alexis's soft brown eyes. Hopeful, but not pleading. What had he thought he'd gain by giving her the third degree? Except perhaps to establish some vital distance between them. They'd hooked the minute they looked at each other on those stairs. She could deny it if she wanted to, but he'd felt it to the marrow of his bones, and he'd bet anything, even his varsity ring, that it was the same for her.

The present arrangement wouldn't work; he didn't want Tara running around in the corridors near their bedrooms. "Tomorrow, I'd like you to move over to that guest room off the garden. It's private and safe, and it's much more spacious. No one can scale that wall without spending a few weeks in a hospital. Furthermore, Tara will be less likely to grow up too fast. Henry will show you to that room."

"Thanks. When you have time, please tell me how you like things done."

He looked at her to see if she might be pulling his leg, and realized that she was serious. In spite of himself, he laughed aloud. "Why would I bother to do that? You'll do what you like. Sleep well."

For some reason, he didn't want to see her walk out of the door, so he went over to the window and busied himself closing first the blinds and then the draperies. He heard her say good-night, but he pushed from his mind the soft caress that was her voice.

He went back to the bar, poured himself another glass of club soda and sipped it, mostly to have something to do. When he'd looked up those stairs and seen her looking down at him, he thought a barrel of bricks had fallen on his head. And as she glided toward him, her motion slow and fluid as if something other than her feet propelled her, a sweet, terrible hunger that he hadn't experienced in his thirty-six years began to churn in him. She stopped just in time, bringing him to his senses seconds before he would have reached out for her.

He brushed his fingers over his curly hair, exasperated at the thought of having that woman in his home for the next two years. He'd had enough of women, beautiful and otherwise. First his unfaithful mother, and then... He pushed the thought from his mind.

"Well, does she stay?"

He spun around at the sound of Drake's voice. "She stays. What else can I do? She has to work, and she has a child. I—"

"That's a great little girl, too. Don't sweat it, Telford. We're in the doldrums; been in 'em for years. I liked sitting at a properly set table. Hell, half the time, Henry serves the food right from the pot so he can wash one less dish."

"I know, but it's… Well—"

Drake's hand clasped his right shoulder. "Don't let it get to you. You'll either like it or it won't amount to a thing. Trust me; I've been there."

He looked at his brother, the person closest to him, and shook his head. For all Drake's apparent frivolousness, his insight into human feelings and behavior could be startlingly clear, so he didn't try to mislead him. "Right. It may take me a few days, but I'll get it together."

"I may be a little late for breakfast tomorrow morning, Tel," Henry called from the door. "I don't suppose that matters, though, since it's Saturday. But I thought I'd run down to Bridge Market and get some of that good double-smoked bacon. We ain't got nothing here but country sausage."

"Isn't that what we always eat for breakfast?"

"Yeah, but Tara told me she likes pancakes with bacon and maple syrup. We got the syrup, but we ain't got—"

Telford held up his hands, palms out. "All right, all right. Get the bacon. Anything else she wants. I hope I get my breakfast before I have to leave for Baltimore."

"Do my best."

Do his best. "Henry knows breakfast is my favorite meal. I have to change my suppertime, eat in the breakfast room, walk around in the house fully clothed with dust flying around in my face, wait till you get home before I can eat and I'll probably have to give up sausage and eat bacon with my grits?" He threw up his hands.

"Don't look at me," Drake said, his white teeth sparkling against his olive complexion. "And quit complaining. Just think of the fun you're probably going to have."

"Man, you're wasting your thought process. I'm not going that way."

"If you say so. A first-class woman is *in the house*."

Drake raced back upstairs, and his thoughts turned inward. If only he were as sure as he'd sounded.

Chapter 2

Alexis crawled into bed long after midnight, having survived a day in which she'd turned her life around, hurtling from society matron to live-in housekeeper, from college teacher to a woman with limited means of earning a living. At nine o'clock yesterday morning, the judge had banged his gavel and finally closed her custody case for all time, thwarting Jack Stevenson's last effort to take their child from her. Jack had badgered and threatened her until she relinquished her share of their joint property in exchange for Tara's custody. A month later, supported by his enormous wealth and high-priced lawyers, he challenged her fitness as a mother, as if to break her spirit by depriving her of her only remaining treasure. All of her savings had gone to lawyers' fees, but she had her child, and that was all that mattered.

She leaned over the sleeping little girl—conscious that they were sharing a bed for the first time—and closed her eyes in gratitude. Tara was hers, and the future was bright, or would be if… She bolted upright and tremors streaked down her limbs as she recalled Telford Harrington and her reaction to him.

She still felt the shock of seeing the man for the first time, of looking into hazel-brown eyes that mesmerized her, of having the stuffing knocked out of her. When she'd finally gotten back in her room, her fingers shook so badly that she could hardly remove her shoes. She didn't know how she'd do it, but she'd deal with it. She had to; her life and that of her child depended on it. She kissed Tara's cheek and turned out the light.

She had a home for herself and Tara and she could save a little money. But what if... Perspiration matted her hair. If he discovered her education and social status in mainline Philadelphia, he'd fire her as an imposter. She prayed he wouldn't investigate her. She hadn't lied, but no sane man would have hired her as a housekeeper if he knew the life she'd lived.

Alexis didn't know how long she counted sheep, but she awoke from peaceful oblivion to hear Tara say, "I wanna go eat, Mummy. Mr. Henry's cooking something for me."

"In a minute, and say please."

"Please."

She dressed Tara and then herself and went downstairs, where Telford and Drake sat at the table in the kitchen. Drake got up immediately and went to the breakfast room to get two chairs.

"I hope you slept well," Telford said when they greeted each other, warily, like two cats who'd lost their night vision.

"Well as could be expected."

He stopped chewing and looked directly at her. "What do you mean by that? If you weren't comfortable, I'll get you some new mattresses. Today."

"I was very comfortable, and the room is delightful. But... Telford, I've just changed my life. It's going to take some getting used to."

She had his full attention then, and her nerves rioted as his piercing gaze focused on her, his beloved sausage and grits momentarily forgotten. "If you have a problem you think I can help you with, let me know. That's what I'm here for."

She hadn't expected that show of compassion, and her eyebrows arched sharply. "I appreciate that, Telford, but if you and I get along well, that's all the help I think I'll need. Now where on earth did Tara go?"

He waved his fork in the direction of the kitchen stove. "She's over there admiring Henry. I hope she can get him to cook something other than hamburgers, steaks and chops. I've begun to hate that stuff." Something suggestive of pain streaked across his face.

"I'll see what I can do about that. Not to worry."

He stared at her for a long time before he asked, "You can cook?"

"Wouldn't you expect a housekeeper to be able to cook? You bet I can."

"Right on!" Drake said, walking back to the table holding two stacked chairs in one hand and Tara by the other. "Maybe we'll get some variety in these meals."

Telford's face creased into a smile. "If Henry hears you say that, we'll be eating cabbage stew until he decides he's had adequate revenge."

"Tell me about it. You going to Baltimore this morning?" Drake asked Telford. "It wouldn't hurt you to take a Saturday off once a year." He took his plate to the stove for more eggs and bacon.

"Can't. That school's going to be perfect if I have to lay every stone with my own hands. The Harrington name will stand for the last word in building again, for the very best. People will take notice, if I die trying."

She didn't like the harshness of his voice or the rage that she sensed just below his veneer of gentility.

"I'll drag old man Sparkman and his gang down to their knees, if it's the last thing I do," he spat out. "That school building is going to be a symbol of quality, and I'll bring it in on time and on budget."

Alexis looked at Telford's clenched fists and the muscles working in his jaw. Her gaze moved to his eyes and the fierce emotion that robbed them of the warmth that had cast a spell over her the night before. Oh, those eyes held fire, all right, but a different kind of fire, the fire of animosity and a hunger for revenge.

She didn't know the reason for his hostility, but she knew that it made him hard and vengeful; no person could be happy feeling as he did.

The fingers of her right hand closed over his left wrist. "If you dislike this man so much, he will occupy your thoughts when your mind should be free for other concerns. Whenever you hate anyone, you're the loser." His glare didn't shake her resolve. "What I said is true," she continued. "Do what you have to do, but don't think about the man; these feelings you have…they're…they're destructive."

"Look here. You don't know anything about this, nor what this man has cost my family. You'd do well not to talk out of turn."

She couldn't let it go at that. This man hurt, and he would go on hurting until he got the better of his enemy, but she knew that when he did, he'd have a hollow victory.

"I don't mean to offend you, but you'll never be at peace this way."

He pushed his chair back from the table and put his hands on his knees in a move to leave. "I don't care for namby-pamby. That's not… Wait a minute, you're not a pacifist or a…" His eyes widened. "A—"

She finished it for him. "A Quaker, a member of the Society of Friends. I am not namby-pamby, as you put it, and I stand up for my rights. But I do not argue or hold grudges, and I don't let anger get in the way of my common sense. Yours is ruling you."

He leaned back in the chair. "Who the… Who'd have thought it? Did you come from a family of Quakers?"

She shook her head. "I was raised a Methodist."

"Why the change? Is your ex-husband a Quaker?"

That was good for a laugh. "I don't know what he is. I joined the Friends because I needed to be with people whose lives were different from the volatile and sometimes violent relationships I witnessed in my parents, and whose values were unlike those of my manipulative and greedy husband."

She supposed she'd shocked him until she saw on his face something akin to recognition. He seemed uncomfortable, as though she'd given him information that he'd rather not have.

"Sorry if I've embarrassed you."

He held up his hand. "No. No. It's all right. I...I was thinking what a difficult life you must have had. Yet you take me to task for being angry. Neither of us has had a happy time of it." He stood. "I hope you'll be happier here. Henry will show you that room by the garden. See you this evening."

"Around seven?" she asked to emphasize their agreement to eat dinner at a fixed time.

"All right. Seven."

"Mr. Telford, I wanna go with you."

She'd almost forgotten that Tara sat quietly at the table listening to their conversation.

"Tell you what," he said to Tara, who'd left the table and was holding his hand. "You and I will take a little walk another day, but not today. Okay?"

"Don't forget, Mr. Telford. We're going to walk."

She hoped he wouldn't disappoint her child. Jack never remembered his promises to his daughter, and she didn't want her to grow up thinking that men were unreliable.

"Did he leave?" Drake asked, pulled out the chair Telford vacated and sat down.

She nodded. "He'll be back by seven."

An amused twinkle danced in Drake's dark eyes. "Oh, yeah. You said we had to be home by seven and eat together. I was surprised he didn't tell you who was boss."

"You make me sound like a bore."

"Trust me, I didn't mean to. Think the two of you will get on all right? Telford's been through plenty, and when he puts himself to it, he can be a real handful."

"He's sensitive, and Tara likes him."

"Tara likes any guy wearing pants, which is why I'm not

jealous of her affection for Henry. He doesn't even *want* people to like him." He buttered a biscuit and spread raspberry jam on it. "Three or four hours after she meets him, she's trailing behind him, and he's going halfway to Frederick to get bacon for her. He wouldn't do that for me or my brothers."

"Why not?"

The expression on his face suggested that there might be some doubt as to her sanity. "What we want doesn't matter a hoot to Henry. He does as he pleases." He reached over and patted Tara's shoulder. "I gotta get out of here. See you later."

She noticed that, although Tara told him good-bye, smiled and waved at him, she didn't hold on to him or ask to go with him. She wondered if Tara had sensed her own reaction to Telford and been favorably impressed because of it. She cleared the table and took the dishes over to the kitchen sink.

"Ain't no reason for you to do that. You hear?" Henry wiped his hands on his apron. "I'll take care of the kitchen. You go get your things ready so I can take you to your new room. You'll like it." He looked down at Tara. "You will, too."

She loved the enormous room with its sand-colored walls, cinnamon-colored carpeting and soft yellow accessories. A wall of windows let her look at the garden, a grove of trees and what appeared to be a river in the distance. She stood by the window and took in the beauty.

Henry took pride in showing her her new quarters. "Swimming pool's at the other end of the garden. When it's hot in midsummer, we just turn on the floodlights and swim at night." He walked to the far end of the room and opened a door. "This is supposed to be a sitting room, but we can put a bed and some furniture in here for Tara. Bath and Jacuzzi right there." He pointed to another door. "That opens to the garden. Don't worry, it's safe. The fence is twelve feet high and has barbed wire on top."

She thanked him. "I'll plan some menus, make a shopping list, and I can write out some recipes for you, if you want me to."

He scratched the back of his head. "I don't know. If it don't broil, and you can't French-fry it, I ain't got no use for it."

She allowed herself the familiarity of a pat on his shoulder. "You'll be surprised how easy this will be."

Henry hadn't been young for a long, long time, she realized when his face sagged and a shadow flashed in his eyes. "I guess I could use a few tips. Ain't easy figuring out new ways to cook the same old thing."

"You don't have to worry about that in the future, or at least not for as long as I'm here. We'll help each other, Henry. I don't know a fifth of what you know." She wanted him for a friend, and she meant to be one.

Telford had been away for several days on a business trip, and Alexis didn't know he'd come home until Tara ran down the hall calling his name. "Mr. Telford. Mr. Telford. Mummy, can Mr. Telford come look at what I drew?"

Telford wasn't pleased that she brought a child to his home, and she didn't want Tara's fondness for him to become tiresome.

"Darling, Mr. Telford just came home, and he's probably very tired. You must wait till he's had time to…to rest."

"I have to put on some work clothes, Tara. Think you can wait a little while?"

Alexis couldn't believe the smile that lit up Tara's face. Her daughter was as impatient as a four-year-old could be, but she graciously accepted whatever Telford offered her.

"You must have magic powers, Telford. I can hardly believe that's my daughter."

"Why's that?"

"Her patience, this new trait she adopted after she came here, boggles my mind."

His wink nearly knocked her off balance. "Some females know a man when they see one."

And I don't? This woman was far ahead of Tara. "I'm not going there, Telford. Not for a second."

With his hands in the back pockets of his trousers and his

feet planted wide apart, his lips slowly exposed his perfect white teeth in a grin. Devastating. But if he knew it, unlike Drake, he didn't show it. Thank goodness she was able to resist grabbing her chest to slow down her heartbeat. If she wasn't careful or very lucky, she'd be the one to break the contract. A little of this man could set a dozen women on fire.

"Suit yourself," he said, winking again. "I've got to check the warehouse. If you're not busy, you and Tara can come along, see one of our operations and meet some of the men working on that building."

"They work on Saturday?"

"It's their choice, and they're well paid for it. Better put on some jeans."

"How about chinos? I don't own any jeans."

"Whatever. Be back here in fifteen minutes."

"I get the impression you're involved in building. What do you do?"

"I'm a builder. We put up buildings. All kinds. Russ, Drake and I work together as Harrington, Incorporated."

"Impressive. I'd like to see some of your buildings sometime." Realizing that a housekeeper wouldn't have said that, she lowered her gaze, flustered.

"What's the matter?" he asked.

This man was sensitive, and she'd better not call attention to herself. If he became curious about her, she might soon be looking for work. Furthermore, causing him to focus on her could precipitate an eruption she didn't want. She knew enough psychology to appreciate that an attraction as strong as his for her was not one-sided. Besides, that wasn't ice she saw in his eyes as he faced her on the steps the day she arrived, nor was it disinterest she was looking at right then.

"Uh…nothing. I forgot I have work to do."

His facial expression dissolved into the picture of puzzlement. "It's after four, so you're off for the weekend. At least I thought that was our agreement. Meet you down here in a few minutes."

"All right. But, Telford, you don't have to take Tara for a

walk. She's…only a little girl, and she has to understand that you're not here to cater to her."

"I told her we'd go for a walk, and nobody forced me to say that. My word is my bond, and I keep my promises. If I tell you I'll do something, count on it. And I expect the same from anyone else. See you in a minute." He whirled around and dashed up the stairs.

Telford swore at himself as he headed for his room. He had to watch his behavior with Alexis Stevenson. She possessed grace, charm and intelligence—traits that he admired—not to mention sizzling femininity. He'd observed her at breakfast a few mornings earlier, when she thought his mind was on biscuits, sausage and grits. Her finesse went far beyond what he'd expect of a housekeeper. Tactful, too. He threw off his outer clothing, kicked off his shoes, put on jeans, a long-sleeved collared T-shirt, alligator boots and a denim jacket and raced down the stairs. To his surprise, Alexis and Tara waited for him at the bottom of the steps.

"I thought I moved fast. You two must have raced back here."

"I ran. Mummy walked. Where're we going?"

She gazed up at him with soft brown eyes, smiling eyes, and reached for his hand. He supposed she touched him the way she did because she expected him to like her or…maybe because he'd once dreamed he'd have a family of his own—sons like him and soft, feminine daughters. He shook himself out of the memory, the residual of his youthful desires.

"I'm going to show you around the place," he told them. "We're building a warehouse down the road there because it will give us greater security. Want to see it?"

Her little fingers relaxed, warm and trusting in his big hand.

"I do, and I wanna see the puppies, too."

He glanced at Alexis, hoping that she knew something about them. "Puppies? I didn't know we had any."

She lifted her left shoulder in a slight shrug. "Neither did I."

Wondering if he was dealing with the fruits of a child's imagination, he hunkered beside Tara and asked her, "Did Henry say we have puppies?"

She nodded. "Uh-huh. And they're brown."

He stood, and she grasped his hand again. "In that case, I'll see if I can find them. When I was little like you, Tara, I played under this tree while my dad worked nearby." Now why had he shared that with them? He pointed to a sycamore tree that towered over the stable. "That one." When he looked in that direction, he glimpsed Alexis's upturned face and her soft kissable lips, and his heart leapfrogged in his chest.

At the warehouse, he introduced Alexis and Tara to the workers. "Mrs. Stevenson, this is Biff Jackson, my project foreman. Biff, Mrs. Stevenson is our new homemaker." As soon as the words left his mouth, he regretted introducing Alexis to Biff, who assumed the stance of a man looking at a woman he desired but for whom he had low regard.

"And this is Tara, Mrs. Stevenson's daughter. If she strays out here, send her back immediately with a man you trust."

"Sure thing," Biff said, his gaze fixed on Alexis. "Howdy, Ms. Stevenson." He extended his hand. "Things are looking up around here."

Telford didn't imagine that she hesitated before shaking Biff's hand, and it was clear to him that the man continued to hold her grip when she'd indicated she wanted him to release her. Her gaze swept to him, furor flashing in her eyes.

"Knock it off, Biff. If you want to play, find someone who's willing."

Biff's shrug was lazy and insolent. "They're all willing, boss. Some just need a little help." He saluted in mocking fashion. "Glad to meet you. Be seeing you around." She didn't respond.

Telford narrowed his eyes. "Just make certain you know when that help is wanted."

He knew Biff regarded himself highly; he'd heard enough of the man's braggadocios of his way with women. Alexis had just dusted him off, and with Biff's outsized ego, he was probably already thinking of a way to make her pay. Wouldn't hurt to keep an eye on Biff.

"Seen any puppies around here, Biff?"

"Puppies? Naaah. Say, wait. I think Henry has some at his place. Some golden retrievers."

He thanked his foreman and guided Alexis and Tara around the structure, pointing out its features and explaining things to Tara, an intelligent child who possessed a healthy curiosity. The warehouse was a relatively simple structure, and he had built suspension bridges, municipal buildings, schools and mansions, yet his pride in showing Alexis and Tara that uncomplicated job—what he did and who he was—eclipsed his regard for his previous accomplishments. As they headed for Henry's cottage, the significance of his feelings worried him.

Henry stopped mowing the grass as they approached. "I guess you come for your little puppy."

Tara looked at her mother, who pinned soft, warm brown eyes on him.

"All right, all right, but we'll have to establish some house rules, and it has to be a male."

Tara squealed and hugged his leg, and Henry disappeared into the house. Telford liked animals, but he didn't keep pets. As a child, he feared losing things he loved, so he hadn't let himself love. His mother, Etta Harrington, used to disappear whenever it suited her, or it seemed that way to a small boy, and when he was in the third grade, his best friend died of the flu. There'd been times when he'd tried not to love his brothers for fear of losing them.

Henry returned with a puppy in a towel-lined basket, his face bright with smiles as he handed it to Tara, and it dawned on him that the little girl gave the old man unqualified love and affection, a new life.

Tara looked up at them as she cradled her treasure, her face the image of pure joy. "Thanks, Mr. Henry. I'm going to name him Biscuit, 'cause Mr. Telford loves biscuits. I like 'em, too."

What a sensitive child. If she'd learned that from her mother… He shoved the thought aside. He rarely walked around the Harrington property or took the time to enjoy its beauty, and he realized that he found pleasure in it now because he shared it with Alexis and Tara. If he was smart, he'd shake off that domesticity right then.

The little girl held her basket with one hand and grasped his fingers with her other one. "Where we going now, Mr. Telford?"

"We're going home. You need to take care of your puppy, and I've…uh got to do some work."

He wanted to ask Alexis if she was always so serene or if… No, that wasn't it. Maybe he just didn't understand her facial expressions. *And maybe you'd better not try,* a niggling voice warned him.

"Thanks for showing us around," she said, as he prepared to leave them at the bottom of the stairs. "And for letting Tara have the puppy. You've made her so happy."

"My pleasure." Remembering his father's words, "Always get it straight in advance," he sat on the steps and pulled Tara into the curve of his arm.

"Puppies need rules. He cannot run through the house. For now, he sleeps in your room, but when he's older, on the back porch. You bathe him at least once a week. Henry will tell you about feeding him. Understand?"

"Yes, sir." To his amazement, her little arms snaked around his neck and she pressed kisses to his cheek. "I have to go take care of Biscuit," she said, cradling the basket. "Bye."

Tara ran off, but Alexis remained there. He looked at her, and this time he could read her, because he'd caught her off guard with her feelings naked in her eyes. He didn't think he saw gratitude there, but with lightning speed, she pulled a curtain over her emotions, leaving him unsure. In that second, she set off something inside him that he couldn't shove aside, and unless he put on the brakes right then…

He jumped up. "See you at supper."

She called it dinner, thanks to her Yankee roots, and the

Southerner in him thought of it as supper. He half smiled. Another of their inconsequential differences.

"Thanks again, Telford."

Her voice, soft and sweet, soothed him, gave him a strange peace, and he had to admit that she represented what he needed and didn't have: a warm and loving woman in whom he could lose himself and his cares.

Suddenly, he spun around. "What am I thinking? I won't be home for supper tonight. Tell Henry, if you don't mind."

He'd been single for thirty-six years and content with his status. Alone, he'd sent himself and his brothers through school, held his family together after losing his parents, and he'd done it on his own, gone through the tough times by himself. These days, life was a piece of cake by comparison. He wasn't about to complicate his life. But what a temptation Alexis Stevenson was! When she fixed her wide, soft brown eyes on him and subjected him to the peaceful air she wore like a cloak, she weakened his defenses. Inviting. Captivating. Her smooth black skin, patrician nose, luscious lips and full breasts did all kinds of things to his libido. He exhaled a harsh breath. Every perfect curve of her body said *woman*. Jack Stevenson had to be either a fool or a modern tragedy.

When he opened his room door, he thought of Tara expecting him at supper. Now what? He waited twenty minutes and dialed Alexis's phone number.

"Mind if I speak with Tara?"

"Not at all. Just a second."

No preliminaries. He liked that. "Hello, Tara. This is Telford. Have you fed your puppy?"

"Yes, and he's already asleep."

"Good. I'll see you in the morning at breakfast." He hadn't lied, and she wouldn't expect him, so she wouldn't be disappointed. He breathed a deep sigh of relief. An hour later, he was in his Buick Le Sabre headed for Frederick.

Alexis finished pulling the red caftan over her head, tied the thongs of her sandals around her ankles, walked over to her daughter and put the phone back into its cradle. "What did he say?"

"He told me to feed Biscuit."

"That's all?"

"No. He said he'd see me in the morning. Can I have my keyboard now?"

She gave Tara the keyboard, opened the door and walked out into the garden. He'd decided not to have dinner with them and, remembering that Tara would miss him, he'd prepared her. A kind, thoughtful man, but he walked alone, and after what she'd suffered the past four and a half years, she preferred to do the same. Whether she'd made a mistake in signing the contract with Telford would depend on how they deported themselves. Worrying about her reaction to him was a waste of time, and she intended to focus on her sculpting.

"Mummy. Telephone."

"Hello," she said, winded after running halfway across the garden. "Velma! I'd begun to wonder if you'd gotten my message."

"I did, but I've been flying around like crazy. What's he like?"

She prepared herself for the third degree. "What's who like?"

"Don't try to bamboozle me, sis. Anytime your mind goes blank, I know you're hiding something. And this time, it's a man."

"Velma, I've been here exactly six days."

"So? You could've conceived sextuplets by now. What's he like?"

She sat down, crossed her legs and prepared for a grilling by her older sister. "Telford Harrington is, so far as I have been able to determine, a gentleman. That's the sum total of my knowledge of the man."

"My, my. And we're so precise. If he's too much of a gentleman, he can be a bore. What do you think of the place?"

She told her, adding, "Nobody who lives here is suffering."

"Does he have any brothers?"

Alexis laughed aloud, figuring she'd get some of her own. "Two of 'em. Drake, the one I met, makes Billy Dee Williams look ordinary."

Velma's whistle burned her ear. "Quit lying, girl. When I look at Billy Dee in those old movies, I just get plain unconscious. *He's da man.* If this brother's in Billy Dee's class, honey, look for me, and soon."

"Trust me. He's a sizzler." She could picture Velma's mental machine at work.

"If he's so hot, what's wrong with him that you're not interested?"

"No chemistry." That much was true. "And I work for these guys."

"Do you think you'll be able to carry it off, hon? That's hard work, and you're not used to it. I could strangle Jack Stevenson."

"As Grandma used to say, 'let him lie.' I have Tara—or did have. She has mutual affairs going with both Harringtons and the cook." Alexis wiped the dampness from beneath her eyes. "Jack ignored Tara, and she is really basking in the attention these men give her. I think she's fallen for Telford."

"Telford, huh? So that's his name?"

"Would you please back up, Velma? I am not interested in these men."

"Of course you aren't. If one of those blood brothers is a knockout, so are the others. That thing runs in families, and I'll bet Telford's good-looking and you're sweet on him. Anyhow, I want to meet Drake."

"No, you don't. He's younger than you are."

"Don't start preaching. If he's of legal age, intelligent, otherwise mature and has everything in the right places, so what?"

Alexis couldn't help laughing. "Drake Harrington is an architectural engineer and time enough for you and a few more women. If you meet him, you'll have to pay me not to tell him what you just said."

"I'm crying a river. What about the other brother?"

He was a question mark, an important one, because she didn't know how he would react to Tara. "Haven't seen him yet, but Drake referred to him as 'old sourpuss.' He's the middle brother. When can you come visit me?"

"Soon as you can get the family together. I want my pick of those brothers."

"I'll bet. How's business?"

"Great. I just signed to cater the Omega convention. And keep your fingers crossed. I'm bidding for the AKA annual."

"I'm proud of you, sis. I wish you'd show me how to make that crisscross lemon-almond cake."

"Get me a Harrington, and I will."

"I'll… I think that's the doorbell. I'd better answer it. Talk to you later."

She rushed down the long hallway to the front door, peeped out and saw a black Mercedes parked in front of the house. She slipped on the chain, cracked the door and peeped at the visitor.

"You can open it," Henry called to her, and she wondered why he hadn't done that himself.

She flung the door open and gaped at the man who continued to stand there staring at her. "I'm Russ Harrington," he said at last and brushed past her.

Forgetting that she was the housekeeper, she left the door ajar in a kind of reprimand and walked past him.

"Just a minute, miss. Where's Drake?"

"Drake? I haven't the slightest idea."

"Then who're…what're you doing here?"

"I'm Alexis Stevenson, and I'm not visiting either one of your brothers. I'm the housekeeper."

His lower lip dropped. "The *what?*"

"The housekeeper. Dinner's at seven." She walked off and left him wide-eyed and openmouthed.

She'd finally met a Harrington she wasn't sure she liked, and she was almost certain that he wouldn't like Tara.

Chapter 3

"Well, I'll be damned. If she's a housekeeper, I'm William the Conqueror." Russ walked into the kitchen hoping that Henry would enlighten him, but he wasn't there. He moved up the stairs at a slow pace. Surely, Telford hadn't lost his mind and hired that woman to... He stopped on the stairs, took out his cell phone and dialed Telford's cell number.

He skipped the greeting. "Man, I just got home, and this woman who looked as if she was about to entertain the governor opened the door and told me she's the housekeeper. Tell me she's lying or that you're having a little fun at my expense."

"Henry's getting too old to look after that big house, and the place needs more than a—"

Russ sucked in his breath and interrupted his older brother. "So what you're telling me is the woman gliding around here in a long red getup is a housekeeper you hired. Have you lost your mind?"

"She's competent. How'd it go in Barbados?"

"More or less as we thought. Five stories and a one-level

basement is the maximum, and don't try to get me off the subject of this glamour girl who's posing as a housekeeper." The more he thought about losing his privacy, the madder he got. "I don't care if she has a PhD in housekeeping, I'm not changing my life for her. You expect me to walk around here fully clothed, keep my room door closed and—"

"Give it a rest, Russ. She and I signed a two-year contract, and it's binding. Besides, she not a housekeeper; the contract says she's a homemaker."

"Whatever. You could at least have hired somebody who *looked* like a housekeeper. Humph. Homemaker. I thought she was Drake's latest conquest, and I think I upset her by acting as if she were."

Telford's whistle pierced his ears. "I'll bet that rang her bell."

"Did it ever. You should have seen how fast her back went up. Where are you right now?"

"I'm in Frederick."

"Well, you'd better come here and straighten out this mess. Give her a big severance check. Anything. She's got to go."

"Not a chance, Russ. By the way, dinner is at seven; hat off in the house; no swearing; no loud voice; we all eat together; and we say grace at meals."

"What on earth are you talking about?" He couldn't believe the snicker he heard coming through the wire, but there it was again.

"New house rules. I'll get in late tonight. See you."

Russ stared at the dial tone. He was having none of it. After dumping his bags in a corner of his room and kicking off his shoes, he charged, barefooted, downstairs in search of anybody against whom he could release a little venom.

"Hello. What's your name?"

He whirled around and banged his head against the antique chest that had stood in that spot in the hallway since before he was born. He was on his way out of his mind. He was certain of it.

"My name is Tara. Who're you?"

He looked down at her and tried to collect his wits. "I don't know. I honestly don't know. Maybe you'll tell me who you are."

"I already told you. Where's Mr. Telford?"

"He's…uh…out of town, but when he gets back here, you will definitely know it."

"You want to see Biscuit?"

"Biscuit?"

"Biscuit is my little puppy. Mr. Henry gave him to me."

He looked toward the ceiling and fought the urge to bare his teeth. Animals did not belong in a house, and especially not if he lived there. "Did he, now? Where's your mother, Tara?"

To his surprise, she took his hand and smiled. "She's around here."

He'd been in a trance ever since he walked in the door, so he submitted to the eerie feeling that he might have lost his mind, allowed her to hold his hand and followed her.

"There you are, darling."

He stopped and waited until Alexis reached him. "I assume this is your kid."

"You assume wrong. She's a little girl, my daughter."

He ran his hand over his silky curls and regrouped. "Didn't mean to be offensive, but this… Well, it's unsettling at best. I don't know what my brother was thinking about. With two females in this… This is a man's preserve, and with you here, we'll have to reinvent ourselves. This isn't going to work."

She folded her arms, as relaxed as if she were unaware of his annoyance. "You'll hardly ever run into either one of us, and when you do, you'll find you don't mind it at all. We'll see you at dinner. Come along, Tara."

"Wait a second. *Didn't* you understand me? I said this isn't—"

This housekeeper had the temerity to interrupt him. "I heard you, but you want to quarrel with somebody. *Anybody* will do, but I never argue. We'll see you at dinner. Seven o'clock."

She took her daughter's hand, turned and left him standing there.

Housekeeper, huh? Queen of Sheba was more like it. He went to the telephone in the hallway and dialed Henry's cottage. When he didn't get an answer, he dialed Henry's room off the kitchen.

"Henry. I'm trying to sleep."

"How are you, Henry? This is Russ. I came—"

"I know good and well who it is, and I still need my sleep."

"And I need some answers. Where did Telford find Alexis Stevenson? How long's she been here, and what about this little girl and this puppy? This is no place for grown men anymore."

"No? Things musta changed since I was your age. She's the housekeeper, and you needn't raise a stink about Tara, 'cause she's got your brothers in her pocket."

"And you, too, I suppose."

"Well, she *is* a right cute little tyke, and just as sweet as anything. Might as well get up, since you broke my rest. Supper's at seven."

Russ hung up and headed back to his room. An outsider in his own home.

Although she was off duty, Alexis set the table for dinner in the breakfast room. The sooner she got Russ Harrington off his high horse the better, though she suspected he'd resist change until a crisis forced him to be reasonable. She arranged the table with embroidered linen place mats, family-heirloom porcelain, silver and crystal goblets, flowers and lighted candles in silver candlesticks. She'd overdone it, but that was her way of declaring war. Her child deserved a peaceful, happy environment, not an atmosphere soured by Russ's disgruntlement. She hoped Drake would be home for dinner, because the prospect of eating with Russ and only Tara as a buffer all but took her appetite.

At seven o'clock, she and Tara took their places at the table, and to her surprise, Russ joined them immediately. No one had to tell her he wasn't motivated by a spirit of cooperation. The man was anxious to strike back.

"What the… Is somebody getting married?"

"I eat at a properly set dinner table," she said, smiling her best smile. "I try to make the home comfortable, a happy place."

"You're kidding. This looks as if you're expecting the president, or some big shot's getting married. I don't call this comfortable."

She looked at him and smiled, though she knew he was vexed. If he took pleasure in eating with them, he had to be the world's best actor. He picked up his fork.

"You have to say grace first," Tara told him. "My mummy always says it before we eat."

Russ looked steadily at the child, but he didn't say grace.

"Would you like to say it, Tara?" Alexis asked her daughter.

Tara offered a long, colorful supplication, and Alexis's respect for Russ mounted with the minutes, for he didn't attempt to stop her and didn't begin eating until she finished. In fact, it was the sound of Telford's voice that ended Tara's grace; she would have dashed to greet him, if Alexis hadn't restrained her.

"How's everybody? Am I late?"

Russ stood, and the way in which they clasped each other tightly told her much about the Harrington men. In spite of Russ's displeasure with Telford because he'd hired her, he greeted his brother with affection.

"You're in time," Alexis said. "We hadn't started eating."

"That's because Tara here treated us to the longest grace I ever heard. I expect she'd still be at it, if you hadn't walked in. Look, man, this is a hefty dose you're pouring out."

Telford ignored him. "Be back as soon as I wash up. That's another thing. Our homemaker says no dirty hands at the table." She glimpsed the twinkle in his eye and realized that he enjoyed jostling with Russ.

"Put a lid on it," Russ said, reaching for his fork. "Who taught you to say grace?" he asked Tara.

"My mummy. Is Mr. Telford coming back?"

He helped himself to a broiled hamburger, tasted it and grimaced. "Henry's losing it," he said in reference to the hamburger, then looked at Alexis. "Is she stuck on Telford? What's Drake's reaction to this?"

"He graciously capitulated."

"Hmmm."

She nearly sighed in relief when Telford sat down, but she knew at once that Russ intended to press for her dismissal when he said, "I'm going to speak to Henry about these meals. And you've got a lot to account for, brother."

"Not till after I eat," Telford said. He spoke in a gentle tone, but she knew, and she didn't doubt that Russ knew, that Telford meant what he said.

"How's Biscuit?" he asked Tara, signaling to Russ that the matter of Alexis's status was closed for the moment.

As if she'd been waiting for him to acknowledge her presence, Tara's face bloomed into a smile. "He's asleep. I fed him like you said." She looked at Russ. "His name is Biscuit 'cause Mr. Telford likes biscuits."

A half smile flashed briefly across Russ's mouth. "In that case, I'm surprised you didn't name him sausage. Or maybe grits."

"Lay off, Russ," Telford said. He looked at Tara. "We'll have to get him a real puppy bed. I'll speak to Henry about it."

Telford had spoken directly to Tara and to his brother, but he hadn't said a word especially to Alexis; indeed, he hadn't let his gaze connect with hers.

Tara thanked him and blessed him with one of her most brilliant smiles. Alexis watched in amazement when Telford smiled lovingly at her daughter. She didn't know what to think. It was as if he wanted her to know that he didn't welcome the intrusion, but wouldn't punish the child because of it. Yet... Lost in her thoughts, she lifted the large Waterford crystal pitcher of iced tea and would have spilled it if Telford hadn't reached across the table and grabbed it. He looked at her then, filled her glass and handed it to her.

"Maybe we should use smaller pitchers. This one's heavy."

"Come now," Russ said. "You don't mind doing it for her, do you?"

"You're way out of line, Russ. You want to say something to me, save it for later. And lay off Alexis."

Her gaze flew to Russ. She hadn't detected any animosity or hostility in his voice, but Telford took offense. She wanted to go back to her room, but she couldn't think of a way to do that without giving the impression that Russ had displeased her. Tara yawned, giving her the perfect excuse.

"You can't go yet," Telford said when she took Tara's hand and attempted to leave the table. "I brought Tara some black-cherry ice cream." He got up to go to the kitchen and stopped beside Tara. "Henry said you like it."

Tara removed her hands from her mouth, where she'd clasped them to prevent herself from squealing, and laughed. "I love it."

"I'm bringing it," Henry said. "You should've bought some cake, Tel. Black-cherry ice cream without cake is as bad as bread with no butter." He gave Tara a dish containing five scoops.

"You didn't tell me she liked cake."

"You bought *ice cream?*" Russ asked, his face the picture of incredulity. "And you practically gave her the whole half gallon," he said to Henry, who stood by waiting to see her eat it. "Are you trying to kill her?"

Alexis raised her head and glanced at Telford with the intention of thanking him for bringing Tara's favorite ice cream, but she couldn't utter a word, only trembled with excitement when she saw the naked desire blazing in his eyes. She glanced past Telford to the knowing look on Russ's face. Telford hooded his eyes, but she knew she hadn't imagined it for she had responded to him from the depth of her being.

Still, she was glad for Russ's presence, because she wouldn't have bet on what might have happened if she and Telford had been alone at that moment. He generated a warmth, a sweetness that wove him into her like an artist's needles subduing yarn. The tremble of his bottom lip titillated her woman's need, shortening her breathing, and he saw it. She knew he did; nothing else would account for the fire of passion that leaped back into his gaze. She had no defense against the primal need that she saw in him. Everything about him beckoned her and claimed her, and she couldn't help shifting in her chair as his heat singed her. With her eyes closed to banish from her presence the man who tantalized her, who represented the living embodiment of temptation…and maybe ruin, she struggled for composure. What had she gotten herself into?

"I turned the floodlights on out back," Henry said, making Telford aware that he and Alexis were not alone. "But the one near the guest room didn't come on. Wouldn't matter, if it wasn't for Tara and Alexis. The light might make 'em feel more comfortable."

"I'll have a look at it. Could be the fuse." Any reason to focus on something other than the woman in front of him.

But Russ clearly had other concerns and didn't hesitate to express them. "When are we going to talk, Telford?"

He narrowed his eyes. If his brother meant to be troublesome about Alexis and Tara, he wouldn't tolerate it. A contract— whether by word of mouth or in writing—was binding. "About Frenchman's Village in Barbados, or about…things here?"

"Things here. We can talk about the village when Drake gets back. Where is he?"

"In Philadelphia. He thinks we need lighter-weight material for the top six floors of the Griffith-Joyner houses, and he's testing some products. I'm going to check on that light."

"Can I go, too, Mr. Telford?"

When she ran to him and took his hand, her little brown face shimmering with delight, her smile said, *I think you're wonderful, extra special.* And though he tried to resist her, joy pervaded his whole being. Before he stopped to consider his action and what it implied, he swung her up on his shoulders, braced her hands on his head and gave the laughing little girl the ride of her life as he strode swiftly to the room she shared with her mother.

Russ's astonished "Well, I'll be…" followed in his wake.

"Mind if I duck out here?" Telford asked Alexis, pointing to the door of the anteroom that was designed as a sitting room, but which was now Tara's room.

"Of course I don't mind." She didn't look at him when she said it, evidence enough that she was as conscious of him as he was of her.

Tara yanked on his hand. "Want to see my keyboard?"

He wanted to give his self-control a break and get out of there, but she took his hand and he followed her into what seemed to be her room. She sat at the portable keyboard and played finger exercises. Then, she asked if he could play.

"I used to."

She moved, and he sat down and played several nursery rhymes and some Beatles songs that she seemed to appreciate more. It was too cozy, too much like his youthful dreams and too dangerous.

"Look, I…I have to be going. That light…"

She reached over and hugged him then, her little arms tight around his neck, communicating a need to which, God help him, he responded with every fiber of his being. When she released him, her little face illuminated with smiles, he stared down at her, suddenly pensive, contemplating a truth he'd just learned: this little girl had plugged up a hole, obliterated an emptiness he'd had in him nearly all of his life. She went back to her finger exercises and was soon lost in the pleasure of them. He patted her shoulders and, humbled by the child's healing love, walked with measured steps out of her room to where Alexis filled his vision, and he received his second shock: tears streamed down her face. And he'd thought her unflappable.

He rushed to her. "What is it? What's the matter? Alexis, why are you crying?"

His hands went toward her shoulders but didn't touch them. She wiped at her tears with the back of her hand and tried to speak, but the strength of whatever she felt overwhelmed her, and the tears became a deluge, cascading down her face.

Her loss of composure cut to the quick, and he thought he'd go insane if he couldn't comfort her. With a groan, he pulled her into the protection of his arms.

"Tell me what hurts you, and if it can be fixed, I'll fix it. I can't stand seeing you like this."

She didn't move from him, and he clasped her tighter, relishing her nearness and the womanly scent that perfumed his nostrils.

"What is it?" he urged.

"Tara. Her...her father never had time for her. Yet, as busy as I know you are, you sat there and played that keyboard for her, giving her what she's missed so badly. I don't know how to th—"

"Don't. Don't thank me. Look, I...I'd better check out that floodlight."

He knew his limit, and he was inches from it. He opened the screen door and stepped out into the garden, still feeling her flesh in his hands, her softness against his chest. He leaned against the side of the house, took deep breaths and counted to ten as he inhaled and exhaled. In thirty-six years, he'd never been so strung out.

Standing where he left her, Alexis, too, let the wall take her weight. Maybe he had herculean self-control, or maybe he didn't want her as badly as she'd thought. Whatever the reason why he could hold her so tenderly and then walk away when her whole being screamed for his loving, she should be grateful. She rubbed her arms and knew that was a substitute for his warmth. It wasn't right, and she would regret it, but she wanted him to kiss her so badly that she burned for it.

He knocked on the screen door. "May I come in? I have to get a flashlight."

"I have one." She handed it to him, keeping a good distance away.

"Could you hold it while I check out this fuse box?"

She stepped outside in the cool spring night and trained the beam on the light meter. After about ten minutes during which he worked silently, he closed the box.

"Must be the bulb, but I can't change that tonight."

"I don't need that light, Telford."

He raised himself up from his squatting position. "Then I'll do it after I get home tomorrow."

The moonlight cast a glow over his face that softened his features, and gave his hazel-brown eyes a sexy, almost wanton magnetism. She stared at him; she couldn't help it. Her gaze darted to his broad chest with its pectorals prominent beneath his T-shirt, back to his square chin and settled on his mouth.

She knew the moment had come, when he took the flashlight from her fingers and she heard the gadget fall to the grass. It didn't occur to her that she ought to move.

"Alexis, if you want our relationship to remain exactly as it is, get back in that house. Now."

She didn't want it to change, but she wanted to be in his arms. Needed the warmth and loving that a faithless marriage had denied her. Her head said *move,* but her heart said *stay where you are.*

"Did you understand what I said? Did you?"

The hoarse, guttural sounds, so unlike his mellifluous voice, excited her, and a strange heat began wafting its way through her veins. She opened her mouth to answer, but no sound came.

Like lightning, he had her in his arms and lifted her until he pressed them breast to chest and belly to belly. One of his big, powerful hands locked to her buttocks and the other to the back of her head. He stared into her face, and then his mouth came down on her, hard and trembling.

"Open for me. Let me in you."

He parted her lips with his tongue, commanding her to take him. And she did. Hot darts danced inside her and her senses whirled dizzily when at last she had him. His tongue danced within her mouth, tasting, anointing, driving in and out in a symbolic act of love. He teased and tantalized until she gripped him to her and moans sprang from deep in her throat. Frustrated, she twisted against his chest, and experienced man that he was, his fingers found her nipple and pinched and rubbed until she cried aloud.

"Telford, I can't stand this."

The tips of his callused fingers brushed her chest before dipping into the scooped-neck caftan and freeing her breast for his rapacious mouth. His tongue, moist, warm and sweet, curled around her erected aureole, bringing a keening cry from her as he suckled her with a wild, animal hunger until electric shocks pelted her feminine core.

Stunned as, for the first time in her life, love's liquid flowed freely from her, she attempted to move away from him.

"What's the matter?" he whispered, as if he feared startling her. "Have I…done something wrong?"

Embarrassed, she buried her face in his shoulder. "It's… I'm sorry…it went further than I… I let it get out of hand."

He eased her to her feet, but his arm stayed snug around her. "I don't want you to be upset. There's no point in that. Both of us knew the minute we first looked at each other that this would happen. Right?"

He caressed her cheek, rhythmically, the way he'd stroked her breast and, to stop his assault on her senses, she covered his hand with her own. But to him, it must have been a gesture of affection, for he kissed her forehead.

"If you had left here then, it could have been a year from now, but I think I would eventually have gone after you."

"Yes, we both knew, but we didn't want it to happen," she whispered.

"In these circumstances? No, we didn't, but I wouldn't exchange it for anything. Still, I'll try to keep my hands off you."

She couldn't help smiling at that. "I don't question your honor."

He stared until she wanted to lose herself in his eyes. Then he tipped her chin with his right index finger. "You are one beautiful woman. And I'm not talking about looks, though there's definitely that, too. I mean you are everything a man needs. I'll see you at breakfast. Sleep well." He opened the screen door, strode through her room and out of sight.

She sat on the edge of her bed, grateful for a moment of privacy while Tara plunked away at the keyboard. Jack Stevenson hadn't known what to do with her or, if he had, he hadn't bothered to apply that knowledge. Maybe she'd asked to be treated as if she were cold porcelain, but she didn't think so. Until tonight, she had no basis for comparison, but she'd always thought petting and sex ought to be both more demanding and more rewarding. When Jack didn't show any concern for her lack of response, she began to resent his own release and finally reached the point where she tuned out, even when they were supposed to be making love. After the first six or seven months, she stopped hoping and, as time passed, she no longer tried to feel anything.

She could think of a dozen reasons why she should stay away from Telford Harrington, including the fact that he liked his life as it was. *Girl, you'd better use some discipline. If you don't you're headed for trouble.* If she didn't use self-control. Precisely what she didn't want to do.

He had hoped that Russ wouldn't broach the matter of Tara and Alexis that night. He didn't have the patience or the will to deal with his brother's displeasure at his having hired Alexis. It wouldn't hurt him to shave every day and observe rules of common decency in communal living. All three of them needed to clean up their acts and stop taking self-indulgence to such extremes. He bypassed the den and headed for his room, but Russ would not be deterred and waited for him at the top of the stairs.

"Look, Telford, I suspect it's useless to ask you to reconsider this. But have you thought about what it'll be like for her in the midst of four men? This isn't the place for her, and what about that child? In two weeks, she'll know every cuss word ever spoken."

Telford loved his brothers, and he valued their camaraderie and peaceful relations, but this matter was not negotiable. "She stays, Russ. I gave her a contract. I don't like our disagreeing about something so fundamental as who lives in our home. She's intelligent, and if she finds that you're not comfortable around her, I'm sure she'll avoid you as much as possible. As for the cuss words, Tara won't learn any in this house."

"Aw, hell, man. I'm not stupid. A five-year-old could feel the chemistry between the two of you. Tara feels it. And another thing, you can break that little girl's heart."

He stared at Russ. "Right. That must be the reason you want me to send her away from here. Don't expect anything to happen between Alexis and me." He couldn't help smiling. "As for Tara, I think she's got my number."

Russ raised an eyebrow and let a smile play around his mouth. "If she's got your number, her mother's got your address. I just talked with Drake, and he thinks I ought to go up to Philadelphia tomorrow and check the new material he's considering. You want to examine it, too?"

"Not unless the two of you disagree, and that isn't likely. I need to keep an eye on that school. That dedication ceremony will go on as scheduled, and the bell will ring for the first day of school on September seventh if I have to hold up that building with my back." He knocked his left hand into his right palm and ground his teeth. "Fentress Sparkman will be sorry he ever heard of our dad, and it will be a long time before he turns the screw on another one or his partners. I've got him this time."

"Yeah. Just be sure you can give it your full attention."

Another allusion to Alexis. Both of his brothers wanted the best for him. He knew that, but he didn't give either of them the right to choose his friends and tamper with his relationships. He told Russ good-night and went to his room, where he paced the floor for half an hour.

She had a wallop like nothing he'd ever experienced. It

scared the hell out of him and yet, it felt like coming home to a warm, welcoming fire when you were practically frozen. Unfortunately, he couldn't let anything happen between him and Alexis Stevenson, though he dared not let himself think about the hot lover she'd be. He shook his head. Not only did she work for him, but she could bring him to his knees the way his mother did his father whenever she got the notion. Besides, he liked his life as it was. He amended that. As it had been, and he'd make certain it stayed that way.

"I'm bringing a friend home for dinner," he told Henry several mornings later. With Russ and Drake in Philadelphia, he figured he had to do something to put a damper on what was becoming a cozy, family atmosphere with Alexis, Tara and himself. He behaved impersonally with her and kept his hands to himself, though at great cost. But they were like missiles, headed directly at each other, primed for a massive explosion. And nobody would believe what passed for conversation between them. Banality hardly described it.

"Does this friend eat a lot, or does she pick at the food like she was scared it was gonna rise up and bite her?"

At times, he would like to give Henry a piece of his mind, but that would be the same as cussing his father. "Just prepare enough for another adult."

"And here I was hoping you'd lost her in some nice place like the Bermuda wrangle."

"You mean Triangle. And, Henry, could you please stop meddling in my business?"

"Humph. Guess you in a hurry for the Fourth of July fireworks. Them two women ain't gonna like this. You think Alexis gonna hold still for that stuff Evangeline…'scuse me, *Miss* Evangeline puts down? I'm gonna eat a big lunch to give me plenty energy. I'll need it for all the laughing I'm gonna have to do." Henry looked up toward the ceiling and started whistling "Takin' Care of Business."

Telford swallowed what remained of his coffee, picked up an umbrella and headed for the Eagle Park High School construction site. Henry had never liked Evangeline, and she'd never been special to *him*. Maybe he shouldn't have asked her to dinner, but what else could he do? Heat flared in his loins every time he looked at Alexis; if he couldn't cool down on his own, maybe after tonight she'd force him to do it. He was halfway across town before he remembered that he hadn't told Tara good-bye.

As soon as he reached the trailer that housed his temporary office at the corner of Mountain and Edgecomb, he phoned her.

"Henry, is Tara eating breakfast?"

"Ain't you supposed to be asking her mother that? Hold on."

"Hi, Mr. Telford. Where are you?"

"I'm at work. I had to leave early this morning, so I called to tell you good-bye."

"Good-bye. When you coming home?"

"I'll be there for supper. See you then."

"Lots of kisses. Bye."

He hung up. He hadn't said what he felt, but enough to let her know he hadn't forgotten her. Somehow, he felt lighter than before. That little girl had gotten inside him, and it wasn't a question of liking it or not. It just was.

Since the night they gave in to the fire burning in them for each other, he and Alexis hadn't gotten close enough to touch, except at mealtime when they had Tara and Henry to help them use common sense. She hadn't made one move toward him, and he knew it was because she didn't think a relationship with him appropriate, much as she might desire it. So if she didn't want him, he reasoned, seeing him with Evangeline shouldn't bother her. *Yeah. And the sun rises in the west.* He'd cross that bridge when he got there.

Alexis sensed a difference before she got to the kitchen; the house seemed empty for so early in the morning.

"Just you and Tara this morning," Henry told her. "Tel had to leave early."

So that was it. If she could sense his absence from a house that big, she had better avoid him altogether. Nothing in her contract said she had to eat her meals with him; indeed, most housekeepers—and that's what she was, no matter if the contract specified homemaker—didn't eat with their bosses. She slapped her forehead. Not being able to eat with Telford would devastate Tara.

From somewhere in the distance she heard Henry's voice. "...and wear that long red thing at supper tonight. Telford's planning to commit social suicide."

"What? What does that mean?"

"Means he's bringing company."

Cold marbles danced around in her belly, and moisture beaded on her forehead. "Are you telling me he's bringing a woman friend home with him this evening?"

She'd learned that Henry never answered a question directly if he could do it some other way. He raised an eyebrow. "Like I said, come in here looking good. Course, you'd make her look bad if you showed up in dungarees. And fix the supper table real nice."

Although she appreciated his gesture of friendship, she was too annoyed to show it. "What makes you think I care who Telford Harrington brings here?"

"'Cause you do. But don't worry none. She won't spend the night. Never has. He ain't *that* crazy."

That conversation weighed on her as she did the morning chores. Put on that caftan? No way. She intended to wear her red silk sleeveless jumpsuit. He'd get an eyeful whether she was sitting down or walking away from him. She set the table with the best Harrington appointments, added candles and a bouquet of red, white and yellow roses and surveyed the result with satisfaction.

She dressed Tara in a jumpsuit that matched her own, combed the child's hair out and sprayed it with a lilac scent. Then she showered, put on the red suit, fastened gold hoops to her ears, let down her hair below her shoulders and dabbed

Obsession perfume where it counted. She didn't believe in going to war unless you meant to win.

For whatever reason he'd brought a woman home with him, he remembered that they ate at seven. It wasn't she, but Henry, who usually opened the door for the brothers, but when the bell rang at a quarter of seven, she beat him to it. Telford gaped at her, speechless and obviously dumbfounded until Tara ran between them and hugged his legs.

"Mr. Telford, I got your telephone call today." Tara held her arms up for a hug, but he didn't see the child. His gaze was glued to Alexis.

"Can I have a hug?" That got his attention, and he reached down, lifted her and stroked her back. "Do you like how I look?"

"You're beautiful, and I like it." She kissed his cheek and he set her on the floor.

"What a touching little scene."

His head snapped around. "Oh. Sorry. Ms. Moore, this is Mrs. Alexis Stevenson, our homemaker."

Alexis sized her up and smiled. The woman wouldn't resist being catty. She extended her hand. "How do you do, Ms. Moore. This is my daughter, Tara."

"Hi, Miss Moore." Tara's greeting lacked enthusiasm.

"Sure you're a housekeeper?"

Alexis let a smile drift over her face. "If you want to know how competent I am, I guess you'll have to ask Telford." With that double entendre, she led them to the living room, aware that she'd made Evangeline Moore blanch. Whether from annoyance or embarrassment, she didn't know or care. "Would you like something to drink, Ms. Moore? Lemonade or iced tea?" She figured that, as homemaker, she was also hostess. And since she was certain that her tactics didn't please Telford, she didn't bother to look at him.

"I'd like a dry martini," Evangeline said, "and shake it well."

Alexis sat down, crossed her left leg over her right knee

and swung her left foot. "That's Telford's domain. I have no idea how to mix a martini."

She had to stifle the giggles that threatened to spill out of her when she finally looked at Telford and saw his murderous glare. She wanted to dance for joy. He'd get her for it later, but she didn't care. He started to the refrigerator, and Tara ran to him.

"Mr. Telford, is Miss Moore your mummy?"

"What?" Evangeline jumped from the chair and pointed her finger at Alexis. "Did you tell her to say that?"

"I didn't, and I apologize for her innocent mistake."

Telford knelt beside Tara. "No, she isn't, Tara. She's my friend and our dinner guest."

"Is she going to stay with us?"

"No. She's just here for dinner."

"Oh." She ran over to Evangeline. "I'm glad Mr. Telford has a friend."

He looked at Evangeline, waiting for her response, and when she didn't say anything, he walked over to Alexis. "Could we have dinner now?"

"What about the martini?"

"I don't have any vermouth."

She promised herself she'd check the bar first thing in the morning. Standing, she took Tara's hand. "Come along, darling."

He nearly laughed when Evangeline walked into the dining room and gasped. As though it were all especially for her, she headed for the place opposite his own as head of the table and found Alexis seating herself there.

"That's Mummy's seat. You can sit here beside me." Tara patted the chair next to hers.

"I'll sit over here."

Tara was too innocent and sweet to realize it, but she was needling Evangéline more than Alexis was. He knew Evangeline wouldn't show patience for one of Tara's long graces, so he took the matter in hand.

"Let's say grace." He did, and when he glanced from one woman to the other, he saw pride and affection in one and furor in the other.

As if to make certain that he had a heart attack, Henry walked into the dining room and put a bowl in front of him and one in front of Alexis.

"Be right back with the rest."

"Hello, Henry," Evangeline called after him.

"Fine," he called over his shoulder. Seconds later he returned with two more bowls, which he placed before Tara and Evangeline, in that order, then set a soup tureen in the middle of the table.

Telford ground his teeth. One of these days he was going to have to fire Henry. "I don't believe this."

Alexis lifted the lid from the tureen and stared at the contents. "Henry," she called.

"Yes, ma'am," he said, arousing her suspicion, since he never addressed her that way.

"I thought we were having lamb chops for dinner and a full, five-course meal."

"Didn't feel like it. Besides, cabbage stew's healthy."

Telford thought about it for a few seconds. Tara didn't need to see adults act ugly, so he served himself a big helping of cabbage, potatoes and smoked pig jowl.

"May I have your plate, Evangeline?"

She pushed it to him and he was certain that she deliberately shoved her soupspoon to the floor. "Get me another soupspoon, Alexis."

He held his breath, but after Alexis's eyes widened with momentary shock, a smile drifted over her face, and he exhaled.

"If you ask Henry, I'm sure he'll bring you one. You always have to ask him nicely, though."

Henry came in with a pitcher of lemonade, and he was glad for the opportunity to lighten the atmosphere. "Henry, would you bring Evangeline a soupspoon, please."

"What happened to the one I gave her?"

"She threw it on the floor, Mr. Henry."

"Tara, please don't interrupt when adults are speaking."

"But she *did,* Mummy."

That settled it. Telford got up and went to the kitchen to get a soupspoon. Silver or not didn't matter. Besides, he had no idea where Alexis kept that silver. He put the spoon beside Evangeline's plate and looked at her, hoping she got his message. *Let's have some peace at this table.*

At least Henry made dessert. Telford thanked him for the apple pie.

"Tara likes it, and she wants me to put black-cherry ice cream on it" was Henry's reply.

"Would you like espresso or regular coffee, Evangeline?" Alexis asked her.

Evangeline looked at Telford. "Whatever you're having, dear."

"He's having regular coffee."

He couldn't say she was deliberately aggravating Evangeline, but the women were so dissimilar that the difference itself had to irritate Evangeline. Why hadn't he realized that Alexis was an upper-class woman? She had some talking to do.

Chapter 4

Serving coffee in the den wouldn't make Evangeline happy, because it meant sharing Telford with Tara and Alexis for what remained of the evening, but Alexis didn't intend to ease the situation for him. They had agreed to keep their distance from each other, but he could at least have told her he'd have a woman guest for dinner if only because it was she who set the dinner table. With all the innocence that was natural to Tara, the child engaged Evangeline in conversation, or tried to, frustrating Tara and annoying Evangeline.

When Telford finally stood and Evangeline Moore sighed in resignation, the evening shot, Alexis walked over to her and extended her hand.

"It was nice meeting you, Ms. Moore. I hope you'll visit *us* again."

"Bye, Mr. Telford," Tara said, raising her arms for a good-bye kiss and, at the same time, saving Evangeline a courteous reply to Alexis. "You coming back?"

"I'll be back before long." He smiled lovingly at Tara, but the look he gave Alexis had the explosive power of a ball of

TNT headed for a target. She wasn't afraid of the retribution his eyes promised; what he incited in her was as far from fear as east from west. She knew that her own face bore a glow of triumph, and she felt like a victor, because she'd taught him that he had to reckon with her. Tara walked them to the door holding Telford's hand, but Alexis went into the kitchen to speak with Henry.

"Why did you serve that cabbage stew? I set a table fit for the president, and you serve cabbage."

Henry's head went back. Then he laughed until he doubled up and finally lost his breath. She had to pound his back. "Crazy, huh? Funniest thing I ever done. Miss Etta's handkerchief linen and her best crystal and porcelain and things... Cabbage. Prissy as she was, I bet the poor woman turned over in her grave."

"But why? Henry, I wanted us to have a nice dinner."

"Humph. You didn't want no such thing. You wanted to show off. Telford knows what I always serve when he done something I don't like. And bringing that woman here... He shoulda knowed he was gonna have to eat cabbage stew." Henry rubbed his hands together gleefully. "I bet that ain't the only punishment he's gonna get."

"You're getting very fanciful, Henry."

"If you want to call it that. I wasn't born this morning."

"Why don't you like Evangeline Moore?"

He turned out the light over the kitchen sink and leaned against the counter. "I lived a long time, and I know people when I see 'em. He ain't serious about her, and that's because he knows she ain't for him."

"Why are you so sure of that?"

"'Tain't difficult. She gets low grades in the manners department, and Tel can't stand rotten manners. She ain't bad, mind you, but these boys here...they come up practically by themselves, except for what raising I done and Telford when he got older... They been through a lot and worked hard."

His countenance darkened with concern, and she could see

that Telford and his brothers meant a lot to Henry and that he took pride in them.

"She ain't got no appreciation for what they been through and what they've done with their lives, either," he went on, "and she don't care. She just wants a Harrington. Now *you*. You ain't asking nothing from no man. My kind of woman, willing and able to make it on your own."

"Thanks. That doesn't explain why you don't like her."

"She just ain't for him. I could stand her, maybe, if she wasn't so supercilious, always pretending to be something she ain't. She can't fool me."

And what about Alexis? Wasn't she an imposter, an upper-middle-class educator posing as a housekeeper?

Her lower lip dropped. Henry was one surprise after another. "If she wasn't so what?"

"Super…oh, you mean that? Well, I want you to know I finished high school, even if that was a couple a hundred years ago."

She paused, wondering how he'd react to her next question. "Did you ever marry?"

He threw his hands up and looked at the ceiling. "I sure did, which is why I understand the Evangelines of this world. First time was plain stupid, but the second…well, the Lord decided he needed her more than I did." He turned his back, but not before she glimpsed his lips trembling and his eyes blinking rapidly.

She patted the bones that protruded beneath his shoulder. "I'm sorry. I'd better get to my room and see what Tara's doing. Good night." She didn't wait for his reply, but rushed from the kitchen to allow him privacy. When she found Tara asleep in her bed, loneliness washed over her. She wasn't jealous, and she didn't want an affair with Telford, but seeing him with that woman wasn't her idea of fun. She walked over to the window and stared at the garden, idyllic in its shroud of moonlight and its blanket of shrubs and flowers, the perfect setting for lovers. She yanked the blinds down and closed them. She might be alone, but at least she no longer had to suffer the indignity of a philandering, lying husband. Anything was better than that, she told herself as convincingly as she could.

What was that? This time the knock sounded louder and lasted longer. "Good Lord. Telford." It hadn't occurred to her that he'd be back in less than half an hour. "I'll bet he's mad as the devil."

Anger barely described what he felt. Indeed, outrage more closely approximated his mood. She opened the door, and he looked at her standing there, a siren with the face of an innocent. If he hadn't been so furious, he would have laughed. He'd never seen her so beautiful as she was that evening. Or sexier, with that décolletage proclaiming the richness of her treasure and her tight-fitting getup emphasizing her nicely rounded bottom. If Henry had cooked the lamb chops instead of the cabbage stew, he doubted he'd have tasted the difference.

A smile crawled warily over her face. "Hi. You wanted me for something?"

"Do I want… You knew I'd come after you, and don't pretend you didn't." Her shrug didn't fool him. She was strung tight as a bow.

"Did I do something to displease you? If so, I'm—"

He stepped into the room and stopped inches from her. "Of course not. You were the perfect hostess. I couldn't have asked for a more charming woman to grace my home and entertain my guest, but—"

She interrupted him. "Isn't that what a homemaker's supposed to do?"

He stared at the rise and fall of her bosom, and when he let his gaze drift to her eyes, he didn't doubt that she knew where he'd been looking and that his attention to her breasts excited her. She wet her lips, obviously without knowing she did it, and her breathing accelerated. *She knows I'm here.*

"You didn't want Evangeline in this house, and you didn't want her here with me. Oh, you weren't rude; in fact you were sweet as sugar. I wanted to get my hands on you—"

"If you had, what would you have done with your girlfriend looking on?"

"I'd have—"

"She's not looking on now."

Of their own will, his left hand went to her sweet little bottom and his right one to her shoulder, and in a second he had her in his arms and his tongue deep in her mouth. Shudders plowed through him, and his blood pounded in his ears as she locked him to her. The hardened tips of her breasts rubbed against his chest, and when he heaved her higher to take one into his mouth and suckle her, she straddled him and rocked against him. Heat enveloped him like tongues of fire from a roaring furnace, as she pressed against the weight that hung hard and heavy between his legs. Her hips undulated in a pulsing rhythm. Wild and reckless.

Her whimpers heightened his need to have her thrashing beneath him with his name spilling from her lips, and when she pressed her crossed ankles against the small of his back, he nearly exploded.

"Alexis. Baby, I'm reaching my limit. Do you want us to—"

Her moans quickened, and her hands caressed his hair as she held his head to her breast.

"Tell me what you want." She held on tighter, and he knew he had to loosen her hold on him and look into her eyes. This was not a time for a gargantuan error on his part. He took several steps away from the door, tripped and fell backward with her across her bed.

He rolled away from her. "Do you want me to leave or stay?"

She ran her fingers across her forehead, as if clearing away a patch of haze. "Both," she said, sitting up. "I don't understand how it is that when you put your hands on me, I stop thinking." She frowned. "What were we talking about?"

He sat forward and braced his elbows on his knees. "You could drive me insane. You know that? One minute you're setting a torch to me and the next you're as cool as spring rain." He'd leave, but he couldn't stand right then. "Did you think I wouldn't ever bring a woman guest here?"

"The other time when you kissed me, you went at me as if women were about to be banned. We backed off from that and said we weren't going that way. But still, you should have told me ahead of time that you were bringing her here."

"Come off it, Alexis. Henry told you. You want me to believe you dressed like this to have dinner with Tara, Henry and me?"

She had the nerve to grin. "I can do better than this. What's wrong with looking nice at dinner? Did she like me?"

He threw up his hands. "*Did she like you?* Of course. Why shouldn't she? She's crazy about you."

She looked at her fingernails, then polished them on the silk that covered her thigh. "Hmmm. Then it's you she doesn't like. Otherwise, you wouldn't have gotten back here so soon."

"If I thought you meant that, I'd teach you a few things." He got up and walked to the door. "I wouldn't advise you to try that again."

"What? You mean I shouldn't kiss you if you kiss first? What do you expect from me? I'm human, and you're…" She licked her lips. "You're indescribable."

"I don't know what I expected to solve by coming here. You're unreasonable."

She gazed at him through slightly lowered lashes and served notice that she could give as good as she got. "You expected exactly what you got."

He wanted to kiss her until she opened to him, surrendered and flowered in his arms, and he wanted to shake her. He did neither. "See you in the morning."

"Sure thing," she said with an airiness he knew she didn't feel. "Good night."

He closed the door softly and headed for the den. *One of these times when we come together like that, I'm going to let her call a halt. If she doesn't…*

If that evening had been a bust, and it had, it was his fault. Evangeline Moore was not and never had been special to him; indeed, he could count three perfunctory kisses as the extent of their intimacy. It was the minimum a man could do when he took a fawning woman home after a reasonably decent dinner. Hell, he didn't even know where her bedroom was and, unless she was confined to bed with a prolonged and serious illness, he didn't expect to find out. He'd been so intent on covering his flank, on proving to both himself and Alexis that they didn't have any ties and were free to do as they pleased and with whomever they liked, that he overlooked one simple thing: when a man and a woman fired each other up and came as close to all-out lovemaking as they had, they had solid ties whether they liked it or not. Besides, he hadn't cleared that agenda with Alexis. She was right when she said he should have told her. He didn't want to think of his reaction if she'd had a man in her room when he knocked on her door.

He sat in the darkened den with his feet on the coffee table and his hands locked behind his head. If he got Alexis out of his system, what would he do about Tara?

The next morning, Alexis opened the liquor cabinet, her heart in her throat. She needn't have worried. Her whole being awakened, rejuvenated like new life in early spring, when her gaze took in the six bottles of dry white vermouth on the bottom shelf facing the door where Telford couldn't have missed them. He had deliberately refused to give Evangeline the martini she asked for. When the woman mistreated Tara with her rudeness, she lost points with Telford, and he took steps immediately to shorten his time in her company.

Several afternoons later, Alexis walked with Tara along the road leading to what would soon become the new Harrington warehouse. They paused at the quaint bridge—logs grayed from the wind and rain and flat from having borne the weight of humans and animals for a century or longer—that straddled the small brook marking what was the end of Harrington land until the brothers bought the adjacent acreage for the warehouse. Tara picked up a few pebbles and tossed them into the moving stream. Lilies of different colors had sprouted up in the patches of briarberries and blueberries that grew on either side, and she wondered about lizards and snakes. A color picture of either one could give her nightmares.

Holding Tara's hand securely, she walked on. With so much free time on her hands and none of the social obligations she'd had as Jack's wife, she longed to take up once more the hobby she loved. She planned to begin by sculpting wood and hoped to find some hardwood on the premises. She stopped short when Tara said, "I'm going to ask that man over there if he has any little children for me to play with."

"Honey, you can't just…"

But Tara dropped her hand and ran to a tall man who was speaking with a much shorter one and told him what she wanted.

Obviously impressed, the man introduced himself to Alexis. "I'm Allen, and I work for the Harringtons. You have a charming little girl. It's too bad they're so fragile." His eyes mirrored a sadness, and she knew at once that his hurt was deep-seated and raw. "I'm afraid I don't have any little girls, and my boys are teenagers."

She didn't know why, but her heart ached for the man. "I'm so sorry we bothered you. Tara thinks the world is filled with people who love her, and she doesn't hesitate to ask them for proof of it. She doesn't meet many strangers."

He looked past her into the distance. "Wouldn't it be great if we were all like Tara?"

"Can't I play with teenagers, Mummy?"

"No, dear," she said, and explained why. She thanked the man and walked on. They'd walked almost to the construction site when she realized where they were.

"Let's go back, Tara. Come on."

Too late. A red Buick station wagon that bore the imprint of a lion's head encircled by the words HARRINGTON, INC. ARCHITECTS, ENGINEERS AND BUILDERS stopped beside them. She knew its driver before she saw him and could have kicked herself for going there.

"Howdy, ma'am. I was wondering when you'd find your

way back." He reached over and opened the front passenger door. "Hop in."

She squashed the urge to smash his ego. "Sorry. We aren't going your way."

He smiled in a way she supposed some people considered captivating—so sure of himself—but he only made her flesh crawl. "You don't know which way I'm going, babe."

She took Tara's hand and prepared to walk on. "No matter *where* you're going, it's opposite from where I'm headed. Come on, Tara."

When it came to walking and looking backward, Tara was an expert. She stopped and turned Tara to face her. "I need your cooperation. So come on."

"I'm cop-ter-ating, Mummy, but I don't like the man."

That squared it; if Tara didn't like a man, he bore watching. Later, she mentioned it to Henry.

"You mean Biff? That fellow goes through women like water through a sieve. Tara got sense. As a foreman, he's first-class, but as a man, he ain't worth poop."

"I'll be happy never to see him again."

"I hope your happiness don't depend on that. He's like a weed. Always shows up where you don't want to see it."

Tara barged in, ending that conversation. "Mr. Henry, do you have any little children for me to play with?"

"Nope, not a one. Sorry to say."

Tara needed playmates. "Maybe I'd better get her into summer camp, or…" She couldn't think of an alternative.

He sorted the potatoes according to size, selected five and began scrubbing them. "Ain't no summer camp around here. This ain't Philadelphia, you know."

She dragged a stool over to the counter and began stringing beans. "There aren't any children around here. What do you suggest I do?"

"The church school is open all summer. Telford teaches music over there a couple of mornings a week. Maybe he can tell you something."

* * *

"Of course she can go with me," Telford told Alexis at supper that night. "You want to learn the violin, Tara?"

"I wanna learn the keyboard. The piano."

"I'll teach you."

Alexis imagined that she gaped at him. "I knew you played the violin, but the piano?"

"I studied that first, starting when I was about Tara's age. I didn't start the violin till I was thirteen, but it's my real love."

"You ain't bad on the guitar, neither," Henry said. "You gonna take Tara to church school with you, ain't you?"

"Sure, if it's all right with Alexis. In the fall, she'll take the bus to school."

She listened to them, weaving her more tightly into their lives. Closing the hatch. If she wanted to get away from them, she wasn't sure she could. They gave her what she'd never had, a world free of ugliness and selfishness. Warmth. Peace. Chills streaked through her when she remembered that she was deceiving Telford, and he'd warned her that he demanded honesty.

"Mummy, what's a unrest?"

"It means...well, it means someone is unhappy."

"Mr. Allen told that man some was coming."

Telford put his fork down and spoke in a voice that was unnaturally quiet. "Which Allen are you talking about?"

Alexis completed the story for him. His demeanor, tense and apprehensive, aroused her concern and compassion, for she had never seen him when he didn't appear to be solidly in control.

"Excuse me," he said. "I have to make a call. I'll be back in a minute."

Telford dashed up the stairs to his bedroom. He wanted absolute privacy for that call. "Allen, this is Telford." He repeated the essence of Tara's story. "What's this all about?"

"Sparkman Manufacturing won't negotiate with the union,

and old man Sparkman's got most of the other builders in the surrounding counties to side with him. If the union strikes on Sparkman and his cronies, it'll force the rest of us into a sympathy strike."

"I hadn't heard anything about this. You know I'd be the last man to join Fentress Sparkman in *anything*."

"Yeah, I know. I just got wind of it this morning, and I didn't call you because it could have been a false alarm."

"What's your take on this?"

"Your employees don't have any reason to strike; we have a good contract. But if the union says walk, we have to walk. You know that."

Fentress Sparkman would paralyze western Maryland's building industry to prevent him from completing that school building on schedule. *Talk about dirty politics. He sank my father, but he'll never trample on me.*

"You'll keep me posted?"

"You know you can count on me, Telford. I'd have called you if I'd been certain that what I heard was anything more than gossip."

The men wanted more overtime work, so he'd give it to them starting tomorrow. If the union went on strike, he'd be ahead.

"Heard from Bob and Will?"

"Last week. Right after they got to Nairobi. Grace and I don't know how to thank you, Telford, for giving our boys this summer in a place where they can walk tall among people black like them."

He didn't want thanks; he wanted to see the boys complete their education and succeed as men. "They're my godchildren, and I intend to do what I can for them."

He phoned Drake in Baltimore to alert him to the possibility of a strike, hung up and trudged back downstairs, weighed down by the prospect of a strike that would make restoring his family's name a near impossibility.

When he returned to the table, Henry placed his warm food in front of him.

"Thanks, Henry. It's when you're thoughtful like this that I forgive you for those times you act as if I'm working for you rather than the other way around."

"Humph. If you're still hot under the collar about that cabbage stew I gave you when what's-her-name was here, it wasn't nothing more'n you deserved."

He could feel her gaze on him. If he dared to look into those warm brown eyes with their inviting sparkles and long lashes, she'd learn more about him than he wanted her to know right then. But he felt the pull of her intense concentration; she willed him to look at her and he couldn't help but obey. The tenderness, the affection he saw there sent his heart into a lurch, riveting him, and his fork remained somewhere between his plate and his lips, while he stared at the feminine heaven that faced him across his table. Immobilized.

He struggled to control his emotions, to put a damper on the hot currents that sizzled between them. The best he could do was open a topic that wouldn't appeal to her. "It's none of my business, but did you have a special reason for going down to the warehouse?" He wanted her to stay away from there, but he didn't think she'd appreciate his telling her that.

He'd never seen anybody switch gears so quickly. She rested her fork on her plate, and he'd swear she took a deep breath. This woman was *not* a wilting violet.

"I thought I might find some wood that I could use for… for my hobby."

He figured he'd better go slowly, since she didn't seem anxious to tell him. A smile lit his face as he savored his chateaubriand. "Henry, you outdid yourself with this steak. It's the top of the mountain."

Henry put a fresh dish of roasted potatoes in front of Telford, stepped back and rubbed his hands together as one does when washing them, obviously pleased with himself. "All my food is first-class; it's your taste buds that's substandard."

Telford glanced at Alexis partly to share some merriment, but mainly because looking at her pleased him. Now what was in that comment of Henry's that embarrassed her? Her facial expression said she'd rather be anywhere than where she was.

"What kind of wood are you looking for, and how much do you need?"

"Hardwood." She gestured with her hands. "About this much."

"I'll see what I got around here. You planning to whittle?"

"She's gonna make people, aren't you, Mummy?"

He admired her patience with the child, giving her every opportunity to express herself. Yet, Alexis was not a permissive parent. "I'm going to *carve* some people, honey." To him, she said. "I'm an amateur sculptor, but I haven't worked at it for a long time."

Not since she married, he imagined. The woman was a bag of surprises. He tried not to appear astonished. "Then you want the wood seasoned. I'll get you a piece tomorrow."

He didn't want her near Biff Jackson, but he dared not tell her that. Still… "Might be a good idea to avoid that area."

"I didn't like that man, Mr. Telford."

Out of the mouths of babes. "What man?"

"The man in the red truck."

He looked at Alexis and waited for an explanation. When she didn't offer one, he leaned back in his chair, pushed his plate aside and stared her down.

Obviously irritated, she strummed her fingers on the table. Finally, she said, "Biff Jackson intercepted us, but we walked on. I can handle the man, Telford."

"Be sure you know what you're up against. He's been known to show that he can't handle himself."

She hadn't given him the right to warn Biff to stay away from her, so he had to stand back. But it wouldn't be long before the man made a false step.

"Why the hell am I whistling?" he asked himself aloud the next morning after chortling through several popular songs. The answer awaited him at the breakfast table, where Tara sat ready for her first day of church school. When he walked into the room, her face bloomed into a smile.

"I didn't want to make you wait for me," she said.

"Where's your mummy?"

"Getting dressed. She had to get me ready for school first. I already ate."

He stared at her. "What time did you get in here?"

"I don't know, but Mr. Henry said anybody would think I'm going to get my marriage license."

Her giggles gave him such a…he couldn't explain it, but some of her happiness always rubbed off on him.

He finished breakfast, and didn't have an excuse to linger there longer, especially when he had to have Tara at the school by eight-thirty. But it pained him to leave there without seeing Alexis.

"Let's go."

"Mr. Henry, I'm gone." To his astonishment, she reached for his hand and started for the front door without kissing either Henry or her mother good-bye. He'd have to give that a lot of thought.

"This is terrible, Henry. I don't know what to do with myself. It's the first time Tara's ever been away from me. Do you know, she left here and didn't even tell me good-bye?"

"She didn't say nothing to me neither. You better be careful. That little girl's adopted Telford for a father figure. If you leave here, she's gonna be in bad shape."

"She's very fond of him."

"She's crazy 'bout him. She told me he's gonna teach her how to play the piano. Where she gonna practice?"

"She has an electric keyboard."

"Shucks. Get a piano. Plenty of space down in the game room."

"Henry, if I had the price of a piano—"

"Rent one. She needs a piano."

An hour and a half later, Alexis looked at her watch. Bennie, the cleaning woman, had a habit of coming to work late and leaving early, neglecting basic cleaning, and the house showed it. Alexis opened the door before Bennie could find her key.

"Morning, Miss Alexis. It sure is hot this morning. I declare, I'm wet with sweat. How ya'll doing?"

"Good morning, Bennie. It's air-conditioned in here, so you should be happy to spend the entire eight hours today. You're supposed to be doing a thorough cleaning, but—"

"I know, I know. Day 'fore yesterday, I wasn't up to snuff, and I just give downstairs a lick and a promise, but—"

"Bennie, you've been promising this house a cleaning ever since I've been here. Beginning today, I want you to make good on it."

"Lord, child, you would talk like this today when my knees 'bout to give way and my back feel like it wanna go out." She looked toward the ceiling. "Well, if I pass out in here, at least somebody'll take me to the hospital. Where's Henry?"

"It's ten o'clock. Henry's over at his cottage this time a day."

"I was hoping for some coffee and a little bite to eat."

She was doggoned if she'd let Bennie get the better of her. She would come to work two hours late, spend an hour in the kitchen with Henry, work a couple of hours and leave the house more or less as she'd found it.

"I'll make you some coffee while you start the cleaning. What do you want to eat?"

Bennie propped her hands on her ample hips. "You can cook? I never woulda thought it. You don't look like you c'n boil water. Henry always gives me pancakes and sausage, but I don't 'spect you to cook that."

She looked at the evidence of Henry's largesse in the form of rolls around the woman's waist. "Not to worry. Fruit, scrambled eggs and warmed-up biscuits."

Bennie pulled off her hat. "I had my mouth all fixed for Henry's pancakes, but… Well, I sure do thank you."

"You can thank me by giving this place a thorough cleaning. Okay?"

Bennie looked toward the ceiling. "Mr. Telford ain't no

slave driver. Ain't nothing I wouldn't do for him." She began humming "Amazing Grace."

Except clean his house properly. I guess that song is supposed to remind me of her saintliness. "I'm sure he appreciates your loyalty." She made the coffee and fixed Bennie's breakfast.

"Ain't no flies on you, neither," Bennie said, as she sat down to eat.

Just please clean the house, Alexis pleaded silently. "I'll be in my place if you need me."

Alexis put aside the bust of Mary McCleod Bethune on which she'd been sculpting for the past week and got ready for dinner. Her workday ended at four in the afternoon, and ever since Telford began teaching Tara music, she sculpted from four to six while Tara practiced the keyboard. She didn't see Tara when she finished dressing, so she rushed to the breakfast room where they ate dinner, got there a minute before seven and came to a sudden halt.

Russ Harrington's big frame leaned against the doorjamb, his hands in his pants pockets and his stance wide.

"Oops," she said. "I thought you were in Baltimore."

"Sorry if I didn't think to clear my arrival with you. Getting here by the hallowed hour of seven was about as much as I could manage."

It wasn't all-out hostility, but he wasn't offering a peace pipe either. She ignored his barb. "I hope you're satisfied with what you accomplished while you were in Baltimore."

He straightened up. "That I am. How'd you make out while I was gone? Got things going your way?"

In spite of her effort to remember her advocacy of brotherly and sisterly love, no matter the trial or the circumstances, she wanted to throttle Russ Harrington. With as much patience as she could muster, she said, "When things no longer go my way, I'm out of here. And don't waste you hostility on me. I don't respond to that."

"Now, that's what I call a queen. Don't get your dander up over anything the commoners say or do."

"You? A commoner? Whatta you know? And I mistook you for one of the Harrington princes. I must be slipping. You seen Tara?"

He flexed his shoulder in a quick shrug. "Yeah. She was with Henry. But the minute her idol, Mr. Telford, walks in here, Henry's had it. The two of you have my brother by the nose."

"I don't like what you're implying."

"You don't have to like it. I call it the way I see it."

Telford and Tara walked into the room laughing and holding hands, and she didn't think she'd ever been happier to see anyone.

Russ permitted himself what he obviously intended as a smile, and gave her a military salute. "I rest my case."

"Mummy, Mr. Henry said he's getting me a piano, and Mr. Telford said I can put it downstairs in the game room. I want it in *my* room."

The affection with which Henry regarded Tara brought tears to her eyes. At last, her child was surrounded by loved ones. Russ's crankiness and sarcasm detracted little, if anything, from Tara's happiness. Even though he'd rather they were someplace other than Harrington House, and she clearly preferred his brothers to him, Russ was never unkind to the child.

She thanked Henry and looked at Telford. "Can we put it in her room?"

His sheepish grin surprised her. "Sure, but then I can't play it."

"Buy your own," Henry advised him.

"You can play mine," Tara assured Telford. She looked at Russ. "Mr. Telford's teaching me the piano."

Alexis held her breath while she waited for Russ to answer. Finally he said, "You're a lucky little girl; Telford's a good teacher."

"Who's that at the back door, Henry?"

Henry went to the door and returned to the breakfast room, where they waited for Drake before beginning supper.

"Rosen, one of the construction workers, wanted me to put his supper in the microwave."

"Well, did you do it?" Russ asked him.

"Sure, I done it. But he ain't fooling me. They been working down there for two months, and all of a sudden they wants their lunch heated and their supper warmed. It ain't their stomach they concerned with, it's the rise in their testosterone."

Telford's head snapped up, and Russ laughed aloud. "Be careful you don't get a riot on your hands, brother," Russ said.

"Well, I'll be…" Telford said. "You can actually laugh. Don't get too happy, though, pal. Tomorrow evening, they'll have their own microwave oven, and they can stay the he—" He looked at Tara, who drank in his every word. "They can stay away from this house."

Laughter poured from Russ until he got up from the table in a fit of hiccups. "I told you to put a microwave oven in there. Add a coffee urn while you're at it. Threaten the king's comforts and you're lucky you don't lose your head."

Telford narrowed his eyes, and his face wrinkled into a frown. "Lay off, will you, Russ? It's best to talk what you know, and you're way off in left field."

"Mummy, doesn't Mr. Russ like… Eeee," she squealed. "Mr. Drake."

"Hey, there. At least somebody around here's glad to see me." He picked Tara up and swung her around. "How's my best girl?"

"We waited for you so we could eat."

He opened his briefcase and gave her a harmonica. "Just don't play it when I'm around." She hugged him and ran to her seat.

"How'd it go?" Telford asked him.

"Great. Couldn't have asked for better. I'd better wash my hands, or Alexis won't let me eat." He flashed her a charismatic grin. "Just teasing."

Alexis watched as Drake greeted his brothers with the now familiar embrace and warmth, and had to stop herself from wishing she were truly a part of the love between them, so strong that she felt it.

"Who says grace?" Tara asked with the surety of one who belongs and knows it. "Want me to—"

"Dear Lord…" Russ began so quickly that Alexis couldn't restrain the laughter. He wasn't willing to suffer through another of Tara's long, rambling supplications.

After Russ finished, Telford rested his elbows on the table and shook with laughter. "I didn't even know Russ knew how to say grace."

His laughter commenced again, nearly uncontrollable. How she loved to see him laugh! When he looked at her, bright lights danced in his eyes, mesmerizing her. Transfixed, she gazed at his face, beautiful in his fit of hilarity, and wanted to round the table and squeeze him to her breast. Suddenly, he stopped laughing and, in the deafening silence, she looked from Russ to Drake and found their gazes glued to their older brother. Unaware of their attention; the hot fire of passion blazed in his eyes as he reciprocated the ardor she must have shown seconds earlier.

When she could think of a way to divert the brothers' attention from Telford, she said, "Henry, do you mind checking on Tara after Telford brings her home tomorrow? It's my day off, and I need to go to Frederick."

"Just leave her with me." He looked at Tara. "How'd you like for us to make cookies?"

Tara showed her delight by running over to Henry, hugging him and slapping her hands together. "Oooh, Mr. Henry, I love cookies."

"Then we'll make two or three kinds."

Russ looked at Henry and winked. "Better watch it. Telford may put a kitchen in the basement and install a dumbwaiter. That way you can cook the food and send it up on the DW without ever going out of there. You'll be like the prisoner of Chaillot."

"Never thought you'd get a running mouth," Telford said dryly.

"I won't say what I never thought *you'd* do."

"Hey, you two," Drake put in. "Didn't anybody notice how good this roast pork is? Good Lord, Henry, what happened?"

"Don't think I didn't taste the difference," Russ said. He looked at Alexis. "Did you supervise this meal?"

She shook her head. "I gave him the recipe."

"Hmmm," he said, savoring some mushroom soufflé. "For this, I'll even break my neck to get here at seven o'clock. Henry, when was the last time I complimented you on a meal?"

Henry appeared to give the question serious thought. "Never. And 'less you want cabbage stew tomorrow, you'll find something else to talk about."

Russ raised his wineglass to Alexis. "Well done. Continue to ride herd on him. Best meal I've had in ages."

She hated to leave the table and Telford, but she had no choice. She pushed her chair back, glancing at him as she did so, and stilled, mesmerized by the savage fire that raged in his eyes. This time, it was Henry who rescued them.

"You can play the piano a little bit for me tomorrow, Tara, while we got the house to ourselves. Anybody want any coffee?"

"Piano?" Drake asked. "When did you get a piano?"

"Mr. Henry bought me a...a what, Mummy?"

"A console. She's had it a week."

"Mr. Henry's my friend, too."

She grabbed Tara's hand. "I think I'll pass on the coffee, Henry. Come along, honey. Good night, all."

"Good night, all," Tara echoed.

She wasn't making herself any promises, if he came after her tonight.

Chapter 5

"Looks like things have been happening these past two months while I was away," Drake said to Telford as the brothers sat in the den drinking coffee and cognac.

"Like what?"

"Man, you shouldn't ask that unless you want the answer," Russ said, "and you definitely don't want to talk about this."

He certainly didn't. What he wanted was Alexis rolling beneath him in his bed. He wanted it, and he needed it, but he'd never allowed himself everything he thought he wanted. He ignored Russ's comment.

"We may be in for a work stoppage." He explained to Russ what he'd already told Drake by phone. "So I'm giving the workers at the school building and the warehouse as much overtime as they want."

"But—"

He held up both hands. "I know what you're going to say, and I know it's against our policy, but I have to finish that school on time. It will be ready for the scheduled ceremonies if I have to hold it up with my back. Sparkman won't drag us under this time."

Drake looked at Russ and a frown passed over his face. "Come on, Telford. Sparkman can't hurt us now. We've re-established ourselves solidly."

Telford got up, walked to the other end of the room and back. "Not quite. I'm the one who gets it in the face when I'm bidding for contracts. You don't know how many times I've been asked, *Sure you can get it in on time?* We haven't lived it down yet."

Russ drained his coffee cup. "But if there's a strike, it won't be our fault."

"Strike or no strike, that building will be ready when school opens in September." Telford downed the last of his cognac. "I'm turning in."

"Mind if I ask where?"

"Buzz off, Russ. And be nicer to Alexis, because she's not going anywhere," Telford said and headed up the stairs to his room.

"I think she's got him," he heard Russ say.

"I sure as hell hope so" was Drake's reply.

But Telford didn't agree with either of them. He'd never been in such a tizzy about anything in his life as he was about Alexis. He took what comfort he could in knowing that she probably lost as much sleep about him as he did about her. Yet, he wasn't willing to declare his feelings. Every time he contemplated it, he could see in his mind's eye his father groveling for the crumbs of his mother's affection, which she doled out like a boy holding up scraps to make his puppy jump.

The one time he'd dropped his fences and gone to a girl he liked and who he thought wanted him, she'd smiled coolly and told him he'd made a mistake. After all these years, the pain of that rejection still hurt. There'd been women since then, but he'd been able to take or leave them. Alexis Stevenson, though, had settled inside him, deep down where he lived. And Tara. He looked forward to her smiling face when he came home every evening, her arms outstretched for his hug and the kisses she planted on his cheek. He'd never thought a child's love could touch him so deeply and make him feel as if he owned the world.

His heart and his body pointed him back downstairs to the other end of the house where he knew he'd find pure heaven, but his head ruled, and he prepared to take a cold shower.

Alexis read Tara to sleep, stepped out into the garden and sat on the stone bench facing the cluster of rosebushes that she loved. Going to sleep right then was out of the question, for she still throbbed with desire for Telford. If only she knew how to deal with it, what to expect of herself and him. Her years of marriage to Jack Stevenson had left her unprepared for the fire that raged in her. *Thank God I don't drink. If I did, I'd finish off a gallon.* Telford hadn't come to her. Maybe she was glad and maybe she wasn't. She only knew that if he walked into her room that night, he would be hers before he left. She jumped up. The mere thought was self-destructive. She went inside and closed the door.

"I don't intend to spend the rest of my life crying because I ignored my common sense." She went to bed.

Telford heard the piano before he put his key in the front-door lock. *She takes to that piano like a fish to water,* he thought with pride. After changing into a pair of Bermuda shorts and a T-shirt, he followed the sound to Tara's room. When his knock brought no answer, he went to the kitchen.

"It's after five, Henry, hasn't Alexis come back from Frederick?"

"If she is, I ain't seen her. I didn't think she meant to stay off all day long. Said she'd be back around three or so."

He shrugged, affecting a nonchalance he didn't feel. "Maybe something came up, or she went to a movie. We know she'll be here by seven, because she risks dealing with Russ if she's late."

"Yeah. Russ don't like having to live normal, picking up

after himself, wearing clothes in the house and eating at special hours, but it sure suits me." He passed the bucket of string beans to Telford. "Here, Tel, don't just stand there. String these beans."

"How much did that console piano set you back?"

"Ain't none of your business. I bought it 'cause I wanted to. I don't have to spend a penny of my salary." He stopped stringing beans and smiled. "Don't she just love it? Never seen such a happy little girl as she was when that piano come in here the other day. She plain jumped nigh to the ceiling."

"She's been here less than three months, and I can't imagine this house without her."

"Me neither. Ain't that somebody at the door?"

He put the handful of bean ends on the counter. "I'll get it." He couldn't believe his eyes. There at his back door stood Biff Jackson.

He didn't like it, and he wasn't about to behave as if he did. "Need me for something, Biff?"

The man was clearly put off. "Well…I, uh…I didn't know you'd be home."

"You came to see Henry? I thought the two of you couldn't stand each other."

"Well, I was, uh, hoping to get a glimpse of your house-keeper."

Telford folded his arms and leaned against the doorjamb. "That's what I figured. Did she tell you to come looking for her?"

"Well…no, but a man likes to do his own chasing. Right?"

He put his hands in the pockets of his jeans and widened his stance, sending Biff a message that said *stay out of my territory*. "I'll ask Mrs. Stevenson if she wants you to come here to see her. If she says yes, I'll tell you. If not, this house is out of bounds. Do you understand very clearly what I'm saying?"

"Uh…sure, boss."

His temper didn't rear up often, but it threatened to surface when he saw Biff's mocking smile. "I'm not speaking employer to employee, Biff. I'm talking man-to-man, and I mean what I said."

Biff threw up his hands in a gesture of defense. "Sure, boss. I get the message."

"Make certain that you do, because you have never seen me more serious." He closed the door and bumped into Henry.

"The man's a toad if I ever seen one," Henry said. "He's forty miles of bad road."

"If he wants his job, he'd better stay the hell away from this house."

"Alexis ain't interested in the likes of Biff, but he'll make himself a nuisance all the same. He thinks a woman says no 'cause she means yes."

"I don't want to have to... Never mind. Biff is not stupid."

Henry put the beans in a colander and ran cold water over them. "That ain't my estimation of him."

"Mr. Telford, Mummy isn't home yet." He hadn't heard Tara enter the kitchen, and he wondered how long she'd been there. He hadn't heard the piano for almost half an hour.

"She'll be here before suppertime. I heard your practicing. You sounded great, but I didn't hear you play the scales."

"I played them first, 'cause I hate them."

He couldn't keep his mind on the small talk. His watch said twenty minutes to six. Where *was* she? He heard the front door and raced down the hall, but before he reached it, Drake opened it and walked in.

"What's this? What's the matter, princess, aren't you glad to see me?"

He looked at Telford. "What's up?"

"We thought you might be Alexis. It's past time she was back here."

"That's right. She went to Frederick today. Has she driven over there before?"

The concern on Drake's face did nothing to reassure him. He told himself to remain calm. "No, but... Look, man, it's only half an hour from here."

"What's the matter, Mr. Telford?"

He didn't want to alarm Tara, but she already sensed their disquiet.

Drake picked her up and hugged her. "Nothing's the matter. She's spoiled us, and one of us may have to set the table."

"Mr. Russ."

Drake's grin fell into place. "You mean let Russ do it?"

Evidently as mesmerized as the average female would be in the circumstance, Tara nodded and turned on her own smile.

However, Telford couldn't enter into their merriment. Alexis was dependable, and she always did as she said she would. He left Tara and Drake, went out front and sat on the steps, something he hadn't done since he was seven and his mother had left them the first time. He needed to be alone, not that he thought it would help; it couldn't, but at least he wouldn't have to pretend he didn't feel what he felt.

At the sound of a familiar motor, he jumped up and immediately sat back down when he recognized Russ's Mercedes. Russ parked in the semicircle in front of the house and got out almost before the motor died. Telford wasn't anxious for Russ's company right then. Drake would allow him privacy, but Russ would wade in with his questions and observations.

"Say, man, what're you doing out here? Shouldn't you be washing your hands?"

He didn't feel like joshing with his brother. "How'd it go today, Russ?"

Russ was about to pass him on the steps, but he stopped and stepped back. "Something wrong? You all right?"

He threw up his hands in resignation. "Something's wrong, and I'm not all right."

Russ dropped his briefcase, sat down beside him and put a hand on his shoulder. "Can you tell me what it is?" When Russ shoved aside his tough, cynical facade, he was compassionate and loving, but he nearly always hid that part of him.

"Russ, it's five minutes past seven, and I don't know where Alexis is. She left here at noon to go to Frederick."

"Did she take Tara?"

He shook his head. "Tara's inside with Drake and Henry. This isn't what I expect of Alexis."

"No. She's like a clock, and she certainly wouldn't give me a reason to taunt her about being late for supper."

"Maybe I'd better go look for her."

"Where would we start? Frederick's a big place, and there're several ways to get there from here."

He stood and Russ did the same. "We could each take a route. I'll take Route 355, you take 85 and Drake can take 351."

Russ frowned and seemed reluctant to speak. After a while, he said, "What the devil would she be doing over on 351?"

"That's just the point, Russ. I...I don't have any idea *where* she is. If she had Tara with her, I might even think she'd taken off for good."

"Come on, now. If you don't have any more faith in her than that, you've misplaced your feelings."

That remarked registered with him, but he didn't feel like dealing with it right then. Russ picked up his briefcase and slung an arm around Telford's shoulder. "Let's go inside."

"Yeah. Let's see what Drake has to say."

"She didn't phone?" Telford asked Henry.

"If she hada, son, you know I'd a gone out there and told you. Maybe she ran out of gas."

Telford shook his head. "I keep her tank full, even though she doesn't know I do it, because I wouldn't like that to happen on one of these deserted roads."

"Especially not with critters like Biff sniffin' around."

"What's he talking about?" Russ and Drake asked in unison.

"Long story. You know Biff can't pass up a good-looking woman, especially if she ignores him."

He felt Tara's arms around his leg and looked down at her

worried little face. What could he say to her that wouldn't be an out-and-out lie?

"Mr. Telford, is my mummy coming home?"

"Of course, honey." He knelt and took her in his arms, but she wouldn't be placated.

"Is it seven o'clock?"

"Around that." He didn't look at Russ, for he knew that in spite of his brother's concern over Alexis's whereabouts, Tara's question would bring a grin to his face.

"We're going out for a little while, Tara. You stay with Henry. All right?"

"You going to look for my mummy?"

He decided not to lie to her. "I'm hoping we'll run into her."

The strength of her arms clasping his neck startled him. "It'll be all right, baby," he whispered. "Now, don't worry."

The facial expressions of his brothers and Henry were not reassuring, and a dull, heavy thumping replaced his heartbeat. He lifted Tara and placed her in Henry's arms.

"We'll be back soon."

"I'll keep the food warm."

"Thanks." If he didn't find Alexis, he wouldn't want any food.

"Should you take your revolver, Russ?" Drake asked. "In case there's any foul play?"

Russ had a license to carry it, but he'd never used the gun. "Naaah. Let's not think like that."

He opened the front door and stood there. Immobilized. But only for a moment, before he dashed out of the door and met her as she stepped up on the brick walk.

"Alexis, where in the hell have you been? I'm out of my mind with worry, and we're on our way right this minute to look for you. Woman, what do you mean by…"

He stared at her, the most beautiful human being he'd ever seen, and her wide-eyed almost helpless expression rocked him to the pit of his gut. "Oh, hell, baby, I was going crazy."

Oblivious to all but his joy in seeing her alive, he opened his arms, and she raced into them. In that moment, he cared for nothing and no one except the woman whose tears dampened the side of his face.

"You're still frightened. I can feel it. What happened? Are you hurt? Tell me how you are."

"I'm…I'm all right. I got lost and I thought I'd never find the way back here. The bridge on that little road going to Route 85 was washed out, and I had to take a detour and then another one till I found myself halfway to West Virginia. Up and down these roads, there isn't even anyone to ask directions."

He closed his eyes and gave thanks. "If anything had happened to you, I…I don't know what I would have done."

Her beloved fingers stroked the side of his face in a loving caress. "I knew you'd worry. I'm sorry."

"Don't be. It made a few things crystal clear to me."

She brushed his bottom lip with the pad of her thumb, and he recognized it for the possessive gesture that it was.

"Kiss me, Alexis. I need it. I need it badly." He bent to her welcoming mouth, not caring that Russ and Drake stood at the door. She opened to him, but when he got his tongue into her warm loving mouth, the thunder and fireworks didn't come. Instead, she loved him so gently, stroking him, easing her fingers through the hair at his nape, gripping his body with hands that generated not fire but sweetness. Adoring him. The hot passion that lived in him for her alone still heated his loins, but a powerful drive to protect and cherish her overrode it. He broke the kiss and stared down at her.

"Do you feel like this about me?" he whispered. "You're telling me something you never told me before. Is this what I am to you?"

"I am what you see and feel. That's all I'll ever be."

He crushed her to him. "I don't know what this means; I only hope it's real."

Her smile, wobbly and tentative though it seemed, was a shower of joy. He felt like beating his chest with his fists. "I guess we'd better go inside. Tara and Henry are probably out of their minds by now. Russ, Drake and I were just about to search for you. We…" His head snapped up. Thank God they'd had the decency to give him privacy. He didn't know what they'd think, and he didn't care.

"Mummy, Mummy." Tara's relief at seeing Alexis told him how distressed the child had been. As they embraced each other, an intense longing possessed him, and he knelt there in the foyer and gathered them into his arms.

"Mummy, Mr. Henry set the table in the breakfast room just like you do. He said you don't like us to eat in the kitchen."

He stood and helped Alexis to her feet. "Excuse me a minute. I need to wash up and get ready for supper." That was as good an excuse as any to get the privacy he needed. So much had happened in the last four hours that he hardly knew himself. He cared for Alexis, and he'd known that almost from the first, but he realized now that it wasn't a sensation he could get over just by willing it. And Tara. He shook his head in amazement as he ambled up the stairs. How he adored that little girl!

"Want to go for a walk?" he asked Alexis after supper as they left the breakfast room. "It won't be dusk for another hour." He just wanted to be with her, to talk, not about anything in particular, but to have some bonding experience other than their passion. She appeared to be torn, and he asked her, "You don't want to go?"

She grasped his wrist, but only for a second, and withdrew her hand. "I do. I'd just love that, but I'm not sure I should leave Tara right now. My getting here so late shook her up."

Shook him, too. "Tell me about it. She seemed fine at supper."

She looked into the distance. Pensive. "Since we've been here, she clings to me less and less, and I know it's because she gets so much love. She's stopped begging for it and accepts it as her due. She doesn't even shy away from Russ."

That was a loaded statement if he'd ever heard one, and when he got to the root of it, he'd know a lot more about Alexis than she'd previously revealed. "Russ doesn't like having to change his ways. If you knew how seldom he got fully dressed before you came here, you'd probably sympathize with him. He's a good man; you'll learn that when you need him, he's there."

"I'm sure he couldn't be that different from you and Drake. What's Tara doing in the kitchen with Henry? You'd think they had a secret."

In spite of all she'd been through, she still generated the serenity that soothed him and him a feeling of contentment.

"They made cookies this afternoon, and she's probably getting some samples for you. I'll walk you to your room."

At her door, she thanked him, opened it and stood between him and the room.

"Thank me for what?"

"For everything. For more than I thought I'd ever have." She stepped closer quickly, clasped his face in both of her hands and kissed him. "Good night."

"*Alexis!* Woman, for Pete's sake!"

Her smile communicated sweetness, but the wink that went along with it was pure wickedness. "Can we go for a walk another evening?"

"Sure. You're clever. You know that? If you waded into me tonight, you'd have to send for a fire engine. Good night, baby."

Meanwhile, Russ and Drake lounged downstairs in the game room with a beer and their cue sticks ready for a game of pool. Russ racked the balls, then put his stick down and looked at Drake.

He couldn't stop thinking about the level of intimacy he'd witnessed between Telford and Alexis. "What do you say to that?"

"To what?"

"Man, you can be dense when it suits you. You know I'm talking about Telford and Alexis. That's gone a lot further than I suspected."

Drake leaned against the wall and rested the cue stick

between his knees. "Based on what I saw out there, I have a feeling it's gone further than *they* suspected. I'm staying out of that, Russ, and you'd better do the same."

Drake walked back to the pool table. "Telford hasn't had much joy in his life; he was looking after us when he should've been chasing the sistahs. And he's still feeling the pain of Mama's stupidity and Papa's ruin. Granted, Sparkman screwed Papa, but Papa was too trusting. And every time Telford meets a woman, he backs off because he's afraid she'll try to make a fool of him the way Mama did Papa."

"He always chooses the ones he can do without, and maybe that's because he hasn't wanted to get deeply involved with 'em."

"Yeah. He didn't choose this one, and…" Drake shook his head as though in wonder. "Did you see… I mean, Russ, that wasn't heat I was looking at."

"I know. It was a hell of a lot more, and I hope he knows what's happening to him."

Drake aimed the cue stick and pocketed three balls with his first shot. "He knows, and he can handle it. The one thing he'll never be able to change is how he feels about Tara. Four men here, and she chose him. This is good for him."

Russ strolled up to the table and aimed. He had yet to be convinced. "We'll see."

Alexis put the last touches on the bust of Mary McCleod Bethune and set it on her dresser. With a broom and dustpan, she cleaned up the last of the shavings. Her enthusiasm for her hobby in overdrive, she took the bust, a piece of chamois and a bottle of oil out into the garden and sat on the little stone bench facing the rosebushes. She polished the bust with all the muscle she could apply, softly humming "Bye Bye Blackbird" as she rubbed. She always found the rhythm of that song a perfect accompaniment to the movement of her arm.

"Well, I'll be. You are really talented."

She looked around at Russ, shirtless and sweating from digging in the far side of the garden where she hadn't seen him. "I didn't know you were a sculptor. You and Telford have a lot in common."

She didn't stop polishing. "You mean because he's a musician, and I do this?"

"No. Because he makes some fantastic things out of wire. I mean, artistic things. He's done that since he was a boy."

She stopped her work, shaded her face from the late-afternoon sun and squinted up at him. "I didn't know that. Where does he keep his figures?"

"They used to be all over the house, but now I think he keeps them in that cabinet in his room. Ask him to let you see them. They're very impressive."

"I will. Thanks." She was about to allude to his overture of friendliness, but he'd already gone back to his work.

"Something told me that if I came around this way, I might find you. Why you been staying away from me, babe?"

She didn't like Biff Jackson, and now was the time to make that clear. "I am not staying away from you, as you put it. I am not interested in you and I don't want anything to do with you. Kindly leave me alone."

"Aw, quit playing hard to get. You know you want it. Meet me down the road by that bridge in about twenty minutes."

"I hope you don't hold your breath." She rolled the bust up in the oiling cloth and stood to leave.

"You think I can't get over this fence? Just dare me."

"*I* dare you. You've lost your mind," Russ growled. "She said she's not interested and told you to leave her alone. Pester her one more time and look for another job. Half a dozen of the men can make as good a foreman as you, but I doubt Telford would exchange Mrs. Stevenson for one other woman. So who do you think he'd choose? You or her?"

It shamed her that Russ witnessed the exchange, but she was nonetheless grateful for his presence. She murmured "thank you" and fled into the house, careful to enter through the kitchen door rather than the one that led to her bedroom, which she reached as the phone rang.

"Alexis, this is Russ. Don't make the mistake of keeping

quiet about Biff Jackson. He isn't going to leave you alone. We've known him and his antics with women for years. If he bothers you again, let one of us know, because he'll stop at nothing. He honestly believes you're playing hard to get, because he thinks there isn't a woman anywhere who wouldn't want him. We can't protect you if you don't ask for help. I'm leaving it up to you to tell Telford. At least for now. See you."

She would have thanked him if he'd given her the chance, but he hung up before she could utter a word. She wrapped the bust in a towel, rolled it in a sheet of plastic and put it in her closet.

"Now who can that be?" she asked aloud as the phone rang again. "Hello."

"Tara and I are going for ice cream. How about I drive by the house and get you first, huh?"

She grabbed her chest as if that would steady her. Every time she heard his voice unexpectedly and his deep, resonant vibrato flowed over her, her heart seemed to take wings.

"Okay, I'd love that, but I won't have to eat black-cherry ice cream, will I?"

His laughter was a cloud of comfort, wrapping around her. "Of course not. You can have whatever you like. Now and any other time. Be there in fifteen minutes."

Dressed in a pink sleeveless T-shirt and a broomstick skirt that had a pink-and-navy paisley print, Alexis combed her hair down and fastened big silver hoops to her ears. As the big Buick Le Sabre rolled to a stop, she stepped out of the door. Telford got out, walked around the car to meet her and pressed a quick kiss to her lips, surprising her. She got in, reached back and hugged Tara.

"You smell good," Tara said, giggling happily. "My mummy's pretty, Mr. Telford."

"She sure is that. Believe me."

He bought cups of ice cream, peach for himself, black cherry for Tara and butter pecan for Alexis.

"Where we going, Mr. Telford?" Tara asked him when they left the store.

"Down to the river."

"But my ice cream will melt, and I want to save some for Biscuit."

"No, it won't. We'll be there in ten minutes, and you shouldn't give Biscuit sweets. He loves you, so he'll eat anything you give him, but sweets can make him sick."

They sat on a bench by the river and ate ice cream.

"All we need is some music. Next time we come here, let's bring a radio," Alexis said.

"Does that mean you want to come back here with me?"

"It's peaceful here, and I'm...I'm enjoying your company."

She couldn't imagine the humor in that remark, but he obviously did, for he laughed aloud. "If you'd said you weren't enjoying my company, I'd be in trouble. Big trouble."

She couldn't respond to that comment, because she tried to be honest with him. It wasn't a topic for jokes, and the truth would probably knock him off balance. She changed the subject.

"I'm curious. You told me you're a builder, but what exactly is it that you do?"

"I'm a building contractor. I figure out how much it will cost to build the building Russ designs and bid for a contract. After we get the contract, I'm responsible for purchasing materials, hiring the workers and overseeing the job. As the architectural engineer, it's Drake's job to lay out the structure of Russ's plans and to make certain that every detail is implemented. Drake's the troubleshooter, and he's a good one."

"Too bad your parents aren't here to see how the three of you work together. They'd be so proud of you."

"I know our dad would. Our mother? Maybe. I don't know."

"I have a sense that, in your childhood, your family might have been similar to mine."

He rested his elbows on his knees and looked across the river. "Your parents…they weren't happy?"

"Not from the time I could understand human relations. They finally destroyed each other."

He didn't look at her, but his hand went out to her and rested on her thigh. "I'm sorry. I thought we were the only kids whose parents didn't know what they were doing when they got married." He glanced over at Tara, who had stopped eating and watched him.

"Yeah. Well…we can come back here one Saturday morning early and see if we can't catch some fish."

"You gonna bring *me,* Mr. Telford?"

She giggled when he tweaked her nose. "If your mother says it's all right."

Tara wanted all of Telford's time, and this was understandable, because he lavished her with affection. But he needed freedom to love her at will without feeling obligated.

"Darling, when he has time, he'll invite you to go with him, but you must give him the freedom to choose whether to be with you or someone else."

That possibility apparently didn't faze Tara. "Mr. Telford loves me."

Stunned, the words flew out of Alexis's mouth before she considered their implication. "How do you know that?"

Telford's head snapped around, and he stared hard at her as if he didn't believe what he'd heard and didn't approve of it. But Tara was unperturbed.

"When I hug him, he always hugs me back, just like you do. And he always smiles at me and holds my hand. He takes me to church school, and he's teaching me how to play the piano. He loves me a lot."

He stood, and Tara immediately reached for his hand. He pitched his empty ice cream container in the nearby refuse bin and, with his other hand, reached for Alexis. "There's a lesson in what she said," he murmured softly for Alexis's ears only. "I've told her I love her, but what impressed her is the way I treat her."

* * *

Her workday ended at four, but she couldn't leave it at that. It wasn't merely a job; it was her home, and she couldn't help treating it as such. So she set the supper table that evening as always and changed from the clothes she'd worn all day to a soft, feminine dress. It wasn't fancy. She didn't have many elegant clothes; she'd stored most of them with her furniture. The black cotton chiffon skirt flowed in numerous folds around her ankles, and the sleeves of the plain yellow top billowed in the breeze. Modest at best. She'd paid seventeen dollars for it at a thrift shop in Frederick a week earlier.

"It's pretty warm," Henry said. "Maybe I'll make some iced tea. Why don't you get some mint from the garden?"

"Right. I was about to gather some roses for the table." She put on a pair of garden gloves, got a pair of scissors, stepped out into the garden and inhaled deeply of the fresh, fragrant air.

"Looking mighty pretty there. Come over here, so I can touch you."

Even before she flipped around, she knew who it was and that it spelled trouble.

"And would you bring me in a few sprigs of… What the devil you doing loitering around here? You after trouble, 'n you gonna git it sure's my name's Henry. You go on in, Alexis, I'll get the herbs."

"I'm staying right here and picking these flowers, and if he comes near me, he'll wish he'd never seen me," she said waving the fifteen-inch garden sheers.

Henry stood at the door, his hands braced on his hips, and shook his head. "In all my life, I never seed a man so anxious for trouble."

"Mr. Henry, where's mummy? She said she'd make Biscuit a bell, so I can find him if I lose him. She said…" Tara stared toward Biff Jackson. "I don't like that man, Mr. Henry."

"You got good and proper taste, girl. We'll wait here till your mummy finishes cutting her flowers."

She'd as soon Tara hadn't seen Biff, because she blurted

out everything she knew. "This ought to do it," she said of the roses she picked, and walked toward the house.

"You'll come around," she heard him snarl. "They all do."

She went inside, arranged the flowers in a crystal bowl and placed them on the dining table between long tapered white candles in Etta Harrington's silver candlesticks. Her efforts brought a cryptic comment from Russ as they sat down to dinner that evening.

"I'd avoid these daily banquets, but the level of the cuisine has gone up so high that I gladly suffer this grandiose setting. Believe me, I love good food."

"Since you ain't complimenting me, I don't thank you," Henry said. "These recipes of Alexis calls for cooking by the clock. When she says ten minutes, she don't mean ten and a half."

"Otherwise," Russ said, "you just put the food on the stove or in the oven and go on about your business. Right?"

"It ain't killed you so far, has it? And it ain't stunted your growth, neither."

"Mr. Telford, that man was here at the fence today when Mummy was in the garden getting flowers."

Alexis nearly choked on the veal cordon bleu.

Telford's fork clattered on his plate. "What man are you talking about?"

"The man from down the road."

She looked at Telford then, because she knew his gaze would be on her. His eyes bore a murderous look, and shudders rifled through her when he began to grind his teeth.

"Don't you go, Telford," Drake said. "Let me talk to him."

"There's nothing you can say to him. I've told him the score. Tomorrow morning, he'll get his severance pay."

"Telford, I told you, I—"

"You can't handle him, Alexis, and even if you could, I told him what to expect if he came back here. He ignored me. I keep my word." He leaned back in his chair and stared at her, his eyes ablaze with the fire of determination. "Do you want him here for some reason?"

He could ask her that in the presence of his family? Without thinking, she blew aside the strand of hair that hung over her eye. He had the nerve to ask, so she'd tell him. "If I have to tell you the answer to that question, you don't have the right to know."

He gazed at her for a long time, and she knew without looking that all eyes were on them. Finally, a smile lighted his face, and she could feel the electricity flowing from him to her. His face radiated happiness, and when she saw the smile on her child's face, she knew that even Tara was relieved that the tension had subsided.

"So he's out of here," Russ said. "I warned him a couple of days ago, but the man's stupid."

"And you didn't tell me?"

"It wasn't my place to tell you. I left that up to Alexis. Anyhow, what can you handle that I can't?"

"I'm not going there," Telford said.

"My vote for foreman goes to Allen Krenner," Drake said.

The bottom dropped out of Alexis's stomach. "Who?"

"Allen Krenner. You met him. He's a good man."

"I agree with you and Drake," Russ said. "Biff knew how to control the men, but Allen will be a much better all-around foreman, and I won't get sick to the stomach every time he starts talking about women. I was getting fed up with Biff."

"I been fed up with him ever since he come here. Good riddance," Henry said. "Here, Tara, I made this cherry pie just for you."

"Thanks, and I'm gonna eat every bit of it, too."

"Oh, no, you're not. All of us are going to eat some of that pie. You mustn't be selfish, darling."

"Okay. I'll give some to everybody at the table, and I'll save some for Biscuit."

Telford raised an eyebrow. "Tara, didn't I tell you that sweets might make Biscuit sick?"

"Oh. I forgot. What can I give him?"

"We'll get some dog biscuits when we come from church school day after tomorrow."

She clapped her hands. "Biscuit's gonna be happy."

Alexis made herself smile, but she didn't feel like it. Not one bit. Surely there had to be more than one family with the last name *Krenner*. At least, she prayed that it was so.

Chapter 6

Alexis soon learned that she had good reason to worry. Several afternoons later, Telford surprised her with a phone call. As they greeted each other, a sense of foreboding crept over her. Why was he calling her two hours before he was supposed to get home, and why did he speak in such solemn tones?

"You'll remember that my brothers and I decided the other night to make Allen our foreman at the warehouse. I've asked him to come to dinner tonight, because that's about the only time the three of us are together."

Allen Krenner. Her blood seemed to curdle, and she had to sit down.

"We need to talk with Allen...the three of us together, I mean. Could you set a place for him?"

"Of course. Would you like me to...to do anything differently? I mean, do you want me to change anything...or, would you like Tara and me to...eat separately?"

"What? Of course not. You and Tara are... Look. The breakfast-room table won't seat seven people, and we'll have to eat in the dining room. That's a lot more trouble for you, but I'd appreciate it if you'd do it."

She couldn't believe her ears. She was his housekeeper, even though he liked to refer to her as the homemaker, and he didn't have to apologize for asking her to set the dining-room table for dinner. It struck her then that Telford didn't regard her as a servant, and that was a complication she didn't need. If she worked for him and lived in his home, if she was his servant, he was honor-bound not to inveigle her into intimacy with him. She didn't like that, and yet it thrilled her.

"It's a simple thing, Telford, provided I can find a big enough tablecloth."

"Look in that old Aetna cedar chest in the game room. That's where my mother hid her precious linens and things like that."

"Not to worry. Everything will be in order."

"I know that. You…you've made that house a home, something it's never been. I'll see you later." He hung up.

He'd uttered the word "hid" with sarcasm or distaste, she wasn't sure which. She suspected that Harrington House held some ugly ghosts. Three handsome, accomplished and eligible men, all over thirty, all single and none committed to a woman. She shook her head in bemusement. The explanation had to lie all around her; when Etta Harrington faced her heavenly maker, she must have hung her head in shame. Alexis opened the storage chest and found a cloth large enough for the dining-room table and a fortune in linens and silver. The woman must have had delusions of grandeur. Not even Jack's parents were more frivolous, and they didn't buy anything unless it was outrageously expensive.

She set the table in the dining room with a little more care than usual, placing two bowls of flowers and candles in three silver candlesticks between them. The feeling that destiny was hard on her heels wouldn't leave her, and she had to fight off increasingly morose feelings.

"Better make this as simple as possible," she told herself when she was trying to decide what to wear for dinner. Finally, she settled on mother/daughter dresses for herself and Tara—pale green, short-sleeved and double-breasted with big white mother-of-pearl buttons down their collarless fronts. Her dress didn't give the effect of a ruffled apron, but it was reasonably modest.

When the doorbell rang, she thought the bottom dropped out of her stomach. *Please, God, don't let the man be Melanie Krenner's father.* She met them in the hallway between the dining room and the den. Tara dashed any semblance of propriety between employer and employee when she ran to Telford with open arms, her face glittering with happiness at the sight of him. He picked her up and hugged her, and when Tara kissed his chin, he grinned with delight and returned the gesture.

"Mr. Telford, I look just like my mummy."

His gaze caressed Alexis lovingly. "Yes, you do, and you're beautiful, too."

She couldn't look at him for fear her eyes mirrored her feelings.

"Mrs. Stevenson, this is Allen Krenner, our foreman down at the warehouse." He didn't bother to say why she was in his house, and she wondered at that.

She had to look at Telford then, and it took every measure of her self-control and all the aplomb she could muster not to betray herself. His eyes burned with warmth and…yes…desire. No other word described it. *Dear Lord, what would it be like to know…* Quickly, she shook herself out of that daydream and extended her hand to Allen Krenner.

"Hello, Mr. Krenner, I'm—"

"Mummy, we saw him down the road when he said he didn't have any little children for me to play with."

She made herself smile. "Of course."

Allen Krenner's warm, solid handshake impressed her that he was an honorable and dependable man. "I'm glad to see you again, Mrs. Stevenson. I felt your impact on this place before we got here."

"How's that?"

"Telford told me a dozen times that we had to be here before seven o'clock."

She nearly laughed aloud at Telford's expression. Krenner was enjoying the chance to needle his boss.

The hole in her widened as she observed the affection between the two men, a bond that transcended their employer-employee relationship. She squelched an urge to get out of their company and made herself stand there and mouth small talk until she could gracefully leave. She didn't follow them to the den, but said they probably wanted to talk business, and turned toward her own quarters.

However, when Telford realized that she didn't intend to go with them to the den, he swung around and walked back to her. "Aren't you going to join us?"

Not quite certain as to what she wanted or, for that matter, whether he was only being polite, she looked around for Tara. Stalling.

"She's in there with Allen," Telford said, making it obvious that he suspected her of procrastinating. "I think she's still on that subject of his not having children for her to play with."

His gaze bore into her, communicating feelings that she wasn't ready to accept and that she suspected he wasn't ready to confirm. "What's the matter, Alexis?" For a second, his strong fingers stroked her arm but, evidently remembering that they were not alone, he withdrew his fingers and jammed his hands into his pants pockets.

"Come on back, I want you there with me."

She hesitated, and his expression darkened, almost as if he were suddenly less sure of himself.

"Don't you—"

Heading off his seeming diffidence, she smiled, took his hand and squeezed his fingers. She shouldn't encourage him, but she couldn't let him feel as if she rejected him, either. Telford served drinks—gin and tonic for Allen and himself, a lime rickey for her and, to her astonishment, he handed Tara a glass of cranberry juice, explaining that to exclude her would be bad manners.

She suffered the meaningless small talk until Russ and Drake arrived and she could relax, because she'd already learned that Russ had no tolerance for it. The warm hugs and back slapping with which he and Drake greeted Allen told her more convincingly than words could have that Allen Krenner was more to them than an employee.

At dinner, Allen looked at the food and gasped, "What happened, Henry? You gone gourmet?"

"Same as the reason everybody's sitting at the table together exactly at seven o'clock and Telford said grace. Alexis here put some class into this place."

As if Allen knew that Henry jealously guarded his position in the kitchen, his eyes widened. "You mean she cooks?"

Henry's withering look would have diminished one with the most robust ego, and Allen appeared properly chastened. "I'm the cook here." He pointed to Alexis. "She's got all these recipes and you have to time 'em right down to the second."

Allen dipped a bite-sized piece of his Maryland crab cake in aioli sauce, savored it and rolled his eyes heavenward. "Telford, man, you're living in a state of grace."

"What was he living in before?" Russ asked, a touch of disdain coloring his speech.

"You don't wanna ask that," Henry said. "Shoes, socks and anything you can name all over the place, from the bedrooms to the foyer, you being the main offender." He looked at Allen. "They asked for sloppy, so I let 'em have sloppy."

Alexis noticed that Russ and Drake frequently glanced from her to Telford, but Telford focused on everybody at the table but her.

He's vulnerable tonight, she told herself, aware that each day she knew him better than she did the day before.

"Heard from Bob and Will?" Telford asked Allen. He looked at her then, but hooded his gaze. "His sons are my godchildren. I'm very fond of them."

Allen's face lit up with fatherly pride. "Wil wrote a few lines. Said they had a chance to visit a Masai group and witness a mating ritual. Said we wouldn't believe the young men form a circle and dance, and the young, bare-breasted girls who've just reached puberty walk around them until they decide which one they want. The men accept the girls' choices."

"Whew!" was Russ's one-word comment.

"Them's two fine boys," Henry said.

"But he doesn't have any little girls," Tara said.

Telford's head snapped up, and he glued his gaze to Allen, who suddenly had a hard time swallowing his food.

"How you like my crab cakes?" Henry asked so quickly that his effort to distract Allen was obvious. The three other men gave their food more attention than was normal or necessary.

Her heartbeat accelerated, and she lost her appetite for the meal.

"Nothing yet?" Henry asked after an extended silence.

"Not a thing. Six long years and not a single word. Well," he said, sighing and smiling gently, "God gives and God takes. I no longer hope."

She wanted to ask, and she knew she *should* ask, but didn't dare. The dawning truth was like a noose tightening around her neck. After dinner, she asked to be excused and headed for her room, practically dragging Tara with her.

"I want to stay with Mr. Telford. I don't wanna go to bed."

"Sorry, darling, but he has to talk business with his guest."

"We've hired a detective, Allen," she heard Russ say as she walked away from them. "If Melanie's alive, he'll find her."

She missed a step and nearly fell, her worst fears confirmed.

"You all do so much for me. I can't ever thank you enough. She was a good girl, and I...if she could have, she'd have been in touch with Grace and me long ago. I..."

Alexis stepped into her room and closed the door, shutting out the damning evidence, confirmation—if she needed it—that no matter how she and Telford felt about each other, they were as close then as they'd ever be.

Never would she forget her wrenching agony and guilt when Melanie Krenner was reported missing from her dormitory room for over a week. She told herself to snap out of it. What was done was done. *Get on with your life, girl. You can't go back, and even if you could, wouldn't you do the same thing?* She straightened her back. Her hands were clean, but who in this house would believe her? If the time came, and the brothers didn't accept her explanation, she'd just move on.

Telford sat in the den with his brothers and Allen drinking coffee and sipping cognac. He wasn't crazy about cognac, but it was as good a way as any to finish off a meal.

He turned to Allen. "We've got sixteen men out there, so we may be able to get far enough along on the warehouse to enable us to start blasting for that hospital." A huge boulder lay embedded a few feet below the site.

Drake put his snifter of cognac on the floor beside his chair and stood, drawing the attention of the other men when he shoved his fingers through his hair, walked to the other end of the room and back.

"Look," Drake began, "let's be practical here. It's enough that I have to split myself between that apartment house in Baltimore, the high school here in Eagle Park and the warehouse. Either we hire another engineer or we postpone work on that hospital until we've finished at least two of these projects."

"Not the school." Telford jumped up and stood facing Drake. "You know I won't permit even the semblance of a slowdown on that."

"I'm with you on that, Telford," Russ said, "but I wish you'd stop focusing on Sparkman and his antics. We'll finish the school on time. And if we don't, nobody'll think to drag up that old stuff. And don't forget, we've committed to starting the Frenchman's Village in Barbados next year."

"Sparkman's engineering this building strike just to get the better of me. But he won't succeed, even if I have to hire myself as a laborer on my own building."

Later, as Drake and Russ stood at the north end of the garden near the empty pool, Drake picked up a piece of brick and threw it across the fence. "I'd hoped that Alexis would help him to see that the world isn't on his shoulders. If he doesn't stop driving himself, he'll be dead before he's forty."

Russ dragged his right hand across his chin. "Why are you so sure she's the one for him?"

"It's how he is when he's with her. It's indefinable. Subtle. But you can't miss the difference in him. And the heat between them could scorch air."

"Tell me about it. I get the willies just watching it. Speaking of hot air, I could use a swim. When are we going to put some water in this pool? It's June already."

Drake didn't have to be urged to open the pool; swimming was his favorite form of leisure. "Until a few days ago, it was too cool to swim. This weekend, all right?"

Russ nodded. "Imagine. *Me* in a damned bathing suit in this pool."

Drake's perfect white teeth sparkled against his dark olive skin. "Sorry. That's too much of a stretch for my mind. I'm turning in."

Drake went inside, but Russ sat on a stone bench among the flowers and enjoyed the summer evening breeze. He knew why Telford hadn't mentioned putting water in the swimming pool, and it was another reason why he shouldn't have hired Alexis. He got up, dusted off the back of his pants—more from habit than necessity—and went inside. He and his brothers rarely said harsh things to each other, though they sometimes disagreed. He figured they would cross each other in a big way tomorrow.

Telford worked side by side with his hard-hat crew that Saturday until three o'clock in the afternoon when the heat of the sun became so oppressive that he feared for the health of the older workers. The first scorcher of the summer.

"Let's knock off," he said to his foreman.

"But, Telford, the men want to work. Most of them need the money."

"Do they need the hospital bills? I said call it off. If they want to work tomorrow morning and you're willing to come, the hours will be six to one, but no longer. You understand. I'd rather they didn't work on Sundays, but they missed two days this week due to rain, and that's a big hole in their take-home pay."

"I'll be here."

He walked into the house pulling off his shirt, remembered Alexis and Tara and attempted to put the shirt back on, but the sweat-dampened garment stuck to his flesh and, in a flash of annoyance, he hooked his thumb in the collar, draped the shirt over his shoulder and ran up the stairs. *A young, attractive woman in a man's house should be his mother, his sister, his wife or his S.O.* He threw his shirt into the hamper and did his best to curtail his annoyance. Failing at that, he took his violin out of its case, sat on the edge of his bed and began to play. Making music with his violin was one act that never failed to give him peace. He forgot the heat, his hunger and his earlier displeasure as "Lovely Night" from Offenbach's *Tales of Hoffman* caressed his ears.

"What on earth brought this on?"

The sound of the human voice dragged him out of this reverie, out of his peace. He looked up from the strings he loved and focused on Russ. His brothers had always treated as sacred the times when he played the violin and didn't interrupt him.

"Uh…what's up?"

"I thought you'd help me open the pool. I need a swim. It's hot."

He put the violin back in its case, taking his time doing it, and looked at his brother. "I know we usually have the pool open by now, but I don't want to have to fish Tara out of it."

"But, man, are you saying we don't open it? What the hell? Somebody can watch her."

"Yeah, right. Every one of her waking minutes? Tell

me, how'd you like to walk out there and find her floating facedown, huh?"

"What do you think I am? If this isn't proof you should have hired somebody else as housekeeper, I don't know what is. Ninety-seven degrees, and I can't get in the water. Teach her to swim."

"And let her go near that pool herself? Come on, Russ."

"Look, I don't want anything to happen to her, but, man, this is a royal pain."

"We can put a fence around the pool," Drake offered as a compromise when they discussed it later that afternoon.

"That'll look like hell. Whoever saw a fenced-in swimming pool?" Russ said, his voice little more than a sneer.

"Shall we vote on it?" Telford asked them.

Russ shrugged. "What's the point? You always agree. All right, one of you come with me and get the fencing. I want to swim."

Drake stared at him. "You mean you're going out there in that heat and put down a fence?"

"Damn straight, and the two of you are going to help me."

"We disagree rather frequently these days," Telford said, more to himself than to his brothers.

"Yeah," Russ said. "And I wonder what...or who...is at the root of it."

"Ah, come off it, Russ. Alexis is good for this place. I don't enjoy behaving around here as if my third-grade teacher were hovering over my shoulder, but I like the changes Alexis has made, and by damn, I like having a woman in the house."

"Of course you do," Russ told Drake. "It's a wonder you don't have 'em jammed wall-to-wall in this place. Come on, let's go get that fencing. The sooner we finish, the sooner I get a good swim."

Telford didn't like the contention simmering beneath the surface and emanating primarily from Russ. Until he hired Alexis, he and his brothers spoke with a single voice, seemingly always able to see each other's point of view. On the rare occasions that they disagreed professionally, personal feelings didn't enter into their exchanges; each respected the others' competence in their fields of expertise. But their differences about conditions in their home displeased and worried him. Yet, sending Alexis and Tara away was unthinkable.

Drake patted his pockets for his keys. "Let's get the fencing from the load we shipped in for the warehouse. We can replace it later. Takes less time than going into town for it."

"Right, and we can get the tools while we're there. Be down in a minute," Telford said and headed up to his room to change into shorts and a T-shirt.

Russ picked up the towel, wiped the sweat from his neck and anchored the last post. "Do I love the sound of that water filling this pool! Hook the fence here, Drake." In the act of pulling off his shirt, he stopped and glared at Telford.

"You wouldn't have a pair of bathing trunks I could use?"

Drake checked the latch on the gate and began clearing the area of the tools they used. Then, as if impelled by some superior force, he took a deep breath and looked across the garden away from Russ. "Wear your underwear."

Telford dropped to the lawn, rested his elbows on his knees and howled with laughter.

With the towel draped around his shoulders to absorb the perspiration, Russ glared at him. He didn't mind being the butt of their jokes; he was used to that. But they ought to know not to fool with him when he was mad. And after three hours in the hot sun pounding those posts into the ground, he was plenty sore. "I'd like to know what's funny."

"Really?" Drake asked dryly. "You ought to be a sight in those red G-strings you call underwear. Come to think of it, though, I doubt that would be the best introduction Tara could have to the mysteries of man."

Russ looked at Telford. "Surely you've got something to say about how that would look to Alexis."

Telford got up. "Didn't occur to me, Russ. You're not crazy. Come on. Let's put this pool cover in the garage."

"But what will I swim in?"

"You can use those boxer shorts Henry gave me for Christmas five or six years ago," Telford said. "They're on a shelf in the game room. I'm going into town and get some swimming trunks."

"Yeah," Russ yelled after him, "and bring some of those water wings kids wear on their arms when they're learning to swim." He found the shorts, put them on and raced out to the pool. Half an hour later, his body soothed and his soul comforted, he stepped out of the water.

"Can I swim with you, Mr. Russ?" Tara sat on the stone bench watching him. He wondered how long she'd been there and thanked God for the fence.

"As soon as we get you something to swim in. Yes."

"Can Mr. Telford swim?"

He couldn't help laughing. She loved Telford, and everybody other than her mother came after him. "You bet he can." He sat on the bench beside her and took her hand. "Don't open this gate, and don't go to the pool when you're by yourself. You understand?"

She nodded. "Okay."

He couldn't let himself leave her there, not even with the fence to protect her. "Let's go inside and get some lemonade." Anything to take her attention away from the pool.

She got up, took his hand and said, "Okay."

He walked with her to the kitchen, her little hand snug in his, and understood why Telford was so attached to her. That little girl made a man feel ten feet tall.

"Want to swim with me?" Telford asked Alexis later that night after he heard Russ and Drake go to their rooms. He hoped they didn't track water over the house as they usually did after swimming.

"Yes, I'd love it. Tara's in bed, but I don't think she's asleep yet. I'll call you back. What's your number?"

"Wait a minute. As long as you've been here, you don't know my phone number?"

"I figured you'd give it to me if you wanted me to have it. Anyway, I never had a reason to call you."

She'd never had a reason to call him! "You certainly know how to make a man feel great."

"Ooops!"

He gave her the number. "Be sure and write it down. And some of these nights when you're having trouble sleeping, use it."

"Does that mean you go sound asleep every night as soon as your head hits the pillow?"

"If I telephoned you every time you got between me and sleep, you'd be thoroughly rest broken by now. Call me when you're ready."

Later, he stepped off the back porch and looked around at the bright night. Where was she? A gentle breeze teased his flesh, ruffling the silky curls he inherited from his mother and stroking his chest, thighs and belly like the tips of a woman's warm fingers. He strolled over to the rose garden and stopped short. She stood amidst the flowers, an ethereal vision in a long, billowing white skirt, shrouded in moonlight. His breath lodged in his throat. The most beautiful being he'd ever seen.

She didn't know he was there, and he didn't want to frighten her, so he squelched his need to touch her. He had an urge to know for certain if she really cared about him. Swaying gently in the breeze, the roses perfumed the night, filling his head with senseless ideas. Outlandish thoughts. To have a woman like her for himself alone…and for all time… Maybe he ought to go back inside and forget about the swim. She turned then, and when her gaze fell on him, she smiled in that way that said he was a special man. Special to her. With slow, deliberate steps she walked to him.

"It's so beautiful tonight. This scene almost takes my breath away."

"*You* take my breath away. You are so lovely. I...I want to drown myself in you."

She lowered her lashes and looked away from him, displaying a diffidence that he hadn't associated with her.

"I'm sorry if I've embarrassed you," he said, "but you're wrecking my common sense right now. Seeing you like this and knowing it's the way you want me to see you... Alexis, you're raising hell with my mind."

I've done it now, he thought, as her arms locked across her bare middle giving him the impression that she felt undressed. He stepped closer and dusted her cheek with the back of his hand.

"Don't hide yourself from me. Not now or ever. To me, you're the essence of beauty."

"S...slow down, Telford. You don't want what you're implying."

Without knowing he'd do it, his right arm shot out and encircled her waist and his fingers knew at last the feel of her silky flesh. "I want it, all right. I'm going crazy for it."

"It's just the moonlight. It's the night. We said we were going for a s-swim, that—"

"I know what we said, but it can wait. Open your mouth for me."

Before his words filled the air, her lips parted, and her arms went around him and tightened. The feel of her full breasts almost naked against his bare chest sent tremors of desire plowing through him. He told himself to think about his workers' possible strike, the atomic bomb, the War of 1812, anything but the woman in his arms as he plunged his tongue into her, and she took him, feasting as if her life depended on it. He turned to his side to prevent arousal, but she moved with him, locked an arm across the flesh of his buttocks and gripped him to her. Heat spiraled straight to his groin, and he jerked away from her, lest he spill out of his skimpy swim trunks. The sound of her hot moans of desire set his heart into a spin, whirling like a barrel on its way down a hill, and he lifted her to fit him. Face-to-face, he stared into her eyes, and the innocence he saw there shocked him back to reality.

"Alexis! My God. What am I doing to you?" He slid her to her feet with great care so as not to upset her. "Honey, I must have gone out of my mind."

"I don't know what you mean."

"I was half a split second from getting inside you, and you… you trusted me not to do that. I think we're going to have a talk about this, but right now, I'd better get into that pool. Are you going in with me?"

"Y…yes, if you still want to."

She untied the long, white skirt, let it drop to the grass and he gaped. The scrap of red cloth below her navel matched her bra and hid only the absolute minimum. He let out a sharp whistle, opened the gate and dived into the pool.

The impact of the cold water tempered his desire, but only its physical manifestations. His head told him that if he ever sank into her, he would no longer have the option of walking away, for the abandon with which she responded to him left him with no doubt that she'd love him uninhibitedly, giving him everything he needed. And he ached for the sweet heat of her body.

Beneath that cool facade, he'd found a passionate, wildly sensuous woman, who… He came up for air, flipped over and did the backstroke. How on earth could a woman with a sex drive as powerful as hers and who'd been married for five years be so naive about a man's sexual threshold? He switched back to the Australian crawl and, with powerful kicks, swam as fast as he could, hoping to deplete his energy.

Alexis stared after Telford as he plunged into the pool. He might as well have hypnotized her. Maybe he had. Her common sense—not to speak of her willpower—seemed to take a walk whenever he touched her. If she had any sense, she'd leave. Her original reasons for wanting to avoid a relationship with him paled in importance compared to her role in Melanie

Krenner's disappearance. When he discovered it, he'd put her as far away from him as possible.

"What are you waiting for?" he called out. "The water's great." When she didn't respond, he needled, "You *can* swim, can't you?"

She kicked off her sandals. "Of course I can." *My hair will get wet, and I'll look like a rat if I dive in there.* She walked to the steps, grabbed the bar and waded in.

"Chicken. I wouldn't have thought it."

"Get me a bathing cap, and I'll dive for you."

Seconds after she shoved away from the edge of the pool, he surfaced beside her. "Swim on my back, and your hair won't get wet."

"No, thanks. I want a swim, not a ride as if I were a baby whale."

"I wouldn't touch that one with a loaded missile."

They swam beside each other for several laps, synchronized as if performing a water ballet. When they reached the south end of the pool, he stopped them.

"Doesn't this seem eerie to you? Our swimming together stroke for stroke as if we'd spent hours rehearsing it?"

She had thought of it, but she wouldn't have dared articulate such sentiments. Too much about their relationship seemed preordained.

"Hmm. That the way it looks to you? I was thinking what a hard time you were having trying to keep up with me. You're pretty good." It was probably just as well that she wasn't looking at him when she said it.

His hand gripped her shoulder. "Liar. You weren't thinking any such thing. Step out of this pool, lady, and I'll prove it to you."

"I don't take dares."

"Who said anything about a dare? You're still thinking about me. About *us*. I'll prove it. If I'm wrong, you name the penalty."

It might seem like a penalty to him, but it certainly wouldn't feel that way to me. She told herself to use some sense. She was already in deeper than was wise. He was asking her to goad him, to give him an excuse to do what he wanted to do but didn't consider prudent. Deciding to move on while she was ahead, she raised herself to her full height, braced both hands on the edge of the pool and flung herself out of it.

"You dived into the water to cool off," she told him. "Stay that way. I have as many concerns right now as I care to deal with."

"And I'm just one more complication. Is that what you're saying?"

She picked up the white skirt that she'd dropped on the lawn earlier, turned around and looked at him. And she saw him then as never before. Covered by water up to his waist, he loomed there as a powerful figure, a modern Poseidon. Her gaze settled on his thick biceps, strong, corded neck, broad chest with water-slicked black hair that revealed prominent pectorals—a dangerous man whose magnetism diluted her willpower. She stared into the hazel-brown eyes that seduced her in the glittering moonlight, although he remained half a dozen feet from her.

"If you were nothing more than a complication, it wouldn't be worth discussing. See you in the morning."

With a pounding heart, she rushed into her room, closed the door, locked it and collapsed against the wall. How many more narrow escapes before she stepped into that bottomless future from which there was no turning back, before they locked together in an irrevocable giving of themselves? She wanted it. Lord, how she needed it! But even if she'd leveled with him when she took the job, if she were able to push aside the still painful memories of her existence as Jack Stevenson's wife and link her life again with that of a man, she couldn't risk the scorn this one would heap on her when he discovered her connection to Melanie Krenner.

The phone rang, and she looked at the clock on her dresser. Nine-forty. She answered, expecting to hear Telford's voice.

"Girl, I've been ringing you for the past hour. What do you

and those brothers do out there for entertainment this time of night? Where were you?"

"Velma!" She didn't know whether she was disappointed or relieved. "How'd it go in Oakland?"

"I'm still in Oakland. Got a minute?"

"Sure. What's happening?"

"I'm setting up a banquet for a writers' convention. Some of the organizers want a purple-and-green color scheme and some others are insisting on purple and lavender. Neither is my favorite combination of colors. Which group should I ignore?"

"Try purple and mauve-pink."

"Good idea. Anything going on with you and what's-his-name?"

"Velma, for the nth time, would you please forget about Telford Harrington? He's my employer. Period."

"Yeah. And Michael Jackson sings opera. How'd you know who I was talking about?"

"Easy. You've got a one-track mind. Let me know how the reception comes off and…and, Velma…honey, it's time you found someone. You…you're so alone."

She listened to the silence, hoping her sister's next words would be that she wasn't alone. Instead, Velma commented with the precision of a champion archer releasing his arrow.

"In other words, you aren't alone. You have a man, and you want the same for me."

Alexis opened her mouth but no words escaped.

"Don't throw away your opportunity, sis," Velma went on. "Not every man is like Jack Stevenson. Indeed, men like him are probably rare. Think about it. Talk to you soon."

Alexis listened to the dial tone. Very little changed with Velma. She said what was on her mind and didn't hang around to argue. Neither of them did. As children, they'd heard too much of it from their parents. Telford was like that, too. Telford. Always Telford. The man occupied too much of her thinking. She showered and went to bed.

She walked into the breakfast room the next morning just

as Telford left the table. "I hope you slept well," he said. "You probably won't see much of me during the next few days, maybe weeks. Allen called a few minutes ago. We've got a general strike on our hands."

"I'm so sorry, Telford."

With his briefcase in his left hand, he brushed her left cheek with the fingers of his right one. "Believe me, so am I. Sparkman will pay for this."

She reached for his hand and held it. "You're a kind, generous man. A loving man. Please don't let your hatred of Sparkman destroy this…this good in you."

For a long time, he gazed into her eyes, his own unreadable. Then he spun around and left her.

Chapter 7

He didn't go to the warehouse, though it was close to Harrington House, and he knew the men were gathered there waiting to hear what he had to say. Instead, he headed for the school construction site at Mountain Avenue and Edgecomb Street in Eagle Park. He couldn't fail, because it might be his last opportunity to vindicate his father. He parked beside the trailer that housed this temporary office, went inside and phoned Allen.

"This is Telford. I'm at the school. I want you to tell the men I know they're loyal and I understand they have to obey union rules, so I'm not looking for strike-breakers. I just want them to show up ready for work the minute that strike is over, prepared for some heavy-duty overtime."

"Don't worry, Telford. They're with you, to the last man. I'm going to Delaware to see what I can find out about Melanie. I haven't been to that university since the week she was reported missing. I—"

"Why don't you leave it to the private investigator we hired? He'll come up with something. What do you say we take half the men from the warehouse and put them to work here at the school when the strike's over?"

"Why not all of them? Anything there I can help you with?"

"Plenty."

"Be over there shortly."

He worked with Allen, driving himself until the muscles of his arms and shoulders tightened in a painful spasm, dust from bricks and concrete interfered with his breathing and the stench of dank rubbish settled on his stomach, but he couldn't stop. Until today, victory had been so close, and he would not be defeated.

"Telford, if you don't ease up, you're going to have a problem. What's driving you, man?"

"This building will be ready when school resumes September seventh if I have to finish it single-handedly."

"If you continue at this rate, you may not be alive to see it. I'll work as long as you do, but I don't want to see you wreck your health in this hundred-degree heat."

He appreciated Allen's loyalty; the man would never desert him, but Allen was years older than he and could get sunstroke. He couldn't have that on his conscience if the school was never finished. "You're right. If we work like this every day for the next three months, we can't finish it in time. Let's knock off."

He hadn't expected Alexis to meet him at the door when he got home, nor did he welcome the sensation he got seeing her there, the feeling that he'd come home to his woman. And when she took his hand, stared into his eyes for a moment and then opened her arms to him, he knew she'd read in him the hopelessness he felt.

"I was listening to the radio," she said as her hands stroked his damp back, "and I heard that the union doesn't expect the strike to last more than a week or two. You'll make it; I know you will. Want some lemonade?"

That and more, but he didn't feel like moving out of her

arms in order to get it. "I'm a mess. Thanks for...for letting me know you're here for me. I'll get a shower. Where's Tara?"

"She and Biscuit went with Henry to his cottage so Biscuit can see his brothers and sisters, as she put it."

What he needed, he realized, was the healing power of the child's smiles and her hugs and kisses. The knowledge that he needed both of them hit him with the force of a sledgehammer, stunning him.

More attuned to him than he'd imagined, Alexis caressed his jaw. "What is it? What's the matter? You're doing what you can to minimize the effect of this crisis. You can't do more. Have faith, Telford."

She'd misinterpreted his reaction, and a good thing, too; he wasn't ready to reveal the power of what he felt for her and for Tara. Perhaps one day. Perhaps never.

After showering, he got a glass of lemonade from the refrigerator. "I'm thinking of going to Barbados," he told her. "I want to see the place where we're suppose to build Frenchman's Village. I can't do anything here till the strike's over."

"How long will you stay there?"

"Three or four days. A week at the most. But the minute that strike's settled, I'll head back here."

He needed a swim. "I'm going to the pool. Feel free."

A grin flashed across her face. "I'd better finish my work. When you come out, I'd love to see some of your wire sculptures."

"Who told you about that?"

"Russ."

"Really? I've known him for thirty-two years, and sometimes he's an enigma to me. Solid as a rock, though, and loyal as a homing pigeon."

"His telling me that surprises you?"

"Actually, no. He doesn't want a liaison between you and me, mainly because you inconvenience him, but he knows what's going on, and he cares about me. I guess he wants you to see me in the best light. Sure you don't want a swim?"

"Later, maybe. I have to finish next week's menus and grocery list. Don't forget those wire sculptures."

He wouldn't, because he wanted her to see them. He raced out to the pool, dived in and wished he hadn't. His neck, arms and shoulders balked at the punishment he'd given them while working on the school. But he swam nevertheless, and soon found the water soothing. After half an hour, he left the pool and went to find Alexis.

"Last night, I said we ought to talk. Feel like it right now?"

She shook her head. "I don't know how much good talking will do, and I don't feel like digging into my psyche. I also don't feel like making promises to myself that I'm not likely to keep."

"I'm not talking about promises, neither to me nor to yourself. I got the impression that you're an innocent, yet you were married and you have a child."

Her lashes hooded her eyes in a display of diffidence. "I…uh… Like I said, I'd rather leave my psyche alone right now."

"All right, but one day we'll talk about this, and there'll be no hedging then. I'll be in the den half an hour before supper with some of my wire figures."

"See you then."

Intelligent, serene, elegant…and a real live wildfire. Yet… he snapped his fingers. Jack Stevenson had left her as he'd found her. Unawakened. "Well, I'll be damned!"

He couldn't wait to… *Down, boy! You're just guessing.*

He ran upstairs to his room and began to pack.

He didn't kiss her good-bye, but he knew his worshiping eyes told her how he longed to hold her and love her. "Take good care," he said in barely audible tones, "and don't you and Tara stray away from the house. If you need anything that isn't here, ask Russ to get it for you. Or Drake if he gets back before I do."

"Does that mean I'm a prisoner?"

"No, but it's easier to prevent a disaster than to repair one." He turned to Tara. "Remember not to give Biscuit candies and other sweets."

"I won't," she said in a teary voice.

He picked her up, hugged and kissed her. "I'll be back in less than a week." He hugged her again and set her on her feet. "Be sure and practice the piano every day." She nodded, her sadness at his leaving painful to watch.

"We'd better go if we're going to make that plane," Allen said with the obvious reluctance of someone who'd observed the tender scene and hated to end it. Telford's fingers squeezed her hand, and his gaze bore into hers. Then he picked up his briefcase, got in Allen's car and left them.

Alexis made up her mind then to go back to Delaware State College in Dover and find out what she could about Melanie Krenner. Several of the professors there remained her friends, and she believed they would help her. She paced in her room until Tara asked her to stop. She needed the papers she'd locked up in her house in Philadelphia, but she didn't think it proper to go there in Telford's absence, as if in stealth. With her hands gripped tightly at her back, she walked the long hallway. Restless.

"He ain't gonna be gone but a week," Henry said, "and them few days ain't gonna kill you."

She swung around and glared at him, annoyed that he'd caught her out. "I can't imagine what you're talking about."

"You can, too, and you might as well accept it. The two of you ain't using a crumb of sense. What you feel for each other ain't ordinary. You been married, so you oughta know that."

Later, in the privacy of her room, she sat on the edge of her bed and made herself face the truth. She wanted Telford, and she had to do everything within her power to make it happen. Her phone call to State U netted her nothing. Most of the professors had left for summer vacation. But she'd made up her mind and, come September, she'd begin in earnest to find out what happened to Allen Krenner's daughter. *You don't have to wait until September,* her conscience needled.

Alexis hadn't tried to prevent Jack from visiting Tara; indeed, she wanted her daughter to know and respect her father. However, Jack hadn't attempted to see Tara, nor had he asked about her since their separation, although he never skipped monthly child-support payments. So, something akin to fear streaked through her when, several days after Telford left for Barbados, she answered the phone and recognized her ex-husband's voice.

"How are things, babe?" he asked, as if they spoke daily.

"Never better," was her flippant reply. "What can I do for you?"

"I thought I'd come down for a visit. This phone's listed to the Harrington brothers. What're you doing for them?"

Her explanation that she was their housekeeper brought a long silence. At last, he said, "If you're living with one of those guys, I don't blame you for covering it up. But don't expect me to believe you're somebody's housekeeper."

"If you'd like, I'll mail you a copy of my signed, two-year contract. It's working out well. Tara's happier than she's ever been. Let me know when you'd like to visit. After all, this is the place where I work." She hung up, stunned by the realization that he had neither inquired about his daughter nor asked to speak with her. She didn't hold it against him, because he seemed unable to sustain relationships. His second marriage had lasted fourteen months, and she'd heard he'd taken wife number three. The thought of seeing him, even for a few minutes, didn't sit well with her. He was a page she'd turned, and she wanted no more of the man who admitted cheating on her for four of the four and a half years of their marriage.

The loud banging on her bedroom door startled her, and she rushed to open it.

"Henry! What is it?"

"It's the strike. It's over. I don't know where Russ and Drake are. You got a number for Telford in Barbados so's you can call him?"

"I'll call him." She dialed the number Telford gave her with Henry standing close enough to hear anything Telford said.

"Harrington." And proud of it, the tone of his voice implied.

"Telford, this is Alexis. Henry said the strike's over." She heard him suck in his breath.

"Who told him it's over?"

"Allen just phoned," Henry said, loudly enough for Telford to hear him.

"Whew! That's great. Just great. Thanks for calling me. I'll be there tomorrow."

"I ought to give him cabbage stew when he gets here."

"Why? What did he do?"

"It's what he ain't done. He could at least said somethin' nice to make you anxious for him to get back. It must be all this grits he eats. I don't know what else it could be, and I ain't cooking no more of it neither."

Laughter bubbled up in her throat and finally spilled out. Glad for the chance to release the tension she felt while she spoke with Telford, she gave the laugher full rein and patted Henry's slight shoulder. "Please don't do that. Telford loves grits, and if he doesn't get them, he'll be beside himself. Stop worrying. When he gets back here, he'll take care of business. Trust me."

The old man braced his right fist on his hip. "You ain't foolin' me? If you are, you'll eat cabbage stew, too. Telford's thirty-six, and it's time he got down to brass tacks." He turned to go and stopped, a smile covering his face. "Ain't it a pretty sound? That little girl loves that piano." He shook his head as if in amazement. "She's learnin' fast, too. I hear the difference every single day. Telford's gonna be right pleased when he gets back."

Alexis walked into the breakfast room the next morning and gasped. "When did... I thought you were coming back today."

"Hello to you, too," Telford said. "Glad to know you missed me. Where's Tara?"

"Brushing her teeth. She likes to get away with not doing it properly. This morning, I caught her at it."

"Mummy, I did it. I brushed them all over again. Want to… Eeee," she screamed. "Mr. Telford!" She ran around the table to him. He stood, lifted her into his arms and hugged her.

The unfamiliar peace that settled over her at the sight of Telford Harrington loving her child turned her heart into a quivering mass and brought tears to her eyes.

"I'll be right back," she said, and rushed out of the room.

"What's the matter with you?" Henry asked when she bumped into him, jarring him and nearly knocking the tray of sausages and eggs out of his hand.

"Er…something in my eye." She continued walking down the hall.

"Surprised you, didn't he?" Henry yelled after her. "You shoulda knowed he'd get back here on the first plane flying outta there."

She didn't answer him. In her room, she washed her face, drank a glass of water and struggled with her emotions. She didn't want to love Telford Harrington and suffer the pain that was bound to come if she did. Her feelings for Jack Stevenson hadn't amounted to peanuts compared to the powerful emotion her heart held for Telford.

The knock on her door, soft but insistent, told her he'd come after her and that he meant to be reckoned with. She opened the door, looked up at him and felt her lips part of their own volition. He stepped into her room with her tight in his arms.

"I wanted to do this when I left here." His tongue plunged into her mouth, and she lost herself in him.

"What's Tara doing?" she asked when he set her on her feet and she could catch her breath.

"She's at the table where I told her to stay. We're going to have to deal with this, Alexis, and it will be sooner than later. I hated every minute I was away from here. Away from you."

"I know, but I…I'll handle it when I get to it."

"Hold on there. You know what you feel for me, and you know what you want to come of it."

She stepped back and looked him in the eye. "Why do you think I understand my feelings, that I've settled on what I want from our relationship, when you haven't gotten that far?"

"I may move with the speed of a tortoise, but when I get to the end of the row, I know where I want to go from there. You left the table crying. Why?"

She'd thought she hid that from him. "The…the tenderness, the… Telford, you can't conceive of what I felt. Do you really love Tara?"

"If you could imagine what having her unqualified love and affection does to me, you wouldn't ask that question. She's precious to me. Of course I love her."

"I don't want her to be hurt."

"She'll never get that from me. Come on back and eat your breakfast. Henry's keeping it warm."

"By the way," he said as they walked back to the dining room, "Tara wants to go to the warehouse with me today. Is it all right with you?"

"Now that Biff Jackson's no longer there, of course, I don't mind."

"Biff's out of the picture. A builder in Corpus Christi, Texas, phoned me for a reference, and I gave him a glowing account. He hired Biff at a good salary, and I expect him to stay down there."

She released a deep sigh. "What a relief!"

"Tell me about it. I'll take Tara to church school and, from there I'm going over to the school construction site. We'll be back around one, and about three or so, she and I will go down to the warehouse."

"If you was eating grits, your breakfast wouldn't be fit to eat by now. I cooked you some fresh pancakes," Henry said and set a pile of them in front of her.

She'd heard that love begets love, but she'd never been sure of it until now that she found herself surrounded with it. She watched Telford and Tara leave and could hardly believe the joy in her life.

"Quit looking a gift horse in the mouth," Henry said as he joined her at the table for his usual breakfast of stewed fruit, waffles, sausage and eggs. "There ain't no flies on Tel. And with that bitter tongue he's got, he ain't about to mislead you. My biggest problem with him growing up was him thinkin' he had to say somethin' just 'cause it was the truth."

"What about his parents?"

"His mother never did decide whether she wanted to be a wife, and whenever she felt tied down, she'd up and leave. Miss Etta didn't let them three little boys get in the way of her freedom. No, siree. She'd be here one day and next morning when everybody woke up, she'd be gone. She come back for good after Mr. Josh died of a broken heart, but by then, the boys didn't care too much."

"And their father?"

Henry looked toward the ceiling and inhaled deeply. "Now there was a man. His family was everything to him. Trouble was he felt like he had to get rich so they could have everything they wanted, and he pretty nigh worked himself to death. Then, old man Sparkman tricked him out of his good name." He let out a long breath and shook his head as though disbelieving what he knew to be a fact. "He was a proud, honorable man, and it killed him."

She stopped eating while she tossed ideas around in her head. *Might as well go all the way.* "Three handsome, intelligent, wealthy and extremely eligible men, but they're not married, and I haven't seen any evidence that any of them has a love interest."

"None but Tel, you mean. Well, if you watched your dad grovel for your mother's affection, while she ladled it out like a prize for his good behavior, you'd be careful about tying up with a woman, too. Miss Etta was somethin' else!" He looked toward the ceiling. "And she got a lot to account for."

As long as they didn't argue endlessly, she thought. Anything was better than living in that environment. Right then, she couldn't think of any reason why she rushed into marriage with Jack other than to escape her battling parents.

"Today is Tara's birthday. I'd like to make her a cake before she and Telford get back here."

"Well, whatta you know? It's Tel's birthday, too. Make two of 'em. He likes chocolate."

She made a cake with caramel frosting for Tara and a chocolate cake with chocolate frosting for Telford, placed them on a shelf in the pantry and put five candles on Tara's cake and seven on Telford's. *Lord, please don't let Henry choose today to make cabbage stew.*

"Let's have that standing rib roast for dinner, Henry."

"You been here almost four months, and you still don't know dinner from supper. What else?"

"Roast potatoes, some fresh green beans—string beans, to you—broiled fluted mushrooms and a salad. I hope you have black-cherry ice cream."

"Always got that. What are we startin' with? You Northerners always have to have something to *start* with. I starts with the first thing I puts in my mouth."

"I'll make some cold-minted pea soup."

He distorted his face. Mocking. "Do tell!"

When Telford and Tara went to the warehouse construction site, she drove into town, bought two birthday cards, a bicycle for Tara and a leather-bound book of the world's best loved poems. He'd never told her he cared for poetry, but a man with his soul and sweetness had to love poems.

"We've spent the day together," Telford told Tara when they returned from the warehouse.

"And I made some friends. Guess what?"

"What?"

"When I'm big, I'm going to have lots of friends, and you will be my best friend."

He did his best to ignore the emotions racing through him. "Thanks. Go practice for an hour. After that, maybe your mother will let you swim." She hugged him and ran off to her room. He stared after her for a few seconds, before going up to his room and getting to work.

He'd just sat down for supper when Russ and Drake walked in. "Happy birthday, brother," they said in unison. He knew it was his birthday, but with Russ and Drake out of town and Henry becoming forgetful, he figured it would pass like any other day.

"I wasn't expecting you two," he said after they embraced each other.

"You didn't think we'd miss helping you celebrate your birthday, did you?" Drake asked him.

Tara ran to him and plastered his face with kisses. "Happy birthday, Mr. Telford."

Alexis raised her wineglass. "Happy birthday. I hope you have many, many more."

"Here's your starter," Henry said, as he served the pea soup. "Another one of them fancy Northern ideas."

Next, he brought in the main course, sat down and watched as Russ, his biggest critic, savored the prime rib. "Henry, you're getting a raise."

"Don't give it to me; Alexis is the one with the recipes and this fixation on the clock. *Oven at four-twenty-five degrees and roast it twenty minutes to the pound,*" he mimicked to a chorus of laughter.

When they finished, Henry darkened the room and Alexis brought in Telford's lighted cake. Russ began to sing "Happy Birthday," and they all joined him. Alexis whispered in Telford's ear, and he left the room as Henry turned out the lights. Tara's screams reached record decibels when Alexis and Henry walked in with her lighted cake as they sang "Happy birthday, Tara," and Henry pointed to the bicycle that Telford had leaned against the sideboard.

"This is what family should be," Telford said to himself as he tried to remember if he'd ever enjoyed his birthday so much.

Alexis handed him a small package wrapped in gold-foil paper and tied with a greenish-brown ribbon. He gazed at it, then at her. She couldn't hold his stare, but lowered her eyelids, communicating to him without even trying. He wanted to take her and hold her. His need to touch her gripped him with a powerful force, bruising his nerves until he trembled. She had him, and he knew that every man in the room was aware of that fact.

Slowly, to get his emotions under control, he untied the package, pressed the ribbon flat, folded it, put it in his shirt pocket and slid off the paper wrapping. A glance around him confirmed what he hadn't doubted: Henry, Drake and Russ looked not at the package but at his face. The small, red leather-bound volume, its lettering gold-tooled, lay in his hands while he stared at it and told himself not to look at Alexis Stevenson.

Tara's little hands clutched his thigh. "Let me see, Mr. Telford."

He handed her the book, got up and walked to the other end of the table. He was making a public statement, but hadn't she done the same? With his right hand, he grasped her shoulder and with his left one, he caressed her head and held it. When she looked up at him, her lips soft and glistening, he bent to her and caressed her welcoming mouth with his own. *I'm not giving her any peck on the cheek, because that's not how I feel.* He increased the pressure, and her arms went around him, leaving no doubt in anyone's mind as to what she thought of his public declaration.

"Mr. Telford's kissing my mummy."

"And doing a good job of it, too," Drake said.

He broke the kiss, looked down at her and grinned. With the happiness flowing through him right then, he couldn't help it. "Thanks. I suppose Henry told you, huh?"

She nodded. "I hope you like poetry."

"I do, but if you gave me a horseshoe, I'd like that, too."

He went back to his chair and retrieved the book of poems from Tara, who still stood there.

"Read me something, Mr. Telford, please."

He didn't feel like reading aloud to that assemblage, especially not love poems. "Later. All right?" She nodded and ran back to her chair. "Let's have some of this cake."

After consuming slices of both cakes, Russ said to Alexis, "You're a genius, because only a genius could get Henry to turn out a meal like this one. And I'm serving notice. On December the first, I'll be thirty-three. I love stuffed, roasted fresh ham, smoked salmon and coconut cake; and I'll definitely be home for dinner."

Drake stood and raised his wineglass first to Telford and then to Alexis. "Mine's right around the corner. In July I'll be thirty-one. I'll eat anything you serve, especially chateaubriand, so long as you make me one of these unbelievable caramel cakes. Let me tell you, this is good stuff."

"What day are we speaking, Drake?" she asked.

"July twenty-eighth, and I'll be home for dinner."

She looked at Henry, and Telford's heart swelled with affection for her when he saw that she wouldn't leave the old man out of it. "When's your birthday, Henry?"

"Day before you come here, and I ain't telling none of you how old I was."

"Let's see. I came to Harrington House the fourth of April, so yours is the third."

"Tara coulda figured that out. Your chocolate cake is fit for a king."

"I made it for a king."

Russ's whistle split the air.

When she would have helped Henry clear the table, he said, "You go on in the den. Me and Tara will bring the coffee."

"How about a stroll along the river?" he asked her later.

"After I get Tara to bed. Will that be too late?"

He shook his head. "No, she'll be asleep long before it gets dark at around nine-thirty." He wanted to be with her, and he'd accept whatever time she gave him.

He sat in the big brown leather chair that his father had preferred and sipped some tawny port, while Russ and Drake nursed their snifters of cognac. He wondered if they realized that they had accepted Alexis as a part of him. He was certain now of what he felt, but he still didn't know what he'd do about it. Russ hadn't uttered a word about his kissing Alexis in a way that couldn't be dismissed as a polite thank-you, which meant that his brother acknowledged its seriousness. He'd meant all that that kiss implied, and both Henry and his brothers had to know it.

He waited in his room impatiently until his phone rang and he heard her voice. They met in the foyer and strolled away from the house hand in hand toward the narrow bend of the Monocacy River, about a city block from Harrington House.

"Thank you for my gift and for that wonderful cake," he said when they neared the river. "I don't know when I've been that surprised or as happy. I saw the marker on Shelley's 'Love's Philosophy.' Did you mean that for me?"

She nodded. "I, uh… Yes, I did."

He repeated the last few lines. *"'And the sunlight clasps the earth, And the moonbeams kiss the sea; What are all these kisses worth, If thou kiss not me?'"*

She gasped. "You knew that poem?"

His fingers squeezed her hand. "I read it for the first time while I waited for your call. It touched me, too. I was looking for a poem to read to Tara. I promised her I would, you know."

"Did you find one?"

"Yes, and I already knew that one. It's Leigh Hunt's 'Jenny Kissed Me.' Funny thing; Tara reminds me of Jenny in that poem."

She projected an aura of quietness that he didn't quite fathom. It wasn't that she didn't want to talk… Maybe she didn't need to and he shouldn't second-guess her.

They sat on a bench facing the river as the sun began setting, and she cleared her throat. "Henry told me about your home life as a child and as a teenager. I've alluded to the similarities in our young lives, but I never told you that my parents argued and squabbled as if they hated each other, or at least it seemed that way to me as a child."

Her hand, locked in his, began to perspire, and he could feel her tension. "Apparently it continued after Velma—my sister—and I left home," she went on. "I never knew why, but our mother finally ran out of the house one night during a blizzard, and they found her the next morning, frozen to death. My father called Velma and said he was going to Alaska. He left before the funeral and didn't give us a forwarding address. We haven't heard from him since he left."

He eased his arms around her and locked her to him. Telling him that had cost her something, and he wanted her to know he appreciated her confidence. "You can't know how sorry I am to learn this. Does it still hurt you?"

"No, but the potential for that in my own marriage was so strong that I… I suppose I became a Quaker to learn how to deflect meanness without letting it be a part of me. Telford, my parents made us so miserable."

"I understand now why you won't argue, not even as polite debate, but try to clean that out of your mind. There are occasions when failing to argue can be viewed as cowardice."

"I know."

She rested her head on his shoulder, and as the night gathered, he held her closer. They sat there, holding each other and not speaking, as the fireflies blinked their approval, a frog croaked out a bass baritone, crickets made their presence known and two mockingbirds battled in song for preeminence in the night air.

Until now, the night sounds hadn't meant anything to him; he'd always had them in his life and accepted them as a part of it. But as her breath warmed the side of his neck and her breast rose and fell against his arm, he felt himself a part of her and of all that surrounded him. In the light of the new moon, her skin glowed like a copper coin, and he listened to the river as it rushed along soft and soothing like a Duke Ellington tone

poem. He wouldn't have been surprised if his heart had burst
with the happiness that suffused him.

What he felt must have reached her, for her lips brushed his
jaw, and she tugged him closer.

"Alexis. Sweetheart." Her hand went to the back of his head.
"Baby…"

She parted her lips and he sank into her and let her have him
while she sucked his tongue deeply into her mouth and feasted.
Heat plowed through him, blistering his veins and setting a
torch to his groin. The sweetness. The pain. *Lord!* He thought
he would explode. He tried to ignore her moans of pleasure, but
when she began to cross and uncross her knees, he broke the
kiss. He wanted to ask her to go away with him for a weekend,
but he didn't think the timing right. His mind would be on
the construction of Eagle Park High School and hers would
be on Tara. Church school would be out mid-August and…
He'd better not make plans until the time was right—if ever
it would be. With their arms locked around each other, they
walked back to the house.

At the bottom of the stairs, she said, "We'd better say good
night right here. Okay?" Then she brushed his lips with her
own, and walked with lithe steps down the hall to her room.

She had mixed feelings about Tara's increasing attachment
to Telford. He hadn't indicated that he wanted a more definite
relationship with her, least of all anything permanent, and she
feared her child might be hurt. Each afternoon, when Telford
went to talk with Allen and inspect the day's work, he took
Tara with him. She rode her bike up and down the road while
he spoke with his foreman.

"Ain't nothing wrong with her lovin' Telford," Henry said
when she mentioned her concern. "It's good for both of 'em.
Tel ain't never happier than when he's got that little girl with
him. Like I said already, he needs her as much as she needs
him."

"But, Henry, when we leave here, she'll be unhappy."

He stared at her as one might look at a Martian. "You ain't going no place, and if you had any sense, you'd know it."

At supper that evening, Russ urged Telford to go back to Barbados and complete his inspection of the site for the Frenchman's Village, and it occurred to her that Russ might use that as a ruse to put some distance between her and his older brother. She wasn't convinced that he accepted her and Tara.

"Look," Russ explained, "in another three weeks, the school will be finished and pristine clean. I can handle what remains to be done there, but we can't start in Barbados until you check out that site, order the supplies and find a foreman."

"Right. We may have to take some heavy equipment over there. That rock bed is going to be a problem."

"You'll know that after you check it out."

"All right, but if there is one single snag with the school, phone me. That building is going to be ready on time."

She made up her mind to speak to Telford about his passion to vindicate his father; no one could know happiness while harboring resentment.

"How long will you stay?" she asked, aware that her voice was less steady than it normally was.

"Maybe ten days. Less if possible. You can bet I'll be back here as soon as possible."

She hadn't thought Tara would miss Telford as much as she did. Several times a day, she would ask when he was coming back. She ran to the front door whenever she heard a car and, disappointed to learn that it wasn't the Buick Le Sabre, would become despondent.

Around four o'clock Saturday afternoon, Alexis intended to take Tara to the pool for a swim but couldn't find her. She phoned Henry. "Is Tara at your cottage with you?"

"Why, no, she ain't. You mean she ain't with you?"

"I can't find her."

"I'll git dressed and be right over."

She thanked him and, after searching the entire house, paced the hallway trying to imagine where her child could be. When she heard the Mercedes, she sped to the front door and unlocked it.

Russ walked in. "Hi. Surely you aren't waiting here to greet... What's the matter? Hey, wait a minute. Something's wrong."

"I c-can't find Tara."

He dropped his briefcase to the floor. "You can't find... don't joke. Where'd you look?"

"Every room and closet in this house, including downstairs and all over the garden. I walked around calling her. She isn't here, and she's not with Henry."

He plunged his fingers through the curls on his head. "Let's look at this thing logically. Let me think. She's been out of sorts ever since Telford left here. First, let's look at the things they did together."

She went down the list, ending with their visits to Bart's ice cream parlor and daily afternoon trips to the warehouse.

"I see. Can I get you to go someplace, sit down and stay there, maybe work on your sculpture, while I look into this? Will you?"

What could she say? "Thanks. I'll be in my room."

In his first true gesture of empathy toward her, he patted her shoulder. "I'll find her."

Russ went upstairs to his room, changed into a T-shirt, a pair of jeans and boots. Then he loaded a rifle, went to the garage and got a hammer, hatchet, screwdriver and flashlight, all of which he loaded into the pickup truck. She wouldn't know the way to the ice cream parlor, so he headed for the warehouse.

The men knocked off at five, and according to his watch, it was six-fifteen. He didn't like this. Giving Tara that bicycle might not have been a smart idea. He parked a few feet from the hard-hat area, got out, slung the rifle over his shoulder, put the hatchet in its holder across his hips and started his search. An hour later, deciding that he might have to go back home, get a hard hat and go in the building area, he walked across the old bridge and stopped, all five of his senses on alert. Where had that hissing sound come from? He picked his way around the massive old olive tree and stifled a gasp. Tara. And coiled three feet from where she sat was a poisonous snake. With his heart in his mouth, he eased away to get a better angle. At least she didn't see the snake and wouldn't move. He took the hatchet from its holder, aimed and let it fly. A second later he had Tara in his arms. His dad had impressed him and his brothers that if you saw one, another was nearby, so he didn't waste time getting out of the way.

"Tara, it's Russ," he said when she screamed. "Honey, your mother's out of her mind with worry." He hugged her close as he raced from the bridge to his truck.

"Mr. Russ, you scared me. Did you throw something at me?"

If only she knew. "Honey, you know I wouldn't do anything to hurt you. I saw a little animal there, and I threw my hatchet at him."

"Oh. Is he all right?"

"Yeah. Perfect." It was against the law, but he had no choice but to put her beside him in the front seat.

"It's fun sitting up here, Mr. Russ."

Suddenly, he had to stop the truck. His heart pounded like a speeding freight train, and his hands shook so badly that he had trouble steering. After taking some deep breaths, he turned to Tara and spoke with all the calmness he could manage.

"Tara, I know you miss Telford, but he'll be back in a few days. If you want to come out here, ask me, and I'll bring you. What you did was bad and very dangerous. You could have been…ki…in serious trouble. How'd you get down here?"

"I rode my…" She slapped her hands over her mouth, signifying her excitement. "Mr. Russ. We forgot my bike."

He turned the truck around. "Just show me where you left it."

He put the bike in the bed of the truck and headed home. In the garage, he lifted her from the truck, and when she smiled up at him, he hugged her. "All of us love you, Tara. Telford,

Drake, Henry, your mother and me. We love you. Please don't ever do anything like this again. Don't get on that bike unless we know where you're going."

She hugged him and kissed his cheek. "Okay."

He took her hand, went into the house and didn't stop till he reached Alexis's room. When she opened the door, he picked Tara up, handed her to her mother and, without a word, walked swiftly away. At the end of the hall he bumped into Henry.

"You found her?"

"Yeah. Three feet from a coiled rattler. If anybody had told me I'd be willing to trade my life for that kid, I wouldn't have believed them. I don't want another scene like that one."

"Whew! You don't think it upset her?"

"As best I could tell, she didn't see it. But it bears watching."

Henry scratched the few strands of hair on his head. "Yeah. Looks like that little girl's an angel sent here to brighten our lives. I ain't never seen nothin' like her. You just can't resist her."

"Tell me about it. She...she's real special. And Telford... Henry, if Alexis leaves here, that child will go to pieces."

Henry waved his hand as if dismissing the idea. "Alexis don't strike me as being that stupid, but you never can tell."

Chapter 8

Her face awash with tears, Alexis clutched Tara to her breast and prayed words of thanks. When tremors racked her body and she shivered uncontrollably, she felt Tara's little hands cup her face.

"What's the matter, Mummy? Did I do bad?"

"I'm just happy you're all right. Where did Mr. Russ find you?"

"Under the big tree near the bridge. He told me I can't go back there, but Mr. Telford always took me there."

"You can't go anywhere alone on your bike. Do you understand? If you do, I'll punish you."

"I won't, Mummy. I told Mr. Russ I wouldn't. When is Mr. Telford coming back?"

"A week, maybe. I'm not sure, honey. But stop worrying about him; he's working, and when he finishes the job, he'll come—"

Now who could that be? Still holding Tara in her arms, she reached for the phone thinking that the caller would be Russ, but the voice she heard belonged to Jack.

"How's it going, babe? Thought I might drop over there in a couple of days."

"We have to settle on a specific day and a precise time. The best time is between two and four in the afternoon."

"You playing hardball, babe?"

"You'd know; you're an expert at that."

"Look, I have to check out of here. Ring you back in a few days."

"Don't you want to speak with her?" He'd hung up. She stared at the receiver, unable to believe he'd done that a second time. When the phone rang again, she prepared herself to give him a piece of her mind.

"What is it this time?"

"Hey! Who rattled your cage?"

When she recognized Russ's voice, shame poured over her. "I'm sorry for snapping at you, Russ. I'll explain that when I see you; it won't do for all ears."

"You mean Tara?"

"Yes."

"I see. How's she doing?"

"She's fine. I'm the wreck. Apparently, she went down to the warehouse site because she goes there most afternoons with Telford."

"Yeah. She misses him. You make certain, Alexis, that she never does that again. I cautioned her, but she can't hear it too often. If necessary, keep her in your room. That was dangerous."

She wondered at the roughness of his voice and its tone of command. "Russ, I don't know how to tell you how much I appreciate your finding her and bringing her home. I was going out of my mind. She's—"

"Don't thank me, Alexis. She's...special to all of us." He hung up.

For all his blunt manners and toughness, he's a tender man, she mused. "Come with me while I set the table for supper, Tara."

"Can't I practice?"

"Not now. Come with me." She couldn't bear to have Tara out of her sight. Another experience like that one and she'd be ready for her grave.

"You care to finish our conversation?" Russ asked her after dinner, while they sipped coffee in the den, and Henry entertained Tara in the kitchen.

"Tara's father had just called suggesting he'd like to come for a visit. That's twice in the last three weeks, but on neither occasion did he ask for a specific date and time, nor did he inquire about Tara or say he wanted to speak with her. I thought he was calling back."

Russ walked over to the bar and poured himself a snifter of cognac. "Maybe Tara isn't the reason why he wants to visit."

She sat up straight, uncrossed her legs and braced her hands on her knees. "Russ, I was Jack's first wife. From what I hear, he may have number three, and I assume he was no more faithful to the second one than he was to me. Every child ought to know his or her father, and that is the only reason I'll suffer Jack Stevenson's presence. He'll have to visit her here, because I will not allow him to take her out of this house or that garden."

"You have sole custody?"

She nodded. "Bought with half of our joint property. That was the bargain. He didn't even specify visitation rights."

His whistle bruised her eardrums. "Supervised visitation is more than he deserves. Set his visits for a time when you know Telford, Drake or I will be here."

Later, sitting in the garden, she shaved the bark from a piece of walnut and tried to envisage the face of Martin Luther King, Jr., emerging from that wood. She enjoyed a sweet serenity, knowing that her precious Tara was safe and unharmed in the next room practicing scales on the piano. She rushed inside when Tara called to her.

"Mummy, somebody's at the door."

"Russ! What is it?" she asked when she opened the door.

Russ had never knocked on her door until that afternoon when he brought Tara to her.

"Telford's been ringing you for the past ten minutes. He asked me to find out if you and Tara are all right."

She knew he caught the excitement in her voice. "Thanks. I heard it and didn't hear it. It's that way sometimes when I'm starting work on a new piece."

His left eyebrow shot up. "Telford's like that when he's working on his wire sculptures. He'll call you in a few minutes."

When the phone rang again, she raced to answer it. "Telford. How are you?"

"Great. What about you? You miss me?"

"Of course I miss you."

"Listen, woman, that is not what I asked. I asked whether you *miss* me."

She couldn't help laughing, though she well knew that part of the euphoria she felt was nervous release, a reaction to the three hours of terror she'd lived through.

"I wish you were here. That better?"

"A little," he grumbled. "Where's Tara? Let me speak with her."

With a lump in her throat, she called Tara to the phone and, for the first time, wished she'd met Telford Harrington before she became involved with Jack. This man had become father to her child. She stood nearby while Tara chatted with Telford, eventually telling him of her adventure that afternoon.

"I won't, Mr. Telford. I promised Mummy and Mr. Russ I wouldn't. I love you, too. Are you coming back soon? I will. Kisses. Bye." She handed the phone to her mother and went back to the piano.

"I suppose you and Russ will tell me more about Tara's mishap when I get home. I want you to put that bike in the garage till I get back. She promised not to stray away from the house, but she's only five. I—"

"Henry stored it downstairs in the game room. Don't

worry. Do you think you'll be able to put up that apartment complex?"

"Yeah, but I'll have to stick close to it for the first couple of months. Fortunately, the school will have been completed before we begin work over here."

She hadn't wanted to ask him the question that pressed most heavily on her mind, but when he didn't volunteer the information, she had no choice. "When will you be home?"

"In a couple of days. Probably Friday night or Saturday afternoon if my luck holds. I'm waiting for some samples of roofing material."

"I'll...uh..." Her voice was a mere whisper, so she cleared her throat. "I'll be glad to see you."

"Same here. I...uh...I'll get back to you soon as I can. How about a kiss?"

Her eyes widened, and she swallowed with difficulty. What did that mean? She made the sound of a kiss. "You'll find a lot more where that one came from."

"Glad to hear it. I hope the supply is inexhaustible, because you're talking to a needy man."

"I don't know how to react to that," she said, and she didn't. "So I suppose I'll have to play it by ear."

His laughter warmed her. "Not to worry. I won't steer you wrong. Good night, sweetheart."

"G-good night, love."

She hung up quickly, because she didn't know how to deal with what had just happened. He hadn't said much, yet what he'd implied filled her heart till she thought it would burst. She went back to the wood on which she'd been working, and marveled that it seemed to glow. Foolishly, she hugged it to her and twirled around. She needed to share it, to tell someone that she loved him, so she rushed into Tara's room and stopped. Suddenly sober. She had to move with care, because her child's well-being depended on her using common sense.

She switched gears. "You're learning fast, Tara."

"I make a lot of mistakes, Mummy, and I don't want Mr. Telford to hear my mistakes."

"Everyone makes boo-boos sometime, honey."

"I know. Mr. Telford told me that." She looked up, her face shining in a brilliant smile. "I love Mr. Telford, and he loves me, too." She played a few more bars and stopped. "And I love Mr. Henry, and Mr. Russ, and Mr. Drake and you, Mummy."

More proof that if she left Harrington House, she'd break her daughter's heart. "And all of us love you," she whispered, her joy of minutes earlier only a memory.

Telford stepped out of the taxi, hooked his finger in the handle of his wardrobe case, grabbed his briefcase and dashed to the house. He didn't mind getting wet in a summer downpour, but he'd rather not be fully clothed. He couldn't get his keys out without setting his luggage on the wet steps, so he leaned on the doorbell.

"Why didn't you tell somebody you was coming?" Henry asked him.

He threw an arm across the old man's shoulder in response to as warm a greeting as he ever got from Henry. "So you could cook cabbage stew?"

"Now, that's a thought."

He dropped everything in the foyer and headed down the hallway to Alexis. Her hair looked as if she'd been pulling at it in frustration; she wore a gray smock that he supposed she worked in while sculpting; her face was free of makeup; and the odor of turpentine perfumed her surroundings. But he didn't care about her disarray, nor did the scent of turpentine, which he disliked, offend him. She was here, looking at him, gaping in surprise, the most beautiful sight he'd ever seen.

"Can I come in?"

As if his words unlocked the door of her mind, she stepped back, opened her arms and gave him the warmth and softness of her body. Her fingers caressed the side of his face, and he stared down at her. He needed some proof, some verification that he was everything to her as he realized she was to him.

"If I'd known you'd be here today," she said at last, "I'd have planned something nice, and I wouldn't be wearing this—"

He held her closer, relishing her nearness. "I don't care about that; it's just window dressing. You're what I need. Kiss me. Let me know I mean something to you."

"You do. Oh, Telford, don't you know how dear you are to—"

He didn't wait for more, but squeezed her to him and bent to taste her lips. She parted them and welcomed him as he stroked her tongue with his own. It wasn't enough. He needed more, and as if she knew it, she sucked his tongue deeply into her mouth and feasted until he lifted her and wrapped her to his body. Her arms tightened around him, and she straddled him, taking over the kiss, cherishing him. He'd wanted proof and she gave it, giving in to her passion. With seemingly great reluctance, she moved her mouth from his and let her lips caress his eyes, cheeks, neck and ears, his entire face as she murmured incomprehensible words to him. Her passion seemed to mount like an arising wind, and she opened her mouth, took in him, loving him while she rocked against him. Her bed stood four feet away, but the sound of the piano made a mockery of it.

Still holding her close to his body, he smiled down at her. "Now, that's what I call a decent welcome." He stroked her cheek. "You realize, don't you, that we have to talk about this and do something about it? I want you to think about us seriously. Don't try to guess what I think and feel, though I suppose you know."

He walked a couple of steps away from her, turned and fixed his gaze on her eyes. "Take a good look at your life, how you feel about me, what you want for yourself and Tara and decide where you want to go from here. I think we both have to do this without each being influenced by the other's needs and feelings."

"I know what I feel."

"But do you know what you want to do about it?" He held up his hand. "Don't tell me now. Think about it."

"Mummy, can I go on the back porch? Biscuit has to... Eeee, Mr. Telford, Mr. Telford." She ran to him, her little arms outstretched and her face shining with happiness. "Mr. Telford."

He picked her up, swung her around, hugged her and loved every one of the kisses she planted all over his face. "I think you grew while I was away."

"I'm five now, so I'm bigger."

"You are, indeed."

"I been practicing, but I make mistakes."

"I told you not to worry about that. If you practice, you will stop making mistakes, but that takes time."

When her expression clouded, her next words didn't surprise him. "Are you going to stay, Mr. Telford? I want you to stay."

He put her down and hunkered beside her. "Sometimes, I have to go, Tara. I have to work. But I will always come back. Do you understand me? I will always come back."

She stared at him, pensively, for a minute. Then, as if the meaning of what he said penetrated, she smiled and hugged him. "Okay. Wanna hear me practice?"

"He's tired after his long trip, Tara. Maybe later, after he has time to rest."

He thanked Alexis with his eyes. Tired hardly described how he felt; he hadn't been in bed since the night before. "Let me rest a few minutes. I'll phone you. Okay?"

"Okay," she said, and he realized she trusted him to keep his word. How could so small a child make a man his age feel as if he could move mountains?

He didn't want to eat dinner at home that night; he wanted to take Alexis into Frederick for dinner, but Henry would be offended. He had to find a way to treat her as she deserved. In that house, she did things for him. He paid her, but that no longer seemed adequate or, for that matter, desirable. He sprawled across his bed and gave in to his weariness. But his thoughts stayed with Alexis. The longer he knew her, the further his unpleasant memories of his mother faded from his consciousness.

The next morning, he parked in front of the church school, got out and opened the back door for Tara. He realized she'd missed the classes as well as her schoolmates, for she jumped out of the car, then raced back to kiss him good-bye, something she'd forgotten in her eagerness to get inside the school building. The incident reminded him that she should be registered for school. He drove off wondering when he'd accepted that he needed more in his life, that he needed his woman and couldn't imagine days without Tara.

A few minutes later, he walked into his makeshift office at the school construction site. "How's it going, man?" he asked Allen, whom he'd transferred from the warehouse.

"You're in for a surprise, friend. Those six extra men have made a big difference. We ought to sweep it clean, mop and polish the floors by next Wednesday."

He grabbed Allen's shoulders. "You wouldn't lie about a thing like this."

"It's true. Nothing else left. Every bit of debris's been hauled out, and McCallister's already working on the landscaping."

"Getting you on this job was a stroke of genius." Now he could make plans for himself and...Alexis.

On Wednesday, August the eleventh, he walked through the school building with the mayor, the Eagle Park buildings inspectors, Russ and Drake, bursting with pride. They'd done it with a little more than three weeks to spare. After they walked out of the building's front door, Drake locked it and handed the mayor the keys.

"We got the best-built, most modern school in the state of Maryland," the mayor boasted. "Now all those who said I should give the contract to Sparkman can eat their words."

Joy and pride hardly described Telford's emotions. He hadn't known he underbid Sparkman, or that influential people in his own town thought him incapable of delivering the school on time. He didn't care who they were, only that he and his brothers had made them look foolish. He wondered if it was over or if he had to continue proving to those who doubted Harrington, Inc. One thing was certain: he'd brought Fentress Sparkman to his knees.

"I'm off to m' sister's," Henry said to Alexis when she entered the breakfast room that morning. "I takes me two weeks vacation every August. They give me a month, but I ain't got nothing to do a whole month, and I can hardly stand m' brother-in-law a day, much less a month."

"You have a good time. Tara and I will miss you."

"I doubt that. I'll be having me a good time big-game fishing, though. If it wasn't for that, I'd stay right here. I'm leaving soon as breakfast is over and Russ is ready to take me to the airport."

Nobody had said anything to her about cooking arrangements while Henry was away. "Does that mean I cook while you're gone?"

"Course not. Telford wouldn't ask you to do that. Everybody leaves here these two weeks." He gazed at her with the look of one who'd just talked too much and knew it. "We needs a break from each other. Ain't you planning going off?"

"Oh, I get a vacation, too, Henry," she said, evading his question.

Russ walked in carrying a suitcase and dressed so casually as to be hardly recognizable.

"Don't tell me you're off somewhere, too," she said as cold tentacles of fear wafted through her. What was going on here?

"Yeah. We close the house the last half of August. Didn't Telford tell you?"

"Didn't I tell her what?"

She spun around and saw Telford standing in the doorway with both hands on his hips. "I didn't realize you closed up here this time of year."

"I'm sorry, Alexis. It's in a separate paragraph in your contract in bold black lettering. I assumed you remembered it and were planning for it. Frankly, I wondered why you hadn't mentioned your plans to me, but I didn't want to invade your privacy."

"You could have asked me what I planned to do. Where're you going?" It occurred to her that she sounded more like an offended lover than an employee, not that she cared right then. She didn't like the feeling—however unfounded—that she hadn't been told because her status didn't warrant it.

If Telford found something amusing in the situation, she wished he'd tell her what it was. His grin broadened almost to a laugh. "I'm waiting to know what you're doing."

Russ slapped his hand on the back of his neck and furrowed his brow. "We're not leaving her and Tara here alone. Suppose they have an emergency."

She wondered at the grin on Henry's face as well, but ignored it for the sake of prudence. "I'll be fine. I should have remembered that clause. No problem. I'll phone my sister, and we'll have a great time together."

"I've got to get to Baltimore to catch my plane," Drake said. "I wish we'd settled all this last night." He hugged Alexis and went to find Tara, whose attention to the piano even before breakfast had become more persistent since Telford's return.

"None of you should worry about this," Telford said. "I'll look after Alexis and Tara."

"Why didn't I think of that?" Russ asked, his mouth curved into a half smile, half smirk. "See that you do, brother."

An hour later, she vacillated between annoyance at Telford and excitement at the thought of nights alone with him in that huge house. With what she didn't doubt was deliberate discretion, he avoided her until around five o'clock, when he telephoned her.

"I'd like the three of us to go into Frederick for supper. Tara will love it, and I'll at last get to take you out."

"I can cook."

"I know that, but I don't want you to. If we leave around a quarter to seven, we can eat and get back here before Tara gets too sleepy. What do you say?"

She remembered Henry's comment that Telford wouldn't

ask her to cook. "All right. Since Tara will be with us, I guess we'll be informal."

"Why? Tara knows how to behave. I'm wearing a jacket and tie."

"Well, 'scuse me. I get the message. Be ready at quarter of."

He cooked breakfast the next morning, and planned for them to eat dinner out. She didn't question that, but she couldn't understand his treating her as if she were his baby sister. After four days of it and thoroughly fed up, she confronted him.

"How is it that you're the only one who doesn't get a vacation? You don't want me to believe this happens every year, do you?" She hadn't previously been in his bedroom while he was in it; and with him barefoot and wearing a robe that she knew he put on when she knocked, his rough masculinity jolted her into a more cautious mood. Yet, she was prepared to finish what she began by walking in there.

"Why didn't you take your vacation?" she pressed.

When he sat down, the robe opened exposing a part of his naked thigh midway above the knee. She swallowed hard, fighting back rising desire, and a smile flickered across his face.

"Did you think I'd go away and leave you and Tara alone here? It didn't even enter my mind."

"I can take care of Tara and me. I appreciate your thoughtfulness, but there's no need for you to stay here."

"I've stated my position, and I won't change it."

She turned to go and stopped. *Don't be chicken, girl.* "And another thing, why are you suddenly treating me as if I were your sister?"

He got up and walked as if in slow motion until he reached her. "You once told me I was honorable, and I'm doing my damndest not to make a liar of you. If you think this scenario isn't getting on my nerves, you're wrong."

"You didn't hear what I said? You're behaving as if I'm

a piece of wood, and you're asking me to believe that's an act?"

Seeing the thunderous expression that leaped into his eyes, she took a step backward. "I lie here every night in physical pain," he said, "twisting and turning in these sheets, imagining your naked flesh soft and warm against mine and knowing that a walk downstairs to your room might bring me relief."

She blanched at that, but he didn't stop. "If you're ready to talk, I'll put on some clothes and meet you downstairs in the den. If you stay up here much longer, talk will be out of the question."

It was D-day, and she knew it. He wanted everything, maybe even that piece of her soul she kept for herself, but she'd forced his hand, and she had to brazen it out.

"See you down there in fifteen minutes."

He didn't offer her anything to drink, nor did he get one for himself, signaling to her the seriousness of his thoughts. After waiting until she sat, he took the big, brown leather chair that he preferred, leaned back and looked steadily at her. The tender expression in his hazel-brown eyes, so unlike his dispassionate looks during the past four days, nearly undid her, for it was what she wanted to see in him, what she'd missed.

"Remember my asking how, after years of marriage and of motherhood, you seemed not to know when a man neared the limit of his control? Remember that?"

She hadn't expected him to return to that, and she wished he hadn't. "Yes, I remember, but, Telford, the truth is so…so personal and…so unpleasant."

He leaned forward. "I suspected that. Just tell me whether you had a…a satisfying relationship."

She didn't know how to answer that, or maybe she didn't want to. How could she confess to this man that she'd been a failure?

"It's all right," he said after her long hesitation. "I have my answer. Try to remember that one person can't sing a duet; for that, you need a partner. Never forget that."

He was telling her that it wasn't her fault, at least not entirely. Jack had never acted as if she were entitled to anything, neither in the bed nor out of it, but she knew it would be different with Telford. That thought banished her disquiet. She supposed the smile that flowed from the depths of her to cover her face was the reason for the lights that suddenly shone in his wonderful eyes.

"I want to take you and Tara to Cape May for a vacation. What do you say?"

She knew she gaped at him. "If you have any more surprises for me, let's have them now. I'd love to go there, but I can't let you—"

A smile played around his mouth, and his eyes sparkled as if he were anticipating pleasure. "Your contract says you get a paid vacation." He got up, walked over to her and knelt beside her chair. "And even if it didn't, I want to take you there. You can't say I'm taking you off for...uh..." He grinned. "To have my way with you. There's plenty of opportunity for that right here. I want to change the scene. Give us a chance, Alexis. Will you, sweetheart? I want you to know me in better circumstances than these."

And she wanted the same, to be with him away from Harrington House, where they would simply be woman and man. "When do you want to leave?"

"Tomorrow morning. It's about two hundred miles. If you don't mind, I'd like to drive, because we'll need the car. Getting around in Cape May without one is just about impossible."

"I'd enjoy that. I haven't been to Cape May." She'd almost added, *Though I taught not too far from there.* That was something she had to level with him about, she realized.

His hand was warm on her thigh, and when he gazed into her eyes, her heart took off in a mad trot and the heat of desire suffused her. How she wanted, needed this man!

"You only need to bring casual clothes and not much of that. The lifestyle up there is very informal."

"We'll be ready to leave right after breakfast."

She could see that her answer pleased him, for he smiled

broadly and squeezed her thigh. "Then, let's leave here at eight-thirty, eat breakfast in town and be on our way by nine-thirty."

"Fine with me. What about Biscuit?"

"We'll leave him at a kennel in town. Okay?"

She nodded.

He stood and looked down at her. He wasn't smiling then, but as somber as she'd ever seen him. "I want you in my arms so badly, but I'm damned if I'll put myself through what it'll cost me later on."

She eased out of the chair, reached up, kissed him on the mouth and whispered. "I need you, too."

She didn't wait for him to react. Her own plan had begun to take shape in her mind, and it didn't include their making love on the floor of the Harrington House den. Within minutes, she'd closed her bedroom door, pulled out a suitcase and started packing. The first item she folded was a dusty-rose silk negligee.

He strapped Tara into her car seat, got in and headed for Highway 70. Exactly nine-thirty. "We'll be there by two. I reserved rooms in a small bed-and-breakfast just off the ocean. Except for the waves, it's quiet, five or six blocks from the tourist hangouts. Do you mind that we'll have adjoining rooms with a door that opens between them? If you do, I'll change it."

He glanced over at her and relaxed when she appeared unperturbed. "I'm sure I'll love the place."

He chose Irene Wheeler's Bed and Board instead of a hotel so that they'd have a sitter he could trust. He always stayed there, because she served him grits, sausage, eggs and biscuits for breakfast and pampered him as though he were her own son.

"Irene, meet Alexis and her daughter, Tara. They're very special to me."

"I figured that out myself, since this is the first time you haven't come here alone. Glad to meet you, Alexis." She took Tara's hand. "I'll bet you love cookies and ice cream."

"Yes, ma'am," Tara said, her face beaming her pleasure at the thought. "Black-cherry ice cream."

As he expected, Tara and Irene embraced each other like old friends. Alexis smiled. "I'm glad to meet you, Irene, and I'm sure I'll enjoy my stay here."

"If you need anything, just let me know. If I don't have it, I know where to get it."

A strange feeling settled over him when he unlocked the door to room number sixteen. Right down to the recesses of his gut, he felt as if he were checking in there with his family. Half an hour later, he hadn't been able to shake the feeling.

He answered her knock on his room door, and every nerve in his body jumped to alert. Her big brown eyes gazed up at him, warm, seductive and, unless he missed the mark, inviting. But she was in his care, and he intended to take his cues from her.

"Hi. You comfortable in there?" Suddenly, he had the unsettling sense that he'd known her someplace. A different setting and different circumstances. He'd had that feeling the night they swam together in the moonlight, though less strongly. Maybe another life. But he didn't believe in that. He shrugged it off.

She nodded. "It's a lovely room. Do you plan to keep this door shut? I know it's a little awkward with Tara here, since she acts as if she owns you, but…"

"Then we'll leave it open and close it when we need privacy. Put on some comfortable shoes, and let's look for some lunch. You're a tempting dish, but right now, I need food."

She looked at him from beneath lowered lashes. "By all means. A man should be fortified at all times." She patted his flat belly. "Not bad."

Hot little needles shimmered through his veins. "Woman, are you flirting with me?"

She leaned against the doorjamb and examined her nails. "Who, me? Would I do such a thing?"

He grabbed her and locked her to his body. "You bet you would."

She looked up at him, her eyes projecting the epitome of innocence, relaxed, offering neither defense nor apology.

"Aw, sweetheart, you get to me. Let's move out of here and find something to eat, before we start something."

The sound he heard was more a giggle than a laugh. "Not to worry. Our little chaperon is the perfect libido-suppressor."

"Yeah. But don't forget she's my friend. If I tell her to go to sleep, she'll do it."

She tweaked his nose. "And if I promise her black-cherry ice cream, she'll stay awake for hours waiting for it."

"And if I get my hands on you," he growled, "you'll beg her to sleep."

His woman walked back into her room, turned and winked at him. "Do what you have to do."

The primate in him roared into action, and he had to stifle the urge to grab her and sink himself as deeply into her as he could get. He told himself to cool down. "Woman, you know precisely how to strip my gears. Meet you downstairs in five minutes."

"I have to tell Miss Irene good-bye," Tara said, as they were leaving the house.

He wanted to encourage the child's good manners, so he took her hand and walked back to the service area, where he knew he'd find Irene.

"Bye, Miss Irene," she said and turned to him. "Are we coming back?" Assured that they would, she smiled. "Tell me when you want to make cookies. Mr. Henry taught me how to make noels. Bye."

"What a delightful child," Irene said. "We'll make some tomorrow afternoon, if that's all right with your mother."

"Okay," Tara said. "Bye now." She took his hand. "Come on. I'm hungry." He didn't laugh, but he couldn't help thinking how feminine she was. She'd detained him, and now she protested that she was hungry. Lord, he loved her!

After lunch, they ambled to the tourist attractions where it was as if all the craftspeople in the region brought their wares for sale. He noticed Tara's fascination with a little polar bear and asked her if she'd like to have it.

Though his question brought an expression of glee to her little face, she looked up at her mother for permission. It hit him then that he wanted that little girl for his own, wanted the right to guide her life. He waited for Alexis's response.

"You must thank him, darling."

Her squeals were all the thanks he needed, but she wrapped her arms around his knee. "Thanks, Mr. Telford." He handed her the bear, and she looked up at him. "Now Biscuit will have someone to play with. I love you, Mr. Telford."

"I love you, too, baby."

They strolled along the shore drive beside the ocean, holding hands. He understood the contentment that enveloped him. They'd finished the school with weeks to spare and, he hoped, restored confidence in Harrington, Inc. And though he had vacationed in Cape May for each of the last seven years, he hadn't previously experienced there the peace and inner joy that he felt now. Alexis and Tara gave his life a new meaning. Walking between them, he squeezed their fingers. When they reached the next bench, he sat down, put his arms around them, stretched out his legs, crossed his ankles and let the sun drench his face. Finally, after his struggles to get his brothers through school, finish his own education and rebuild the business that had cost his beloved father his life—though the memory of that girl from long-ago college days stayed with him—he knew what happiness was.

Chapter 9

After dinner, with Tara asleep and the day spent, Alexis stood with Telford on the balcony off her room and looked out at the dark waters of the Atlantic Ocean. In the glow of moonlight, the waves danced ferociously as if at war with each other, and she said as much to Telford.

His arm slipped around her waist and tugged gently. "I was thinking that the waves were vying for the moon's affection. What do you make of that?"

He's here with me because he wants to be. Maybe I'll be sorry, but I want to be alive. He'll help me to achieve what I've missed. I know he's different from Jack. I love him, and I'm going to trust him. Lord, please don't let it sour. I'm going for it.

She leaned against him. "Anything personal in that statement? I mean, are you vying for anyone's affection?" It was a leading question, and that was what she intended.

He put both hands on her waist and turned her to face him. "In a way, yes. But I'm after more than affection; I can get that from Henry and my brothers. I'm after you. All of you. And I'm not going to resort to tricks to get what I want."

Unprepared for that declaration, she gazed at him, tongue-tied, but only momentarily. "Tricks? What's that supposed to mean?"

"I mean I'm not going to try seducing you into doing anything. You told me you needed me, and I haven't kept my feelings for you a secret."

"I'm a wounded bird, Telford."

Holding her close and stroking her as though his hands would heal her, he whispered, "I know that, because you've told me in many ways. Do you trust me?"

"Yes," she said, and buried her face against his chest.

With his index finger, he tipped her chin, urging her to look at his face. "I'm egalitarian. You know that. But when you lie in my arms, let me lead you." His face softened, lights danced in his eyes and she could see that the thought fired up his emotions.

"When we get it perfect," he went on, "you can have your way with me all you want. Trust me, I'll be your willing victim."

She'd think about the meaning of that later. Right now, she had to level with him. "I always felt used, be-because my interests were never considered."

He sucked in his breath. "I halfway figured something like that. And there's never been anyone else?"

Telling him about it wasn't as painful as she'd thought it would be. She shook her head. "No one."

"When you're ready, you'll come to me. Try to stop thinking about that phase of your life. Tara is a product of it, but she isn't part of it. It's over."

"What makes you so sure I'll come to you?"

"Because you have the courage to do anything you want to do. Don't think I'm being noble; I am not. You're very important to me. I want to show you a new world, and I want you to be sure you're ready for it, because it will change our lives."

He walked her to their connecting door. "We'd better say good night before I forget about my good intentions."

His kiss on her cheek didn't thrill her, but she hadn't indicated she wanted more, and, indeed, from her perspective, the time wasn't right. "I think I *do* understand. Good night." *He's leaving this up to me because he doesn't want me to think he brought me here and is bearing all the expenses for the express purpose of getting me in bed.* As much as she wanted to kiss him, she didn't think it prudent considering the conditions he'd just laid out, so she brushed the side of his face with her right hand, went into her room and closed the door.

However he looked at them, his days with Tara and Alexis could only be described as idyllic. They ate breakfast at the Bed and Board, roamed the tourist area and perused the numerous handicraft stalls, museums and gift shops until lunchtime. Then they rested, mostly for Tara's sake, for an hour or two after lunch, after which they swam and frolicked in the ocean. He'd learned more about her in those six days than in the five months he'd known her.

"I can hardly imagine that three days from now I'll attend the dedication of the Eagle Park High School," he said, sitting with her on his balcony that evening. "It's one of the most difficult jobs we've had, and definitely the one that put the most pressure on us."

"I'm happy for all three of you. You can't help being proud."

"What I'm going to enjoy most is seeing Fentress Sparkman eat crow, and by damn, I'm going to wash his face with his lies. After screwing my father royally, he fed the rumor that Harrington, Incorporated, was undependable, that we overspent our bids, didn't bring our buildings in on time and used substandard materials. The superintendent of buildings promised me he'd comment on each of those points."

Her hand stroked his left forearm, but he didn't pay too much attention. Indeed, he tried not to focus on it. She touched him frequently the last couple of days, almost as if she had to have her hands on him. Whether she realized it or not, she was telling him something with her possessive little moves, and he'd be ready when she made good on her promises.

"Telford, honey, your hatred of Sparkman worries me. You've won the battle, restored your firm's credibility and still you're bitter. Honey, happiness and bitterness don't go together." She took both of his hands into her own, and her voice took on a pleading tone.

"You can't love and hate at the same time. How can you be at peace and feel this way about another person?"

"It isn't easy to love your enemy, especially one who attempted to rob you of your livelihood."

"I know. But promise me you'll try it my way. If he's at that ceremony, seeing Harrington's success will probably give him the toughest lesson he's ever learned. You can afford to forget about him."

"That isn't so easy."

"It will be if you concentrate on me."

"I've spent the last six days trying to avoid that."

"I would have thought you were smarter than that."

"What did you expect me to do, break down your door and burst in there like a deer in the rutting season?"

She looked at him with sparkling eyes, and her shrug had an air of nonchalance. "Hmmm. I expect those deer get what they're after."

"Yeah. Every time."

He'd never been slow to get a message, so he stood and took her hand. "Let's check on Tara."

They looked down on the sleeping child, and he spoke softly, yet his words were unmistakable. "I wish she were mine." Her gasp let him know that she heard and understood him, but he looked at her steadily, unconcerned about the disclosure.

Her mind made up, she allowed herself a yawn. "I'm getting sleepy."

He gazed at her, but she knew he couldn't read her expression, because she didn't want him to. "I've got a bottle of Moët & Chandon cooling in my room." He leaned against the wall, and his beautiful eyes sent her what could only be described as a challenge. "Interested?"

No tricks, huh? "Maybe. Right now, I need a shower."

A half smile rippled around his full bottom lip, and she knew he had her message. "Sure. Take all the time you need. See you later."

She didn't answer. As his slow, sexy gait took him through the connecting door to his room, she felt the first stirring of desire. She'd come prepared, and she didn't doubt that he had, too. After finishing her ablutions, she dressed in the silk-satin rose gown that dipped to her hips in back, exposed her full bosom in a deep décolletage and barely topped her rose-colored silk mules—items she'd purchased in the hope of putting some spice in her marriage, but which she was never motivated to wear. She put big, silver hoops in her ears, let her hair down in a wild mass, put on the negligee that matched her gown, dabbed Fendi perfume in strategic places and headed toward the connecting door. Remembering past failures, she had a moment of uncertainty, but said a word of prayer and knocked.

He hadn't misunderstood her; he was sure of that. If she'd wanted to go to bed alone, she'd have said good-night. He got the iced caviar, smoked-salmon sandwiches and pumpernickel squares out of his refrigerator and placed them on the little round bistro table in front of the picture window. After adding flatware, napkins and champagne glasses, he checked the espresso coffee urn and headed for the shower. He'd have to remember to give Irene a sizable tip; she'd provided just what he wanted.

What's keeping her? he wondered later, standing by the window in a white dress shirt, red tie and gray slacks. He'd dressed that way so that she wouldn't think he'd tried to second-guess her. He dried his sweaty palms on the sides of his slacks and plowed his fingers through his silky curls. Finally, when the tension became nearly unbearable, he opened the door and walked out on his balcony. But for the strong breeze whipping in from the ocean, he'd say the night was idyllic. Not one on which a man should be alone. He turned on the radio, didn't like the program and flipped through the CDs Irene kept there.

He chose a Henry Mancini recording of instrumental love songs that included "I'm in the Mood for Love," "Paradise," "You Were Meant for Me," Duke Ellington's "Solitude" and similar titles, though none of them satisfied him. He realized he needed his violin. With that, he'd have no trouble communicating to her the mood in which he wanted to envelop her.

Where *was* she? Perhaps she really did mean "maybe." He glanced at his watch and couldn't help laughing at himself. Only thirty-two minutes had passed, and he was as strung up as if an hour had elapsed. *Get it together, man. You may be facing some heavy-duty work.* Not that that worried him. It wasn't a task at which he'd ever failed. He looked at his watch again and laughed. Thirty-three minutes.

Gershwin's "Love Walked In" filled the air, and almost simultaneously what sounded like a banging reached his ears.

"I never thought I was stupid," he said aloud. "How the devil could I hear her from that balcony with the wind howling and the waves sloshing." He dashed to the door and jerked it open.

"I thought you'd decided you made a mistake. Could you have been out on that balcony?"

His breath lodged in his throat, his blood flew through his veins and he was sure she could hear the wild, half-crazed beating of his heart. "I uh… Hell, I don' know. *Good Lord!*" Beautiful. Sexy. One-hundred-percent woman. And she was his!

She looked down at her feet, displaying her vulnerableness. "Can I come in?"

He supposed he shook himself to try to get his senses back.

At least he thought he did. "Yeah. Woman, you poleaxed me. Come in here."

She walked in slowly, and he wanted to hold her, to put her at ease, but he couldn't risk spoiling what he planned for them, and that meant he wasn't going to rush her.

"You're so…so beautiful, so—"

"Thanks. You're a sight for sore eyes yourself. Where's the bubbly?"

She appeared in command, but he knew her now and didn't miss the slight tremor of her voice. *She'll brazen it out,* he said to himself, *but I'm not going to let her sweat.* He reached for her, held out his hand and when she moved to him, he began to dance.

"Do you know the name of this tune?" When she shook her head, he told her, "'Love Walked In.' Funny thing; it started playing when you knocked on the door."

He danced until they reached the little bistro table. "Have a seat," he said with a gesture toward one of the white, wrought-iron bistro chairs.

"Telford, this is wonderful. All of it—the champagne, food, this table, the picture window, the moon and the ocean. I'll remember this for—"

He stopped pouring the champagne and interrupted her. "I want you to remember this night for as long as you live. I will."

She lowered her gaze until he clicked their glasses, and she had to look at him as they drank together.

"You've nothing to fear. If anything happens between us tonight or any other time—and God knows I want that—you'll have to give me the signal."

After selecting a sandwich and eating it, she put some cream cheese and caviar on a slice of bread and ate that. Then she twirled the glass in her fingers, took a sip of champagne and set the goblet on the table.

"Telford, what kind of signal are you looking for? I don't ordinarily entertain men or let them entertain me in this getup."

"I hope the hell not. I can hardly stand to look at you."

She took another sip and let a smile crawl slowly across her face. "Turn out the lights, and you won't have to."

He threw his head back and enjoyed the best laugh he'd had in weeks. After draining his glass, he put the remainder of the food in the refrigerator and stood beside her.

"This is the most important step of my life, Alexis. I know it took me a long time to recognize my true feelings, but you're what I've needed all my life. If you don't feel the same way about me, let's drop it right here. I don't want a sample. I want a commitment."

In spite of his strength and power, she saw his vulnerableness for the first time. She didn't know how to deal with it in this man, but she loved him, and she had to make him know it.

Cupping his face with her hands, she said, "I didn't want to get involved with you or with any other man, because I didn't want to suffer what I went through with my ex-husband. And I know you didn't want to start anything with me. But I've known greater love since I've lived in your home than I thought I'd ever have." His frown didn't deter her. "And you. Love begets love."

He grabbed her wrist. "Are you telling me you love me?"

"To the far reaches of my soul. Don't you know it?"

"I hoped. I—"

She reached up to him with open arms and stilled his moving lips. His big hands gripped her body and pulled her to him. She didn't care about the strength of his hold, only that he held her as though he'd never let her go.

"Love me," she said. "Just…just love me. For once in my life, let me know what it is to be loved."

He lifted her, and she could feel the shudders plowing through him as he bent to her lips and rocked her with the force of his kiss. Gone were his once soft caresses, genteel kisses, tender brushes of her cheek, controlled thrusts of his tongue. He gripped her hips and fitted her to him, held her and plunged into her when she parted her lips. Wild, like a

suddenly unfettered animal, his left hand roamed over her back
and his tongue danced a lover's rhythm in her mouth, letting
her feel the way he intended to love her. Hot little needles
shimmied through her veins and her blood churned on its dash
to the seat of her passion. When she undulated against him,
he freed her left breast, took its aureole into his mouth and
suckled her, sending hot flames of passion roaring through
her body. She held his head to increase the pressure, and he
moved into her, stroking, rocking.

He's out of control, she thought—joy scooting through
her—when, for the first time, he bulged against her and moaned
aloud. "Honey, take me to bed; do something, anything."

He suckled more vigorously, and she grabbed his hips and
strained against him until he jerked away from her. "Hold
off that, sweetheart. You move fast, but I have to go slow.
Understand?" He eased her to her feet, slipped the negligee
from her shoulders, turned back the covers and laid her in his
bed.

"May I?" he asked, standing at the edge of the bed.

She nodded and focused her gaze on him as he bent to ease
the gown off her. When his hands skimmed her thighs all the
way up to her love nest, deliberately, she knew, he set her on
fire and she had to force herself to wait and let him take the
lead as he'd asked. He stared down at her nude body for a
second, and she closed her eyes.

"Look at me, sweetheart. Whatever goes on between us is
good and right." Methodically, he jerked off his tie, got out of
his shirt and trousers and reached for his bikini underwear.

Emboldened by her need of him, she reached out. "Let
me."

He stepped closer, and she eased the garment down and
gasped in awe when he spilled into her hands, big, strong and
ready. She glanced up to see him staring into her face, his eyes
ablaze with the fire of desire, and raised her arms in invitation.
He rested one knee on the bed and went into her arms. Skin
to skin, breasts to chest, belly to belly, she felt him.

His arms enfolded her, protecting her. Reassuring her.

"Kiss me. Open your mouth and kiss me," he said, his tone breathless. She sucked his tongue into her mouth and let him know she wanted him. The hairs on his chest teased her nipples into hard little peaks until she squirmed and spread her legs. She pulled at her aching nipple, and he bent to it, hungrily, as if it were the sustenance of his life, until, nearly out of her mind, she grabbed his buttocks and tried to pull him to her body, to drag him into her aching void.

"Easy, sweetheart. We're not nearly there yet."

His lips planted kisses on her neck, ears, cheeks and lips, while his hand eased downward over her breasts to her belly. She stilled in anticipation, but when his fingers skimmed over the inside of her thigh, her body jerked upward. His mouth brushed her breast before settling on her left aureole and suckling it, and she thought she'd go crazy when his left hand trailed up her other thigh and stopped at its apex. By then, frustrated beyond sanity, she shifted her body to meet his hand and, as if he'd been waiting for her move, his fingers parted her folds, found the nub of her passion and began their torrid dance.

She bucked beneath him, but after the initial surprise, she stiffened.

"Give yourself over to me, baby. Let me have you."

Slowly, she forced herself to relax and let him have his way. Then, his educated fingers began strumming her as a master guitarist strums his guitar. She wanted to scream as the tension mounted, and her hips swung like a hammock in the wind. He left her breast, and trailed kisses down her middle to her belly.

"Ooooh," she yelled, when he hooked her knees over his shoulder and kissed her. "Telford! Oh, my Lord!"

"Don't deny me this, baby. I want every last bit of you." He took her then, kissing and sucking until she screamed.

"Honey, I'm getting so full. I want to burst, but I can't."

"You will, sweetheart." He moved up her body, but continued to stroke her until love's liquid cascaded over his fingers. He removed the packet from beneath the pillow, opened it and handed her the condom. "Slip this on and take me in. Baby, take me."

She sheathed him, led him to her portal and lifted her body to meet his thrust. He lingered for a second, and drove home. Oh, the sweet sensation! The almost unbearable ecstasy of feeling him inside her, in the pit of her where he belonged.

"Are you all right? Comfortable?" he asked her.

"Yes. Yes."

He began to move, slowly at first and then with fast, hard thrusts. Almost immediately the swelling, pumping and squeezing began.

"Telford. Honey, I'm...something's happening. I'm...I'm going to burst, I can't... I'm—"

"Easy, love. Relax. We can't miss. Raise your hips a little bit."

He let her have his power then, as the terrible and sweet clutching began.

With his right hand beneath her hips, he brought her up to him and increased his pace. He'd give her her birthright if it took the last ounce of his strength. Her heat sucked him deeper into her, and when she began to swell around him, he thought he'd lose his mind.

"Sweetheart, don't hold back. That's right. Give yourself to me."

"I will. I am."

Her hot love tunnel gripped him, pulsing against him while he struggled for control. At last, he heard her cry of love and felt her erupt all around him, firing his groin and filling his heart with love.

"Telford, honey. I'm dying. I'm... Oh, Lord. I love you. I love you. I love you," she shouted as he demanded her total surrender.

She soared. Flying. Was she falling? Lord, maybe she was dying. She clutched at him, but her passion sapped the last of her strength, and she tumbled head over heels into the whirlpool of ecstasy into which he plunged her. With her arms flung wide, she screamed his name, gave herself to him and came alive at last.

"Alexis! Oh, love!" he shouted, no longer able to contain his passion. Shaken to the core of his being, he collapsed in her arms and gave her the essence of himself.

Strung out by the force of his release and the power of what he felt for the woman in his arms, he braced himself on his forearms and rested his head on her breasts. Her arms enfolded him, and a peace such as he'd never known swept over him. After a while, he rose up and kissed her lips. Humbled by the electrifying power of her passion and the abandon with which she'd loved him, he lingered at the heights they scaled together. He couldn't put into words what he felt for her at that moment, so he tried to show her in the gentleness of his kiss, the tenderness of his caress and the look of adoration in his eyes. Her fingers stroked his face and head, and then her arms tightened around him.

"I love you, Alexis." The words rushed out of him as if demanding to be said. "You're... Are you... Am I right in believing that you are completely satisfied? Tell me. It's important to me."

Her smile, radiant and happy, gave him his answer, but he needed to hear the words. "Oh, yes. Everything I could have hoped for and more. If there's anything better, I don't think I can handle it. It was so...so intense and so...wonderful. I can't describe it. What... What about you?"

"I told you before we left Eagle Park that you're what I need, and you are. I don't think I'll ever be the same after this, and I don't want to be. You're perfect for me."

He attempted to separate them, but she threw a leg across his buttocks and restrained him. "If you stayed right where you are forever, I wouldn't mind. I love being with you this way."

He gazed down at her, proud and not caring if she knew it, and a grin spread over his face. "You may be sorry you said that. I've been starved for what seems to me like years."

He loved the smile that bloomed first around her lips, then

over her cheeks and flashed in her eyes. His body quickened at her audacious wink, and he hardened within her.

"If you'd just discovered gold," she asked, "would you close the mine and walk away? I intend to make up for lost time, starting now."

"Deal me in. I'm with you, sweetheart, all the way. Love me?"

She nodded. "You know I do."

He flexed his buttocks, gathered her close and took her with him on a short, hot ride to paradise.

Hours later, she left him and went to the bed she shared with Tara, and this went against his grain as few things ever had. When something didn't suit him, he usually changed it or altered the circumstance, but his hands were tied. He didn't like hiding his behavior—not even from a five-year-old—and, until then, it hadn't been necessary. But Tara would broadcast everything she knew, and she didn't choose her audience. He wanted to shout it to the world, but Tara's tattling to Henry and his brothers would humiliate Alexis.

The next day, the early afternoon temperature soared to ninety-seven degrees. "A perfect day for swimming in the Atlantic," Irene said to Alexis. Thanks to the heat, they had returned to their air-conditioned rooms rather than walk along the ocean after lunch.

"We'd better wait a couple of hours before going out there," he said. "It's too hot."

Walking between them, he grasped their hands, and the three of them headed up the stairs to their rooms. *Why do I have this need to protect her? She's a capable woman, and I like that about her. Yet, this primitive feeling that I should shield her from...from...* He told himself to snap out of it.

Alexis understood her reluctance to leave Cape May; she had found there a fulfillment that had eluded her, a coming into her own as a woman. And she would always remember the place where Telford first told her he loved her. What she couldn't fathom was Tara's gloominess when the child saw her packing their belongings.

"Where are we going, Mummy?"

She explained that their vacation was over and they had to go home.

"I don't wanna go home, Mummy. I want to stay here."

She sat on the edge of their bed and put her arms around her daughter. "Don't you want to see Mr. Henry, Mr. Drake, Biscuit and—"

"I wanna stay here where we can be with Mr. Telford all the time."

"We'll still be with him," she told her, though she knew what Tara meant.

They'd been a threesome in Tara's eyes, a family, and their idyll sent the wrong message to the child. She knew she failed in her attempt to explain, because she didn't believe her own words.

Tara's lethargy and quiet during the drive home distressed Alexis, and she mentioned her concern to Telford.

"Don't you feel it, too? We're toppling her little world, and we're also losing the freedom we had these past two weeks to be ourselves with each other." He glanced at the rearview mirror for a look at Tara and spoke more softly. "Unless we're going to tell Henry and my brothers that we're lovers, we can plan on one hell of a job of acting."

And a lot of good that would do. Aloud, she said, "No job of acting will fool Russ."

He glanced at her, and the twinkle in his eyes heated her blood. "Won't fool any of 'em, but what do we care? They'll have to keep their thoughts to themselves." As if in afterthought, he added, "They'd better."

"All except Russ," she insisted.

"Try to like him, Alexis. I... He's... I love my brothers."

Didn't he realize that she and Russ came to terms when Russ rescued Tara? "Russ and I are straight. I think he stopped resenting us that day when he brought Tara to me. After that,

I'd like him no matter what he said." She spoke softly so that the child wouldn't hear her.

"That incident shook Russ up plenty. You know, he's never wanted to love anyone, even pulls back from Drake and me sometimes. You might say that's our mother's legacy to the three of us. Russ has always been a loner but, as you said, 'love begets love,' and he couldn't resist her any more than the rest of us could."

He turned into John Brown Drive and, minutes later, swung into the circle at number ten and stopped.

"Thanks for a wonderful vacation." She pointed to her forehead. "The memory of it is embedded up here for all time."

As he stared boldly into her eyes, his own blazing with knowledge of her as a woman in her most intimate self, she lowered her gaze and fidgeted with the hem of her T-shirt.

"Don't you dare thank me. If you knew what I'm thinking and what I'm feeling, you'd tell me to thank *you*." He got out of the car and went to open the back door for Tara.

"Why can't you come and stay with Mummy and me?" she heard Tara ask him as she walked around the car.

He unstrapped her and lifted her from her car seat. "I... have to stay in my own room."

"You can have my room, and I can sleep with Mummy like we did in Cape M-May. I want you and Mummy and me to stay together."

Telford's glance toward her held a touch of panic, an obvious call for help. When he attempted to set Tara on her feet, she clung to him, as if she were desperate.

He stroked her back. "Baby, this is something your mother and I have to work out."

Tara looked him in the eye. "What does it mean, 'work out'?"

Alexis's antennae shot up. She wouldn't mind having the answer to that herself.

"It means we have to talk about it."

Tara continued to look at him for a minute and then, as if she understood, a smile lit her face. "Oh. When are you going to talk about it?"

Figuring that he'd had enough of Tara's inquisition, Alexis reached for her, but the little girl clutched Telford's shoulders. "Honey," Alexis pleaded, "we can't stay together now, but he'll be near us. Please don't cry."

"I'm not going to cry," Tara said and pushed at Telford's shoulders.

He released her. "You're precious to me, Tara. I love you, and I'll be right here."

His tone, when he said the words, bespoke his dilemma, and Alexis vowed at that moment not to drift into an affair with him. She knew they had failed to pacify Tara when the child strutted past them, walked up to the front door, reached up and rang the bell.

"What a difference from age four to age five," she said to Telford. "Did you ever see the like?"

He lifted his left shoulder in a shrug. "You asking *me?*"

"Mr. Henry!" Tara screamed in delight, as if she'd never been at odds with Telford and her mother. "I was in the Lantic Ocean, and the water is colder than the swimming pool."

"You mean *At*-lantic Ocean, don't you?" Henry said. He looked past Tara to the two adults unloading luggage from the trunk of the car, left the front door ajar and walked into the house holding Tara's hand.

"If I had the nerve, I'd fire that old coot, but Drake and Russ would murder me," Telford said, the grin around his mouth belying his words.

"You wouldn't...would you?"

"Naah. I don't remember life without him. He was always like a father to me, even when Dad was alive. He's just such a smartass sometimes."

They walked hand in hand into the house and found Henry and Tara in the kitchen eating black-cherry ice cream.

"Any messages?" Telford asked Henry.

Henry took his time answering. "I got back a couple a days ago. Since then, Allen Krenner called twice, and the mayor wanted to remind you about the ceremonies day after tomorrow. The way he went on, anybody would think he built that school building with his own hands. Russ come back this morning, and he said Drake will be here this evening, though I ain't heard drip nor drop from 'im."

At the mention of Allen Krenner's name, one of the reasons why she'd been reluctant to become involved with Telford pounded her senses like a hard-rock drummer. In the euphoria of her Cape May idyll with Telford, she'd forgotten about Melanie Krenner.

"You want me to take this to the men down at the warehouse?" Telford asked Alexis the next day when he returned from work. He never bothered to guess at Alexis's motives.

She nodded. "They're working double time, sometimes longer, so I thought they'd appreciate this."

He opened the box and sniffed. "Gingerbread? I love this stuff. You giving it all to—"

"Of course not. There's another pan of it in the pantry. Will you take it down there? If they haven't eaten since lunch, they're hungry by now, and I thought...well, you know."

Every day, he learned more endearing things about her, and it occurred to him then that her compassion set her apart from other women he'd known. "I'll be glad to take it down there and you can bet it'll make you a bunch of friends."

"Can I go with you, Mr. Telford?"

He picked Tara up and hugged her, basking in the adoration she always bestowed on him, and his gaze settled on Alexis, a question in his eyes. He had no rights where this child was concerned, and that fact had begun to gall him like the taste of bile. Loving the little girl as he did meant that he was vulnerable and susceptible to pain and disillusionment.

She must have discerned his feelings, for she said, "You don't have to ask me. Just let me know where you take her."

Her words should have given him relief, but he couldn't say that they did.

"Let's ride in the truck, Mr. Telford. I love to sit in the front seat."

He raised an eyebrow. "Really? When did you do that?"

She slapped her hands together, her face beaming. "With Mr. Russ."

"I see. Well, not today." She wasn't going to con him into doing that.

Allen met him at the gate. "Great, man. This comes right in time. One of the men just made coffee. I...uh...meant to tell you I went up to the university—hardest thing I ever did—but I didn't get one crumb of information about Melanie. Not a single soul could tell me anything." He blinked rapidly. "Telford, nobody was interested."

Telford hurt for his friend. "I'm hoping our investigator will be able to tell us something."

That night at dinner, he mentioned it to Russ and to Drake, who got back from his vacation precisely at dinnertime.

"That's the only way to go about it," Russ said, "and it's what we should have done when this first happened."

"What's the matter?" Drake—always sensitive to another's discomfort—asked Alexis. "You all right?"

She shook her head and got up. "No, sit," she said to Telford. "I'll be all right in a minute."

He had a hard time preventing himself from going after her, and he exhaled a sigh of relief when she came back to the table looking as if nothing had happened.

To his delight, Tara's normal ebullience resurfaced during dinner, though he didn't much care for the course of her mind when she asked, "Where did you have your vacation, Mr. Drake?"

"Mallorca, off the coast of Spain."

"Mr. Russ went to the Cod, and Mr. Telford and my mummy took me to Cape Cod. Did you see what I brought you?"

"You mean Cape May," Alexis said.

Telford looked around the table at the little boxes of peanut-filled saltwater taffy that Tara must have placed beside the plates belonging to Henry, Russ and Drake. "You hid it," Drake said.

Her smile reminded him of the wicked streak he'd discovered in Alexis. "I know. Mr. Telford gave me a 'lowance, and I spent it all on the presents," she explained to the surprised men. Then she dropped the bomb he'd dreaded.

"I want Mr. Telford to stay with me and my mummy all the time."

"I've told you that's not possible, sweetheart," Telford said.

"You said you and mummy had to…to…to what, Mummy? To…work it up."

"Did you swim in the ocean?" Russ asked, smothering a laugh and diverting Tara to a less sensitive subject.

"Yes." She giggled. "In the Lantic, and it was cold."

"*At*-lantic," Telford corrected and sent Russ a look of thanks.

Later, they gathered in the den, sipped coffee and cognac and related as much of their separate vacations as was appropriate to the circumstances. Henry gave Tara a box of multicolored seashells, Drake handed her a Spanish doll and Russ gave her a miniature Shaker rocking chair.

She ran around the room kissing each of them, her whole demeanor a vision of delight. When she stopped before Telford, put a hand on each of his knees and said, "Everybody loves me, Mr. Telford," he wanted to shield her from all the sadness she would ever face.

The next morning, he sat with his brothers and Henry on the dais in the new high school's auditorium, and it pained him that Alexis was not beside him to share his victory publicly.

The mayor's speech was longer than it had a right to be, but he didn't mind having the public blessings of the town's highest elected official.

"This school is the finest building ever to stand in Eagle

Park," the mayor said. "I'm proud of it. We owe the Harringtons a debt of gratitude for bringing it in at a price the people of this town could afford and in time for the beginning of this school year. I hereby proclaim today Harrington Day in this town." He walked over to Telford. "Telford, my boy, on behalf of yourself and your brothers, would you accept this key to our great town? For today, it unlocks everything but Bart's Bar, the YWCA and the jail." He laughed heartily in appreciation of his own cleverness.

Telford hadn't expected the mayor's accolades; neither had he anticipated the feeling of humility that pervaded him. "On behalf of my brothers, I thank you, sir," he said when accepting the key. "We all wish our father could have been here to witness this moment."

He sat down and looked in the face of Fentress Sparkman, who sat in the first row among the notables, but the sense of triumph, the feeling of victory, of having made the kill did not materialize. Instead, and in spite of the hatred he tried so hard to summon, he couldn't help admiring the weather-beaten old man who had the courage to face his mockers with head high and shoulders back.

That evening, he and Alexis sat beside the pool, holding hands, their first minutes alone since returning from Cape May. "I don't understand it," Telford said, "I didn't feel a thing. Nothing. All this time I worked my butt off for revenge." He turned to face her. "Fentress Sparkman might as well never have existed."

"You don't know how glad I am to hear you say that. You're not a vindictive man." She squeezed his fingers. "Admit it."

He watched her poke her tongue in her right cheek as that wicked light flashed in her eyes.

"A little bit set in your ways, a trifle conservative, maybe…" She spread her hands as if to suggest that his shortcomings could easily be remedied. "But…er…in the department that counts, there aren't any flies on you, love."

"In the department that…" He locked her in his arms and bent to her mouth.

"Mummy. Telephone. A man wants to talk to you," Tara called.

A man! He released her, took her hand and walked with her to her room door. "I'll wait out here. If he's an admirer, tell him you're taken." *Let her digest that.*

Chapter 10

Alexis rushed inside. A man. It couldn't be Jack; he would have identified himself to Tara. An eerie feeling slipped over her. Something could have happened to Velma, or maybe to her father in Alaska. She quickened her steps.

"Hello. This is Alexis Stevenson."

"Hi, babe. Thought I'd drop over there sometime tomorrow. I'm here in Frederick."

She nearly sat on the floor. "You mean you didn't tell your daughter who she was speaking with? How could you?"

"Easy there, babe. It's been a long time. Be there tomorrow around noon."

Not in this life! He'd bartered away his right to see his daughter at all, and she wasn't going to let him set the visiting hours. She sucked air between her front teeth. "I don't think so, Jack. Tara will be home around four. You may visit her from then until six. No longer."

"You mean I'm not invited to dinner?"

She battled her rising furor. After ignoring his child for years, he'd decided to be a nuisance. "I work here, Jack.

Invitations to dinner are issued by the Harrington men, not by their housekeeper. I assume that if you wanted to speak with your daughter, you'd have done so when she answered the phone. See you around four." She hung up.

Tara had resumed playing the piano, oblivious to the drama unfolding around her and in which she was about to become embroiled.

"That call didn't make you happy," Telford said when she rejoined him on the stone bench beside the pool.

He'd begun to read her moods and reactions. She kicked at a little mound of sod. "That was Jack. He'll be here tomorrow around four for a two-hour visit with Tara. I'm not looking forward to it."

His face wore an expression of incredulity. "Didn't she know it was he on the phone?"

"He didn't tell her, and she doesn't recognize his voice."

"Damn!"

The next afternoon, after sculpting for an hour, she changed from the smock she wore into a pair of white cotton pants and a pale green T-shirt. Jack hadn't wanted her to wear pants, claiming they weren't feminine, and had demanded that she wear dresses and skirts. He arrived minutes before Telford and Tara returned from their daily trip to the warehouse, and the three of them met at the front steps.

"I'm Jack Stevenson," her ex-husband said to Telford. "Which brother are you?"

From where she stood just inside the open door, she noticed that Telford's top lip curved in what could only be described as a snarl. "I'm Telford Harrington, and this is Tara, your daughter."

Ouch! Tara, who knew no qualms about presenting herself to strangers, gazed steadily at the man who had sired her and didn't say a word.

"Well?" Telford said to Jack.

Jack's eyebrow shot up. Accustomed to deference and stunned by Telford's put-down, Alexis wasn't surprised when

Jack narrowed his left eye and said, "Looks like you're full of attitude."

"Yeah. I won't say what you're full of."

Jack saw her then. "Well, hi, babe. You're like fine wine, more heady with age."

Before she could answer, Telford needled Jack again. "What's the matter, man? Don't you recognize your child's name?"

That comment might have humiliated a man of greater substance, but it didn't surprise her that Jack finessed the remark with the deftness of a self-satisfied person. He hunkered beside Tara and grinned his most charming grin.

"And you're a big girl, too. Want to give Daddy a hug?"

As if she didn't understand, Tara's face darkened in a frown, and she looked up at Telford. "You want to hear my music lesson now, Mr. Telford?"

Telford's face bore an expression similar to the pain in her heart. As a father, Jack had no meaning for Tara.

"We'll have to skip lessons today," he told her.

Tara's bottom lip trembled, and she rubbed her index finger beneath her nose fighting off tears. "But I practiced, and I know the whole thing."

She could almost feel his desperation when he gathered the child up, held her briefly and hugged her. "We'll do it tomorrow. Okay?" With that, he set Tara on her feet, brushed past Alexis without speaking and trudged up the stairs.

"Now, wasn't that a touching little scene? Playing house?"

She hadn't imagined that he'd be discourteous, because that had never been his style, but she no longer knew him. *I'm not going to entertain him,* she said to herself. "Jack, you may visit with Tara in the living room and in the garden."

"Not in your room?"

She imagined that the look she gave him would have curled a horse's mane. "You're two wives too late, buddy."

"Mummy, can I go play the piano?"

"Not now, dear. Your daddy wants to visit with you. You may tell him what you do every day, what you're learning in—"

She stared, wide-eyed, as Tara shot past her and raced to the kitchen.

"It will take time, Jack, so try to be patient."

"Yeah. Look, babe, why don't you and I go for a spin?"

If anyone had told her that her tolerance for Jack Stevenson had dropped to the point where it was practically nonexistent, she wouldn't have believed it. Fired up with more anger than her religious beliefs permitted, she put her hands on her hips and glared at him.

"I thought you came here to visit your daughter."

Alexis spun around at the sound of Telford's voice, harsh and wrathful. "Telford!" she exclaimed.

"May I speak with you, please?"

Now what? "Of course. Excuse me, Jack."

She walked with Telford into the dining room, which he began to pace from one end to the other. "He's got a right to see his child—more for her sake than his—but she's in the kitchen crying her eyes out, and he doesn't give a damn." He balled his right hand into a fist and shook it. Unapologetic about his blatant furor, he stopped in front of her. "If he has your permission, he can visit Tara as long as she lives in my home, but you tell me this minute whether you want to...to be with this fellow."

Stunned, she directed to Telford her annoyance at Jack. "What do you mean? He's the father of my child. What should I do, pretend I never saw him before? I did what I thought was right. If Jack Stevenson's a dunce, it's not my fault." She poked her right index finger against his chest. "Figure the rest of it out for yourself."

From the expression on his face, one would have thought he'd never seen anyone or anything like her. However, dealing with the vagaries of the male mind wasn't a priority right then. She charged into the kitchen, and it didn't surprise her to find

Henry with one arm around Tara's shoulder and his other hand holding a spoonful of black-cherry ice cream.

"If she won't eat this, somethin's wrong, and I bet it's male, walks on two feet and ain't got good sense."

She took Tara's hand. "Thanks, Henry, but she has to obey me. Come with me, Tara."

The child hung her head and refused to move. She'd never known Tara to display protracted recalcitrance. Her occasional stubbornness rarely lasted longer than a few minutes, for she had learned that good behavior brought rewards.

"I want you to go in there and talk with your daddy. Do you hear me?"

"I don't want to, Mummy."

To her amazement, Tara dashed out of the kitchen and up the stairs, where she wasn't allowed to go and never went.

"Mr. Telford," she called. "Mr. Telford."

Alexis reached the top of the stairs in time to see Telford open his door and step out of his room. She thought her heart would break when her daughter ran to Telford, locked her arms around his leg and sobbed. He gathered Tara into his arms and tried to soothe her. This man gave Tara the only fatherly love she knew.

Alexis whirled around and raced down the stairs to where Jack leaned against the mantelpiece in the living room.

"Quite a stunt this kid pulled off."

Anger would solve nothing, she told herself, took a deep breath and dropped her hands from her hips. "We'll have to do this gradually. I refuse to force her. You ignored her when we lived in the house with you, and she's seen you less than half a dozen times since you walked out nearly three years ago. What do you expect?"

His face broke into the boyish smile she had once believed to be a promise of the gentleness and sweetness she needed. "Listen, now, babe. You and I have to talk. How about we get out of this dinosaur and go someplace else?"

So he still thought he could charm her. Well, she'd show him. "I'm not going anyplace with you. Next time, plan on a half-hour visit, and we'll increase it as she feels more comfortable with you." She opened the front door and, as he sauntered out, it struck her that he hadn't objected to the shorter visiting time.

She trudged back to the stairs wondering how to handle Tara's disobedience. The child knew what daddies were, and she witnessed their relations with their children every day when they brought them to church school and picked them up when it closed. As Alexis started up the steps, she looked up and saw Telford coming down with Tara in his arms.

"Let's you and I sit down and talk with him while she gets to know him. If we're there with her, she'll be more comfortable."

"I sent him away. He'll visit another time."

"Then we'd better prepare her for it. All right? What happened today was a fiasco for both of them and doesn't portend well for their relationship."

Telford had served noticed that he wouldn't abandon Tara, that he was there for her, no matter what or who, and Tara had known that. Alexis nodded her agreement. Jack possessed a mean streak, and she knew he'd stoop low to get what he wanted, but Telford's presence lessened the likelihood that his tactics would succeed.

Still holding on to Telford's shoulders, Tara asked her, "Mummy, is the man gone?"

Exasperated and uncertain as to the right course of action, she said in as stern a voice as she could muster, "That man is your daddy and, yes, he left. I'm going to have a talk with you about your behavior."

"Can I go play the piano?" Already gifted in the art of deflecting the sword, Alexis thought.

She nodded. Tara kissed Telford's cheek and, when he set her on the floor, she blessed them with her smile, radiant and loving, and dashed toward her room.

"I don't know what to make of it," Telford said. "Drake swears she likes any man who wears pants, and usually she does."

"Not quite," Alexis said. "She walked up to Allen Krenner and talked with him as if she'd known him all her life, though she'd never seen him before. Less than five minutes later, she disliked Biff Jackson on sight."

"She has good instincts about people. But I can't understand this absolute antagonism toward her father."

She took a step backward. Even in her dilemma about Tara's behavior, Telford's nearness got to her.

She found a spot past his shoulder and focused on it. "When Tara was two and a half, he wanted an end to the marriage so that he could marry his boss's pregnant daughter, and I gave him a divorce. But for a full year prior to that, she and I rarely saw him. He claimed to be on business trips, building a future for his family, but as I discovered, he was busy impregnating Loren Ingles."

Telford shrugged both shoulders in a show of impatience. "The man's missing a lot." He looked away, draping his face in an unreadable expression. "A rotten father and a philanderer to boot. Enough about him."

After supper that night, Telford sat with his brothers in the garden at the edge of the pool. "Pretty soon, it'll be too cool to swim at night," Drake said. "What's missing around here is a good party."

Russ stretched his legs out in front of him and locked his hands behind his head. "A party. Just what I need." His sarcasm wasn't lost on his brothers.

"Don't knock it, man," Telford said. "It's not a bad idea. We've finished the school, and in a couple of weeks, the warehouse will be behind us, too. I'd say that calls for a celebration."

"Works for me," Drake said. "Life's too somber around here. I'll bet Alexis can plan a great party, and if she can't she'll know someone who can. That dame's first class."

Russ got up, dusted off the back of his swimming shorts and stretched his long frame expansively. "Yeah. Which makes me wonder how she got tied up with a man who'd give up custody and all rights to his daughter as a condition for keeping all of his wealth and property."

Telford waved his right hand in dismissal. "The man's a jerk." Saying it gave him a better feeling than he'd had all day.

Russ's head snapped around. "You've met him?"

"Yeah. Biggest bag of wind that ever blew into Eagle Park." He looked at Russ. "Are we celebrating or not?"

"Sure," Russ said, in an offhand manner. "Drake will be able to show off, and you need to take Alexis someplace special. Fine with me, so long as it's top flight. If we're going to do it, let's go all out."

"You're asking me to plan a gala?" Alexis leaned against the blue refrigerator and gaped at Telford, a white-shirted silhouette against the monotonous blue of the walls around them. "For a group of more than fifty people, I'm out of my element. My sister's a professional party and banquet planner. She can handle as many as two or three thousand."

"I'm considering three or four hundred. Would you see if she's available?" He gave her several acceptable dates. "And pick one on which you'll be free to go as my date."

She let that pass. "I'll let you know what she says."

"If she can't do it, please find someone who can."

After finishing her morning chores, she went to her room, started to work on the bust she was sculpting and remembered she had to call Velma. She wrapped the piece in a beach towel, put it in the box she kept for that purpose and covered it. She didn't want anyone, including Tara, to see it till she'd finished it.

Velma answered the call immediately. "You bet I'll do it. What kind of money are we speaking here?"

"Just make it first-class."

"Standing up or sitting down?"

"Standing, but there should be small tables around for those who need to take the weight off their feet."

"Better to make it all a seated affair. Waiters can pass the drinks and hors d'oeuvres. Classier that way."

"You're the boss."

"Let's see. Since the hosts are men, I'll start with an old rose and dark tan color scheme. You're in Maryland, and it's crab season. So it's little Maryland crab cakes, broiled bacon-wrapped chicken livers, tiny buttermilk biscuits, broiled scallop kebabs, barbecued buffalo wings—"

"Right on, girl," Alexis interrupted. "I'm impressed. If you need any contacts here, let me know."

"Nothing. Just the phone number of someone at the chamber of commerce who's got good sense. I'll take it from there."

She hadn't brought an evening gown to Harrington House, and she didn't plan to waste on a ball gown the money she'd saved since coming there. The next Thursday, her day off, she drove to her house in Philadelphia and after a brief visit with her tenants, collected from a storage closet in the basement two evening gowns, accessories and several elegant street-length dresses, lingerie and a nightgown set. It amazed her that she had no emotional attachment to her home, no sense of belonging in that place.

Late in the afternoon, she parked in front of Harrington House and lingered in the car as the uncertainty of her life pressed heavily on her. She hadn't lied when she told Telford she'd burned her bridges. She looked up at the Harrington brothers' imposing colonial house, closed her eyes and leaned against the steering wheel. She was home, the place where she knew she belonged. Home, where she loved a man who loved her. Home, where she worked as a housekeeper. She dried her tears and drove into the big four-car garage.

Velma arrived a week before the reception, though she had already organized the affair. "Girl, you trust me up here with those three hunks?" she asked her sister when Alexis settled her in the upstairs guest room. "Sleepwalking is something a person can't control."

Velma had always enjoyed making practical jokes, and

Alexis tolerated her sister's off-the-wall sense of humor, but she meant to make it clear that pranks involving Telford were out of bounds.

"Just be sure you don't wake up in a mahogany-colored sleigh bed. Fratricide has been around ever since Cain knocked off Abel."

Velma stroked her hips and allowed herself a hearty laugh. "You used to cover your corners better than that, honey. You just told me where Telford sleeps. He *is* the one, right?"

Alexis nodded. "Looks like it, but nothing's definite."

Velma leaned her head to one side and contemplated her sister. "No? Well, if he's an upstanding citizen, looks and acts sweet, got a nice slow hand and it swings right in the sack, put a lock on it. If you don't, a smarter sister definitely will." She rubbed her hands together, and an expression of pure glee seemed to change her face into a charismatic neon sign. "Which one's the tallest?"

"Telford's the tallest, but not by much, and they'll be here by seven, because that's when we eat."

"Hmmm. Wonder whose rule *that* is," she said dryly, as if to herself. "What time does Tara get home from school?"

"Around four if she comes on the bus; a bit earlier when Telford brings her."

Velma stopped hanging up her clothes, walked over to her sister, who was taller by two inches, and looked up at her. "You love this man. It's on your face, in your voice when you say his name, in your whole demeanor. I can't wait to see him."

Alexis set the dining room table for seven people that evening and added a centerpiece of yellow and orange chrysanthemums, autumn-colored oak leaves, evergreen branches and candles. "Why do I enjoy doing this so much, when I hated entertaining during my marriage to Jack?" she asked herself aloud. She knew the answer. Jack used her, but although they paid her, Telford and his brothers treated her as if this were her own home.

Velma looked at the table with an expression of approval. "Mama flunked out when it came to human relations, but she definitely knew the requisites of an elegant home. I've often wished she'd been as meticulous about giving me a hug once in a while as she was about the shine on the damned silver."

"I know. Me, too, but she's gone now, and I forgive her."

Velma walked around the table as if she were inspecting it, but Alexis knew her sister's mind was in the past. "Good for you. I wish I could embrace the Quaker teachings, because I think it has something to do with this peacefulness in you. Not me though. My mouth is never going to be still, and I can't imagine forgoing a chance to tell it like it is. I'll die a Presbyterian."

Alexis hugged her sister, reveling in the joy of having her near. "You're something of a nut, but I love you just like you are. Don't overdress for dinner. I'm wearing an ankle-length rust-colored T-shirt."

Velma raised an eyebrow. "Yeah. And you'll look like a fashion model. If I put that on, somebody would mistake me for a butterball. I'm going with my green caftan."

"At least we won't clash. I've got a few things to do in my room. See you a little later."

When Telford brought Tara home that afternoon, the child's squeals filled the house. "Aunt Velma. My mummy told me you were coming."

Alexis introduced Telford and her sister. When he grinned, Alexis knew he understood the blatant once-over Velma gave him.

"Hi," he said, his facial expression reminding her more of Drake than of himself. "Do I pass muster?"

She could have told him that, when it came to freshness, he'd met his equal. "And with plenty to spare," Velma said. "A regular number ten. Any more where you came from?"

He laughed aloud. "I have a feeling I'm out of my league here. There're two more, but they don't think I'm like them. Thanks for helping me out." He looked at Tara. "We'll get to your lessons as soon as you drink some milk and eat whatever Henry's got for you."

"Okay," she said, blew him a kiss and ran off toward the kitchen.

Drake greeted Velma with the warmth and charm he reserved for females, and Velma responded in kind. One ladies' man and one coquettish woman, Alexis decided. Nothing there. At dinner, she waited for Russ to show annoyance at Velma's presence. He hated inconveniences, and with Velma occupying the guest room across the hall from his bedroom for the next eight days, he'd have to clean up his act.

"So you're an entertainment manager," he said to Velma.

Velma focused her attention on the rack of lamb, fluted mushrooms, spinach and potato croquettes in her plate. "That's what I do."

"Any good at it?" he asked her.

"Uh-huh, and I'm well paid for it."

"Say, don't get your back up. I'm just making conversation. Where do you live?"

"I pay rent in Wilmington, Delaware, but I work all over the country, so I'm not there much."

"Who's older? You or Alexis?"

"Me, by a year and eight months."

Alexis listened to them talk, suddenly aware that no one at the table joined in. *He's not hostile toward her.*

Her gaze swept around the table. Henry, Telford and Drake ate as if dining alone. For Russ, laconic by nature and never one to lead a conversation, this amounted to a barrage of words and, what was more, it was he who propelled it.

"Hope you enjoy your stay here," he said.

Velma finally looked at him, though with little more than a quick appraisal and none of the impudence she displayed when jostling with Drake. "I'll take any help I can get. And thanks."

Alexis managed to catch her fork before it clattered on her plate. *That wasn't flirtation; it was a come-on.*

"Don't expect no help from him," Henry put in. "He thinks house guests is some kind of virus."

"Knock it off, Henry," Russ said, but without his usual bite.

"Don't pay any attention to him, Velma. *He* thinks that if he keeps his mouth shut for a few minutes, he'll get lockjaw."

"Oh, Mr. Russ." The adults stared at Tara as if they'd forgotten she was there. "Mr. Russ, please. Please don't say that. Mr. Henry will cook cabbage stew, and I don't like cabbage stew."

Telford explained the comment to Velma, and a chorus of laughter ended the meal.

Telford leaned against the marble fireplace in the den, sipping espresso and watching Alexis. Who would guess that she wasn't mistress of Harrington House, but a paid homemaker? He no longer signed her checks; in his eyes, that demeaned her. He left that job to their business accountant. *We can't continue this way. She avoids being alone with me, especially after dinner, and I know it's because she fears having an affair. She's erected a barrier between us, subtle and troublesome.*

He glanced around the den. In one corner, Drake accused Tara of cheating in their game of checkers. In another, Velma was apparently charming Russ, who laughed more than he'd known his brother to laugh. Alexis sat alone in a tan-colored wing chair, her legs crossed at the knee while she swung her left foot, the essence of self-possession and tranquillity.

He ambled over to where she sat. "You're a soft rain after a long summer's draught. You light up my world."

She looked up at him, and he knew the second he got to her. Eyes that had been clear pools of serenity flashed with the heat of desire, the fire of a woman who knows what's there for her.

"Get your coat, and let's go for a walk. Want to?"

She made an effort to hide her eagerness to join him, shrugging her shoulder and swinging her foot, but her eyes and the way she shifted in her seat betrayed her desire to be with him. He leaned over and brushed her forehead with his lips.

"Come with me. I'll wait for you in the foyer."

Without a word, she stood and walked over to Tara. "I'm going for a walk. Be back in a few minutes."

Tara looked up at Alexis. "Mummy, Mr. Drake's supposed to be teaching me checkers, but he's cheating."

"That's a strong word, honey, and I'm sure you're wrong."

Tara looked at Drake. "Are you cheating?"

Drake pulled one of Tara's braids. "No, and you stop accusing me of it. Friends don't cheat each other."

Her bottom lip protruded. "Then how come I don't win?"

"You will when you learn the game," Drake said.

Love, warmth and camaraderie shouted at him from every corner of Telford's home, and he had no trouble tracing it to Alexis.

She didn't make him wait long for her. She never did, and it was one of the habits that drew him to her—her respect for others. Wrapped in a red woolen shawl, she smiled when she stepped into the foyer and saw him, spontaneously, as if she hadn't expected to find him there.

He reached for her hand. "Would you rather walk or go for a ride?"

They stepped out into the brisk late-September evening, made bright by the glow of the full moon.

"It's such a beautiful night. Let's walk."

He wanted to stop right there, take her into his arms and love her, but he knew that, with the uncertainties dominating their relationship, he'd better leash his feelings lest they get the better of him. As they strolled arm in arm along Old Liberty Road toward the warehouse, their shadows stretched far ahead of them, elongated and thin, he thought, like figures in an El Greco painting. A breeze stirred the red, yellow and golden leaves that swirled around their feet, dancing like magic creatures of the nearby woods. He stopped suddenly when a doe and her fawn crossed the road half a block in front of them.

"I never knew this until I came here," she said, almost as if speaking to herself. "This quiet. The stillness. The beauty. It's almost unbearable."

When she would have walked on, he restrained her. "I've lived here all my life, but I didn't see this." He waved his left hand around to indicate what his eyes beheld. "None of it, until I looked at it through your eyes."

She looked up at him with a question in her gaze. "How could you not see it?"

"Easily. As a child, I wasn't often happy, so I guess I didn't know beauty when I saw it. Besides, I've done the work of a man ever since I was seventeen. I didn't have time to appreciate nature."

She squeezed his fingers. "But it's everywhere." She tugged at her shawl, wrapping it more tightly over her shoulders.

Tugging that shawl close, she was like a little bird bracing itself in a blustery wind, and the need to hold and protect her slammed into him. "Are you cold? Let me warm you."

When he gathered her to him, he intended to hold her close, nothing more. But she gazed up at him, her eyes brimming with fire-hot want. Lustful and yielding. Unmistakable desire.

"Alexis!"

Her hand, soft and delicate, stroked his face, and heat sprinted from its touch, boiling the blood that shot through him, blistering his veins and stoking the furnace in his groin. Her lips parted, and he plunged into her, ready to drain her of that sweet potion that fired his manhood.

In a second, she called his number. Always the giver, but not this time. She pulled him into her, demanding that he give, pressing the tips of her fingers into his body, straining him to her. *Give yourself to me,* she seemed to say. And forgetting his own needs, he gave, glorying in the loss of himself to her. She pulled his tongue deeper into her mouth, and with one hand on his buttocks and the other on his upper back, she locked him to her and demanded surrender.

If he didn't set her away from him, his passion would roar out of control, yet he knew it was no use. She tried to climb his body, to get closer to the source of sweet satisfaction, and he lifted her and let her have her way. Her long legs straddled him, and when she brought his hand to her breast, her breathing changed to a pant and she moaned her frustration.

With the little energy she hadn't sapped out of him, he loosened her hold and set her on her feet. He had never made love standing on an open road or even contemplated it and, if he did it then—as badly as she wanted him—she'd be gone when he got up the next morning. And worse, she would dislike him.

"Alexis, sweetheart. We need to get a few things straight. Your head doesn't want an affair, but your heart and the rest of your body are all for it. Furthermore, you aren't even sure you want *more* than an affair with me. I don't want to go on like this."

She passed her hand over her eyes, as if to clear away a haze and improve her vision. "You haven't offered me anything more permanent than an affair."

"You haven't encouraged me to do that, either. In fact, honey, you've discouraged me in subtle ways." He took her hand and started back to the house, their passions cooled by the somber business of looking at their lives. "I'm thirty-seven, and it's time I put my house in order. You have this wonderful little girl. I can't even lay claim to that happiness."

She didn't answer, but her silence didn't perturb him. Not yet. She loved him, and she wanted him. A man hardly needed more powerful weapons.

And I'd better get my house in order, too, Alexis admitted to herself that night as she helped Tara get ready for bed. And she would start by doing what she'd procrastinated about for the past four months. The next morning, she telephoned Dr. Eleanor Shaw, her former colleague at State University.

After they greeted each other as old friends who had long been out of touch, Alexis cut to the chase. "Eleanor, do you remember the case of Melanie Krenner? I know it's been a long time."

"Remember? Who'd forget it?"

Alexis explained that she'd met the girl's father and that

her whereabouts remained a mystery. "Allen Krenner is still distraught after all this time."

"Hmmm. Is he special to you?"

"Only in that he's very close to someone I…uh…dear to me."

"I see. I think he recently inquired about her. My daughter knew Melanie's roommate, but it's possible they've lost touch. I'll see what I can find out. How may I reach you?"

Alexis told her. "This means a lot to me, Eleanor. More than you can imagine."

"Don't mention it, friend, I'll be in touch soon as I have something to tell you."

The following Saturday evening as she dressed for the Harrington reception, the phone rang. "Mummy, it's a lady." Tara loved answering the phone and considered it both her right and her duty.

"Hello. Alexis Stevenson speaking."

"Hi. This is Eleanor. I may have something for you, if you've got a minute."

Alexis took the portable phone from its cradle and sat on the bed. "What's the story?"

After listening to the incredible tale, she asked the doctor's name.

"Lawrence Duckwilder. Can't be too many of those around."

"Right. I'll follow this up. I know it's going to take a while, but I'm going all the way with it. It might be best if word of this doesn't get back to your daughter's friend. Thanks is a poor expression of what I feel."

"I know. Let's try to meet somewhere for old times' sake."

"I'd like that, and I'll stay in touch."

She sat there for some minutes after Eleanor hung up. She'd always been honest in her dealing with others. Knowing what she knew, she shouldn't let Telford touch her again. If he never knew, she could go on, letting him love her and reaching out for the true happiness she craved. She exhaled a long breath. *I can't worry about Telford's reaction to my role in that fiasco. I have to do what I know is right.* And that meant taking whatever steps she could to ease Allen Krenner's awful load. It might take months, but until she could face Telford, she would try to keep a distance between them.

She finished dressing, inspected the long, strapless red silk sheath and checked her makeup and perfume. In view of the revelation of the past half hour and what she'd decided to do about it, it might have been better if she'd worn something more subtle, but she didn't have that option.

Taking Tara's hand, she headed for the living room, where she expected to find Velma, Henry and the Harringtons. "Miss Bennie's staying with you until we get back. I want you to obey her."

"Okay, Mummy. Can Biscuit sleep with me tonight?"

What a con artist! "Biscuit cannot sleep with you tonight or *any* night."

"Oh." She smiled as if she'd just been given a priceless gift. "Can I have some black-cherry... Uh...no, thanks. I'll ask Mr. Henry."

She stopped and looked at her daughter. Five years old and able consistently to wind every man in the house around her finger.

They reached the living room where Telford relaxed against the door, resplendent in a black tuxedo with a red-and-gray paisley cummerbund and matching accessories. He walked to meet them.

"Oh, Mr. Telford, you look so nice." Tara gazed up at him as if he were her beloved black-cherry ice cream. "My mummy's pretty, too."

Telford gazed at Alexis. "She's...beautiful. Woman...what have... Oh, you're wearing makeup." He let go a soft whistle. "I've got a siren on my hands."

"Where's Velma?" she asked him, trying not to react to his words and the praise that he heaped upon her with his eyes.

"Velma left about an hour ago. Russ took her."

She hadn't considered that possibility. "I'm getting suspicious of those two."

Telford poked his tongue in his left cheek. "Don't. With this kind of business, you can't second-guess Russ. He treads so softly he wouldn't make a footstep in a pile of sand." He rubbed his chin as though in thought. "Can't tell, though; every Samson meets his Delilah. Sooner or later."

He looked down at his watch. "Let's go, Henry."

The old man ambled into the living room wearing an oxford gray suit, white shirt and red tie and looking as if years had fallen away from him.

"Close your mouth, Alexis," he said. "I know how to dress, but trussing m' self up so folks'll stare at me ain't in my racial DNA. I leave them monkey suits to the younger ones, but there ain't no poop on me."

Alexis smothered a laugh. Henry had a habit of caressing her funny bone without even trying.

Tara clapped her hands. "Mr. Henry, you look…oh!"

Tara's remark brought a big laugh from Telford. "You're right, sweetheart. He looks great. Yeah. Henry cleans up real good." He looked at Bennie. "We should be back by midnight."

Alexis threw a black, cut-velvet shawl around her shoulders and took Telford's arm.

"You're so somber," he said. "I shaved, got a manicure and put on my best tux. Don't I rate a smile?"

"You shave every day," she said.

"Didn't used to," Henry said. "Don't seem like too long ago when his hair hung down to his collar, and them scrawny strands on his face looked like the whiskers on a wet rat."

Telford laughed aloud. "Are you trying to ruin my image? I'm trying to impress this woman, and you're talking about my adolescence."

"You ain't going about it the right way. If it was me, she'd a changed rooms long ago."

Telford seated Alexis and Henry, got in and pulled away

from the curb. "Henry, a wise man doesn't say everything he thinks."

"Yeah? Then how does anybody know he's wise if he don't say what he thinks?"

Alexis laughed, enjoying the easy camaraderie between Henry and Telford. *No wonder I love him. It would be strange if I didn't.*

A twinge of guilt pricked her conscience when Telford took her hand and entered the reception with such obvious pride, but she'd deal with that later. The people stood back as they passed on the way to the head table and, for the first time, she understood that Telford Harrington was head of Eagle Park's leading family, what that status meant to him, his brothers and the community. She banished the feeling of guilt and reveled in the pride he took in being with her.

"You two took your time getting here," Russ said, though his broad grin took away the bite of his mild reprimand. He stood, as did Drake and Adam Roundtree.

"Thanks for coming, Adam," Telford said. "Where's Wayne?"

"Hadn't you heard? Banks is expecting, and Wayne's treating her as if she's breakable. He hardly goes to work for fear she'll drop a piece of paper and he won't be there to pick it up. He's driving Banks crazy."

"I can imagine. Give them my best." He reached for Alexis to introduce her, but Drake was trying to get her attention.

"Alexis Stevenson, this is Marla Sinclair," Drake said of the woman beside him, and she judged at once that, though Drake liked the woman, she wasn't special to him.

Telford introduced Alexis to Melissa and Adam Roundtree, explaining that he and Melissa were college classmates, and that the Roundtrees lived in Beaver Ridge, a tiny hamlet about twelve miles from Eagle Park.

"I'm delighted to meet you, Alexis," Melissa said. "Something tells me Big Tip is finally going to take the plunge, and believe me, a lot of…"

Alexis didn't hear the remainder of Melissa's words. Big

Tip, Melissa Roundtree's college classmate. She put on her best smile and the best acting performance of her life. Big Tip. She had to be sure.

"Where'd you go to college?" she asked Melissa as soon as the others at the table became absorbed in their own conversations.

"Howard University."

The muscles of her belly contracted violently, but she wouldn't let herself clutch her middle. "We have something in common," she said and immediately switched the conversation to include her sister, complimenting her on the decor, the band and the table settings. Having successfully deflected Melissa's thoughts from Big Tip and Howard University, she plastered a smile on her face, laid back her shoulders and prayed that she could get through the evening with her pride and composure intact.

Big Tip. The boy she'd craved from a distance while a college freshman, the boy she'd made a fool of herself over. Without the long wavy hair, mustache, beard and horn-rimmed glasses, and with the added height, weight and physical maturity that came with age, she would never have recognized him. She'd poured out her soul to him in a note, telling him of her longing for companionship with him, the boy who haunted her thoughts day and night. The boy who was so kind to her, the one time she was near him.

In those days, she hadn't had any self-confidence, and when he came to her with the note she'd written him, embarrassed, she swore she hadn't written it. Obviously crestfallen, he never spoke to her again. One more reason why only pain could come out of their relationship. God forbid he should ever discover that she was Alexis Brighton, the skinny girl who wore contact lenses to change her eye color from light brown to gray, who didn't have a date during four years of college and who was so foolish as to fall for Howard's Big Man on Campus. *Lord, please let this evening end.*

Chapter 11

Telford tried to decide whether Velma's seemingly natural ebullience accounted for Alexis's subdued behavior. Somehow, he doubted that she would pay such deference to her older sister in that gathering. And surely she didn't think she took a backseat to Melissa Roundtree or any other woman. Still, her unnatural quiet disturbed him, and he studied her with slightly hooded eyes. One who didn't know her would see a regal, self-possessed woman who listened and didn't talk, but the Alexis he knew held her own in any company. When he glanced around, he noticed that Henry, too, studied Alexis. He tried to shrug it off. Maybe he imagined it.

"Time for you to say something, isn't it?" Drake asked him.

"What's your hurry?" he asked under his breath. "You're not spending the night in Frederick," a reference to the fact that Marla lived in Frederick.

"If somebody drugs me, I might," Drake said, standing to greet a passerby. "Good of you to come, buddy."

Telford went to the microphone, got the guests' attention and cleared his throat. He hadn't planned a speech. "My brothers and I completed the school, finished our new warehouse and got plans approved for a complex in Barbados. With all that under our belt, what was there to do but give a party? Thank all of you for coming. As I said at the school's inaugural ceremonies, we'd give anything if our dad could be here. Everybody, have a good time."

Telford couldn't decide how to respond when Adam Roundtree winked at him and said, "When you walked in here with Alexis, I thought you'd planned the party to announce your engagement to her. What's holding you, man?"

He didn't want to give his friend a flip answer, and he wouldn't say anything that suggested Alexis wasn't important to him. He decided to treat it lightly. "Man, you need a woman's permission when you broadcast to the world that she's agreed to marry you, and I don't have her consent."

"Think you'll get it?"

"It hasn't gotten quite that far."

"She's the kind of woman a man wants to be seen with, and face it, buddy. You're bored with bachelorhood. Grant's five years old. Who's he going to marry, if you don't get busy?"

He sat forward. "Did you say he's five? Alexis's daughter is five, and she needs a playmate. Mind you, if Grant roughs up Tara, I'll whack his behind. That little girl wound me around her finger the minute I saw her."

"Whoa, buddy. You may be telling me more than you'd like me to hear."

Telford raised an eyebrow. "You didn't mean that. No word ever comes out of my mouth that I don't plan to release. Bring Grant over one Saturday morning, and we'll take the kids fishing."

"Great idea. Good as done."

Tara would have a playmate, but what about him? Alexis had barely looked at him all evening, and when he did catch her gaze, she quickly looked away. Something had happened since they entered the reception hall, and she had some explaining to do.

* * *

Telford didn't hold her hand or put an arm around her as they left the reception, and she understood why. She hadn't been able to hide her despondency, and he'd interpreted what he saw as the deliberate erection of a barrier between them. She didn't blame him, but the awful ache inside her choking her breath and tearing at her insides was real and painful. He would understand that she didn't remember him from their school days, because he didn't remember her. But straitlaced as he was, he'd damn her for lying to him.

She could still see in her mind's eye the disappointment mirrored in his eyes years earlier when she rejected him. Several days prior to that, he had befriended her quite by chance, though he had no idea who she was. But she knew him, for she had cherished him from afar throughout her freshman year. Newspaper reports of Big Tip, Howard's great star quarterback, hung on the walls of her dormitory room. He was her secret love, and she daydreamed endlessly about him.

One day, she poured out her affection in a letter to him that she signed *A. Brighton* and addressed it to him as *Big Tip* since, like most other Howard University students, she didn't know his real name. But she lost the sealed letter, and someone found it and delivered it to Big Tip. He sought her out, but in her embarrassment, she claimed that she didn't know anything about the letter. He'd been unable to hide his hurt and humiliation.

"Sorry. My mistake" was all he said. He never went near her again.

And how she regretted that lie! All during her disastrous marriage, when she longed for love and genuine affection, her thoughts went back to Big Tip and what she might have had with him.

"Feel up to letting me in on the reason for this…this mood, Alexis?" Telford asked, bringing her back to the present as he began to drive home.

Surely he didn't plan to discuss their differences in

Henry's presence. "You seem to have forgotten that I'm your housekeeper. Well, I remembered, and I expect your guests couldn't figure out why I was with you," she said, the only answer she could give.

He slowed down, and a glance at the speedometer confirmed that he'd been speeding. "I'll think about that, and you can bet believing it will take some doing. You're a housekeeper in name only. Besides, I didn't introduce you as our housekeeper. Think again."

The trajectory of his voice served as notice that he was in an aggressive mood and didn't plan to let her off easily. If they were to preserve the element of their relationship that was so important to her—the love and trust—they had to talk in private.

"Do you mind if we postpone this discussion at least until we get ho…uh—"

"What's the matter?" His voice carried an icy challenge. "You can't make yourself refer to my home as your home?"

Four months of heaven, and it had all slipped through her fingers. From the euphoria that only a woman in love can know down to the valley of despondency, and in no more time than it took Melissa Grant Roundtree to say "Big Tip."

She thought her head would explode, alarming her, because she couldn't remember the last time she'd had a headache. "Please, Telford, don't say hurtful things. I don't think I can stand it."

He spared her a quick glance. "What you're hearing is how *I* hurt. Nothing could provoke me deliberately to hurt you."

"Fine, when that's mutual," Henry said, reminding them of his presence. "But according to what my eyes seen tonight, your intentions needs some fixin' up, Alexis, and you'd better get to work on it."

"Henry, will you please butt out of this and stay out?" Telford said.

"Like I said, Alexis, make up your mind. Won't do for Tel to harden his position, 'cause he ain't never learned how to… to…reverse himself."

She knew Henry cared about her and that he loved Telford, so she didn't complain about his interfering. "Thanks, Henry. I'm trying."

"You ain't trying hard enough."

She dreaded the way the evening would end and, as things transpired, her intuition proved right.

"Thanks for your company," Telford said as they walked into the foyer. "I'll drive Bennie home. Good night."

"Wait," she said, head high and shoulders back, "I have to pay her."

His smile amounted to a benevolent exercise of authority. "Of course I'll take care of that. Good night."

She slept fitfully, reliving missed opportunities. He didn't give her a chance to tell him that they'd known each other briefly in their college days. No, that wasn't true. If she were honest, she'd admit he created an opening but, scared of the consequences when he discovered she'd lied to him, she didn't take advantage of that opportunity. Yes, she'd had the chance and she'd blown it. She wasn't used to fear, and she didn't know how to handle it. *If only she had leveled with him.*

The brothers usually slept late on Sundays, and so did Velma. Alexis had breakfast with Tara, left her daughter with Henry and drove to Frederick to look for a stand and glass case for the bust she'd almost finished. With luck, she'd have it ready by Christmas. She bought a gray, antique marble pedestal and had it stored in the trunk of her car, where it would stay till she needed it.

"You don't seem to be up to snuff," she said to Henry when she went to get Tara from his bungalow.

"Little tired. Old men ain't got no business gallivanting around with these here young turks. Feels a little like a cold's coming on."

"I'll cook dinner, then."

He threw up his hands. "For goodness' sake, ain't you never gonna learn? Down here, we eats supper at night."

She hugged Henry, startling herself and probably embarrassing him, but it was too late; a person couldn't retract a hug.

"Were you mad at Tel last night?"

She shook her head. "Nothing like that, I gave him my reasons."

"I heard you, and I didn't believe you no mor'n he did. If Telford ever loved any other woman, he didn't bring her here and I ain't seen her. You 'bout to send him right back into that shell he lived in 'fore you come here."

"Don't look for anything to materialize between us, Henry. It wasn't meant to be."

"Rot. You knocked the wind out of each other. Still…" He scratched his head. "If you want to be stupid, I can't stop you."

She ignored that. "I'll fry some chicken, make some potato croquettes and cook some asparagus. Do you have anything for dessert?"

"I made a couple of apple pies, and Tara can have her ice cream. Thanks. I'll spell you sometimes. Tara can stay over here and play with the puppies."

Alexis set the table for supper, went to her room and worked on the bust, molding and chiseling the clay. She couldn't wait to see the final figure, cast in bronze.

"Where you hiding out down here?" Velma asked, knocking and entering simultaneously.

"Suppose I had company," she countered in a mild reprimand.

Velma allowed herself a deep yawn. "Oh, I knew you didn't. He just now got into that Buick and drove off."

Blood squirted from the middle finger of Alexis's right hand. "Ow."

After cleaning and bandaging the cut, she returned to her work. "You can stay, but ignore this piece I'm working on. It's a surprise, and you can't see it."

Velma buffed the nails of her right hand on her slacks. "He spent a lot of time gazing at you last night, puzzledlike. The rest of us watched first one of you and then the other. What are you going to do about him?"

"I don't know. I'm not going to chase him. If we work it out, I'll be happy; if we don't, I won't lie down and die." Brave words, but after the trials of her marriage, she figured she could weather an earthquake.

"What's going on with you and Russ?" Alexis asked.

"I like him. He's a nice guy—like Drake and Telford."

In other words, nothing yet.

For dinner, she dressed in the red silk, floor-length T-shirt that Telford liked, caught her hair up with a white-ivory comb and dressed her daughter in a red pantsuit.

"Where's Mr. Telford?" Tara asked, as they sat at the table waiting for him. "Is it seven o'clock?"

"He's fifteen minutes late," Drake said. "I say we eat."

The phone rang in the dining room, and Tara raced to answer it. "Hello. Mr. Telford, dinner's ready. Oh. Oh. Okay. See you at breakfast. Bye. Kisses." She ran back to the table and sat down. "Mummy, Mr. Telford called to tell me he wasn't coming home for supper."

That took care of her appetite. Not only was Telford not eating at home, but he'd phoned late in a deliberate act of defiance.

After supper, Russ asked, "Anybody want to go to the movies? How about you, Velma?" *Come along, but it's nothing special* was his message. Velma went, but Alexis declined.

The next morning, Alexis skipped breakfast. She knew Telford would either put Tara on the school bus or take her to school.

However, Tara raced back to their rooms crying, "Mummy, Mummy. Mr. Telford didn't come home last night. Mr. Henry told Mr. Russ his bed's still made up."

When her shock subsided, she hugged Tara. "Don't worry, he's got business to look after." If only she could assuage her own fears with that explanation. "I'll put you on the bus."

She got Tara off to school and went into the kitchen for a fortifying cup of coffee. All she could think of was that sometimes nothing went right. Just when she needed her sister's company, Velma was headed to Detroit and another job.

"It's been great, sis," Velma said. "I'll stay in touch. Drake's working in Baltimore today, so he's driving me to the airport."

"What about Russ? Think anything will happen between you two?"

"Doesn't seem likely, though we might have clicked if I'd stayed around longer."

"Don't cross it off. I've developed an enormous respect for Russ. Did he kiss you last night?"

Velma licked her lips and rolled her eyes. "Yeaaaah. And, honey, that man knows what he's doing."

"Then, what—"

"A slow man with a slow hand. I could get used to him, but the minute you sat down at the table and began talking with Melissa Roundtree, something went out of the party. Russ was so distracted by what was, or wasn't, going on between you and Telford that he couldn't pay attention to me. All of us at the table knew something had gone wrong. Knowing how tight-lipped you are, I won't ask. But, girl, Telford Harrington's a forty-karat man, and he's besotted with you. Don't louse up."

"You've decided it was my doing, and the onus is on me?"

"You got it. Give me a hug. Drake's waiting, and Russ might be somewhere around the front door, too." She laughed aloud. "How's that for humor? You stay here. I might get a kiss with Drake there, but I can't imagine Russ kissing a woman in front of two witnesses. Bye, hon."

As the day wore on, she stopped pretending. Though Drake and Russ went to work as usual, she knew that they, too, were worried, because they phoned Henry several times to ask whether he'd heard from Telford.

She went to his room to look for clues as to where he might be and saw his cell phone on top of his chest of drawers. "That explains why he doesn't call," she told herself. At three-thirty, she asked Henry if he knew where Evangeline Moore lived.

"Why you want to know? Tel ain't there and he ain't been there. He might a been mad with you, but I didn't see no evidence that he'd lost his mind."

"Shouldn't we call the police?"

"That's somethin' we oughta let Russ do, and he ain't thinking 'long them lines."

"Then what? I can't just do nothing. I'm on my way out of my mind. If he could, he'd call. He wouldn't put us through this."

At four o'clock, Tara came home from school, took one look at her and said, "Mummy, where's Mr. Telford?"

She was about to say he'd be home soon and thought better of it. She never lied to her daughter. "I...I don't know, honey. I just don't know." It didn't surprise her that Tara ran to the kitchen to receive comfort and black-cherry ice cream from Henry.

She set the table for dinner as if Telford were expected home at his usual time, but she had no faith in what she did and could hardly move around with the weight pulling on her heart.

The banging on the front door sent her charging to it with a speed she hadn't exercised since she played high-school basketball. She flung the door open without checking the keyhole and stared at Russ. "Hold it open," he said, his tone breathless, and motioned to two men who carried a stretcher.

"What is it? Russ, oh, my Lord, what happened?"

"Easy now. He'll be all right."

"But—"

"Shhh. He'll tell you all about it."

She looked down in his face, as they brought him in, his eyes closed and his body still. Her heart raced wildly, and she grasped the doorjamb for support. "Russ—"

But Russ had gone inside, she discovered later, to insure

that Henry kept Tara in the kitchen where she couldn't see the men bring Telford into the house.

"Russ, please tell me something. I can't bear this suspense."

He draped an arm around her shoulder. "When three big guys hold you up, don't bother to fight. Remember that. He's going to be all right. Just get things straightened out between the two of you. If you don't, both of you will regret it for a long, long time. Been there."

Easier said than done. "Can I... Is it all right if I go up there and...and stay with him?"

Russ stared down at her, his face inscrutable. He was Telford's brother, and Telford came first. After a minute, his face softened. "I don't know what went wrong between the two of you, but something did, and it's not a simple problem. You know how you feel, so do what you think best, so long as you don't distress him. He should be in bed a couple of days. If I were you, I'd use this time to good advantage." About the longest statement she'd ever heard him make.

"Thanks. I love him, Russ."

"That's what I thought. I'd better go talk to Tara and Henry."

She headed to her room to freshen up and say a prayer of thanks and reached it as the phone rang. "Hello."

"Hi, babe. I thought I'd drop over tomorrow afternoon if you're not busy."

Keep your temper under wraps and control your tongue. "Well, let's see, it's been...hmmm, six weeks since we last heard from you. How do you expect Tara to get acquainted with her father if she never sees him?"

"I'm busy. You know that."

"Yes, I suspect you are. The question is, busy at what?"

"Now, babe, those days are behind me. I'm straightening out my life. I slipped up a time or two, babe, but you know I'd go to the end of the world for you."

"I'd appreciate that if I were confident you'd stay there."

"Now, come on. You've got a lot of mouth these days."

"You bet. And guts, too. You can't visit Tara this week or next." She didn't know how long Telford would be recuperating and until he was well, she couldn't risk a visit from Jack, temperamental and unpredictable as he was.

"If you waited six weeks," she told him, "two more won't hurt. Besides, I need time to prepare her for your visits. Send me a couple of your pictures."

"One of those brothers is giving you a lot of self-confidence. I'd like to—"

"You asked me for a divorce so you could marry your pregnant mistress, and I gave it to you. You're out of my life, Jack, and you're going to stay out. Call me next week, and we'll set up a day and time for you to visit with your daughter. Oh, by the way, would you like to speak with her?"

"Uh…re… Look, what's to say on the phone?"

"That's what I thought. Call me Saturday." She hung up.

Telford looked around and tried to focus on his surroundings. *Where the devil was his car?* He tried to sit up in bed and fell back. It hurt to breathe, and something tight around his chest constrained his movements and seemed to pin him down. In his mind, he fought the intruder with all his might until darkness closed in.

"How do you feel now?"

The words, soft and loving, so much like Alexis's sweet voice, pierced his consciousness. He wanted to smile, but wasn't she mad at him? Or something. He couldn't quite remember what.

"Telford, honey, talk to me, please. How do you feel?"

He opened his eyes, and her faced loomed above. Her lips grazed softly across his cheek, and he did his best to smile. If only he wasn't so hungry. He recognized his room and realized that he was in his own bed and that Alexis hovered above him, tears in her eyes and an anxious look on her face.

"Hi. What's all this about? I was… Oh, yes. Looks like they did a job on me."

"Let's not think about that right now," she said. "You're

safe, and you won't have any permanent damage. Do you want anything?"

"Thank God for that. Water. And something to eat, if you don't mind. I feel like I haven't eaten in years."

"A little more than thirty-six hours, I would guess. I'll fix something light."

"Don't make it too light. I'm starved."

He struggled to sit up and collapsed to the flat of his back. Though exhausted from the effort, he refused to give up and tried to roll to his side. That didn't work, either, and he had no choice but to lie there on his back. He relaxed when Russ entered the room.

"Alexis is cooking something for you, and you'll have to sit up," Russ said. "I brought some pillows." Telford tried again to raise himself up. "Look, Telford, if you try to sit up by yourself, you'll bust up something. I'll prop you up."

"Thanks, but this is a pain in the rear." He took a deep breath and winced at the stabbing hurt.

"Now maybe you'll do as I say. You might be older, but you're flat on you back, brother, and I am in charge."

Telford looked at the grin of satisfaction on Russ's face. "Well, hell. You don't have to act like you're enjoying this."

A grin took its time crawling over Russ's face. "I'm sorry you got messed up, but this is the first time I've been in a position to tell you what to do and make you do it. Feels good."

"Russ, would you put this little table beside Telford's bed, please?" Alexis said.

At the smell of food, his mouth watered.

"Sure. Soon as I have him sitting up." He eased Telford into a sitting position, looked at him and grinned. "Simple as rolling over a baby."

What would she do if he grabbed the plate from her while she took her time putting a cloth and place setting on the little table? Daintiness he didn't need, starved as he was. He managed to restrain himself. Grits perfectly cooked, toast and scrambled eggs. No sausage.

"You're an angel," he said. "I suppose it would take too long to cook some country sausage."

"That, too, but I thought sausage would be a little too heavy." She offered him a spoonful of grits.

"You're going to feed me? Now, look here. I can feed myself."

"Russ told me you shouldn't use your right arm. If you can eat with your left hand—"

"Sorry. I appreciate it, but I can't stand feeling helpless." He took the spoon from her and helped himself to the grits and eggs. "Sweetheart, this is good stuff. I was starving."

"Feel up to telling me what happened?"

"Well, as I remember it, I got a flat on Route 84 right about dusk, and was changing the tire when a car pulled up behind me. Three big guys got out, and I knew right away that they didn't plan to help me with the tire. When I wouldn't give them my money and credit cards, one of them socked me. I let him have it right back and gave him a few kicks for good measure."

He stopped talking long enough to savor his food. "I don't remember much after that, except that one of them was lying on the ground. From what Russ told me, they took my money, car, car keys and watch and left me to bleed to death. I remember propping myself up against a highway sign with my hand out, though I can't say how I got there. Next thing I knew, I was in a hospital, and Russ was sitting on the side of my bed."

He looked toward the door to see who had entered the room. "I don't want Tara to know about this, Russ."

"What'll we tell her? She senses something unusual, and she wants to come up here."

"Make up something. You're creative."

Russ spread his hands, palms out. "Sorry. When I realized I couldn't keep my lies straight, I quit telling them. I'll just say you're not feeling too hot. You handle the rest. Here, let me take that tray down, Alexis."

He wanted to lie down, but he didn't want to alarm Alexis, so he called after Russ. "Come back up before you go out.

"Alexis, I don't want Tara to see me bruised and bandaged. It will frighten her and undermine her sense of security. Russ is so smart; he ought to realize that."

"I'll talk to her, but I don't think anything I say will pacify her. Tell me how you got to the hospital."

"I'm told a lady and her two teenage sons came along, drove past me, backed up and stopped. The boys got out, saw that I was hurt, put me in the car and they took me to the hospital. Since I didn't have any ID, the authorities didn't know who to call, but Russ said he phoned every precinct within a fifty-mile radius and that's how he found me. I've got several broken ribs, a gunshot wound in my right shoulder and less blood than I'm supposed to have."

Why was she so subdued? He fished around in his mind for an explanation of her solemnity, and couldn't find one. "If the expression on your face is any gauge, I must look a mess."

She'd been perched on the side of his bed, leaning toward him with one hand beside his hip and the other across his body, but as if she suddenly realized the intimacy her posture created, she straightened up and braced her hands on her knees.

"You're not your normal pretty self," she said, "and I'm scared that if I touch you, you'll break, but that wasn't on my mind. I can't help thinking how I'd be feeling if you hadn't come back here. You know what I mean."

"Yeah, and something tells me it was a lot closer than either of us realizes." He had to lie down. "I…would you please call Russ?"

"Would you like to stretch out? Sitting up must be tiring." She leaned over him, put her arms around his shoulders and smiled that wonderful smile that always made her face a living promise of love.

"Slide down. Just draw up your knees, put all your weight on your hips and push downward."

He did, and in a minute was flat on his back. She eased her arms away, but the feel of her body brought back the ache he'd been trying to shake when he skipped supper at home that Sunday night, and he caught her hand.

"Be straight with me, Alexis. I let you into me, deeper than any other human has ever been." He pointed to his heart. "This is where you live. Only once in my life have I felt complete, and I was in your arms, deep in your body.

"Either something happened that took the shine off what you feel for me, or there's something you think I won't understand, and you're retrenching out of self-preservation. If I've done something, I'll try to repair it and make amends, but if it's in your court, trust me to understand."

Right on the money. "I don't think this is the time to discuss serious things. You've done nothing to discredit yourself."

He nodded. What she didn't say told him more than what she said, because he knew he hadn't done anything untoward. "I know. So what we're facing is whether you trust me. That it?"

"Not quite. It's time you got some rest. I'd better check on Tara."

"Yeah. Tell her I said I want her to practice her music. If she learns that piece well, I'll play the violin along with her."

Her face lit up. "You promised to let me see your wire sculptures."

"I did, but you haven't let me see what you've been doing lately."

"I will, though."

"I'll hold you to that." She leaned forward and pressed her lips to his. His chest hurt, and his arms felt like lead, but he had to hold her, this sweet love of his life.

"You'll hurt yourself."

"It'll be worth it," he said, as she wrapped her arms around his shoulders and let him taste her. Her woman's fragrance mingled with the man-made perfume she wore, her soft cheeks caressed his face and her lips moved over every exposed part of him. With a will of its own, his sex began to stir.

"Sweetheart, you're lighting a fire down below, and since I can't even sit up without help, we'd better let that fire die out as quickly as possible. Woman, you pack a wallop. I may have lost a lot of blood, but my testosterone is at peak strength."

That mischievous crinkle appeared around her mouth, and she winked her left eye at him. "Peak strength, huh? Well, may it'll always be that way. See you later."

He tried to twist around enough to watch her walk out of his room, but the pain in his shoulder wouldn't allow it. Alexis could give lessons in how a woman ought to walk, free and easy, but elegant, regal. He closed his eyes, and in his mind's eye, he could see her glide. A pair of hips that rolled like ocean waves, and the sharpest pair of props he'd ever seen. *Down, boy.*

"I gotta get out of this straitjacket," he told himself as he fought the increasingly heavy weight of his eyelids.

At the bottom of the stairs, her mind still with Telford, Alexis nearly collided with Russ. "Oh. Sorry," she said. "Where's Tara?"

"Henry took her over to his cottage to play with the puppies, as he calls them, though they're big dogs. She said Biscuit missed his brothers and sister."

"I don't know what to tell her about Telford."

Russ leaned against the banister and rested his right elbow on it. "When I was a kid, our mother fed us all kinds of untruths when it would have been easier to level with us. Dad was away from home, and she said he was off on a business trip. He called Telford and said he was in the hospital. It's best to tell children the truth in words they can understand and accept."

"Telford wanted to protect Tara from unhappiness about his condition."

"Yeah, I know. He loves that little girl more than anybody, except maybe you. I'll never understand it, but she's crazy about him, too."

"Neither do I, but he zonked both of us the minute we saw him."

Russ's face broke into a smile. "Well, what do you know?

And I always thought Drake was the lady-killer. Never can tell. I'll look in on Telford, but I expect he'll sleep for a while."

Watching him take the steps two at a time, she wished Velma would have the good fortune to find a place in his heart. She walked back to her room, put on a smock and began to etch the features of the bust she'd hoped to finish that day, but she made so many mistakes that she wrapped it and put it away. Telford had admonished her to be straight with him, but with two strikes against her, being straight wasn't enough. She needed to find Lawrence Duckwilder, but she didn't have a computer, and if she went to Frederick or Baltimore while Telford was recuperating in bed, she'd send him the wrong signal. Maybe she could use Russ's computer while he was at work. Telford would let her use his, but she couldn't risk his getting up and peering over her shoulder.

She phoned Russ. "I need to look up something, but I can't leave the house while Telford has to stay in bed. And I don't want to disturb him. May I use your computer tomorrow? I won't change any settings."

"Uh… Sure. Log on to Mind Spring and use the password *hkeeper*. You got that? I'll set it for you."

She wrote it down. "Thanks, Russ. I appreciate it." And while using the computer, she'd find a foundry close by that would cast in bronze the bust she was sculpting in clay.

The next morning, she gave Telford breakfast, and planned to spend a few minutes with him before starting her morning chores, but Telford had other ideas.

"Don't do any chores." When she insisted they had to be done, he countered, "I'm the boss, and I say don't do any chores. Stay here with me."

"What will Russ and Drake think when they come home and find their rooms just the way they left them? I'm sparing Henry because he's looking after Tara."

"They'll think you were looking after me," he said with a twinkle in his eyes. "Besides, it won't hurt 'em to straighten the sheets."

"But all Russ needs is an excuse to revert to being sloppy. You're being unreasonable."

"Aw, sweetheart, I hate lying flat on my back like this. Now if you'd—"

"Don't even think it, Telford. I am not getting in that bed with you. Henry would be scandalized if he came up here and... Besides, it would be indiscreet. Period."

"Tantalizing thought, though, isn't it?" he asked with a wide grin. "I can just see you teasing me, peeling off one thing after another till you get down to your shoes, and then crawling slowly between these sheets. A breathtaking *naked Maja* as beautiful as Goya's painting." The laughter seemed to stab him and he winced, but still he laughed. "Get as furious at me as you like, but I can dream, and that is one fantastic dream."

She startled him with a kiss on the mouth and moved from his reach before he could react. "See you later." It wasn't difficult to see where Tara learned some of her traits.

She finished her morning chores, discussed the supper menu with Henry, went into Russ's room and closed the door. He'd left the computer running, so that she wouldn't have to figure out how to turn it on. She couldn't find a Lawrence Duckwilder under the domain name. All right, so maybe he didn't have a website. She typed in the name and hit the search button. No luck.

"I'm not going about this correctly," she said. "I'm wasting time." She found the names of three foundries within a reasonable distance, made a note of them and logged off.

She reached the bottom of the stairs as the phone rang. "Harrington House."

"Hi. This is Velma. Just wanted to let you know I'm in Detroit, and it's cold. I've gotta go out and buy a couple of warm sweaters. Danged if I'll buy an overcoat."

"With your raincoat, two good sweaters ought to be enough." She told her about Telford's encounter with the three thugs.

"Good Lord. You need me, and I'm stuck here in Detroit."

"He's getting on fine." She remembered Velma having

said that half the members of her nutrition classes in graduate school were doctors. "If you wanted to find a doctor, and you didn't know where in the United States he was, where would you look first?"

"The American Medical Association and the National Medical Association. Every African-American doctor belongs to the NMA, and most also belong to the AMA."

"Thanks. By the way, Russ has a birthday coming up— December the first."

"Whatta you know! I'll send him a strand of my hair."

Alexis's lower lip dropped. "You'll what?"

"Just kidding. I'll let him know I remember it. A Sagittarian, eh? Hmmm. Lover boy. I'll have to rethink him." Her laughter rolled through the wires. "Trouble is, if you slip up with one of those brothers, you've had it. No second chance. Still…"

"Rethink him?" At times, Alexis forgot how much she enjoyed her sister, so full of wit, fun and pranks. "Velma, you're full of it, but you're the top. I gotta go check out these medical associations. Give me your phone number." She wrote it down. "Thanks, I'll call. Bye."

She went back to Russ's room, logged on to the computer, searched the NMA site, noted the contact for information and hung up. She tiptoed into Telford's room and found him asleep. An hour later, she knew that a Dr. L. T. Duckwilder lived in Oakland, an L. O. Duckwilder in Nashville and an L. Duckwilder in Boston. She went back to the computer and checked the internet yellow pages for addresses and biographical sources. By two o'clock she knew that the Lawrence Duckwilder who lived in Nashville had graduated from Howard University School of Medicine, class of 1996. *Bingo!*

When she attempted to write down his street and email addresses, her fingers shook so badly that she couldn't recognize her writing. Her breath seemed to clog her throat as sheer black fright swept through her. She dreaded what came next, but she saw no alternative.

Chapter 12

I'm sick of this bed, and I'm getting up. But just as he made up his mind to test his strength, he heard footsteps that could only belong to Tara. So he pulled himself up in bed, though not without more effort than he anticipated, and drew the sheet up to his neck.

She knocked twice and called him. "Mr. Telford, I wanna come in."

When he answered, she rushed in and dashed over to his bed. "Mr. Russ said you had a accident, but you weren't too bad. Are you too bad?"

He hadn't realized how much he missed her. "No, I'm not. But I had to rest and be quiet. Have you been practicing?"

She braced both elbows on the bed, cupped her chin with her hands and nodded. "Every day. Mr. Henry and my mummy said I couldn't come see you, 'cause you had to rest."

What he wouldn't give to hug her. She wanted him to know that she would have come to see him if she'd been allowed to do so. "I know you wanted to come see me, but I was supposed to be quiet. Where's your mother?"

A grin spread over her face and she leaned toward him, obviously about to share a secret, and whispered. "Mummy's doing her scupter. She thinks I'm in the room."

He didn't want to encourage Tara to disobey Alexis, and he had to fight hard to stifle the laugh that bubbled up in his throat. "The word is sculp-ture." He pronounced it slowly.

Suddenly, she raised herself up on the bed, kissed his cheek and scampered down so fast that he nearly missed it. "I'll be back," she whispered and ran out of the room.

How he adored that precious little girl! He turned on his side and, with his left elbow on the bed, propped himself up and braced his head with his left hand. Alexis and Tara. Tara and Alexis. His world. He threw back the covers, gripped the headboard and stood up. Spots flashed before his eyes, dizzying him, but he took as deep a breath as he could and drew himself up to his full height of six feet four inches. The longer he stayed in that bed, the longer he'd have to. He left his bedroom door open, made his way carefully to the bathroom, turned on the shower and let the warm water stream over him. One of life's true luxuries.

With effort, he dried off, pinned a towel around the wet bandage, dressed and stretched out on the bed. Alexis had implied that they'd talk after he recovered. As far as he was concerned, that was now.

Alexis wasn't thinking along those lines, however. Her thoughts were occupied with ways of getting to and from Nashville, Tennessee, without creating suspicion. She didn't think a telephone call would gain her more than a polite turn-down. If Melanie wanted to be found, she would have written or called her parents or her brothers. After checking her funds, Alexis decided to ask Telford to let her take her two days off consecutively. Instead of Thursday and Sunday, her usual free time, she'd ask for Thursday and Friday. However, that would pique his curiosity, so she'd have to tell the truth: she was trying to solve a personal problem, and she would discuss it with him as soon as she could.

"When do you want to leave?" he asked her, several days later when, after deciding the course she'd take, she told him what she wanted to do. Nothing in his demeanor betrayed his thoughts.

"I was thinking about next Thursday, but I'm not yet sure that's the best time for me to go."

"All right. When you're ready to make plans, let me know. Will you take Tara with you?"

She glanced down at her hands, unsteady and thus incriminating. But to her relief, his gaze didn't move from her face. "I hadn't gotten that far, but I guess it would be simpler if I didn't have to, and I don't want her to miss school."

"Lay out what she's to wear each day, and I'll take care of her. One thing: Is this trip aimed at getting things straight between you and me?"

She nodded. "I'm hoping that...that it will help us reach an understanding."

"If you need any money for hotel and transportation, I'll be glad to spring for it."

"Thanks, but I've saved some money since I came here. I can handle that. One more thing: Jack wants to visit Tara, but I didn't think it wise for him to come here while you're still recovering. Jack's unpredictable."

"Maybe, but I doubt he's fool enough to take me on whether I'm well or not."

A half laugh slipped from her lips. "Unfortunately, he is. He'll probably want to come next Friday, and I may not be here."

The frown that darkened his face reflected more than puzzlement, and she knew as much. "The guy's been here once in the almost seven months you've been here. What's his hurry? If he really wants to see Tara, he won't care whether you're here or not."

"My sentiments precisely."

"Whatever you do, I'm with you. You understand what I'm saying?"

She reached toward him, but withdrew her hand. *I can't let him think I'm looking for someone to lean on, because I'm not.* But when he narrowed his eyes, obviously drawing the wrong conclusion, she grasped his hand.

"This isn't a time for second-guessing, Telford, because I'm finding my way as I go. Right now, I'm slightly preoccupied with what my next step will be."

He appeared to release a lot of tension. "I'm not in this because I'm bored and don't have anything else to do. I believe you're straight with me, but I need the answer to two questions: Is your divorce final, and does Jack Stevenson have any hold on you?"

"My divorce has been final for three years, and Jack has remarried. I don't owe him anything and don't want anything from him. Believe me, if he wasn't Tara's father, he wouldn't know where the dust on my shoes came from."

"So you feel nothing for him."

"Not even pity."

At the airport, Telford held her hand until they reached the security checkpoint, and he couldn't go any farther with her. He moved to the wall, dropped her carry-on luggage and grasped both of her shoulders. "Call me if you need me."

His fingers pressed into her flesh, and his lips on hers jolted her senses. She parted her lips, but he didn't accept the invitation. Instead, he picked up her bag and put it on the conveyer.

"See you Sunday." With that, he strode off.

During her life, she'd treaded rough waters and weathered a lot of storms. None of it had frightened her. But as the plane landed at Nashville International Airport, her nerves fought a war among themselves, sending tremor after tremor shooting through her body. She closed her eyes and slowly repeated "Tara and Telford" over and over. Still, her stomach rolled like a ship on a turbulent ocean.

Get a grip on yourself, girl. Don't lose your cool. By the time she checked into the Marriott Courtyard, she'd forced her nerves to settle down. "I'm not drawing this out," she told herself, as she sat on the edge of the bed and dialed Baptist Hospital.

"Doctor Duckwilder gives physical therapy from ten to twelve on Wednesday and Saturday mornings," the cheerful voice drawled. "If you need individual attention, call his office at…"

Alexis hung up after verifying the information she'd gotten in Eagle Park, and at ten o'clock the next morning stood at the information booth in Baptist Hospital.

"Why, yes, Ms. Brighton, I have your reservation right here. Just sign this."

She'd used her maiden name in order to hide her identity and prevent Duckwilder from excluding her. Needing a medical reason for taking the therapy, she told the truth, that she had sustained a whiplash some time back, and that after long periods of sculpting, fatigue set in.

His piercing gaze darted to her from time to time as if verifying a flash of recognition. At the end of the period, Alexis detained the doctor.

"May I speak with you privately?"

Displaying genteel Southern manners, he smiled. "Yes. What may I do for you?"

She took a deep breath. "I've been years getting to this point, Doctor, and what I'm about to say concerns something that has kept me awake many nights…and for years."

His eyes widened, and she thought she detected a look of recognition in them. "Perhaps we'd better go into my office."

Once there, he closed the door, and his hand lingered on the knob for a while, almost as if he feared releasing it. "Have a seat."

The ball was in her court. "Thank you. I hope you'll hear me out before you decide anything."

She could see from his expression that he knew what was coming and that, like a cornered man who'd been on the lam for years, he was tired of running from his demons.

"My real name is Alexis Stevenson." He gulped and his Adam's apple bobbled furiously, but she plunged on. "I'm the teacher who gave Melanie Krenner the failing grade that prevented her graduation from State U. I followed school rules and wouldn't change the grade. Recently, I've come to know her father, and—"

He sprang forward. "Is he… Is anything wrong with him?"

Her heartbeat returned to normal. This was indeed the man she sought. "Only that, after all this time, he is still dying of a broken heart. A few weeks ago, he went back to State U to try and trace her, but got nowhere. I used a different route and learned about you and your connection to her. Is she well?"

He nodded slowly, stood, locked his hands behind him and began pacing the floor. She didn't say anything more, just waited. Finally, he stopped in front of her.

"After months and months of pleading with her to call her folks, I stopped pestering her about it. Her father mortgaged their home to send her to college, and she fooled around and flunked out. At first she was just scared, but as time went on and she began to accept responsibility for what she'd done, she became ashamed. She misses her parents and her brothers, but she's petrified at the thought of facing them."

"Maybe if I talk with her, tell her about her father, how he looks and how he and her mother long to see her, she'll change her mind."

He started pacing again, this time with faster steps, no doubt nervous and indecisive. Her own nerves laid siege on her body, and she silently repeated the rhythmic phrases of Poe's poem, "The Raven," a nerve-calming trick she learned when Jack would stay out all night.

After what seemed like hours, though it was barely more than a minute, he stopped pacing. "I'll leave here about six today. If you'll give me the name of your hotel, I'll stop by for you at about six-thirty."

She gave him the name and phone number of the hotel, aware that she had no choice but to trust him. As she walked to the door, a thought occurred to her, and she stopped and turned around. "Does your wife like surprise guests?"

He reached past her for the doorknob. "I'll phone Melanie and tell her I'm bringing a guest for supper. And, no, siree, she does not like for me to surprise her with a mouth she hadn't planned on feeding."

He'd answered the question foremost in her thoughts. Melanie was his wife, and as long as he practiced medicine Alexis would be able to trace them. Nonetheless, that knowledge wasn't sufficient to banish her anxiety. No matter what happened that evening, she'd go back to Eagle Park with some good news, but she wanted to be able to tell Allen Krenner that Melanie would telephone him and that she would visit him soon. That was her goal. So she left the hospital less wary of failure, but too familiar with disappointment to let herself feel ebullient.

Finding a way to pass the next six hours proved a trial. After wandering around midtown for an hour, she boarded a little red trolley for a short sightseeing trip, walked through a crowded mall, bought a bag of boiled peanuts and went back to the Marriott Courtyard.

Dressed in a nonthreatening Dior blue woolen suit, she waited for Lawrence Duckwilder in the hotel lobby while marbles scrambled for space in her belly. Aware that, even then, he could be hiding Melanie. Though the lobby was barely warm, perspiration forced her to remove her coat.

"I hope you haven't waited too long."

Her head snapped up, and relief flowed over her, palpable in its significance. "Why, no. Thank you. You're right on time."

He drove away from the city's center, and took her past rows of elegant homes all of which belonged to African-Americans. The Cadillac Seville came to a halt in front of a pale gray, two-story stone house, modern in design and set far back from the street. Elegant by any measure.

"Here we are," he said, as if aware that she'd expected less.

Her first thoughts were that no one would willingly give up a place such as that one and that Melanie wouldn't force Lawrence to move away simply to avoid her family. If for no other reason, Allen Krenner would get his daughter back.

She missed a step, and he grasped her arm. "You all right?"

"I guess. You told Melanie to expect company, but you didn't tell her to expect *me*."

"If I had, she'd have worn herself into a frazzle by now." He shrugged. "She might even have disappeared."

She recognized Melanie at once, even with the glasses, though she was obviously more mature than in her college days. A petite woman with smooth dark skin and short, natural hair.

Lawrence Duckwilder hugged his wife and kept an arm tight around her in a gesture of protection. "Melanie, this is Ms. Stevenson. Remember her?"

Melanie gasped and clutched at her chest. "Steady, honey," he said. "It's all right. I didn't tell you because I didn't want to worry you, but I'm glad she came. I can't begin to tell you had glad I am."

"Hello, Melanie. Do you mind if we…talk a little? I have some news for you."

"Come on in," Melanie said. "You're the last person I was expecting. I fixed supper. Hope you haven't eaten."

Nervous chatter, but Alexis understood that the woman couldn't help being disconcerted, and she wondered if, in similar circumstances, she would have been as polite or as self-possessed.

"She's in contact with your folks," Lawrence said, as they began the meal.

Melanie's lower lip dropped, and she gripped the edge of the table. "Is there… Are they—"

"They're fine, all of them," Alexis said, "at least insofar as their health is concerned. I've only met your father, and he's the reason I'm here."

Melanie glanced at her husband before fixing her gaze on Alexis. "What is it, Mrs. Stevenson?"

This is it, and I've got to make a real statement, or else. "Every time your father mentions your name in my presence, tears pool in his eyes. Recently, he went back to State U for clues as to your whereabouts, but as in other times he'd gone there, he hit a dead end, and the life seemed to seep out of him. It's time you ended his needless suffering and let him know you're alive."

She spoke in barely audible tones. "He doesn't know?"

Alexis shook her head. "Of course not. You covered your tracks well. I didn't know, either, until this morning. If you had a child, how would you feel not knowing whether it was living or dead, happy or starving to death?"

Melanie sniffed several times, pushing back tears. "I don't know how to face them."

Alexis exhaled a long breath, impatience threatening to emerge. "Stop pampering yourself, Melanie. You made a mistake, and you have to face up to it. Your family deserves better from you. With all these colleges and universities in Nashville, you can still finish school."

"I've thought about it lots of times."

Alexis stood, aware of the danger of overstaying her visit. "When I get back to Eagle Park tomorrow, I'll tell your father where you are and about my role in this fiasco." She handed Melanie a slip of paper. "Here's his phone number and address. It's your duty to get in touch with him."

"She'll call him," Lawrence said, "and she and I will visit him. You can depend on that."

Alexis thanked them both. Allen Krenner's problem may be nearing a solution, but only the Lord knew how Telford would react to what she had to tell him. He didn't even know she'd been a college teacher, much less the one who gave Melanie the failing grade that prevented her graduation.

* * *

"I'm not hanging around here waiting for a call from Jack Stevenson," Telford said to himself. "It's Friday afternoon, and if he hasn't called by four-thirty, Tara isn't on his schedule for today." He gave Tara her piano lesson and played the violin for her while she gazed at him in rapt attention. After supper, he phoned Adam Roundtree. Nothing like a morning of fishing to guarantee he wouldn't spend all day Saturday worrying about Alexis. He didn't expect her to call him until she was ready to leave Nashville, because he figured she had her hands full doing whatever it was she went there to do. In any event, she wasn't likely to tell him anything important until they were together.

"Adam, this is Telford. How about you and Grant going fishing with me and Tara tomorrow morning? Alexis is out of town."

"How's about eight o'clock? Bait early if you want fish," Adam said.

"Right. We'll be over there by eight."

Grant wasn't overjoyed at having a girl for a playmate and showed it. Tara caught a second fish before Grant caught any, gave the second one to Grant and said, "I don't think I like you, but I caught two and you don't have any. If you lived with us, Mr. Henry would cook you cabbage stew."

"Looks like they don't hit it off," Adam said.

Telford waved a hand, dismissing that idea. "You don't know Tara. Just wait."

He explained Tara's remark about cabbage stew to Adam and thought he'd have to give his friend first aid. Adam laughed uncontrollably. Then the two men watched, dumbfounded, when Grant went over to Tara and baited her hook with a worm.

"Worms are yucky," he said. "My dad always puts the bait on for my mom."

Tara's face bloomed with a brilliant smile. "Thanks, Grant. I don't like worms."

Telford looked at Adam. "See what I mean?"

He closed his eyes, waiting for the fish to bite, enjoying a rare respite from his many business concerns. A tug at his line proved to be a false alarm, but he didn't care; a good nap out of doors in the fresh air would make him as happy as a mess of fish.

"Mr. Adam, can Grant go home with me?"

Telford's brow furrowed. Minutes earlier she'd told the boy she didn't like him, and there she stood in front of Adam holding Grant's hand, and… He scratched his head in wonder. Damned if he'd ever understand the opposite sex. He busied himself checking his line.

Adam cleared his throat. "That would be all right, Tara, but Grant's mother is expecting him home in—" he looked at his watch "—twenty-five minutes."

She persisted, her smile intact. "Then, can he come to see me?"

"Uh…yes, if he wants to."

"I want to, Daddy."

"Then it's settled."

Still holding hands, the children went back to their fishing lines. Adam cocked an eyebrow. "Man, she's started early."

Telford threw out his line and reeled it back a bit. "She practices daily on the men in our house. Doesn't surprise me one bit."

"Her mother must be some woman. By the way, did you and Alexis straighten out your differences?"

"You're saying we had some?"

Adam pulled in a little fish and threw it back into the river. "Absolutely. I was there. Remember?"

"We're working on it. She's very important to me, and if you don't mind, I won't discuss her."

Adam let go a sharp whistle. "Go for it, man. I wish you well. Bring her with you next time you come to Beaver Ridge."

Telford thought for a bit. "Thanks. I'll do that."

* * *

Alexis stepped into the terminal and let her gaze sweep over the individuals waiting for arriving passengers. She saw him at once, a full head above the crowd. He smiled when she saw him, the smile of a man whose fear equaled his hope, rushed to meet her and opened his arms. She reveled in the feeling of his arms strong around her body and let him cherish her. Who knew how he'd feel by daybreak the next morning?

"Tara wanted to come with me, and I would have brought her, but Henry talked her out of it. I think they're making a surprise for you. How do you feel, honey?"

So he wanted some indication of what to expect. "So far, so good, but there's more to go. We'll talk when we get...when we get home."

He grasped both of her shoulders. "Alexis, I'm aware that you work for me, but you *live* at Harrington House. That's your home, and it goes against my grain that you can't accept that."

She expected that his eyes would mirror the annoyance in his voice, but they held a warmth and a sweetness that made her heart race. Silky lashes emphasized their dreamy beauty, mesmerizing her, and without thinking, she dropped her bag, reached up and hugged him.

"You're so...so... Heck, I don't know. I'm glad you're back," he said. With her bag in one hand and his other hand at her waist, they headed for his car.

"I rented this one," he explained. "I've ordered a new Le Sabre. It ought to be here in a week or so."

"Did the police find your other one?"

"Not yet. I'm told it's probably been chopped and sold for parts." He flipped on the radio and headed for Route 70.

She knew his mind was on her trip, but he'd wait till they were at home and she found the appropriate time to talk. She closed her eyes and enjoyed the music and his nearness.

In her short absence, Tara seemed to have grown another inch. Her greeting to Telford, who'd only been away a couple of hours, was as effusive as that to her mother. Dancing with excitement, she said, "Mummy, Mr. Henry and I made something for you. I went fishing, and I have a new friend. Do you know Grant Roun...?" She looked at Telford for help.

"Roundtree," he said.

"Grant Roundtree. He's going to be my friend. I caught three fish, Mummy, and Biscuit's sister is going to have babies."

Alexis hugged Tara, glanced up at Telford and saw love shining in his eyes. *I'm almost happy,* she said to herself. *If only...*

"Let me change my clothes, and see what Henry has for me to do," she said to both Tara and Telford.

"Ain't nothin' for you to do."

"Henry. I was just going to look for you. Thanks for helping take care of Tara while I was gone."

"She ain't needed much takin' care of."

"We'll talk after dinner," Telford said. "I'll take your bag to your room."

"Thanks, but it's not heavy. See you at dinner."

Alone in her room, she tried to organize her thoughts, to choose what she'd say to Telford and how she'd say it. *I can't be artificial about this. I'm dealing with my life.* She threw up her hands and decided to roll with the punches.

"Hope you don't mind if I don't join you in the den," Telford said to Russ and Drake after dinner. He looked at Alexis. "Call me when you're free. I'll be in my room."

In other words, he'd wait until Tara was asleep and they wouldn't be disturbed. On that night, however, Tara's excitement was at fever pitch, and she didn't sleep until around ten o'clock. *What's he thinking?* she wondered. At last, she could phone him.

"Is Tara asleep?"

"Finally. She was as revved up as a jet engine. Where can we meet?"

"The den. Russ is in his room."

Alexis sat in the beige-colored wing chair that she favored, feeling as if she were on her way to her execution and hoping she didn't show it. Telford watched her for a minute and then dragged the Moroccan tooled-leather pouf over to her chair, sat on it facing her and took both of her hands.

"I can see that this is difficult for you, but try to remember that what I want most is an understanding with you, a relationship that isn't marred by the past or what either of us anticipates for the future. And that's possible only if we level with each other. What happened in Nashville?"

In his face, his whole demeanor, she saw warmth, friendliness and, yes, love. His eyes told her that she was precious to him, and she had to believe what she saw.

"I'd better start at the beginning." She told him that she taught at State U before marrying and after her marriage broke up and, it didn't surprise her that his eyes widened in astonishment.

"At the end of the second semester of my first year there, I posted grades and sent the record to the dean of my department and the dean of students. I had three failures..." She stopped and took a deep breath, for he had shifted to the edge of the ottoman and his hands squeezed hers as though he anticipated her next words.

"Go on."

Hearing the edge in his voice, she felt her nerves begin to rearrange themselves. "One of...of those students was...was Melanie Krenner."

He jumped up. "And all this time you didn't say a word? You knew how crazy—"

"Please sit down, if you want to hear the rest of it."

Still holding both of her hands, he did as she asked. "I'm sorry. I...I don't know what got into me."

"I had given her three opportunities to make up her midterm papers, but she didn't bother and didn't offer an excuse. If she had been doing well in her other classes, that D wouldn't have failed her. Without a reason acceptable to the dean, I couldn't change the grade, although she begged me to. Indeed, there was no reason to change it.

"Her sudden disappearance was a campus calamity. After I met Mr. Krenner, I decided to try and find out what happened to Melanie and began an inquiry. As I was dressing for your reception, I got news that she was afraid to face her parents and tried to commit suicide. No. No, not that," she said when his bottom lip dropped and a frown darkened his face.

"Her girlfriends revived her and called her boyfriend, who was a senior medical student. He got medicine for her, rented a room off campus and kept her with him as his wife until he finished his internship at a local hospital the following year. I got the name of that doctor and used Russ's computer to trace him. Since I found three doctors by that name, I was only about seventy-five percent sure I had the right one when I left here."

"Was he the one? Did you see him?"

"Yes, and he took me home with him to talk with Melanie, his wife."

He jumped up, picked her up and twirled around with her. "Honey, are you sure? Are you sure? Let's…"

"Not so fast. I'm positive it was the Melanie Krenner I knew, because I ate dinner with them and talked with her. She looks the same, only more mature. She's still scared of facing her family, but she promised me she would call her father, and her husband, Doctor Lawrence Duckwilder, gave me his word that he will bring her here. I believe he'll do it. I liked him."

"You mean you're suggesting I shouldn't call Allen and tell him. Are you serious?" he asked, his face shrouded in a look of incredulity.

"No, I'm not suggesting that. I was hoping she would call him. Anyway, I'll give Mr. Krenner her address and phone number."

Suddenly, Telford braced the back of his neck with his right hand, narrowed his left eye and stared down at her. "Why was it difficult for you to give me this good news?"

"It hasn't sunk in yet, I guess. I thought you'd hold me accountable for not speaking up about my relationship with Melanie, that you'd accuse me for having flunked her. And I hadn't told you that I have a master's degree in health sciences and taught at State U for two years before I married and another two years after my marriage broke up."

When he started pacing the floor, she knew his mental wheels had begun turning, and that she was about to get the backlash she'd dreaded.

"Why did you leave there?"

"Beginning this year, all teachers in all departments must have a doctorate. That let me out."

"And you don't think that just knowing what happened to Melanie would have been some comfort to Allen?"

"I didn't know any more than he did. What good would it have done to tell him she flunked out? I had no idea as to her whereabouts, only that the school couldn't locate her."

He threw up his hands. "Look, I don't mean to give you the third degree. You've done something good, and you took a big chance on my understanding all this."

"I didn't think of it that way," she said. "As soon as I got that information, I began the next step. I had to do what was right, even if it meant you'd send me away from here and I wouldn't see you again. And believe me, that would have been a life sentence."

Suddenly, he stopped in front of her and grinned. "Get your coat. We're going to Allen's house right now."

"All right, but I'm drained. You tell them." She looked at her watch. "It's almost eleven o'clock."

"So what? He wouldn't care if it was three in the morning, and I don't, either."

She needed to know where she stood. "Does this mean you don't blame me for…for anything?"

He'd started toward the stairs, but stopped and walked back to her. "I'm feeling too good to think about blame. You said you were hoping to remove one of the things that hampered our relationship. Honey, you did more than that. Get your coat, and let's go."

If only Allen Krenner's verdict would be as generous.

* * *

"I know we're bringing them good news, Telford, but, honey, it's after midnight. Suppose they're asleep."

He could hardly believe she'd said it. "You're kidding."

He parked in front of 311 Hatch Drive in a lower-middle-class neighborhood of Frederick and scrutinized the little green-shuttered white bungalow. Not a light.

"Come on, sweetheart. The only thing Allen and Grace can do to you is love you." He walked with her to the door, rang the bell and waited. He rang it again, and after a while a light flooded the little porch.

The door opened slowly, as if the person inside feared the visitor. "Good Lord! Telford! It's you. What's the matter?"

Holding Alexis's hand, Telford walked past Allen, who stood rooted to the spot as if in shock. "Good news, Allen. Is Grace asleep?"

"Good news? Whatta you talking about?" Allen grabbed the lapels of Telford's leather jacket and jerked at them. "Talk to me, man."

He laid a hand on Allen's arm. "Sit down, friend. Alexis has found Melanie. She's seen her and talked with her."

"What?" Allen clutched Telford's arms and attempted to shake him. "Don't lie to me, man." Suddenly, his hold on Telford slackened, and he sank into a chair.

Alexis dashed over to him. "Is something wrong, Mr. Krenner? You—"

"Allen, what are you doing down there? I thought you were asleep."

A short, frail woman, aged well beyond her forty-eight years, Grace Krenner entered the living room tentatively, holding her powder-blue robe at her waist as if to secure it.

"Why, Telford," she gasped. "What's the matter?"

Allen pulled himself up with obvious difficulty, as if the weight of the world hung around his shoulders.

"Melanie is alive. Our baby is alive."

He clasped his wife in his arms, as powerful sobs racked

their bodies. Alexis turned away, and he didn't doubt that the scene moved her, because tears threatened to spill from his own eyes.

After moments of tearful reminiscences, expressions of gratitude, tears and laughter, the Krenners settled down and he recounted to them Alexis's story.

"She's in Nashville, Tennessee, and she and her husband assured Alexis that they're coming to visit you soon."

Allen shook his head, obviously perplexed. The fingers of his left hand moved back and forth across his chin as he gazed into the distance. "I just can't understand it. She's all right. She's well, and I guess since she's married to a doctor, she's well-off. *Didn't she know...didn't she realize we've worried ourselves almost to death?*"

What could he say to that? To his amazement, Alexis went over to the sofa, sat between the two people and put an arm around each of them. He'd never known another woman who possessed such compassion. "Knowing the sacrifice you made to send her to college, when she flunked out, she was scared to face you," Alexis said, "but that's all in the past." Her voice took on a huskiness. "When she comes, open your arms to her."

There it was again, that feeling that he'd known her before. It kept cropping up, though it didn't make any sense.

"Yes, of course we will," Grace said. "Allen, I think we ought to call the boys and tell them." She looked at Alexis. "God bless you, dear. Oh, my manners! Would you like some coffee or tea?"

Alexis stood and shook her head. "No, thanks. We'd better be going. I'm so happy for you."

Telford was on a high, and he knew it was temporary, because he'd have to come down and settle at least one issue that remained between Alexis and him. He didn't believe her role in Melanie's disappearance accounted for the way in which she froze him out at that reception. How could it? She wasn't culpable; a teacher is honor bound to give a student the grade deserved, not more or less. He pasted a smile on his face, shook hands with Allen, kissed Grace, took Alexis's hand and left.

"Russ is going to kill me," he said, not without some glee at the thought of being able to disturb Russ's sacred rest with impunity. "But I can't help it. I have to wake him up and tell him." He opened the door of Harrington House and stopped himself as he was about to lift Alexis and carry her inside. *I need to straighten out my head.* He hung his leather jacket and her coat in the guest closet near the door, remembered that her coat didn't hang there and shrugged it off.

"I'm wrung out," Alexis said. "I…uh…I'd better turn in."

She lacked her usual aplomb, and he could certainly understand that. "I'll walk with you to your room."

They didn't speak as they walked down the hall, slowly, as if by agreement, each seemingly in a private world.

At her door, she turned to face him and, with both hands braced above her head, he trapped her between himself and the wall. He hadn't planned to do it, but his mind had suddenly begun a war with his feelings and emotions. And she knew it. Her eyes, her whole bearing said she expected him to pull back, and that she had prepared for it.

"I can't tell you what this means to me, to all of us. Allen is like my third brother. But, Alexis, my head's full of questions. I don't want to detract from the importance of what you've done, so…we'll talk tomorrow. Okay?"

She stood tall before him, gazing into his eyes, her dignity intact, but all at once that magnificent self-possession that set her apart, that always marked her every move was missing from her demeanor. His heart constricted, and he gathered her into his arms.

"Honey, is there…anything else you need to tell me about this?"

She shook her head, her eyes sad. It nearly unglued him. He loved her. No matter what. He loved her. His blood pounded in his ears, and when her glossy, unpainted lips parted and waited to welcome him, a groan dragged itself from the pit of his belly, and he plunged his tongue into her waiting mouth.

Heat sliced through him and aimed arrowstraight to his groin, as her beaded breasts rubbed against his chest and her fingers gripped his shoulders with unnatural force.

He wanted hot passion and fire, but she softened and gave him tenderness and sweetness in a gentle kiss, loving, caressing and adoring him as if he were the most precious person alive. He backed away from her seconds before he hardened to full readiness.

"Honey… Oh, Lord," she whispered.

He needed her. He would always need her. The ache in his belly burned out of control, and he pushed open the door, picked her up and carried her to her bed.

As light filtered through the Venetian blinds, he looked down at the sweet woman in his arms and prayed that they could straighten out whatever it was that made them both reticent.

"Are you awake, sweetheart?" She only snuggled against him. He had never demanded so much of a woman, and none had ever given him so much. He kissed her eyes until she opened them and smiled.

"I'd better get out of here before Tara awakes, comes in here and finds me."

She stretched her body like a sated feline. "Then you'd better go before I think of something for you to do."

He couldn't help grinning. "You're the best medicine my ego ever had. See you at breakfast."

She sat up, leaned over him and brushed his lips with her own. "Do we still need to talk?"

The somberness in her tone of voice was all the reminder he needed of their unfinished business. "When I get home from work. But don't stew over anything. I think we just need to get rid of the remaining debris. Love me?"

"Oh, yes. I love you."

His kiss was hard and swift. "And I love you."

Drake was in Baltimore, thank goodness, because he could hear a footstep on any surface. Telford got to his room without

Henry or Russ having seen him. He took pride in Alexis's love for him, but unless and until they spoke promises to each other, he'd soft-pedal the nature of their relationship.

Chapter 13

Alexis buried her face in the pillow and inhaled his scent, stretched, rolled over, pulled the sheet over her face and breathed in the musty scent of their lovemaking. She had to get up and get Tara ready for school, but his fingers teased her flesh and her body vibrated from his powerful, rhythmic strokes. He possessed her still. *I'm in deep trouble. He hasn't quite forgiven me for not telling Allen Krenner of my relationship with his daughter. What will I do when he learns I'm that girl who humiliated him, that I lied because I was so embarrassed?* She crawled out of bed, half drunk on the memory of him in her arms.

"I'll be in Baltimore today," Telford told her at breakfast. "I'll take Tara to school, but she'll have to come back on the bus."

"I can pick her up this afternoon," Russ said. He looked at Alexis. "When do you think Melanie will get in touch with her folks?"

Alexis sensed in Russ an ally, and she expected to need one. "She should already have done that by the time I got back here yesterday. If she doesn't call them soon, I'm going to phone her."

Telford concentrated on his grits, eggs and sausage, but Russ leaned back in the chair, sipped coffee and seemed to scrutinize her. Not that it made her uncomfortable; Russ always seemed to dismember people with his piercing gaze.

"You've done your part," Russ said. "If she doesn't call them today, I'll buy them a ticket to Nashville. I can't believe this thing's solved. And she's all right. Fantastic!"

"Phone for you, Tel," Henry said. "It's 'bout time you got one of those phones that goes from place to place."

"Thanks. Tell me why I should walk around here with a mobile phone. I've got a cell phone."

"Humph. Then give whoever's calling your cell number. I'm not the butler. I'm the cook."

"Yeah," Telford said, getting up from the table. "And you're getting cranky. Excuse me," he said to those at the table. When he passed Tara, he pulled one of her braids.

Alexis had the feeling that Henry enjoyed needling Telford.

Tara giggled. "Mr. Telford likes to pull on my braids. Why don't you wear braids, Mummy?"

Russ responded to that with prolonged laughter. "Do that, Alexis," he said, gasping for breath. "I can picture Telford taking his frustration out on those braids."

"That was Allen," Telford said, taking his seat. "Melanie and her husband phoned, and they'll be here on Thanksgiving. He's so excited, I could barely understand him."

He stopped Alexis in the hallway after they'd finished breakfast. "You okay this morning?"

"Other than being a little drunk, I'm fine."

He stared at her. "Drunk? Did you say you're drunk?"

He could behave like an innocent, could he? She lowered her left eyelid in a slow wink. "Honey, you pack the punch of straight tequila. I had a shot of that in college, and I've been an almost teetotaler ever since."

A grin spread slowly from his lips to his wonderful eyes.

"Tequila, huh? Not bad. I've had a few of those. Remember we'll talk when I get back this afternoon."

She nodded. "Kiss me."

Before she could prepare herself, he gripped her close to his body, and took her mouth in a quick, drugging kiss. "Tara's waiting in the car. See you later."

She blinked rapidly, staggering under passion-induced vertigo, and tried to regain her equilibrium. "I'd like to punch him," she said aloud. "He knows exactly what he did to me." But, Lord, it felt good. One minute in his arms was like pouring gasoline on a fire that was already burning out of control.

"I need to go to Frederick," she told Henry later. She wanted to take the bust she'd finished to the foundry to have it cast in bronze.

Her phone rang as she was dressing to leave. "Hi, babe. What do you say I come over this afternoon?"

She took a deep breath. The man was hell-bent on driving her crazy. "Jack, that won't be possible, unless you want to visit with Henry. Come tomorrow at four for half an hour. Tara will be here then."

"You've gotten to be a hard woman. All right. See you tomorrow. Say, look, babe. I'm a changed man. Give me a chance."

She didn't believe he'd said it. "Jack, I can't count the number of second chances I gave you in the four years that we were married. The lies you told me would fill up the New Orleans Super Bowl. Get real!"

Hard or not, he had no claim on her, and she intended to keep it that way. She got back from Frederick a few minutes before Russ brought Tara home.

When she met them at the door, Tara kissed her and raced to the kitchen to find Henry and black-cherry ice cream.

"Did I detect a strain between you and Telford this morning?" Russ asked her and, without waiting for her reply, added, "If he's sore because you hadn't told him you knew Melanie, don't let it upset you. He demands a lot of people. He'll get over it. Anyway, it's time you two made up your minds."

"Are you suggesting we…that we… I mean—"

He laughed at her obvious surprise. "Yeah. Get married and quit fooling around. It's painful to watch."

"Don't *you* upset her." She whirled around at the sound of Henry's voice. "Russ don't never bother to contain his opinions. Course, it wouldn't hurt you none to build a fire under Tel."

The grin on Russ's face was that of a man savoring a tidbit. "Yeah, and I want to be there when you light that fire. That'll be the day."

"You're such a loving brother," she said, and his laughter followed her as she walked off to her room.

"Hi. I just got in," Telford said a few minutes later when she answered her phone. "Can we talk now?"

"All right." She agreed to meet him in the game room where the brothers played billiards, darts and table tennis and they were unlikely to be interrupted.

He walked in, kissed her on the cheek and cut to the chase. "Sit over here on this couch with me. I need to know what caused you to back off from me at that reception."

She wanted to move her hand out of his so she could think straight, but he held it as if it belonged to him. "I explained it to you once. The setting, your friends, who I should have been and who I actually was—that, and what I'd just learned brought home to me forcibly that no matter how we polished it up, I was your housekeeper. A servant had no place in that company. I was playing a dangerous game." She didn't lie to him. Learning that he was Big Tip after the news she'd just received about Melanie had everything to do with it.

"I see. And what about last night? What changed?"

She was still trying to deal with the wild, possessive and explosive way in which he'd made love to her the night before, deliberately, almost as if he were teaching her a lesson. And then, he'd shattered in her arms as never before, giving her every bit of himself.

Shaken by the thought of what she'd experienced with him, her words came out in a whisper. "You know the answer to that. I…I needed you, and…and you were so near. I…" Why

should she explain it? Her temper threatened to break loose.
"You know darned well how I feel about you, so that question
doesn't make sense."

He released her hand, leaned forward and rested his elbows
on his thighs. "I can't help feeling that there's more to it. You've
always been so open, so natural, and to suddenly clam up like
that..." He shook his head as though perplexed. "This thing
has to clear up sooner or later, and when it does, I'll know it.
I'm not giving up. You mean too much to me."

Thank God for that! "Jack's supposed to visit Tara tomorrow
around four," she said, glad to get off that subject.

He slapped his thighs and looked toward the ceiling. "It's so
pathetic. If only he'd come to see her regularly and she could
get to know him. Right now, she's dead set against having
anything to do with him. I can't figure it out."

"You implied that you weren't crazy about your mother."

"I wasn't, but I was old enough to know why. Tara's going
with her instinct."

"Jack's superficial. He smiles readily and in many ways
he's charming. My guess is that children respond to sincerity
and know when you're faking."

He took her hand as he stood. "Whatever. I'll make sure
I'm here, in case you need me."

Jack's visit the next afternoon didn't improve his relations
with his daughter. Where she'd previously been indifferent,
she seemed to have developed a dislike for her father. Alexis
decided that Jack wasn't aware of it or, if he was, he ignored
it.

"Why don't you try talking with her, Jack?" she asked him
when Tara used going to the bathroom as an excuse to leave
Jack.

"She's a child," he said. "I'm not going to cater to her.
You've spoiled her."

"A single parent is subject to do that to make up for the
other's absence."

Later, at Telford's suggestion, Jack agreed to visit Tara every

Wednesday afternoon. "If she knows she can depend on seeing you, she's bound to soften up. She needs consistency."

"What's your interest in this?" Jack asked him.

"I had a flighty mother who took off for weeks at a time whenever she got bored, and I bear the scars of one who, as a small child, couldn't depend on a parent. I'd like to spare Tara that pain."

"Maybe if you left the three of us alone to work out—"

"Don't kid yourself, man. The only reason Tara stayed in this room with you as long as she did is that I told her she had to do it. Will you be here next Wednesday?"

"Yeah." He looked at Alexis. "How about taking a ride, babe?"

She shook her head. "I'm sorry, Jack, but I'm not going to socialize with you. You're here to visit Tara, not me."

With a smile that didn't quite make it to his eyes, he saluted her. "See you next Wednesday, babe."

He didn't surprise her when, on his visit the following Wednesday afternoon, he proposed a different scenario. "Let's you, me and Tara go for a ride, and let the big guy do his own thing. I don't need him."

"Sorry. The deal is that you visit with Tara in the living room, or the garden, and it's too cold for her to go out in the garden. Tara," she called, "tell your daddy the name of the latest piece you learned to play."

With her eyes downcast, she leaned against Alexis's knees. "'Songs My Mother Taught Me.'"

"Tell him how you learned it."

"Mr. Telford played it on his violin, and I asked him to teach it to me. I been practicing it."

If she'd known Telford first played it on his violin, she wouldn't have mentioned it. She had hoped Tara would tell him that she'd practiced it every morning before school and every afternoon. The little devil. She knew what she was doing. And so did Jack.

"We just can't get away from the great *I am,* can we?" he said.

"Can I go now, Mummy?"

What was the use? "Ask your daddy to excuse you."

Tara's face bloomed into a smile. "Excuse me." She ran from the room.

"We'll see you next week?" she asked him with as much civility as she could muster. He hadn't said one encouraging word to Tara about her playing; instead, he'd focused on his dislike of Telford.

"I'll call you."

She closed the door behind him and took a deep breath. Being with Jack for a mere half hour could ruin her entire day. As a man, he paled in comparison to Telford's decency, sweetness and strength. She took the vase of withering flowers from the table in the foyer and went to the kitchen.

"Whatta we having for Thanksgiving?" Henry asked her. "It's usually turkey, but I don't know how you feel about turkey. Never did care for it myself."

"I'm not crazy about it either. Tell you what. We'll make it a gourmet feast. Let's get a goose."

Thanksgiving morning, she set the table with autumn flowers, candles and Harrington heirloom table appointments. Since all the brothers were at home, she finished upstairs later than usual, took Tara for a walk down Old Liberty Road halfway to the warehouse and returned with the view to getting some work done on the sculpture she'd just started.

"Want to watch some football games with us?" Drake asked her. "Around here, football is as much of a ritual as the Thanksgiving meal. We'll be in the den."

Henry put a large bowl of roasted chestnuts on the coffee table, sat on the floor in a lotus position and starting eating.

"Who're we watching?" she asked.

"You can't be serious," Drake said. "We're going to watch Howard University and Grambling at Howard's homecoming. Tonight, we'll watch UCLA and Cal Tech."

She shelled a chestnut, savored it and reached for the ginger ale Henry had placed there for her benefit.

"What's that?" Henry asked.

"They're getting ready to show some clips of past homecoming activities," Drake said. "They always do that."

"Humph. Why don't they just get on with the game?"

Her belly began to roll and a chill shot through her, though she sat three feet from flames that blazed in the fireplace. She put the ginger ale on the table.

"There you are, brother," Drake said, his voice filled with pride. "Big Tip himself. Alexis, you should have seen Telford sling that football down the field."

"Yeah," Russ said. "Put Telford and Big Train out there together, with Telford throwing 'em and Big Train pulling 'em in like ordinary fly balls. Man, nobody beat Howard U in those days. You should have seen him, Alexis."

Didn't she know it, and hadn't she seen his awesome feats with that football! "I'll be doggoned" was as much as she could manage, and she made certain that she didn't look any of them in the eye.

"He was so skinny and had all that long hair on his head and all over his face," Henry said. "Used to make me want to take a pair of scissors to him."

"Yeah," Drake said. "Couldn't see much of anything except his eyes and nose, but this brother could throw a football."

The pregame ceremonies merged into the game, and the play melted into the halftime ceremonies. Finally, it was over, and the men raised their glasses to Howard's twenty-one-to-seventeen win. She drank the warm ginger ale without tasting it. She couldn't admit that she'd attended Howard, known him, fallen for him and loved him from afar, because he'd know who she was, and he wouldn't forgive her. Secrets. How she hated them. Even more, she hated the thought that when Telford learned who she was, he would despise her.

"Man, I used to be so proud that my name was Harrington," Russ said. "I was four years behind him, but my professors would ask me if I was Big Tip's brother, and I wouldn't have been more pleased to say yes if they'd asked me if I was related to Einstein."

She'd been proud of him, too, but he would never know it.

"I'd better get back to Barbados," Telford told Alexis after Thanksgiving dinner, as they stood beside her room door. "We've been sending materials and heavy equipment over there, and I have to check on it. Drake will be in Baltimore much of the time, but Russ will be working here at home. We're putting in a bid for a project in North Carolina, and Russ is drafting the design."

"How long will you be there?"

"A week, maybe two, depending on what I find there. I wish you could go with me."

"It would be nice, but—"

"I know. We can't take Tara out of school." He tipped up her chin with his right index finger. "What's wrong, sweetheart? It isn't like you to be subdued. Look, I'm leaving here day after tomorrow, and when I come back, you're going to tell me where I stand with you. I want my life in order, and you should want the same. Hell, I can get a housekeeper. A dozen of them. And I'm tired of this arrangement, anyhow."

She risked looking straight at him, knowing that if she did, the heat between them would burst into flame. His eyes mirrored the compassion, love and, yes, the fire-hot desire that he felt for her. She sucked in her breath as a longing for his warmth, heat and loving swept over her.

For a minute his gaze hypnotized her, his eyes stormy pools of pure want, and all she could think of was how wild he could be in bed. She swallowed hard, and suddenly, he picked her up, fitted her to him and plunged into her open, waiting mouth. He trembled against her, and his groans shocked her into awareness of their surroundings and of the possibility that, at any second, Tara could have opened the door. Stunned both by the force of what she felt and by her carelessness, she slumped against him.

"You're right. We need a resolution to this, but right now, I'm doing the best I can."

"It isn't always necessary to go about things the hard way. When you trust me, really trust me, there won't be a problem." He looked at his watch. "Want to go to a movie? I don't know when I last saw one."

"If Henry will look after Tara, I'd love to go."

I've got to learn how to enjoy life, Telford told himself as he walked with Alexis into the theater. Being with her like that, just walking along the street and holding hands, laughing and telling each other jokes made the whole world warmer, friendlier. He felt more carefree, more alive than he ever did as a child. *She's good for me.*

He got in the line leading to the popcorn vendor. "Want some?"

"I sure do, but no butter, please."

"What do you mean, 'no butter'?" he asked her, patting the back of her neck. "Since when were you allergic to butter?"

"Okay, I'll have butter on my popcorn if you promise to discipline your tongue."

He laughed aloud. "I wouldn't touch that with a guided missile."

They took seats near the aisle, and he put the open bag of popcorn between his knees, clasped her shoulder with his left hand and waded into the popcorn with his right one.

"Isn't it good?" he asked her.

She nodded. "Uh-huh."

He wanted to kiss her, but settled for a hug.

"All right, you lovebirds up there, be still."

He recognized that voice and, hard as he tried to dismiss the incident, knowing the man was in the vicinity put a damper on the evening. At the end of the movie, he took his time getting up, and when he did stand and turn around, he didn't see anyone he recognized. He'd parked two blocks from the theater, and as he turned in that direction, he saw him.

"Well, whatta you know, boss. Surprised to see you at the movies."

Alexis stiffened and moved closer to Telford, and he put his left arm tight around her waist. "Same here. I thought you were down South."

"I was." The man's gaze swept over Alexis with what was just short of a leer. "Howdy, ma'am." Her response was to move closer to Telford's body.

He didn't care about Biff, but a man should make it a point to know as much about his opponent as possible, and any man who coveted Alexis Stevenson was his opponent.

"What brings you back up here?" he asked Biff.

Biff lit a cigarette, blew the smoke away and leaned against the lamppost, his swagger and outsized ego still intact. "We finished the job. You got anything?"

"Not a thing."

"Keep me in mind for your next project, will ya?"

Didn't the man remember why he'd fired him? "If I hired you, Biff, that would create a rift between Russ and me, and nothing's worth that."

"I, uh… I thought he'd get over that…uh…little incident. I didn't mean no harm."

"Little incident? If Russ hadn't been there, you'd have followed through on your threat to impose yourself on a woman who told you she didn't want anything to do with you. I don't compete with my employees, Biff, and Mrs. Stevenson is my woman."

Biff kicked at the pavement, his eyes downcast. "Guess I tore it all the way 'round." He looked up. "I'm a good worker, boss. Nobody can say I don't do my job."

"Competence doesn't compensate for a lack of morals, Biff. All the best."

She didn't speak as they walked to the car.

"I'm sorry we ran into him," he said.

"Me, too. Would you hire him again?"

"No, indeed. Besides, Russ wouldn't hear of it, and Drake

always had low tolerance for the man. I'm going to see that he gets a job as far away from here as possible."

Her laughter rang like a tinkling bell. "Wishful thinking, but I like it."

He opened the passenger door, waited until she got into the car and hooked her seat belt.

"No way," he said, easing away from the curb. "And I aim to take care of that before I sleep this night." He looked over at her and grinned. "That is, unless you've got something else you'd rather I did."

She cast a side glance at him, slowly raised her eyelids, winked and looked straight ahead without uttering a sound. Man, oh, man, this black woman could really turn it on.

"Watch that, baby. You're putting notions in my head that I couldn't discuss with a priest unless I was at confession."

"I didn't know you were Catholic," she said, filling her voice with awe. "When do you go to Mass?"

"You still don't know it, but what I said holds nonetheless. And don't try to knock me off the subject."

"Really? Wonder if Melanie and her husband visited her parents today."

"I went in the dining room to tell you. You mean I didn't? Indeed, they did. I imagine that was one emotional scene."

"I'm...so happy for them."

She didn't sound happy. At best, her tone was wistful, maybe even a little strained. She could deny it as often and as vehemently as she liked, but she was keeping something from him. And he'd bet it was her sense of decency and fairness that forced her to pull back whenever their relationship seemed too much like the real thing, as if it were destined for permanency. She would never commit to him as long as she held that secret. *I'll worm it out of her if it takes me a year.*

At home, he parked in the garage, and they entered the house through the side door near the dining room. Hand in hand, they walked to her room. He didn't know what she was thinking, but his own mind conjured up images of the two of them silver-haired and still holding hands as they walked through life. He shook himself, but the pictures stuck in his head.

"I enjoyed being with you," she said. "I feel like a teenager…I think. I didn't have many movie dates when I was growing up. Velma and I didn't want kids to come to our house, so we kept to ourselves."

"Why? Did your parents drink?"

She shook her head almost with reluctance, as if drunkenness would have been preferable to what they experienced. "Worse than that. They fought all the time. Almost every meal ended in an argument."

"Oh, yes. I remember your telling me something like that. I'm sorry, Alexis." He needed to hold her. "How about a kiss? And unless you want company, don't lay it on thick."

She poked her tongue in her right cheek and let her gaze travel over him slowly and deliberately. "Does that mean I call the shots?"

"If you play your cards wisely, yes."

"And you're not telling me what wise means in this case. Right?"

"Wouldn't think of it. You're batting a thousand without any help from me."

With gentle sweetness her lips brushed his, and she quickly moved away. At his inquiring look, she explained, "I'd rather not learn how to resist responding to you. Thanks again for the movie and the popcorn."

"What about the company?"

"First-class. 'Night." With a grin, she went into her room and left him gaping at the closing door.

Musing over what had just transpired, he shrugged first one shoulder and then the other one. She was so right. The woman burned whenever he touched her, and he wanted it to stay that way. He went to his room and called Armand Wright, a contractor and close friend who worked in Oregon.

They greeted each other as friends would. "What're you doing right now, buddy?" Telford asked him. Learning that the man was recruiting workers for an underwater tunnel he was about to begin constructing, he recommended Biff. "He makes a first-class foreman, but keep him away from your women."

Armand's laugh crackled through the wires. "Man, he'll be so far from any woman that by the end of the four years, he'll have forgotten what they look like. Tell him to call me."

"I'll do that." He hung up, barely able to contain the laugh that bubbled in his throat. *Talk about justice!*

At a quarter of ten that Friday morning, he dropped his flight bag and suitcase at the bottom of the stairs and headed for the kitchen to speak with Henry. The phone rang. "I'll get it," he yelled to Henry.

"Telford Harrington."

"Hi. This is Velma Brighton. Is my sister there?"

"Sorry, she isn't. She went to take Tara to school and hasn't gotten back yet. I'll leave a message for her."

He went to the kitchen. "I should be back in a couple of weeks at the latest, but in any case, you'll know where I am. Take care of yourself."

"Alexis, too?"

"Yeah. And tell her that neither she nor Tara should go walking around here unless Russ is with them. I ran into Biff Jackson night before last, and although I told him what's what, it wouldn't surprise me if he did something stupid."

"I'll tell her, and Russ, too. You take care of *your*self."

Several blasts from an automobile horn got his attention. "That's my car service. See you."

His plane was forty minutes from Barbados when it hit him. Brighton. She'd said her name was Brighton. Something back in the recesses of his mind told him that name had importance for him. He tried to recall it, but couldn't. "I'll get it, though," he promised himself. "Sure as my name is Telford Harrington, I'll get it."

* * *

"Henry, where are you?" Alexis called when she returned to the house after taking Tara to school.

"I'm right here doing my work. Where you been so long? Tel ain't happy leaving here with Biff Jackson roamin' in these parts."

She hugged him and quickly moved away. Henry could stomach just so much sentimentalism. "I went into Frederick to do some grocery shopping. Tomorrow is Russ's birthday, and we have to make him a nice dinner party."

"Humph. Mr. Gourmet. If he ain't careful, I'll cook—"

"You'll do no such thing. We'll have smoked salmon with red onion slices, capers and sour cream, herb-stuffed roasted fresh ham, sweet potato soufflé, asparagus tips, Cajun corn bread, coconut layer cake and vanilla ice cream. Tara will have to give in."

"I'll be a monkey's uncle. Russ'll stretch out and die. Did you bring all that?"

"I sure did."

"I ain't gonna eat nothin' from now till tomorrow night."

"Oh, come on, Henry. It's just a good meal, and I remember he said that's what he wanted for his birthday."

"Well, you give Drake and Tel big birthday celebrations. If we skipped Russ, he'd be hurt."

"Wouldn't think of it."

"Mummy, what's that gonna be?" Tara asked Alexis as she grated the coconut for Russ's cake.

"Honey, it's a secret. Okay?" Telling Tara something was tantamount to publishing it.

"Oh. If it's a secret, I can't tell?"

"That's right, love."

"Maybe Mr. Henry doesn't think it's a secret. I have to go practice, so I'll know my piece when Mr. Telford comes back."

The next evening, she dressed herself and Tara in green jumpsuits, went to the dining room and was admiring the table she'd set when she heard the front door open.

"I almost got arrested trying to get here on time," Drake said. He picked Tara up and swung her around. "How's my princess?"

She kissed his cheek. "Mummy's been making secrets today, Mr. Drake, and she wouldn't let me see."

"And I know why. Where's Russ?" he asked Alexis.

"Upstairs in his room. I was hoping Telford would call."

"He will."

"Hey, brother," Russ said as he loped down the stairs. She looked on as they went through the ritual that never failed: a returning brother was always greeted with an embrace.

"Mr. Drake is gonna say the grace tonight, 'cause Mr. Russ has a birthday."

Drake didn't dare refuse in Tara's presence, but he made quick work of it, and finished just as the doorbell rang. He went to the door and returned with a package.

"Something for you, Russ. FedEx overnight mail. I'll get you a sharp knife."

Tara ran around the table and leaned against Russ's knee while he opened it. Her mouth formed a small O, and her eyes widened. "Gee. Mummy, look!"

"Well, I'll be," Russ said, shaking his head as he held up a gray stuffed tabby kitten. He read aloud the tag that the little cat wore. "'My name is Hugs, and there's more where I came from.'" He turned the tag over and gazed at it.

"Mummy, Mummy. It's from Aunt Velma. It says Velma. It says Velma, Mummy."

Russ looked at Tara. "Isn't it a good thing I don't mind if they know who sent it?"

Tara slapped her hand over her mouth. "Is that what means secrets, Mr. Henry? I forgot."

"It wasn't a secret, Tara," Russ said. "I'll have to call Velma and thank her."

"You remembered what I wanted," he said to Alexis as he savored the cake and ice cream. "This was one great meal."

"I let her cook this stuff, too. Sweet potato soufflé. My brain burned trying to imagine what it would taste like. Pretty good, too," Henry said.

"Wasn't better than the one she cooked for my birthday," Drake said. "And that caramel cake. Man, I can still taste it."

"Drake, you and I are not smart," Russ said. "We could have this stuff regularly. Get another housekeeper, build a fire under Telford and tell him to do the honorable thing toward our…er…sister here. Then, man, we could—"

"I haven't left the table, and neither has you-know-who," Alexis said, reminding the two men of Tara's presence.

"Sorry," Russ said, "but I was dead serious. Not about the cooking, though that would be a bonus, but I want to see this mixture jell."

Drake stopped eating and looked at Alexis. "You're the one holding this up, aren't you? I know Telford's stubborn, but he isn't crazy. I'm going to have a real good talk with you."

What could she say? "Russ, Drake, Henry. I love all of you. Please don't upset me."

The phone rang, and Drake jumped up. "I told you he'd call." He handed the phone to Russ.

"Thanks, brother. Yeah. She pulled out the stops and cooked all my favorites. Sorry you missed it, because I doubt it can be duplicated." He passed the phone to Drake, then to Henry and then to Tara.

"Mr. Telford said to tell you he'll call you later, Mummy. He talked to everybody else. Is he mad at you?"

There were times when she'd like to muzzle her daughter. "No," Henry answered for her. "He wanted some privacy."

"Oh."

"Come on," Drake said. "Let's all take this stuff into the kitchen and straighten the place up. I've got a couple of bottles of Moët & Chandon, and we're all going to drink champagne."

"Me, too?" Tara asked, giggles spilling out of her.

He rubbed the tip of her nose. "I got you some bubbling grape juice."

Henry stood and stretched to his full height, which even he admitted wasn't much. "This is a great family. Perfect with all six of us, and ain't nobody should break it up."

When she got a minute to herself, she'd try to digest that. She drank two glasses of champagne with them, told them good-night, went to her room and put Tara to bed. If Telford had been there, if would have been perfect.

Chapter 14

She couldn't control her restlessness, and a cold December evening wasn't a time for walking in the garden where she always found peace and tranquillity. If she lived to be a hundred, she wouldn't get used to waiting on a man's telephone call; indeed, she had rarely done it. But this one had a hold on her. She looked at her watch. Dinner had been over for nearly two hours, and he still hadn't called her. She wanted to be annoyed but, instead, she was worried as to whether something had happened to him. *Oh, for goodness' sake, girl, get yourself back on track.* She stripped and headed for the shower, mainly for want of something to do, since she'd had one earlier. As soon as she turned on the water, the phone rang. She grabbed a towel and raced to answer it.

"Hello," she said, with a huskiness that embarrassed her.

"Whoa. From the way you sounded, I take it the big guy isn't there. How about I come out tomorrow, since I'll be away on business Wednesday?"

She hadn't thought her heart could hit the bottom of her belly so fast and so resoundingly. Recovering as quickly as she could, she agreed and added, "Four o'clock for half an hour." If he put forth some effort to help Tara like him, she'd lengthen the visiting period, and she told him as much.

"Bring me one of your recent photographs, and I'll frame it and put it in her room."

"What if I bring you one for your room, too?"

"No, thanks, Jack. See you tomorrow."

She started back to the bathroom, glimpsed herself in the mirror and let the towel drop to the floor. What did Telford see when he gazed at her body? Did a man focus only on what his eyes beheld? She looked at the tiny stretch marks on her belly and the upper part of her thighs, barely visible, but sufficient to mar the beauty of her flat belly, narrow waist, full bosom and flared hips. She picked up the towel, drew it tightly around herself and walked slowly back to the bathroom. She was as she was.

After the shower, she patted herself dry, applied some lotion and crawled into bed. Immediately the phone rang, and she reached over and lifted the receiver. *If it's Jack, I'm going to hang up.*

"Hello."

"Hi. How are you? Sorry I had to miss that great banquet you gave Russ. It blew his mind."

She rolled over on her belly, luxuriating in the sound of his voice. "It was as perfect a meal as I ever cooked. The only thing it lacked was you."

"How'd it happen that Henry let you do that, cook a whole meal, I mean?"

She twisted the telephone cord around the index finger of her right hand. "He said if I wanted to get that fancy, I could do it myself, but I sensed he was tired."

"That doesn't sound like Henry. Tell Russ to check on him, will you? Henry acts like he's a piece of iron. I'll call him tomorrow. Seen or heard anything of Biff?"

Hmmm. So Biff was on his mind. "Not a thing, thank the Lord."

"Good." His voice vibrated with relief. "I wouldn't walk out on that road alone or with Tara. Biff's devious. You miss me?"

"Do birds fly?"

Though miles away and with half an ocean between them, his laughter warmed her and a delicious, sweet feeling snaked through her body like a searching wind. "Unless their wings are damaged," he said. "How're your wings?"

Oh, talking with him was so good. Liberating. Joy suffused her, and she wrapped her free arm around her middle and burrowed beneath the covers. "My wings? Never better."

He laughed aloud. "When I get back there, we'll fly together." Her nerves shimmered in anticipation, and she tingled from head to foot.

She kicked up her feet and let laughter peel from her throat. "Promises, promises," she teased.

"If I was with you right now, you'd scream 'uncle' before I left you."

"Talk, talk. My grandfather always said, talk's cheap. It takes money to buy land."

She knew she was getting to him when he said in a voice minus the rich vibrato she loved, "You are one fresh woman. What happened to that decorous female who came to my home last April?"

She flipped to her back, crossed and uncrossed her legs. "I've wondered about that, and all I can come up with is that mind-altering experience she had with us...Tel...er, what's his name? Turned her inside out."

"Yeah? She's not bad at mind-blowing herself. Listen, sweetheart, I'll call you in a day or so. Give Tara a hug. Kiss me?"

She blew him a kiss. "Take good care of yourself, hon."

"Thanks. You do likewise."

She hung up and lay there staring at the phone that she gripped in her left hand. Where was her resolve? She'd better remember the price she had to pay when he learned of her schoolgirl folly, of her lie. He'd had her understand that he placed a high value on honesty. She'd been dishonest, and she'd hurt him. Sleep came slowly.

"Jack, I can*not* force Tara to like you," she told him during his visit the next day. "You have to teach her to love you. Where's the photograph you promised?"

He leaned against the doorjamb at the entrance to the foyer, his arms folded as if he lived there, and gazed at her in the way of a man cataloguing the assets of a woman he wants.

"I forgot the photo," he said, as if it were of no import.

Tara walked up to them and pulled on Alexis's arm. "Mummy, Grant wants me to come over to his house and see his new computer. Can I go, Mummy?"

"After your daddy leaves, I'll call Grant's mother and we'll see what's what."

With neither deference nor embarrassment, Tara looked up at her father. "How soon are you going? I have to tell Grant."

"Look," Jack said in a tone that signaled a rising temper, "I'm getting out of here."

"Stay right where you are, Tara," she said when the child turned to leave. "You said you wanted to go to the bathroom, but you made a phone call."

Alexis hurt for Tara, because even at so young an age, the child didn't like to compromise and usually made that clear. She couldn't remember Tara disobeying or being uncooperative, except in connection with her father.

"I'm sorry, Mummy, but I promised Grant I'd call him, and you said I have to keep my word."

"Who's Grant?" Jack asked.

"Grant Roundtree, her playmate. They're good friends."

"Fast company. Where's the big guy these days? What's his name? Telford?"

"Mr. Telford is working in Barbaby."

"You mean Barbados, darling," Alexis said.

"Barbados. Mr. Telford calls me lots of times."

"I'll just bet he does. How about you, your mother and me going for a ride in my brand-new car?"

Tara hung her head for a second and then looked straight at him. "Sorry. I have to call Grant."

Jack shrugged, but the scowl on his face bespoke anything *but* indifference. "Five will get you ten there's something going on here that they don't teach in Sunday school."

His gloved hand was already on the doorknob, and he simply turned it and left without another word. Not a hug or even a pat on the head for his daughter. It occurred to Alexis that she had never seen him hold and kiss Tara, not even as an infant. She flung open the door and raced after him.

"Why do you come here? I have never seen you show Tara the affection a child expects from a father. Don't you know she sees other children with their fathers and understands what fathers are supposed to be? No wonder she rejects you: you don't try to teach her. And another thing, when are you going to introduce her to her half brother?"

He stared at her almost as if he didn't understand. "What was I supposed to do with a baby? As for Pierce, I never see him, because his mother and I don't speak."

"Mummy, here's your coat."

She spun around and saw Tara standing in the open door holding a coat. In her anger, she hadn't thought of the cold. She ran back inside, taking Tara with her.

"Thanks, honey." She took the coat, hung it in the closet and walked with Tara to her room.

Sitting on the edge of her bed, she positioned Tara between her knees, and Tara smiled up at her, the essence of sweetness and the innocence of a child. Her heart brimmed with love, but if she didn't discipline Tara, she would become a replica of her cunning, self-centered father.

"Because you told me an untruth, Tara, you can't visit Grant today, so phone him and tell him you can't come."

"Yes, ma'am."

Tara dialed the number and asked for Grant. "Hi, Grant.

I was bad, so I can't come over today. Nope. Just don't invite me on Wednesday. I'm always bad on Wednesday. You will? Oh, great. Bye." She walked over to her mother. "Mummy, can Grant come to see me next Wednesday?" Before she could say no, Tara added, "After he leaves."

"We'll see." *He!* It struck her that Tara rarely referred to her father and that, when she did, *he* and *him* were the only titles she gave him. *My goodness, and she won't even be six for several months.*

At first, Telford called her every other evening after dinner. But by the end of the first week after leaving for Barbados, he'd begun calling her daily and at different times during the day. His phone call awakened her the following Sunday morning.

"I know I woke you up but, heck, I've been waiting for daylight for the last nine hours. Talk to me."

"Hmmm? What time is it?" She pulled the pillow over her face. "I'll be there soon as I…" She rolled over, imagining being closer to him so that his fingers could reach her body, but his arms didn't seem long enough. "Honey, stop moving away from me."

"You can believe me, if I could, I'd be as close to you as a man can get to a woman."

"You're teasing me."

"You're the one teasing, baby, and my blood pressure's rising by the second. You're still asleep. I'll call back in a couple of hours."

"Huh? Oh! Telford?"

"Yeah. I'll call back."

"No. No, I'm… I'm awake." She sat up. "How are you?"

"I'm not sure you want to know. Tell me about you. Anything. I just want to hear you."

"Will you be home for Christmas?"

"You bet. No matter what, I'll be there."

"Do you mind if I invite Velma? There're only the two of us, and—"

"Of course you may, but be sure to let Russ know."

She hadn't thought of that. "Thanks. I will."

No matter how long they talked, she never wanted their conversations to end. "Bye, love. Hurry and come home."

"On the first day possible."

Several days later in midafternoon, Russ looked up from his drafting table and turned on the light. A glance at the windows revealed a blackened sky and trees bending in the wind. He closed all the windows, brought candles and lanterns up from the basement and put boxes of matches in strategic places. Then, he put Alexis's car into the garage, locked the door and dashed into the front door to escape the storm.

"I don't see how I can leave here in this storm," Jack said to Russ and Alexis. "For the last few minutes, the wind's been blowing so hard it's bending those trees, and it's pouring rain out there."

Russ rested his hands on his hips and stared at Jack. "This storm's been forecast for the last three days, so you knew it was coming and you should have arranged your visit accordingly. You'll have to spend the night. I'll show you your room."

Good grief, Alexis said to herself. *You can almost cut the hostility between these two men with a knife.*

"Alexis can show me," Jack said.

With his left hand on his hip and his other one braced against the wall above his head, Russ stared at Jack. "I say what goes here, and *I* will show you where you'll sleep. We eat at seven, not later." He headed up the stairs, leaving Jack to follow him or sleep on the floor wherever he could find space.

"If I was his type, I'd introduce him to my fists," Jack muttered beneath his breath.

"That would be foolhardy. Never try it," Russ said without stopping or looking back. "If you were my type, you'd be reading your daughter bedtime stories."

Alexis didn't know how she got through dinner that evening. For once, Tara didn't declare the necessity of saying grace before they ate, though Russ said it anyway, and cabbage stew tasted like gourmet fare. Not even Tara complained about it.

To her amazement, Jack asked her, "Where's your room?"

She was about to slap her hand over Tara's mouth when Henry answered for her. "Why you asking? That ain't none of your business."

Alexis strummed the table with the fingers of her left hand. "Run into the kitchen and get Mummy a paper napkin, please," she said to Tara.

Jack's face contorted into a scowl. "I've got a right to know where my child sleeps."

"You wasn't asking about Tara. Exercise yer rights some other place, some other time," Henry said. "At this table, we don't speak of nothing unpleasant."

"For a cook, you got a lot of mouth."

"Sure have. Everybody in this house is equal, so don't pull your highfalutin stuff on me."

Tara came back and took her seat at the table. "Here's three napkins, Mummy," she said, pride in her accomplishment evident from her expression.

"Thanks, honey."

Russ, who hadn't uttered one word since saying grace, laid his fork down and looked at Henry. "What are we having for dessert?"

"Apple turnovers."

"I'll get mine later. Thanks for a great meal, Henry. I can't tell you how much I enjoyed it."

And he said that with a straight face. She had to stifle the laugh that threatened to burst from her throat.

She folded her napkin and prepared to leave the table, but Tara jumped up ahead of her. "Ask to be excused, Tara," she said.

Tara looked up at her and forced a smile. "Excuse me."

"Please."

"Please."

She couldn't believe her eyes. Tara scooted off to her room without hugging Henry or Russ or saying anything to them, and Henry's knowing look told her that the child's unhappiness hadn't escaped him.

Good manners dictated that she not leave Jack alone, and she might have remained with him if he hadn't slammed both palms on the table.

"Where the hell is everybody going?" He looked at Russ. "And who do you think you are looking down your broad noses at Jack Stevenson? I can buy and sell the lot of you."

Russ doubled up with laughter, though only he knew how he managed it. "I don't doubt it for a second, man. You gave away your daughter in order to keep your fortune. Don't tempt me. Hike it on upstairs, and for God's sake, *get a life!*"

The next morning, Telford stepped out of the limousine, took his bags and started up the short walk to the front door of Harrington House. Suddenly, the strangeness of his surroundings registered—the silver-gray Lincoln Town Car parked in the circle, several saplings uprooted, limbs detached from older trees and a shattered garage window. He'd seen the storm's damage along Route 70 as the driver brought him in from Baltimore International Airport, but he hadn't considered the damage it might have done to his home. Seeing that it was minor, he heaved a sigh of relief, walked into the house and dropped his bags, his only thoughts being Alexis and his craving for her.

His foot touched the first step of the stairs, and he looked up and stopped, rooted in his tracks, as Alexis floated down to him, followed by her ex-husband. Grinning. Triumphant. Arrogant. Alexis stopped.

"Telford. Oh, Telford, I didn't realize you'd be back today."

Hold your tongue, man, and don't say anything you'll be sorry for. Jack Stevenson is baiting you. Before he could greet her, Jack plunged in, playing his cards close to his chest.

"Thanks for the hospitality, buddy," Jack said. "All of it."

His resolve to remain unperturbed deserted him. "What do you mean 'all of it,' and what the hell are you doing up there?"

The man's grin widened. "It's where I slept last night."

She whirled around. "What are you insinuating? You slept up there because Russ told you to."

"So you were visiting Tara when the storm hit, and Russ allowed you to spend the night. Well, the storm's over, pal."

He dashed up the stairs to where Alexis stood, fit to explode, folded her in his arms and covered her mouth with his own. Warm and pliant, she melted into him, gripping his shoulders and lower back. With parted lips, she took him in and gave him what he needed.

As if Jack Stevenson were not standing there, he took her hand, walked past him up the remaining three stairs with her, went into his room and closed the door.

"I'd like to rearrange that guy's face. Where's Tara?"

She stepped closer and rested her head against his chest. "Russ took her to school. I was up here doing my work. I didn't even know Jack was walking behind me."

"The guy's cunning. I didn't appreciate his attempt to implicate you."

Both of her arms went around him, and she nuzzled his chest. Coming home. This was what it really meant to come home. "He no longer surprises me," she said, her voice muffled by the fabric of his jacket. "How'd you leave things in Barbados?"

"I'm satisfied for now, but that is definitely not where my mind is. I missed you."

She stepped away and looked up at him, her stance provocative and inviting. "Wherever your mind is right now, I guarantee it is not alone."

"If I put my hands on you right now, here in my room, three feet from my bed… Look, I'll be down in a minute." He opened the door. "Wait up here. If he hasn't already left, I'll see him out."

He ran down the stairs. *Let's see who'll be wearing an arrogant, mocking grin now.* As he turned toward the foyer, the front door closed, and Russ locked it and wiped his hands along the sides of his trousers as if brushing away some unwanted matter.

"Damned nuisance," Russ muttered, looked up and saw him. "Say, brother, when did you get here?" They rushed to each other, and Telford knew again the strong, welcoming love of his brother.

"About twenty minutes ago, just in time to catch Jack making an ass of himself."

"Don't tell me. If anybody's an expert at that, he is. I just sent him off, and I wouldn't care if I never saw or heard of him again."

"Same here, but we have to tolerate him for Tara's sake. How's Henry? When I talked with him a few days ago, I sensed that he lacked his usual vigor."

"This is flu season, and he may have had a touch of the virus. Drake will be here tomorrow, and I understand from Alexis that Velma will get in Christmas Eve morning. I guess we'd better get her some presents."

He wasn't going to laugh at that, he told himself, but when had Russ become so transparent? "Yeah. I'm going into Frederick this afternoon and do some shopping."

"I figured you'd forgotten I was still upstairs waiting for you to say something like—" Alexis pursed her lips and put a bland expression on her face. "Like yoo-hoo, hey, pig. You know what I mean."

He walked back to the bottom of the stairs, where she stood and draped an arm around her waist. "Quit mugging. A man would have to be out of his mind to forget about you."

She raised both eyebrows. "Enough said."

Russ blew out a long and loud breath, as though he'd practiced doing that for their benefit. "You two either get your show on the road or break it up. Watching it is like seeing a bunch of people gazing at a wildfire and praying for rain instead of plunging in and doing something about it."

Telford didn't allow himself to get irritated at his brothers, so he waved a hand at Russ, dismissing the remark.

He'd already made up his mind that when January the first came, there'd be no debris cluttering up his life. Happy or not, he'd at least know where he was headed.

"You believe you ought to say whatever you think?" he asked Russ, though he imagined that, as much as his brother loved things tied in neat packages, the ill-defined relationship between Alexis and himself bothered him.

"You're smart," Russ said. "So you know nothing stays the same. Any welder will tell you to strike when the iron's hot." He strode past them and dashed up the stairs.

Since he wasn't ready to settle issues with Alexis, he hugged her, dropped his arm and gazed down at her. "I'd better let Henry know I'm back. See you later."

He found Henry in the pantry, humming. "Going to Chicago," a song popularized by the Count Basie Band six decades earlier, and slung his arm briefly around the old man's shoulder. "How's it going, Henry?"

"Same as always. If you want I should stay here cooking you meals, see to it that I don't have to fix another morsel for Jack Stevenson."

"You could always give him cabbage stew."

The frail old man stared up at him with the look of incredulity on his face. "And you think I didn't?"

He laughed aloud, a good cleansing guffaw. "You just made my day. Don't I wish I'd been here."

"This is subject to remake your day. Old man Sparkman called here a couple of times wanting to speak with you. Said it's important." He took a piece of paper from his billfold. "Here's his number."

"Thanks." He stared at the number. So familiar, though he knew it had been years since he'd used it. "This seems like... Say, this is Mercy Hospital in Frederick." How often he'd dialed that number during his father's last illness.

He dialed the number, and when the voice identified the hospital, he hung up. "I'll get hold of him later. Right now, I need to unpack and get a briefing from Russ. You need anything from Frederick or Eagle Park?"

"Nope. I done my Christmas shopping in Florida last summer. Don't wait till the last minute to do things. Didn't teach you to do that either."

He brought Russ up to date on their operation in Barbados, got a look at Russ's design for their next project and phoned Alexis. "I'm going to Frederick. How about dinner tonight? If it's yes, tell Henry not to count on the two of us for dinner." He told her good-bye, got into his car and headed for Frederick.

He was of two minds, curious as to why Sparkman considered it important to see him and tempted to let the old hatred resurface and have its way. But Alexis's words haunted him: *"Happiness and bitterness don't go together. You can't love and hate at the same time."*

After finishing his shopping and completing several errands, he started home. But his conscience flailed at him, and he turned around and drove to the hospital where he found Fentress Sparkman sitting up in bed watching a soccer game on TV looking years older than when Telford last saw him in September.

He walked up to the foot of the bed. "You wanted to see me?" he asked him.

Sparkman turned off the television set. "Yes, I did. I thought you'd call, but I'm glad you came. I like to talk to a man face-to-face."

"What's on your mind?"

Sparkman trained fierce eyes on him and patted the edge of his bed. "Sit down so I don't have to yell. We've had some rough times testing each other. I tried to throw you flat on your face, and I don't apologize for it even now. I did it, and what's done is done."

"Why're you telling me this? I know—"

"That's just it. You don't. All you know is the war between me and your daddy. We hated each other, and tried to ruin each other, and I succeeded. I'm not proud of the way I did it, but it's done. It was him or me, and putting up buildings didn't have a thing to do with it."

Hairs seemed to stand up on the back of Telford's neck as he stared at Fentress Sparkman. His mind's eye dragged him back twenty years, and he was gazing at his own emaciated, terminally ill father, aged by illness beyond his years.

"Run that past me again, will you?" he said, as fear seemed to curdle his blood. "Why did you and my father hate each other?"

Sparkman turned fully to face him. "Because we had the same daddy."

"*What?* Are you crazy?"

"Sane as you. I was born out of wedlock a couple of weeks before your daddy, Josh Harrington, was born, and your grandfather refused to acknowledge me publicly. He was scared to death your grandmother would leave him, and from all reports she would have. Your father and I knew each other well, were even in the same class all through school, and believe me, I suffered. In those days, being what they called an illegitimate child was as scandalous as being a child molester is today.

"We fought all the time. Josh Harrington went to proms, courted the town's best women, went to Yale. And he had the Harrington name. I never went to a prom in my life, not that the man who sired me wouldn't have bought what I needed, but my mother didn't know how to do anything, and didn't bother to learn." He sucked air through his front teeth. "She didn't have the mother wit of a rat's tootoo."

He'd give that comparison some thought later on. "How did you get where you are? Your mother couldn't have been all bad."

"She wasn't. She filled my head with the desire to get even, as she hadn't been able to do. I told myself I'd do it for her. I sent myself to Harvard, working like a dog to get there and stay there, and when I graduated head of my class, by dang, they knew who Fentress Sparkman was.

"I want us to bury the hatchet, Telford. I don't have a soul but myself. Never had any children, and my wife's been dead for years. I'll be checking out of here in less than six months myself. At least, that's what these doctors tell me. I ruined your father just like I set out to do, and losing the benefits of forty-some years of work killed him. I can't make up for that, but I want to leave what I have to you and your brothers. That alone won't get me into heaven, but it might help."

Telford got up and walked over to the window, wishing he could open it and get some fresh air. For a long time, he gazed down at the street, at the people rushing along with their Christmas packages, oblivious to the fact that he'd just had the wind knocked out of him.

He turned around and looked at the man he'd spent over half of his life detesting. "You're telling me that you're my uncle?"

"If you don't believe it, it's easy to prove. DNA doesn't lie."

He shoved his hands in his pockets and walked back to the bed. "Oh, I believe you. A tale like that one has to be true. Besides, when I first looked at you in that bed, I thought I was hallucinating. Without those horn-rimmed glasses you've always worn, you look enough like him in his last days to be him."

"I heard he got pretty sick. You think over what I want to do. As I see it, I'm just giving back to Josh what I took away from him. And…and if maybe you can see your way clear to… to overlook some of the things I've done—"

He had no desire to see the man eat crow, but he needed the answer to two questions. "What prompted you to go to the ceremony for the completion of Eagle Park High School and sit in the front row?"

"I know how to play rough and dirty, and Lord knows I've done plenty of that, but I'm a gentleman. You beat me fair and square. I tell you the truth, I couldn't help admiring you. Nobody thought you'd pull it off. Three major projects in three different places, and you took that little three-man company and made us all stand up and take notice."

"What about that strike? It came close to ruining us."

The old man brushed his hand across his brow. "I know. That was too much even for me, which is why I settled it. My conscience gave me a good beating." His rate of speaking slowed down and his eyelids drooped.

"I'd better not tire you out."

"Come back if you can, but don't take too long."

Memories of his father came back to him as he stared down at the man who claimed to be his uncle. "I'll be back. Thanks for telling me. It couldn't have been easy for you."

"Once I...decided to do what's right, I was relieved. Give my regards to your brothers. Josh raised some fine men."

"Thanks. I'll tell Russ and Drake all that you've said."

He barely remembered walking from Fentress Sparkman's hospital room to his car, but he was sitting in it staring through the windshield and seeing nothing. If he'd ever received a tougher wallop, he didn't remember it. He drove home with great care, left his car in front of the house and headed for the kitchen where he knew he'd find Henry.

"Henry, could you put that aside for a few minutes? You and I have to talk."

"Later. I got to..." He glanced at Telford. "What's wrong, Tel? What's come over you?"

Henry walked over to the table and sat down. "Come over here. Whatever in the world's the matter?"

Telford sat on the edge of a chair and told Henry what he'd learned. From Henry's gaping mouth and widened eyes, he had the answer to the question he'd intended to ask. Henry hadn't known.

After a while, Henry leaned back in the chair, fingered his chin and shook his head. "Damned if that ain't enough to send a righteous man to the nearest bar. You told Russ yet?"

"No. I thought I'd wait till Drake gets here and tell it once. I can't get over this thing, but somehow, I don't doubt it."

"I'm sitting here thinking back a lot of years. Your daddy was so much taller than Sparkman, but... Well, I 'spect he took that from his mother's side," Henry said. He got up and went back to the counter where he'd been peeling asparagus. "Don't git high and mighty and look that gift horse in the mouth. Your daddy suffered plenty at the hands of Sparkman, so you take that money. It rightfully belongs to the three of you."

Telford spread his legs and rested his crossed forearms on

his thighs. He didn't know when, if ever, he'd been so outdone. "Even if I wanted to tell Sparkman no, Russ wouldn't let me. I disliked the man so intensely, spent such a chunk of my life driving myself in order to beat him at one thing or another and now—"

"He's your uncle. If that ain't something!"

Telford slapped his thighs and got up. Canceling his dinner date with Alexis didn't sit well with him, but he couldn't lay a bomb like that one on Russ and Drake and then calmly leave home.

He phoned Alexis. "Honey, I'm sorry I have to break our date, but you'll understand when I explain. I want us to get together later and talk. Okay?"

"Of course. I hope your reason isn't distressful."

"Well, it doesn't make me dance, but I'm dealing with it. I'll tell you all about it."

After dinner, he sat with Russ and Drake in his bedroom and told them what he'd learned. They stared at him, and neither said a word.

All of a sudden, Russ lunged to his feet. "I'll be damned." The words exploded from him as if they'd been shot from a cannon. "Under the heel of his boot all these years, and he's got the nerve to...to... Oh, what the hell! It was Dad's war."

"Yeah," Drake said. "I never felt the animosity toward him that you did, Telford, though that was probably because I wasn't the one in direct conflict with him. Let it lie, brother."

If they had seen that wasted old man, his black skin leatherlike against those white hospital sheets, they would have empathized with him as he did. "I can't hate anybody in his position. In fact, I've only been sorry for him since we licked him with the school; he had to sit there and listen to the mayor say that was the finest building in Eagle Park, and Sparkman must have put up half a dozen buildings in the town. I'm over it."

One issue could set him and his brothers at odds, but he wouldn't act contrary to their wishes. It wasn't worth it. "What about the inheritance? Do we accept it?"

As Telford had expected, a look of incredulity spread over Russ's face. "If he said it's rightfully my father's, that means it's rightfully mine. Period."

He looked at Drake for his response. "I'm not in the habit of knowingly and deliberately doing stupid things," Drake said. "He's in Mercy Hospital? What's his room number? The least I can do is go there and thank him."

"I've been thinking of doing the same," Russ said. "Let's run over there tomorrow morning. I'm tied up Christmas Eve."

Telford got up and started for the door. "Give him my regards. See you later."

"While you're with her, get a commitment," Russ yelled after him.

"He's got a commitment," Drake said. "The problem is getting her to follow through."

But those days will soon be over. I'm not starting the new year with my life screwed up like this. I need her as I need air, but if she's not going my way, I'm going to know it.

He knocked on her door, and she opened it with a look of expectancy on her face, the face he loved, and extended both hands to him.

"You don't look unhappy. What happened?"

"I suppose I'm getting used to the shock."

He repeated what his uncle had told him. "You can imagine I felt as if a locomotive rolled over me."

She moved her head up and down as if she were in deep thought. "Sounds like a true story. What do you think?"

"Oh, he's telling the truth, all right." He put an arm around her and felt her warmth as she moved to him, nestling close. She never failed to welcome him. Whenever he touched her, he could feel her melt into him, making him soar like an eagle. *She makes me feel ten feet tall and rising.*

"I remembered what you said to me about hate being incompatible with love, and that's why I went to see him. I'm glad I did. Not for the inheritance, but for the relief of not feeling that bitterness and ill will."

Her slumberous gaze roamed from his eyes to his lips and back to his eyes, and then she dampened her lips, making his blood quicken and head for his loins. "I don't think we'd better start that, honey. Tara's in that room and likely to come in here any minute, and I'm not in the mood to torture myself. Besides, a couple of hours with you will only be a tease. I want more. A lot more. You think about that." He brushed her lips quickly with his own and left.

And she wanted more, but how could she risk what he would certainly do, if he ever learned her maiden name? She could never forget the crushed, crestfallen expression, the pain on his face when, in her embarrassment, she had lied to him. She'd wanted to retract it, but it was too late. He'd closed up like a clam. "My mistake," was all he said. After that, when he saw her on campus, it was as if she didn't exist.

If he discovered that she'd kept one more thing from him, that would end it. On his own, he'd learned that her ex-husband was rich; circumstances forced her to tell him she had two university degrees, had taught in a university, that she knew Melanie Krenner and was the reason for her disappearance. And following the shock of learning that Fentress Sparkman, a man who'd nearly caused his ruin, was his uncle... She couldn't subject him to yet more pain.

A thought occurred to her, and she telephoned her ex-husband.

"To what do I attribute this pleasant surprise?" he asked her, and she wondered why he didn't ask if anything was wrong with Tara since she hadn't telephoned him in the seven months since their custody settlement.

"Tomorrow is Christmas Eve," she said without preliminaries, "and I want to know whether you're planning to visit Tara."

"Look, babe, don't be so hard on a man. I was just headed out to see my folks. They're getting old, you know."

"And Tara is getting older, but don't worry, she'll have a

great Christmas. You're missing an opportunity, Jack. Don't blame her for loving the men who live here; they never forget her."

"What do you want from me, Alexis? You demanded full responsibility for her, and I gave it to you."

"Sure. And you gave it to me without a fuss in exchange for your money and property. My father was there for me, taking care of my material needs, but he seemed unaware of my emotional ones. I want more for my daughter, for her to love and respect her father. But we can forget about that, if you don't change your style. It's up to you."

"I wanted to take the two of you out in my new car, but you refused."

"I will not socialize with you. That's over. As for the car ride, Tara would have to sit in the backseat and you'd spend the time talking to me. Oh, no."

"Look, I'll send her something by FedEx."

"If that's your solution, fine."

Fighting a moroseness she hadn't experienced since the day Jack walked out of their home, she dialed Loren Ingles Stevenson, Jack's second wife.

"Hello, Loren, this is Alexis Stevenson. I hope you don't mind my calling you." She knew she'd stunned the woman, but she wanted to set one thing straight.

"Alexis? For goodness' sake, this is a surprise. What's up?"

She cut to the chase. "Loren, I asked Jack to introduce my daughter to her little brother, your son, and he gave me a thin excuse. What do you say? They ought to know and learn to care for each other."

"I've thought that, too, Alexis, but I didn't know how you'd feel about it, all things considered."

"What's done is past. As I look back, I'm the winner. I'll call you right after New Year's Day, and we'll work it out. All right?"

"Good. Merry Christmas, Alexis."

"Thanks, Loren. Merry Christmas to you."

She prowled around her room, testing in her mind ways of telling Telford that she was the A. Brighton he knew at Howard University, but no matter how she phrased it to herself, in her mind's eye she saw none of the warmth and beguiling sweetness that she loved in him, but eyes clouded with icy fury. Needing assurance as to the depth of his feeling, she phoned him, but for her trouble she got a busy signal. "Just as well," she placated herself.

Minutes later her phone rang. "Hi. Telford. You called me?"

Why hadn't she remembered caller ID? What could she say to him? "Yes, I did, but it was…uh…just a spur-of-the-moment thing."

"Our parting earlier wasn't satisfactory to me, either." His voice, low, urgent and sexy, had the ability to make her heart do complete somersaults. "You want to talk awhile? It won't be enough for me, but it's as much as I'm willing to deal with right now."

"Hmmm. You're the one who set the limits."

"One of us had to do it. As I recall, I've always been the one who puts on the brakes. When you get going, lady, you've got a one-track mind."

"What *I* recall is that my mind never has a thing to do with it. If the music's sweet, why should I stop dancing? If a player's winning, he wouldn't leave the gaming table if he starved."

"Touché. But before the place closes, he cashes in his chips. He knows he can't *spend* chips. You get my message?"

Did she ever! "I'd better let you get to sleep," she said, aware that they'd neared the danger zone, dangerous for her, at least.

The laugh that reached her ears contained no mirth. "Until I'm satisfied that you and I won't go any further together, I will remind you constantly that I need order in my life, and you are a part of that order."

Chapter 15

Christmas Eve arrived with snowflakes and a plummeting temperature, and an aura of excitement engulfed Alexis as she went about her morning chores. She checked the guest room for tidiness and straightened up Russ's room. For months, Telford had made his own bed, and she understood his reasons for it, just as he no longer signed her checks, but had his accountant do it. Bennie cleaned Drake's room once a week; at other times he took care of it himself, insisting that that was the way he wanted it. So, by nine-thirty, she'd finished her upstairs chores and could help Henry with the extra holiday preparations.

She pulled back the curtains in the guest room to look out at the snow, saw Russ's black Mercedes pull into the driveway and galloped down the stairs to open the door.

"Hey, girl," Velma exclaimed, dropped the two shopping bags filled with wrapped packages and flung her arms around Alexis. "Honey, you sure are a sight for these eyes."

Shivering in the gust of cold air, she hugged her sister, looked over Velma's shoulder at Russ and wondered at his expression, the look of one who'd been caught filching from the cash register. "Thanks for meeting Velma," she said to him.

"My pleasure." He closed the door and put Velma's suitcase at the foot of the stairs. She'd have loved to ask him about the truth of that remark.

"Where's Tara?" Velma asked.

"She went with Telford to find a Christmas tree. They ought to be back any minute."

Russ took the two shopping bags, picked up the suitcase and started up the stairs. "I'll take your things to your room, Velma."

Velma looked in the direction of the stairs. "Thanks," she called to him, "and thank you for braving this weather to make that trip into Baltimore." She looked at Alexis. "How'd it happen that Russ came to meet me?"

Telford had cautioned her not to read anything into Russ's behavior, so she shrugged in an offhand manner. "He volunteered, and I didn't question him. Why look a gift horse in the mouth?"

"What did he say about the kitten I sent him for his birthday?"

"He must not have been displeased, because it sits on his night table. Imagine sending a man a kitten named Hugs. That didn't leave a thing to his imagination."

"I didn't intend to," Velma said in her best come-hither voice and drew a hoot from Alexis. "What's going on with you and Telford?"

"Long story."

"Well, you're still here, so I guess that means the two of you didn't split up. I'm going back there and say hi to Henry."

Having completed her morning chores, Alexis went to her room and changed into a pair of beige woolen slacks and a burnt-orange sweater and went into the kitchen, where she found Henry rubbing herbs into the inside of a goose.

"Drake's gonna bring some dame he ain't interested in. With your sister, that's a total of, let's see, eight. I made three pumpkin pies yesterday, but it sure would be nice if you could mix up one of your caramel cakes."

They worked together on the meal, which the Harrington family traditionally ate on Christmas Eve, and she had her hands full of caramel icing when Henry looked at her with the phone in his hand.

"Tel wants to speak with you. She got her hands full of stuff," he said into the receiver. "Why don't you just come on in here if you want to talk to her? I won't hear a thing."

She'd been ready to wash her hands and meet him in the hallway where she'd at least get a quick kiss, but Henry had deprived her of that pleasure. Telford strode into the kitchen with Tara trailing behind him and didn't stop until he reached her.

"You didn't come to breakfast this morning. Anything wrong?"

She shook her head. He stood before her, quintessential man, strong and vibrant, his curly-lashed, hazel-brown eyes filling her head with ideas that had nothing to do with caramel cake. As if he knew that his aura curled around her and his masculine heat had begun to mate itself with the fire simmering in her, he let a grin form around his lips and winked. She swallowed her breath, and he grabbed her and let her feel his mouth and know once more the quick thrust of his tongue. As quickly, he set her away from him, leaving her to wonder if it had happened or if, stoned by the sight of him, she'd imagined it.

Remembering that they were not alone, she glanced down at Tara, whose gaze shifted from one of them to the other. "Do you like it when Mr. Telford kisses you, Mummy?"

When she didn't answer, a grin spread over Telford's face. "You can answer that, can't you?"

"Do you, Mummy?"

"There are times when I'd like to sock him."

Tara's eyes widened, and then her face wrinkled into a frown. Telford knelt beside her, and she looked at him for an explanation.

"When you're a grown-up beauty like your mother, you will

understand that women keep these things secrets. She loves kissing me, but she doesn't want me to know it."

"But, Mr. Telford, I was looking at it. I know when you kiss *me*."

Laughter poured out of him. "Tara, we are wasting time. We have to decorate the tree."

He left, holding Tara's hand, and the child looked backward at her mother as though uncertain as to what had just transpired.

"He shouldn't have done that in Tara's presence," she said aloud.

"Why not?" Henry asked her. "It's good for the child to see the love between you two and accept it. You should've told her you like it, 'cause you do. You ain't supposed to let a man kiss you if you don't like it."

"This is true, but after an encounter like that one—"

"I know. You wasn't thinkin' straight. A man will stay in a relationship with you forever if you don't shake him up. You and Tel needs to get married."

She put her hands on her hips and glared at Henry. "What makes you think Telford's the one who can't make up his mind? If I said yes, he'd get married tomorrow." She clapped her hand over her mouth.

Henry stared at her. "You telling me you're stupid?" He looked to the ceiling. "You the last woman I would've accused of that. Keep it up. Dig a hole for yourself. If he shuts the door, you believe me, he ain't opening it. Never."

Alexis set the table for their Christmas dinner with festive arrangements of mistletoe, holly and red celosia and placed large vases of the arrangements in the den, living room and foyer. The fireplaces in the living and dining rooms crackled with roaring flames, and the scent of bayberry perfumed the air.

Alexis paused as she passed the den, and tears pooled in her eyes when she saw Telford lift Tara above his head so that she could place the star at the top of the tree. As he lowered her, she wrapped her little arms around his neck and kissed him.

Velma, Russ and Drake helped them decorate the eight-foot Douglas fir.

For lunch, Henry set platters of assorted fruits, cheese and bread on the breakfast-room table, and they stood around it helping themselves. Alexis thought Henry appeared tired and was certain of it when he sat down, and Tara asked him if he wanted her to bring him some milk.

Henry patted Tara's shoulder as she leaned against him, her forearms resting on his thigh. "No, but I'd love some tomato juice." She ran off to get it.

"She's a little angel," he said, "and this is the happiest Christmas this house ever seen."

Alexis looked up to find Telford's gaze locked on her, his soul shimmering in his eyes, all he felt for her exposed to anyone who cared to look. Without giving what she did a thought, she walked around the table to where he stood and wrapped an arm around his waist. She wanted to tell him that her heart was full of him, but she couldn't say what she knew he wanted to hear, and the words stuck in her throat. Yet, she couldn't stop looking at his eyes, eyes dark with love and smoldering with passion. He gazed down at her, his face solemn, and locked her in his arms.

"I brought you the juice, Mr. Henry. Did I do good?"

Alexis didn't hear Henry answer, and when neither Russ, Drake nor Velma complimented the child, she knew their eyes were focused on Telford and her.

Tara confirmed it. "Is he going to kiss you again, Mummy?"

She didn't answer Tara and played down the remark. "Are you?" she asked Telford.

But he remained serious. "Not with all these people gaping at me, I'm not." That told her he wasn't in a playful mood, and his brothers recognized it because they didn't tease him.

"Let's finish this good stuff and get back to the tree," Drake said. "Pretty soon, I'll have to go for my date."

Henry cast Drake an anxious look. "Mind you don't get stuck somewhere."

"Come on, Mr. Henry, and dress the tree with us. Please." Tara tugged at his hand.

"I ain't never... Oh, all right."

Tara took his hand, walked with him into the den and handed him ornaments. "It's fun. Mr. Telford showed me how."

If Harrington House hadn't been the scene of such a joyous Christmas Eve, Alexis hadn't witnessed one such either, and when they were left alone in the breakfast room, she said as much to Telford.

"For us, you and Tara are the difference," he said. "We are all precious to her, and she shows us in so many ways that we make her happy." He looked toward the doorway, sheltering his feelings. "I don't know what I'll do if you take her away from me."

She didn't want to deal with her fears right then. Lord, just let her enjoy this Christmas with him, maybe the only one. "I don't have an answer right now," she fudged. "Can you be patient a little longer?" Until she got the strength to do what she could no longer postpone.

Waves of heat washed over her when his fingers grasped both of her shoulders. And he knew it, for an answering fire burned in his eyes.

"Do you see how you react to my touch? I wasn't trying to seduce you, but I get to you without trying. You do the same to me, and I want the right to hold you, touch you, take care of you, kiss you in front of a priest if I feel like it."

His hand went to the back of his neck as if he battled frustration. "Don't expect me to continue this way. It'll never happen. Never."

"I know. Oh, Telford, I know."

After the brothers cleared the snow from the front of the house that afternoon, Telford phoned her. "How about dressing Tara and yourself warmly and let's go outside?"

They helped Tara build a snow girl, frolicked in the white winter mist, among the snow-covered trees from which icicles dangled like Southern summer moss, threw snowballs and pulled Tara on the sled the brothers enjoyed as children.

"I just love the snow," Tara told them and looked up at her mother, her expression plaintive. "Mummy, why can't Mr. Telford come stay with us?"

What could she answer when the same question tortured her own mind?

Telford dusted the snow from Tara's woolen cap. "We'll be together, sweetheart. I promise, but—"

"You said you had to work it up."

"I said we would work it out."

"Did you?" Tara asked.

Alexis could hardly bear the pain she felt at the sadness in her child's voice.

"We're doing that right now," he said, sending Alexis an accusing look. "Nobody wants us to be together more than I do." He spoke to Tara, but he fixed his gaze on her. "So, don't worry, sweetheart."

"Okay." A child's faith was a thing of wonder. "Let's sled some more."

When the cold seemed to have seeped all the way to her bones, she suggested that they go inside, and they walked back with Tara dancing between them and guilt weighing on her like wet cement.

Russ stopped her as she was hanging her ski jacket in the foyer closet. "Can I speak with you a minute?" She nodded. "I didn't want to bring this up in front of Tara. Is Jack coming here today or tomorrow?"

She refused to cover for Jack. "He said he had to visit his parents in Philadelphia, so he's not coming."

She didn't imagine the distaste expressed on his face. "I see. Did he send Tara a gift?"

"It hasn't arrived yet. The snow—"

He waved a hand, dismissing the excuse. "The snow didn't start till after midnight. I take it he lives in Philadelphia. What's his address?" She gave him that and Jack's phone number.

"Thanks. That guy doesn't add up." He unhooked the cell

phone from his belt and dialed a number as he walked away. "Jamal, this is Russ," she heard him say. "Check out this guy for me."

She went in the kitchen to find out whether Henry needed help with the dinner. "Think we can eat a little before seven?"

He bent to look in the oven. "I ain't serving nothin' till Drake gets back here."

She pulled a chair out from the table and sat down. "Is Drake your favorite?" She hadn't thought that Henry had a preference among the brothers, but it was possible.

"I ain't got no favorite. Drake, Telford and me, we always worried 'bout Russ, 'cause he kept to himself, wouldn't open up to none of us. He's still a loner, which is why I was glad to see your sister come back."

He poured a cup of cold coffee for himself and sat in the chair facing her. "Tel was shy and couldn't reach out to people right up till he was in his mid-twenties. Unlike Russ, he was always glad to be with the kids when they took him in. Now, Drake, he's got an angel sitting on his shoulder. He loves people, and everybody loves him."

Her mind remained on what he'd said about Telford. How terribly she must have hurt him because she, too, was scared and shy!

"But the brothers seem so close," she said.

"Oh, they're thick as thieves. You want trouble, just mess with one of 'em, and you have to deal with all three. Plenty love there. They're just different from one another."

With Tara practicing her music lesson, Alexis took the opportunity to get their presents and place them beneath the Christmas tree. "I had a lot of nerve doing this," she said of the contents of a large box. "I hope they like it."

Telford dressed for Christmas Eve dinner and looked at his watch. Just five-thirty, so why was he rushing the time? He prowled around his room, fingering objects, picking up his wire sculptures and books and putting them down. Exasperated, he dialed her number.

He skipped the preliminaries. "Whatever your reason for not committing to me, tell me flat-out, and don't coat it. I can take it." Restless and on edge, he plowed his fingers through his hair. "By now, you know what you don't like about me and what you're not willing to settle for. Lay it out for me. If you can't tell me, write it down and let me read it."

Her answer came slowly, as if she had to shift gears. "This... isn't about you, Telford. It's about me. A woman knows a man like you once in a lifetime. If she's blessed, she can welcome him into her life without hesitation."

"And you're not that blessed?"

"Unfortunately. But for today at least, can we enjoy being together? Neither in my parents' home nor in my own home did I ever experience such a warm, loving Christmas. I know I have to deal with our relationship, but not today, please. And I thank you for letting Velma share this with me."

"Whatever you ask me for is yours, if it is mine to give. See you when I get downstairs."

He hung up, looked out the window at the snowflakes that drifted lazily past and let himself relax as Drake's white Jaguar eased into the driveway. He hadn't thought it wise to drive into Frederick in such conditions, but you didn't tell a grown man what to do. He loped down the stairs and opened the door as Drake and his friend reached the house.

"Welcome, Pamela," he said, and meant it, when Drake introduced him to the tall, dark woman who smiled with a friendliness that appealed to him. He knew he'd like her. But when she extended her hand and accorded him a deference he hadn't expected, he was taken aback.

"I'm glad to meet you, Telford. Thanks for the welcome. I've been a nervous wreck ever since I told Drake I'd come."

"Why were you nervous?"

"Because he talks about you, Russ, Henry..." She looked up as one does when trying to remember. "Oh, yes, Alexis and

Tara as if his world revolves around you. I can't wait to meet Tara."

"We're glad you agreed to have dinner with us." Finally. Drake had a down-to-earth woman who could see past his money, status and good looks.

For half an hour before dinner, the brothers, their women, Henry and Tara sat around the lighted tree in the den—where the flames sparkled, and the odor of roasting chestnuts, fresh Douglas fir and fragrant potpourri teased their olfactory senses—getting acquainted and swapping stories. His heart kicked over when Tara sat on the floor beside him and supported her back with his leg.

"Mr. Telford, are you going to play the violin?"

He rested his hand on her shoulder, assuring her of her welcome. "After dinner, if you want me to."

She smiled and laid her head against his leg in as possessive a gesture as he'd ever witnessed.

"What about some Christmas carols? Does anybody in here sing?" Velma asked.

After a long silence, Pamela said, "I sing," and with a full and melodious soprano filled the room with "Oh Holy Night."

Tears streamed down Henry's cheeks. "My wife sang that song just like that. God rest her soul." He wiped the tears with the back of his hand, and in a quick change of mood announced, "It's time to eat."

Alexis and Velma helped Henry put the food on the table, and with "Silent Night" playing softly on the radio, Telford said to Alexis, "Tonight and hereafter, guests or not, you sit opposite me at my table."

"I usually do."

"In the breakfast room, yes, but when we eat here, you don't."

"But…that's reserved for—"

"The woman of the house," he said, his impatience showing. "Damn convention. I'm sick of these games."

Her soft brown eyes gleamed in the candlelight, and when

her hands moved restlessly up and down the sides of her shimmering silk dress, he knew she wanted to touch him. Two quick steps took him to her side, and she gasped when his arms went around her and his lips brushed hers. He stepped away, watched her grope for equilibrium and grinned with male satisfaction.

"Serves you right," he said, gloating shamelessly.

She took the seat opposite his and tossed her head. "Absolutely. And I aim to get all of that that's coming to me."

"You two stop dallying with each other and let's eat," Russ said. "Velma, they get on my nerves."

She treated him to a smile labeled for him alone. "*Your* nerves? If you ask me, they're getting on their *own* nerves."

After a meal of oyster stew, roast goose, wild rice, asparagus tips, mesclun salad, Stilton cheese, pumpkin pie, caramel cake, champagne and, for Tara, black-cherry ice cream, they all cleared the table, straightened the kitchen and went to the den, where the brothers paired off with their women.

"Do you think you ought to drive back to Frederick tonight?" Telford asked Drake.

"It isn't a good idea, but we've already got a full house," Drake said.

From that, he gathered that Drake didn't plan to share his bed with Pamela. He hoped his brother intended to cultivate that relationship, because the more he saw of Pamela, the better he liked her.

"If it's a question of sleeping arrangements, she can bunk with me," Alexis said, and slapped her hand over her mouth when she glanced at him. "Ooops!"

Talk about sticking your foot in it. He grinned at her obvious discomfort.

Drake put a log on the fire and went back to his seat on the sofa beside Pamela. "I was thinking Pamela could have my bed, and I could crawl in with...uh-oh."

"Look," Velma said, certain that she could clear up the problem. "Nobody knows who's spending the night where or with whom. Russ and I are not—" she looked at Tara "—uh, you know, so Pamela can stay with me."

"Really?" Russ tugged at a clump of Velma's hair. "How do you know I want everybody to think that? I don't spill my business. Besides, if you wanted to broadcast it, you should have said, *As of now*. So—"

She interrupted him, her smile luminous. "Well, honey, all you have to do is let me know…uh…what's what."

A roar of laughter erupted, but Russ stared down at her for a long minute, his face the picture of sobriety. Inscrutable. "I just might do that. Drake can open this sofa up and sleep down here in the den…provided that suits them."

Telford picked up his violin and adjusted the strings, checking the tune. Tara didn't remind him, but he knew she hadn't forgotten. Sitting at his feet, she turned and faced him as he produced the strains of "Meditation," to his mind, the sweetest music ever written. From the corner of his eye, he saw Russ put his arm around Velma and brush her lips with his own, while Drake clasped Pamela's hand, leaned back and closed his eyes. He didn't dare look at Alexis for fear he'd miss the notes.

At the end of the piece, Henry got up, walked over to the fireplace and stood with his back to it, his hands clasped behind him. "I ain't prayed much in my life, but I will this night. I can quit worrying about the three of you. You…you're all doing just fine."

They sat around the fire, telling tall tales, drinking coffee and aperitifs and opening gifts. Tara received presents from everyone, including Pamela, and her squeals filled the house. Telford wanted to be alone with Alexis when he gave her her gift, but with everyone staring at him, he had no choice. She opened it and gaped. As she stared at the pearl necklace, her lips quivered, and he hoped she wouldn't cry. She went to him, hugged and kissed him.

"Mummy, how come you always kissing Mr. Telford?"

"Because I love him. Isn't that why you kiss him?"

"Oh, my," was as much as the normally loquacious Velma seemed able to manage.

Henry thanked Alexis and Tara for his deep-sea fishing rod, laid it across his lap and shook his head. "I couldn't have picked out a better one myself."

Playing Santa Claus gave Telford a great feeling, even if it was mainly for adults. Maybe one day, he'd have his own children around him on a night like this one. He reached for the remaining package.

"Whoa! This thing must weigh forty pounds. What's in it?" He read: "'To Telford, Russ and Drake from Alexis and Tara with love.'"

The wrapping fell away from it, and he stared at it, unable to speak. His brothers rushed over to look at it and gaped, as he did.

"Will you just look at this?" He held up the bronzed image of his father.

"It's just like him," Drake said. "I won't try to thank you, Alexis. It…it's wonderful."

"Yeah," Russ said, blinking rapidly, and hugged her. "You're one classy lady. I'll never forget that you did this for us."

"I knowed you was a smart woman," Henry said. "Mr. Josh would've been real proud of this."

"Let me see," Tara said. "Mummy wouldn't show it to me. She said I tell everything."

He wanted to carry her to his bed and love her, love her until she gave up her reluctance and reservations and told him she would be his forever. But he sat still, catatonic-like, looking at her, letting her see through the walls of his soul. His lips moved with the words "I love you." She smiled, and it was as if their hearts joined and beat as one.

"I have to put my child to bed," Alexis announced. "I'll fix breakfast, Henry, because you're probably tired after that dinner you cooked."

"I'll help," Velma said.

"Me, too," Pamela chimed in, "if you'll give me something to put on."

"Sure," Alexis said. "Breakfast at nine."

She put Tara to bed and went back to the den with a gown, robe and toothbrush for Pamela, glad for an excuse to linger with Telford. He walked with her to her room.

"Want to come in?"

He shook his head. "If I did, I'd wake up in there tomorrow morning."

"What's wrong with that?"

"I'm beginning to choke on these crumbs you feed me."

"Are you refusing me?" She stood erect, her chin up and shoulders squared. "You told me I could have anything I asked for if it was yours to give. Right?"

"Yeah. I said it."

She tossed her head to emphasize her point. "What I want right now is you. Down here or upstairs in your room. I don't care which. I need you."

His Adam's apple bobbled furiously, and he swallowed hard. "If you knew how hungry I am for you, you'd run into this room and close the door. I doubt I'm capable of finesse tonight."

Just the way she wanted him. Hungry and wild. Without that veneer of polish and good breeding that he wore like a banner. Yes. She wanted the primal man, unadorned.

"If that's what you're offering, it's exactly what I want. I'll take whatever—"

His mouth was on her, hard, demanding and fire-hot, as his hands roamed her back, her hips and her erected nipples. He walked through the door with her in his arms, kicked it shut, closed Tara's door and slipped down the zipper of her dress. Seconds later, she lay on her bed, skin bare, while he stood above her tearing off his clothes.

She raised her arms to him, and her hips began to rock as she anticipated the feel of him, hard, bare and every bit of him hers. He went into her arms and gripped her to him, leaving nothing between them but the sweat that beaded on his chest, bathing her breasts. Musky. Erotic. Filling her nostrils with the scent of man.

She twirled her tongue around his left pectoral, squeezed his buttocks and tried to swing her body beneath his.

"Slow down, sweetheart," he said.

Heedless of his words, she went after the prize. She'd take the niceties some other time. Impatient, she lifted her left nipple to his mouth and held his head as he suckled her and with her other hand found him and stroked in that way he loved. He moved to her other breast, sucked it greedily into his mouth and let his hand drift slowly down, teasing and tantalizing until she thought she'd scream. At last his fingers captured her feminine folds and began their talented dance, stroking, twirling, raiding the pit of her soul. She raised her body up to him, sheathed him and spread her legs for his entry. His moans thrilled and excited her, and she tried to pull him to her, to hasten that moment when she would again feel the driving force of his powerful body.

"You're not ready, honey."

Exasperated, she cried out, "Then get into me and make me ready."

She stroked him with skillful hands until he capitulated, moaned her name and flung wide his arms. "Do whatever you want to me. Take me. For God's sake, *take me*," he moaned. She urged him on to his back, straddled him and took him into her. He went at her then like a roaring storm, his movements wild and uncontrolled, and she gloried in his earthiness, matching him move for move and stroke for stroke.

The clenching and swelling began, sucking the energy out of her, and he flipped her over on her back and drove with rapid strokes, unleashing a power he hadn't previously shown her. He moved up higher on her body and swallowed her screams as he hit that special nerve and she locked around him, claiming him, owning him. Then, he was over her, in her, all around her, unleashed. A human hurricane driving her to one explosion after another until at last, he shouted his own release and collapsed upon her.

Tears cascaded down her cheeks. She couldn't live without him. So she had to take a chance and tell him everything. But not now when she was so full of him, when she didn't know the difference between him and her. But tomorrow. She'd tell him tomorrow.

Hours later, Telford stared into the darkness. The sexually naive woman he made love with in Cape May had become a hot, possessive lover, and she wouldn't stop there. She bloomed from his touch the way seedlings rise to the sun, and as if he'd deliberately nurtured her and shaped her to his tastes and preferences, she suited him to perfection. And she'd changed him, altered his needs and the ways in which he wanted them satisfied. What if, in the end, she refused him? He told himself he was bigger than anything that could happen to him, and he had consoled himself with those words many times. But he no longer believed them.

When she dragged herself into the kitchen Christmas morning, shortly before eight-thirty, Pamela and Henry had the breakfast ready. It amused her that Velma, who was as punctual as a clock, hadn't come downstairs. Neither had Russ. Figuring out who slept with whom wasn't difficult, especially as Drake was outside shoveling snow.

After a lazy day, she told Telford, "It's unreasonable to expect Henry to cook a big meal again today. Let's fix something for supper."

He agreed and made sandwiches while she cooked leek soup. After supper, they cleaned the kitchen.

"I hope Drake's interest in Pamela is serious," he said, "because I like her a lot, and I can't say that about any of the others."

She saw a chance to get some of her own and took it. "What does Drake think of Evangeline Moore?"

He blunted that barb with three words. "Evangeline. Who's that?"

Velma walked into the kitchen. "Sis, I was looking all over for... Well, if this isn't old-fashioned domesticity, my name isn't Velma Brighton."

Fear hurtled through Alexis. She didn't look at Telford and

hid her anxiety by asking as casually as possible, "What time are you leaving tomorrow?"

"In the morning. Russ is taking me, and I'd better turn in because he wants to leave at a quarter of seven."

Telford seemed preoccupied, even pensive. Like a robot, he flicked out the light above the sink and kissed her cheek. "Drake will be working in Baltimore tomorrow, and I have to speak with him. If I don't get back down here, sleep well."

Velma gazed at him as he walked away. "What was that about?"

Alexis held back the sigh that wanted to emerge. "I'm not sure. Is it all right with you and Russ?"

"Yes," she said, her tone wistful. "I could love that man. Oh, Lord, I could love him."

"Be careful, hon."

Velma shrugged. "You're right. I should, but I suspect it's too late for that."

Telford waylaid Velma the next morning as she waited for Russ to bring his car around from the garage. "It's been good to have you here, Velma. Come back anytime."

Her smile held a measure of skepticism, of uncertainty. "Thanks. Russ may have something to say about that."

"I gathered as much. Russ said you went to Spellman College. Were you and Alexis there at the same time?"

Her eyes widened. "Alexis went to Howard University. Why?"

"Just curious. My brothers and I went to the same school as undergrads. Our father went there, too."

Getting the information he sought was a snap. He took her bags to the car, told her good-bye and ambled up the stairs to his bedroom where he could be alone. He closed the door, walked over to the window and looked out at the wintry scene, but his eyes didn't see it. The view before him was of a slim, bespectacled college girl who swore she hadn't written him a letter. He had admired her from a distance the whole term but, for fear of rejection, hadn't gotten the nerve to let her know it.

Getting that letter had given him the thrill of his young life, and he'd rushed to her. But she had denied writing it, crushing him.

She was no longer the thin girl who wore the black horn-rimmed glasses, her hair straight down her back, always racing across campus—alone. To him, a kindred soul with whom he'd longed to share his free moments. After almost two decades, he still loved her. No wonder he fell for Alexis Stevenson the minute he saw her; she was already deep inside him. He sat on the edge of his desk, musing over it. He'd deal with her, but he was in no hurry to do it.

Chapter 16

The snowstorm shut down building construction, and Telford worked at home the next day, though he ate breakfast early to make certain that he wouldn't encounter Alexis. He had a lot to say to her, and he suspected she knew it, because she hadn't contacted him all morning. And he intended to stay away from her until he worked it out. Around ten o'clock, he put on a mackinaw and struck out for the warehouse where he'd be alone, away from telephones and the temptation to phone or see her. He had to think. However, walking in twelve inches of fresh snow soon became tiring, and he turned back.

"What the...?" he said aloud, releasing a stinging expletive when he saw the Lincoln Town Car in front of his house. When he reached the driveway, he quickened his steps as fury possessed him. He strode into the living room and stopped.

"Yesterday was Christmas, buddy. Where the hell were you?" he asked Jack Stevenson.

"What business is it of yours?"

"Plenty. You couldn't get here yesterday, Christmas, to see your daughter, and somehow, the mailman forgot to bring her your gift. But she didn't miss it; she found a dozen under the tree in the den."

"Will you chill out, man? I brought the present with me."

Telford sat down and told himself to cool off. "I don't know what your problem is, but how can you willingly let this child grow up not knowing you? And you don't know her, because the only time she misbehaves is when you come here."

"What's it to you?'

"Plenty. As long as she's in my home, nobody is going to mistreat her, and that includes you." He softened his tone. "Why don't you love her, Jack? She's so special."

Jack stretched his legs out in front of him and rested his head on the back of the sofa. "I don't know. All my life, I had everything…and nothing. It's like… I don't know.

"My parents sent me to boarding school in Massachusetts while they spent the fall in Europe, the winter in Florida and the spring in Bermuda. When I was in Philadelphia, a nanny, a cleaning woman or maybe nobody looked after me. My dad told me he'd never wanted any children. Alexis was the only good thing I ever had in my life."

"And you screwed up."

"Go figure."

"Get to know Tara. She'll change your life. But don't hurt her, Jack. Don't promise her anything you won't give or do. You'll have me to deal with."

He walked out, leaving Jack alone, and bumped into Alexis. "Where's Tara?"

"She's over in Beaver Ridge. Grant and his mother came for her while you were out."

He began to smolder. Anger wasn't a frequent companion of his, but it gripped him now. "Then what's that guy doing in there? I get it, now. He doesn't come here to see his child; it's you he's after."

"She was gone when he got here. You're wrong, Telford."

"The hell, you say." The doorbell rang, and he spun away from her to answer it. When it rang again, he stopped his fist just before it crashed the glass.

"Hey, man, what's wrong?" Russ asked when he stepped inside. "You look like a thunderhead."

He nodded toward the living room and headed up the stairs. If he had been a fool, he intended to find out and soon.

Knowing he'd find Jack in there, Russ started to the living room, thought better of it and went to his room. If a man was going to hunt, he should have a loaded gun. He phoned Jamal, the private investigator with whom he roomed while at Howard University.

"Russ here, man. What did you get on Jack Stevenson?" He wrote as Jamal talked. "Thanks, buddy. If we don't speak again before the new year, throw one down for me."

"You can bet on it."

Russ read over the notes he took and made up his mind. Whatever concerned his brother was his business, and he'd bet anything Telford didn't know what he was dealing with. But he would.

"I won't be home for dinner, Henry," Telford said, "and it'll be late when I get home." He wasn't ready to settle things with Alexis, and he also didn't want a confrontation with Jack; he'd already stretched his patience with the man.

"You ain't going somewhere to self-destruct, I hope. Don't think I don't know what's going on. If you got a problem with Alexis you oughta talk to her about it. You hidin' out, she's mopin', and Tara thinks her world collapsed. Black-cherry ice cream don't make up for it, no matter how much she try to eat."

Henry's interference in his personal life no longer irritated him. He'd probably miss it if the old man suddenly decided to mind his own business. "If you need me, call my cell number."

He drove into Frederick, parked at Mercy Hospital and went up to Fentress Sparkman's room. He handed his uncle a small parcel and took a seat.

"How're you feeling?" he asked him.

"About the same. Russ and Drake came by to see me earlier today, so I was kinda expecting you. I don't have to tell you how good your visits make me feel." He opened the package and took out the CD player and CD recordings by the Howard University and Mormon Tabernacle choirs.

Tears wet the old man's lashes, but Telford couldn't help being amused when the teardrops hung at their tips, but wouldn't drop. *Stubborn old cuss.*

"Till this Christmas, the last present I got was from my late wife." He pointed to the cabinet beside his bed. Drake gave me the complete works of Langston Hughes, and Russ gave me a leather-bound copy of the Bible. Enough to make a man shed tears."

He left his uncle, checked into a room at the Rutherford Hotel, opened his laptop and got busy. He wanted to call Tara and reassure her, but he'd have to talk to Alexis and he didn't want to be rude to her. He answered his cell phone.

"Mr. Telford, it's me, Tara. Hello."

He bolted out of his chair. "Hello, sweetheart. Are you all right?"

"Yes, sir. I just wanted to tell you good-bye, so Mr. Henry gave me your phone number. Where are you?"

"I'm in Frederick. I'll be late getting home tonight, so I'll see you at breakfast. I love you, sweetheart."

"I love you, too, Mr. Telford. Bye."

She hung up, and he shamed himself for not having called her even if it meant small talk with Alexis.

The atmosphere at breakfast the next morning was not conducive to camaraderie, though he tried, for Tara's sake, to act as if the relationship between Alexis and him had not changed. But since everyone at the table, including Tara, ate quietly and spoke only when spoken to, he figured he flunked at that effort. Alexis's failure to ask him why his ardor seemed to have cooled or to take him to task for it vexed him as much as anything.

"Got a minute?" Russ asked him as they left the breakfast room.

"If it can wait an hour, I'd appreciate it. I have to make a call to Barbados."

"Sure. I'll be in my room."

He had reason later to wish he'd taken time to hear what Russ had to say. Around ten o'clock that morning, he bounded out of his room at the sound of voices, loud, rising and very angry, an anomaly at Harrington House.

"You're lying," he heard Russ say in as strident a tone as he'd ever known his brother to use. "You cheated on Alexis with Loren Ingles. You hadn't been married to Loren for a year before you were unfaithful to her with Gina French. You married Gina when Loren kicked you out, and Gina sued you for divorce the day after Thanksgiving, because you hadn't been home for a week and her private investigator caught you in the act. Worse, your son by Loren Ingles doesn't know who you are. Either you need a psychiatrist or a horsewhipping."

"What I do is my business, and I don't believe Alexis Brighton is your housekeeper or anybody else's," Jack said. "She's had servants from the day she was born. She's a convenience for you and your brothers."

"You…you get your ass out of here. If you ever put your foot across this threshold again, I'll…I'll—"

"I have a right to visit my daughter."

"*Rot!* You don't care any more for her than you do for the son you don't know anything about." Russ yanked the door open. "Get out of here." He slammed the door behind Jack.

"What was that I heard?" Alexis's voice floated up to him.

"I just told Jack to get out." Russ repeated what he said to Jack. "Today isn't Wednesday, his scheduled visiting day; neither was yesterday, and he behaved as if Christmas was just another day. That guy doesn't come here to see his daughter."

At the top of the stairs, Telford leaned against the wall, Russ's words to Jack still ringing in his ears. Three marriages, and the man couldn't be more than thirty-two or -three. He went back into his room, closed the door and mused over Russ's charges against the man. Visiting on consecutive days without clearing it with Alexis meant that he was taking his chances on seeing her, not Tara. He needed Alexis's permission to see Tara.

He gave Tara music lessons on Fridays, and he wouldn't think of canceling them and disappointing her. He dialed Alexis's number. If she answered, he'd deal with it.

"Hello. My mummy is busy."

"Hello, sweetheart, did you remember that you get your lessons today?"

"Mr. Telford! Oh, no. I didn't forget."

"Ask your mother if I can come down now."

He listened to their exchange, hooked his cell phone to his belt, picked up the new music he'd chosen for Tara and headed toward the other end of the house.

Tara opened the door. He didn't see Alexis, and he didn't have to be a genius to know she was deliberately avoiding him. After the lessons, he walked to the door holding Tara's hand.

"My mummy isn't talking much."

He knelt beside her and hugged her. "Sometimes, we grown-ups have a lot to think about. You played nicely today."

"I did?" Her laughter gave him a light, happy feeling. She was a gift.

After dinner, he walked down to Alexis's room and knocked. He'd wrestled with it until his head had begun to swim. When she opened the door and saw him, it was as if her engine fired up and she girded herself for battle. He wasn't interested in a fight; he needed an understanding, a resolution. His mind told him he was dealing with the issue that had marred their relationship from the beginning, and he wanted it aired.

"We need to talk. I've wrestled with this till it's practically strangling me. May I come in, or would you rather we go to the den?"

She stepped back. "Come on in."

He cut to the chase. "It's my opinion that Jack Stevenson

is not coming here to see Tara. He's interested in you, and I believe you know it."

Was that anger or relief flickering in her eyes? He wasn't certain, and he wouldn't appreciate either reaction.

"It occurred to me today for the first time," she said.

He stared at her, annoyed with himself that her feminine allure, the scent of her perfume, her beauty and regal elegance could get to him even when he was displeased with her.

"You want me to believe you haven't realized that man isn't interested in Tara?"

She bristled. "Is that what Russ told you? I want her to know her father and respect him."

"So do I. But the most meager of minds could sum up Jack's behavior over Christmas and figure out that Tara isn't his reason for coming here. And another thing. Russ is my younger brother. He respects me, and he wouldn't speak to me about you in that way."

Fire leaped into her gaze, and he watched, fascinated, as she won the battle with her temper. "Good for him. Would you like me to leave?"

He couldn't believe she'd said it. "*What?* Is that what we do? Check out at the first sign of trouble? No, I do not want you to leave. I want you to level with me about this and everything else."

She slapped her palm against her forehead, and he recognized it as evidence of exasperation. "Then, will you please stop badgering me?"

"Badgering you? Woman, I love you, and you profess to love me. I'm tired of sleeping upstairs while you sleep down here. Even Tara sees the ridiculousness of it. Do you want Jack or not?"

"Of course not, and you ought to know it."

"All right. I'll phone him, ask him to come here and we'll sit with him while you tell him the rules under which he continues to see Tara. Now—"

"Yes?" She rushed to the door. "Russ!"

"What is it?"

"It's Henry. Is Telford here?"

His heart thundered like horses' hooves. "What's the matter with Henry?" he and Alexis asked simultaneously. But Russ dashed down the hall, leaving them to follow him to Henry's room beside the pantry.

"It may be a heart attack," Henry said.

Alexis grabbed a telephone book. "What's the number for the ambulance?'

"It's on the way," Russ told her.

"Can you swallow this, Henry?" Telford asked, holding an aspirin and a glass of water. Henry nodded, and got it down, though with difficulty.

Looking down at Henry, Telford was more afraid than he'd been since their father had died. As he waited with Russ and Alexis, they didn't speak among one another as if, by tacit agreement, words counted for nothing. Anxiety etched the faces of Russ and Alexis, and a sense of helplessness pervaded Telford.

Hours seemed to pass while they waited for the ambulance. Finally, with tears drenching her face, Alexis turned to him, buried her face in his shirt and wrapped her arms around him. He could enjoy her need of him only for a few minutes before she raised her head.

"The front door!" With that, she sped from him to answer it.

The paramedics examined Henry and determined that he hadn't had a heart attack, and that his pulse rate was an acceptable seventy-one. "He ought to see a doctor, but he doesn't need to be hospitalized. Too much holiday, probably."

Telford thanked the men, went back to Henry's room and sat on the edge of his bed. "How do you feel?"

"Fine, except when them schoolboys poked in me. Never could figure out why doctors try to make holes in your skin with their fingers. You'd think that from four hundred years before Christ—when Hippocrates was laying out the rules—up till now, these doctors woulda figured out that probing into people hurts."

"They're paramedics," Alexis said, both eyebrows raised. "Hippocrates, eh?"

"I may be old, but I ain't ignorant. When I ain't working, I'm reading."

"His sharp tongue is working fine," Russ said. "Sorry I interrupted you two, Telford, but—"

Telford lifted his shoulder in a slight shrug. "What else would you do?" He opened his cell phone. "I'm going to call Doctor Jenkins."

"Yeah. An ounce of prevention…"

"He shouldn't be alone," Alexis said. "If one of you will wait till I make a pot of mint tea, I'll sit with him till the doctor comes."

Later, he walked up the stairs along with Russ. "Try to straighten things out with Alexis. I…I don't want to see you split up."

"We've got some work to do."

"But you can do it. You have to, Telford. She belongs with you. With us."

"I know."

"A lot of fuss about nothing," Henry said the next morning, as he sat in the kitchen with Alexis. She got there early to relieve him of the job of preparing breakfast, but as long as he could walk a few steps, he'd be in that kitchen.

"Indigestion, is what the doctor said. If I'd remembered I ate them Belgian endives, I could've saved y'all a lot of trouble."

"You said we're all family, Henry, so how could taking care of you be trouble?"

"It sure gave me a good scare. Like I said, I'd better start watching what I eat."

She made biscuits, cooked the grits, country sausage and scrambled eggs and cut up a large bowl of mixed fruit for Henry, Tara and herself.

"I see you flipped yer lid," Henry said at breakfast when she served him the fruit. "I wants me some good old buttermilk biscuits and country sausage. Now, *that's* food."

"Me, too. I want some of everything," Tara said. So much for that ploy.

Russ drained his coffee cup and went to the stove to refill it. "I have to do some research in the museum in Frederick this afternoon. Mind if Tara goes with me, Alexis? She'll enjoy it, and with school closed for the holidays, it's a convenient time."

"Can I, Mummy? Can I?"

"I think it's a wonderful idea. You love galleries and museums."

"Good. Tara and I can have lunch in Frederick."

"Can I dress up, Mummy?"

Tara looked up at Henry, her face beaming, when he patted her shoulders. "Well, I'll be switched if she ain't a chip off the old block. Got a date, so she's dressing up. Humph. I never put on a tie till I was twenty."

Alexis watched Russ drive off with Tara and counted her blessings. Jack wasn't all a father should be, but the child had wonderful adopted fathers who loved her and took care of her.

"Come with me."

She looked around to see Telford with one foot on the first step of the stairs and his right hand extended to her. He said nothing more until they were in his bedroom and he'd closed the door.

"Last night, I thought I was losing Henry," he began, "and I hurt something awful. On top of it, I faced the prospect of losing you. Then you came to me, in tears for Henry, and I felt how deeply a part of me you are. I knew I had to find out why you won't commit to me. Why it's so hard for you."

"Oh, Telford. There's so much."

He took her hand and walked over to the bed. "Let's sit down. We've got nothing but time. Russ and Tara won't be back till suppertime. I want us to stay up here till we know whether we're going to make it or split up.

"For starters, on Thanksgiving Day, when we watched Howard University's homecoming football game with Russ and Drake, why didn't you say you were a Howard University graduate, that you, Russ, Drake and I are fellow alumni?"

Her stomach clinched as fear rioted through her. The moment she'd dreaded, and she couldn't back away from it. But she refused to hang her head and looked him in the eye. "There's more to it. If it had been simple, I would have happily acknowledged my Howard degree."

"But think how great it would've been, an added bond, if we'd learned we had that in common."

"You're getting at something, aren't you?"

He didn't intend to spare her, because he meant to clear it up, to know where he stood. "You bet I am. When Drake and Russ pointed me out as Big Tip, you knew who I was, and you didn't open your mouth. Why, Alexis?"

"I was scared you'd remember that awful time when I... when—"

"When you lied? Why did you?"

Her eyes widened as she experienced the shock of the truth she dreaded. So he knew. "Because I didn't think a big shot like you, the most popular man on campus, could like me. I wasn't a glamour girl. I hadn't had one date since I arrived at Howard."

He plowed on, ruthless perhaps, but he had to know. "Then why did you write that letter? My best friend was walking behind you when you dropped it. It was addressed to me, so he gave it to me. When I went to you, riding on a cloud that you quickly ripped open, I knew you were lying when you denied writing it, and it hurt. I never forgot it. I was so shy, and I didn't know how to tell you I liked you. I read that letter, and it was as if heaven opened up."

"You? Shy? Every girl was after you."

"I wasn't aware of it. I didn't see them. I saw you."

She was staring at him, eyes wide and lips parted. Open. Vulnerable. He wanted to... He told himself to remember his goal.

"You liked me? You're kidding," she said in a voice tinged with awe. "I had a dozen pictures of you hanging in my dormitory room and a scrapbook filled with your exploits as Big Tip, the quarterback with the bullet arm. I was crazy in love with you."

"What a mess," he said. "All that pain for nothing. You changed so much I didn't recognize you, though once in a while, you seemed familiar in some way."

"At school, I wore gray contact lenses, thinking that would make me more attractive. But you. Telford, you're as different from Tip as wine is from water."

He got up and began to walk from one end of the room to the other. "Talking about plural ignorance. Now, I want to know your reason for not committing to me. Give it to me straight."

She walked to where he stood and faced him. He had to know that every word she said was true. "When I met you, I had decided that I never wanted another man within twenty feet of my body. I'd been used and psychologically abused, and I'd promised myself never again. You changed that, but I was still afraid to trust without reservation.

"Then I learned about Melanie, and I figured that if you knew I'd flunked Melanie and prevented her graduation, you'd walk away from me. You're straitlaced, and you don't forgive easily, and I couldn't forget that fact. At your reception, Melissa Roundtree greeted you as Big Tip, and the bottom dropped out of my life. I didn't believe you'd forgive me for lying to you and sticking my nose up to hide my embarrassment."

"So that accounts for your freezing me out at the reception. Well, I'll be. After the way we loved each other in Cape May, you didn't believe I loved you? Honey, everything else we've said up here is trivial by comparison."

She wanted to get close to him, to let his arms, his loving, make her live. Soar. "I never felt loved until you loved me, and I couldn't risk losing it."

"Are you still afraid?"

"I'm...I don't understand what I'm feeling. Maybe I'm scared to death, and maybe I'm excited and relieved that it's all out in the open."

He stepped closer and wrapped his arms around her. "Is there anything else between us?"

She shook her head. "Just too much air and too many clothes."

Passion leaped into his eyes, a blazing banner of desire that sent currents of heat plowing through her body. He stepped away from her, and she saw the war he waged with himself. His fists curled into balls and hung at his side, and his Adam's apple worked furiously in his throat as he widened his stance, commanding from her all that she would ever be. Why didn't he do something? The hazel-brown eyes that she adored darkened, and he took in his breath through parted lips. Drunk on his mesmerizing masculinity, she closed her eyes and laid back her head to hide the hot feminine want that she knew he could see.

"Telford, don't do this to me." She wanted to run to him and wrap herself in his body.

At last, he said, "I'm yours. If you are committed to me and no other man, I need to know it."

"You're my man, Telford. You. Nobody but you." She didn't know how it happened, but she was tight in his arms, locked to his hard body.

"This is it for me, too, baby," he whispered in deep guttural tones and plunged his tongue between her parted lips. Preparing her for the prize that awaited them, he anointed every millimeter of her mouth, stroking, teasing, plunging in and out of her in a demonstration of what was to come. His hand squeezed her buttocks as he moved against her, short-circuiting her senses, and electrifying her insides. She heard her moans and didn't care as she rocked against him. His heat encircled her, arousing in her the need to have him inside her, and she felt the blood coursing through her like a rushing river of steam. He lifted her and fitted her to him, pressing his bulging promise against her portal of love. She quivered as the musky sent of him furled up to her nostrils. Her telltale nipples began to ache and she rubbed them shamelessly until he dipped his hand into her dress and brought the gleaming aureole to his mouth. Hungry. He went at her like a man starved, and she cried out as she undulated wildly against him.

"Honey, I'm going mad," she said.

"I want you mad. Mad for me." He moved to the other breast, kissing, pulling and sucking until he stripped her of her inhibitions, and she grabbed his belt buckle, unhooked it, unzipped him and tried to take him inside her.

He lifted her and put her in his bed. Within seconds he'd strewn their clothes in every direction.

"Now," she begged, "now," but he knelt above her and began kissing his way down her body while his fingers skimmed the insides of her thighs, wandering upward to stroke the damp folds of her treasure, and she thought she'd fly out of her mind. When his tongue swirled over her belly, her hips began to rock.

"That's it, sweetheart, let me know you want me." He kissed her inner thighs at her vee, and she stilled. *Lord, if he'd only...* He hooked her knees over his shoulders, parted her inner folds and kissed her until a keening cry flew from her lips. He went at her then, kissing, nibbling, pulling and sucking until she couldn't hold back the scream that poured out of her.

"Telford, I can't take any more of this. I... Honey, if I don't explode I'll die."

He kissed his way up her body and she sheathed him and brought him to her. He stared down into her face. "You're mine. Do you understand that? And I'm yours. Take me in, sweetheart."

She raised her body to him and he drove home. Immediately the swelling and clinching began and with her legs locked around his hips, she swung with his rhythm. She grabbed his buttocks and, as if that were his cue, he gripped her to him, increased the pace, driving powerfully, demanding and claiming her for his own. He found the nerve guaranteed to drive her insane and stroked until heat seared the bottom of her feet. Her whole being fixated itself on her love canal, tremors streaked through her and her body clutched him, pumping and squeezing until she tumbled into a swirling vortex of ecstasy.

"Telford. Telford. Oh, Lord, I love you! I love you. Honey…"

He shouted her name—"Yes. Yes. Alexis, my love"—gave her the essence of himself and came apart in her arms.

He let his elbows take his weight as he stared down into her face. How could one human being give so much to another one? He thought his heart would burst with joy.

"I've never loved a woman other than you. I haven't even imagined I did. And believe me, Alexis, I do love you."

"I can say the same. I realized within weeks of my marriage that I'd made a mistake, that I had married in haste to get away from my battling parents. I was looking for peace, but I didn't find it until I came here. Don't ever doubt that I love you."

"I don't doubt it, because I feel it. Have for a long time. Excuse me." He got up, opened a drawer, took out a box and got back into bed. "I want to read something to you."

"'Dear Tip, Saying dear Big Tip doesn't sound right. It's too impersonal. Everyone calls you that. I wish I knew your real name. I think about you all the time. You're different from most of the other fellows here, quiet, scholarly and genteel. And you never use bad language. Being a hero doesn't seem to go to your head. When you picked up my books that day, I almost had convulsions. I couldn't even say thank you. I think you're very special, and I like you an awful lot. A. Brighton.'"

"Did you write this?"

Her smile lit up his world. "I sure did. I can't believe you kept it all this time."

"Oh, yes, and sixteen years is a long time to remember a woman you think you'll never see again. When can we get married?"

She sat up. "Is that all the proposal I'm getting?"

"Baby, I'll get on my knees, if it will make you happy."

"Honey, I don't need that. Give me a month."

He kissed her nose. "Can I tell Tara we finally worked it out?"

"Tell the world, honey. I feel like posting it on the internet."

* * * * *

REQUEST YOUR FREE BOOKS!

2 FREE NOVELS
PLUS 2 FREE GIFTS!

KIMANI™
ROMANCE

Love's ultimate destination!